Book Cover: Zuchal Rosyidin from Kamaji Studio (@zukalnid)

Editing: Tracy Pope

Formatting: Marja Graham

ISBN: 979-8-9907088-0-8 (paperback)

ASIN: B0CW9CCZGM (e-book)

First Edition: August 2024

Content Warnings

Your mental health is very important to me. Before reading *Fortunate Misfortune*, please be aware of the warnings. This book is considered 18+ for its explicit content. It contains grief, mourning the loss of a parent (past, off page), anxiety and panic attacks (on page), one manipulative former partner (on page), tense relationships with parents (on page), explicit sexual content (two chapters), medical anxiety, and describes some changes that can come with a new medical diagnosis.

Playlist

Tonight You Are Mine — The Technicolors
Slip Away — Ryan Ritual, Mating Ritual
You Don't Know — Katelyn Tarver
Future Games — Fleetwood Mac
What You Mean — Rome Hero Foxes
So Caught Up — The Teskey Brothers
If You Were Mine — MINOVA
Yellow — Myles Cameron
You Are the Right One — Sports
Older Than I Am — Lennon Stella
Sunshine — The Brummies
Green Eyes — Coldplay
Roddy – Djo
I'm Not Perfect (But I'm Trying) — Rachel Chinouriri
Friendship? — Jordy Searcy
Confidence — Ocean Alley
Junk Of The Heart (Happy) — The Kooks
Kiss Goodnight — I DONT KNOW HOW BUT THEY FOUND ME
Like Real People Do — Hozier
Easier Said Than Done — Thee Sacred Souls
Feeling For You — Milky Chance
I Feel for You — Prince
Right Down the Line — Gerry Rafferty
More — The Greeting Committee
Nothing — Bruno Major
Until I Found You — Stephen Sanchez
Somewhere Only We Know — Keane

To those who constantly strive to prove their worthiness of love and rest,
please know that you are inherently deserving of both right now,
just as you are.

This is a reminder for me too.

CHAPTER ONE

I HATE WATER.

Not drinking water, of course. I love my kidneys too much for that.

I'm talking about bodies of water. Oceans, seas, lakes, rivers, ponds, and pools. Most people don't consider swimming pools to be bodies of water, but they should. They're disgusting.

Spring semester of my junior year is three days away. According to the law of college, a blowout bash to bring in the New Year and spring competition season is justified. The hotel's indoor pool is filled with athletes from various sports, their howls echoing through the stale wooden beams above. The basketball team's hoop is fished out of the pool for the fourth time in the last hour. The track team huffs along the pool's edge, catching their breath after another relay race. Chicken fights are in full swing, people gripping handfuls of slippery skin in hopes the other will topple over.

I, on the other hand, am as far away from the dirty pool water as one can be. I probably look a little bored and sober, which I definitely am, but my favorite pastime activity is in full swing—people watching.

Blocking my view of the pool, blinding bands of metal against pearly white teeth fill my vision. "Did you miss me?" Shay, my best friend and roommate, asks, placing her wet hands on my thighs.

I tug an earphone out and shove her away. "Don't touch me!"

Shay gives me a look I'd describe as lovingly annoyed. As much as she wants me to swim with her, water and I will never get along. When I was five, I was stung by a jellyfish. When I was nine, a turtle bit my ass. But the worst experience was my thirteenth birthday party when Nathan Dooley pooped in the pool.

That floating, brown lump still haunts me.

"Relax, Mally. It's safe! I checked it out myself. No turtles, jellyfish, or poop."

I stare at the gray water in disbelief. There are bound to be at least ten band-aids floating around. I'll pass.

"Pools are essentially public bathtubs, Shaylene. You willingly submerged yourself in a cesspool. You could get sick!" I pull my shirt over my nose. "We need to get you to urgent care right now."

Shay snatches the unused towel from my lap to dry her hands. "Are you ever not dramatic?"

I shrug. There are three well-known things about me: I'm competitive, I'm inflexible, and I'm emotional—which apparently makes me dramatic.

"If it weren't for me, your life would be dull. I keep you on your toes, Shaylene."

Ignoring me, she releases the bun at the top of her head. Box braids fall down her short torso and curl at the ends. Ebony skin glows like midnight under the fluorescent lights, contrasting perfectly against her pale pink bikini. Her eyes match her skin, surrounded by equally dark lashes. Shay is utterly gorgeous.

I, on the other hand, look just as tired as I feel. Tomorrow is wash day, which means my dark coils are frizzy and wild from North Carolina's humidity. A Clear Lake University Soccer shirt hangs to mid-thigh, showing the strong curve of my legs while hiding bikini bottoms that should have been donated years ago.

"Really?" She snorts. "Then why are you hiding away and being nosy? You're listening to Prince at a college party."

"Don't say it like that. Prince is acceptable for all occasions." I pull out my other earphone and twirl the cord around my finger. "And I'm not hiding away."

"You didn't deny the nosy part. At least you're self-aware."

Add that to my running list of traits. I'm nosy as hell.

The rickety chair heaves as she curls into my side, her skin cool and damp from the nasty water. "So, what have you learned so far?"

I nudge her shoulder with a smirk. "Who's the nosy one now?"

"Still you. Now get going before I throw you into the pool."

Shay may be six inches shorter than me, but I've learned to take her threats very seriously. So, on that note, I begin. "Brock and his girlfriend broke up. By the look of it, she ended things. There's a sea of blue texts in the reflection of his glasses, and I don't see one response in sight."

"Sunglasses indoors?" Shay sucks in a sharp breath. "Probably to hide his tears."

"Nice catch." I tip my head toward the captain of the tennis team and six-time loser of slap-the-bag. His torso is in the chair while his legs are splayed across the tile. "Marcus still can't handle his liquor, but him and Jenny? They're on again. Caught them making out when I went to get my charger."

"At least they didn't ask you to join them like they did last time."

To our left sits a duo taking shots. The women could pass as twins with their pale blonde ringlets and sun-kissed skin. "Aubrey and Letty made up. Looks like they're done fighting."

"Finally," Shay mutters. "Fourteen years of friendship almost down the drain over a *Chad*."

"Chicks over dick," I vow. Our fists bump in agreement.

My gaze jumps across the pool to my next target. Alongside many swimmers I know and respect stands one I know but definitely don't respect.

"And You-Know-Who? He didn't get laid over the break."

The dimple in Shay's cheek deepens into a crater. "Neither did you, hypocrite. And you can say his name. He isn't an evil villain."

"Are you sure about that?"

My teeth meet with a hard click as I focus on Kenneth Gray. Five plum bruises stand out along his left arm and shoulder from a recent cupping session. Mild amusement and worry dance across his strong features as he runs a large hand through scarlet waves, watching bubbles pour from his teammate Grant's nose. I swear a few girls swoon when his smile appears.

Shay says because I like the man as far as I can throw him, I'm blind to "the truth." Sure, years of being an elite athlete have sculpted his shoulders into boulders, you can wash clothes on his abs, and he could totally snap someone's neck with his thighs, but that's not the point!

I roll my eyes, refusing to give him any more of my attention. Before I can refocus on my next finding, I'm caught. Emerald eyes lock with mine, narrowing slightly. The coolness that radiates between us would give Jack Frost a cold.

A thick, red brow lifts, and I can basically read his mind: *Can I help you, Edwards?*

I roll my lips together. *Yes, Gray. Fuck off for all eternity.*

The bruised boulder shoulder rises. *Ladies first.*

Before I can flick him my favorite finger, he swiftly ends all brain talk and mouths, "Stop pouting."

"Shut up," I mouth back, pushing my tongue out like a petulant child.

He does the same because he is also a petulant child.

We've been at each other's throats since the first day of freshman year when he called my yellow sneakers and multicolored cardigan "rainbow vomit." After that, I was determined to avoid him, but we were thrown together at every turn. Things really went downhill when we both chose majors in the Hilliard School of Public Health.

What started as off-hand comments about who got the higher grade on the Bio 101 exam morphed into something much more, with planned point opportunities and a score sheet to meticulously track our wins. Everything is a point up for grabs in the Brain Bowl: the highest test scores, athletic national championship wins, canned food drives, community trash pickups, candy donations, dodgeball, party games, spelling bees, and more.

I won freshman year, 13-9. Kenneth won sophomore year, 11-14. Moving into the new semester for junior year, he's currently in the lead, 8-9. Junior year is on the line.

Dammit, my pride is on the line.

"Mally!"

My body convulses in a way that's not attractive at the shrillness of Shay's voice, and the back of my head smacks the chair with a painful thwack. "Ouch!" I shout, rubbing the sore spot. "Who the hell died?"

"Your youthfulness. Stop letting Kenneth give you frown lines at twenty-one." I relax my face, because I refuse to let him be the reason for my wrinkles, but they deepen when Shay speaks again. "By the way, your mom called me earlier."

A dry laugh slips out. "Of course she did."

"You know she calls me when you don't answer." She doesn't sound annoyed, even though this happens at least twice a month. "With Kenneth bragging all day, I didn't want to pile on more bad news. Especially after your endocrinologist appointment yesterday. It was rough."

Understatement of the year.

A little over a year ago, I was diagnosed with type 1 diabetes. Even though we've only been together for a short time, I describe it as my other half. The partner I can't leave behind or take a break from. It's always there and always will be.

I suck in a breath, holding it for three seconds before exhaling slowly.

Breathe, Mallory.

Releasing my jaw, I focus on my best friend's scowl and not the messy state of my brain. "You and I both know it's better that you didn't tell me earlier because I wouldn't have come out tonight. I would've stayed home and listened to sad music with my hand deep in a bag of tortilla chips. You did the right thing."

Lifting my phone from my tote, I hand it over.

"Shit." Her eyes quickly scan the screen as she scrolls through the missed calls and messages from my mom. "I thought things were getting better."

I did too. Then we spent my two weeks at home for holiday break on opposite sides of the house. Things have been uneasy between my mom and me since my dad passed away five years ago, and everything turned into a full-blown shit-show when I was diagnosed with type 1 diabetes. I wanted one night to not feel like a failure.

I open my continuous glucose monitoring app, and my shoulders relax when the number shows my blood sugar is in range.

I'm a perfectionist. To a fault if you ask most people. I used to believe there wasn't anything I couldn't do well. Managing my diabetes has proved me wrong. Day after day I feel like a failure, struggling to put up a fight against the all-consuming monster in my head: anxiety. Sometimes it hides, biding its time in the darkest and deepest corners of my brain, and when it comes out to play, good luck to me.

"I need to..." I trail off, crawling out of our shared seat. "I'm going to the restroom. I need a—"

"Breather," she finishes for me. Shay takes my hand and gives it a squeeze. "I love you big."

"I love you bigger."

Keeping my eyes on my phone, I make my way through the jam-packed aisles, maneuvering through drunks who forgot their inside voices at home. My favorite sandals are ruined by the puddles of stale water, and if one more person with wet hands touches me, I'm going to lose it.

"This is why I hate pools—" I choke on air, yanked backwards by my shirt as the restroom door blows past me with a gust of foul air.

"Seriously, MalPal? That door could've taken your head off! You and that damn phone."

I know that silly voice and Black dad warning from anywhere. Suddenly, I no longer care about my soggy sandals when Cade whirls me around. Locs hang to his shoulders, swaying gently like the rest of his body. Tonight's eye color is more green than brown, the tell-tale sign that my hazel-eyed friend is wasted. "A penny for your thoughts?"

"Come on, Cader Tot. You know it isn't smart to ask a lady what's on her mind, because it probably isn't very kind."

"When are your thoughts ever kind?" He hands over a package of candy before I can flick him. "I missed you, Mal. I just want to make sure we're starting the year with me as your favorite Guardian of the Blood Sugar."

Cade looks over my head at my other guardian, who is dozing off in our seat where I left her. Friends with benefits is what Shay and Cade are calling their little arrangement, but I'd bet a million dollars they'll be a couple by the end of the semester.

I pop a red fish into my mouth, savoring the burst of sugar on my tongue. "I have another reason you shouldn't be friends with Gray."

"Other than the fact that he's beating you?" Cade ignores my glare and bops my nose. "Give me your best shot."

"He's too pale!" I say. "Aren't you worried he's secretly a vampire?"

"Not everyone is blessed with melanin like us. In a few months, he'll be nice and tan and you can stop stressing."

I cross my arms. "Does that mean my request is denied?"

"Yup."

"Well, I'd like to make an appeal."

Cade lets out a drunk giggle before his attention lands above my head. "Hey, Kent! We were just talking about you! Weren't we, MalPal?"

I narrow my eyes at Cade. If I had laser vision, he would be a pile of dust at my feet.

"Of course you were," Kenneth says, the warmth of his body acting like my own personal space heater. My back feels like it's in a damn sauna.

Although Cade's mouth doesn't move, his eyes shimmer, darting down to me and back up. One curse of the two guys being friends since kindergarten is their ability to talk telepathically.

At five-ten, I'm above average height. Standing here between Kenneth at six-three and Cade at six-five, I feel tiny. I inch to the left slowly, desperate to slip out of this awkward, tall-people sandwich.

Cade jabs a finger over his shoulder right as I'm close to freedom. "Did you guys hear someone call my name?" he asks.

Hell no.

"Yeah, that's Shay. She probably needs me to... do something... I should go," he says, unable to keep a straight face.

"I will strangle you where you stand, string bean," I hiss.

Kenneth groans. "We can literally see her sleeping."

"You can't see anything! Bye!" Breaking pool rules, Cade sprints away and dives into the shallow water.

Cade Owens is dead to me. Dead dead *dead*.

"Edwards," Kenneth says in that overly formal tone that makes me want to salute.

Bracing myself, I turn around and salute anyway because I know he hates it. I tip my head back slightly to meet his eyes. What makes this worse is that I've always had a thing for tall men. If it was literally anyone else, these five inches would be perfect.

That's what she said.

When my lips quirk upward at my own joke, he pinches the bridge of his nose as if my presence alone exhausts him. "You need to be careful. Cade won't always be there to make sure you don't get concussed."

I chuckle. "How cute. You watching me, Gray?"

"Always, *Eddie*." Angling his body down, the limited space between us shrinks, giving me a front row seat to his shit-eating grin. I have hated that nickname since freshman year, which makes him love it even more. "Have I told you that you're cute when you pout? I can't imagine how good you'll look when I win junior year."

Now it's my turn to pinch the bridge of my nose. If it were any other time, I'd probably engage in this witty tango. Sadly, I don't have any fight in me tonight.

"Did you just come over here to brag? I get it, it's our thing. Annoy the shit out of the other current loser, but I can't do this tonight." Even though I step back to give him ample space to walk through, he stays rooted like the annoying weed he is. "Fine. I'll leave."

His brow lifts at my unusually defeated response. This isn't the reaction he's used to. Our interactions are exclusively related to the game. On the unlucky days we're forced to mingle, it always ends with a head-splitting migraine.

There's a weird tightness in his freckled forehead when his eyes meet mine again. "I wanted to make sure you were okay. That's all."

"*Okay*?" I ask, blinking hard at the man above me. After he spent the entire holiday break bragging about his lead and incessantly reminded me all night, now he wants to check in? Yeah right. I'll admit, our game isn't bad. I'd even consider it a fun distraction from my host of problems.

Then I remember how badly I need to beat him.

Winning the Brain Bowl would give me infinite bragging rights, but even more than that, I'm desperate to prove something to myself. That I am still me. Maybe a win will convince my brain I have my shit together, and I'll finally stop feeling like the epitome of an overachieving failure.

However, Kenneth doesn't need to know any of that. Not now. Not ever.

"I'm fine, Gray," I say. "Now, if you'll excuse me."

I fling the restroom door open, step through it, and leave him on the other side because I need peace, and Kenneth Gray is everything but that.

Chapter Two

Kenneth

"Hey, Grandpa." Cade's legs hang over the arm of the loveseat, his eyes glued to the television in our living room. "Who's the lucky lady tonight?"

I scan the endless stacks of boxes on the bookshelf. It's a good thing neither of us are big readers. If we were, where would my ladies go? A cluster of stars ranging from brilliant white to fiery red catches my eye, and I pull the puzzle down. "The nebula. She looks pretty."

"Great choice. I bet the guy who got it for you is sexy."

"He's also very conceited." I dump the contents of the box onto the dining room table. Cade gets me the coolest puzzles. "How long until they get here?"

"About an hour, so you better get going. And no timing yourself tonight."

I pat my pockets and glare at him. "Seriously? Did you take my timer again?"

Cade shrugs, reaching into his shirt to pull out my blue timer. "Relax. Set a world record another day."

With classes starting tomorrow, Cade and I spent our last free Monday deep cleaning the house for Mallory and Shay's arrival for tonight's Brain

Bowl activity. In an hour, Mallory will saunter in, bringing chaos and color into our home. I already bet Cade five bucks she'll wear a shade of orange.

After our run-in at the pool party on Friday night, I wasn't sure if she'd still come. Then I remembered Mallory Edwards doesn't flee. She runs straight toward competition with open arms and a cheek-splitting smile.

I've always secretly admired that about her.

"Can you at least give me a hint about tonight's game? I am your best friend after all," I plead, pressing my hands together.

Cade and Shay take their roles as gamekeepers seriously, which explains why his lips are zipped tight. I thought about bribing him with a cupcake from his favorite bakery because he's weak for desserts, but I decided against it. I'm competitive. Not a cheater.

"Nope. You'll have to wait like MalPal."

"You've known me longer."

He shrugs. "True, but we both know I love her more."

I flick a puzzle piece across the room at his head and hope it doesn't disappear forever. Cade and Mallory becoming best friends on the first day of freshman year was a dream for everyone except me. It was assumed they would become the 'it' couple, but by the end of the first week, they were nothing more than best friends. Attached at the hip and wreaking havoc on my life.

While Cade snagged a lifelong friendship, I scored a rival.

I refocus on the scattered pieces in front of me. Abstract puzzles are my favorite. A challenge to complete with no solid shapes, only a kaleidoscope of colors and patterns that I must assemble with nothing more than a glimpse of the box and a lot of patience.

The puzzle border is nearly complete when the doorbell rings. Mallory is chronically early, but never this early.

Cade slides off the couch and disappears down the hallway. The silence that follows the creaking door is my first clue that Mallory isn't standing on our doorstep. If she were here, her wild cackle that she calls a laugh would be bouncing off the walls at a joke Cade made.

I push my seat back and stand, grabbing my wallet from the table. Girl Scout Cookie season just began, so Cade's likely about to buy the girl's entire inventory.

When I step into the foyer, there are no cookies and no smiling Cade. Instead, my father's intimidating aura fills the whole room. His tailored dress pants, white button-down, and perfectly styled copper hair taunt my pajama bottoms, tattered hoodie, and damp hair.

Sharp green eyes snap to me. "Hello, Kenneth."

Cade awkwardly steps around my father, jamming his thumb over his shoulder. "I'll be in the other room. Nice to see you, Mr. Gray."

My father's stoic demeanor vanishes, bright white teeth splitting his scowl. "How many times have I told you to call me Theo, Cade? I've known you for years. I think we're past the formalities."

Cade gives my dad a polite, tight-lipped smile before making his escape. He gives my shoulder a supportive bump as he moves past me. Part of me is jealous he can get away, but I'd hate to expose him to Theo Gray for any longer than necessary.

The moment Cade's bedroom door closes, I speak. "What brings you to town, Dad?"

Clear Lake is thirty minutes from Cade's and my hometown of Bryan, which is too close to my father if you ask me. I should've left North Carolina when I had the chance.

"We're starting a new project in Clear Lake. Thought I'd come by before heading home." He gives my shoulder a too-hard squeeze before strolling past me into the dining room. He studies the unfinished puzzle on the table. "Can't a man stop by and see his son?"

Maybe other dads can, but mine would never.

Truthfully, I can't remember the last time he checked in. Unless Theo Gray needs me, I'm nonessential. I bide my time hiding in the shadows, enjoying the calm until something happens that forces him to reach out.

Which means this random drop-in is not random at all.

I gesture for him to take a seat and do the same. "Sure. How are you?"

His eyes sparkle, elated to talk about his favorite things. Himself and his company. "Incredible. I have a few important meetings scheduled this week, and business is great. Our expansion plan is going well because your brother is doing great with our out-of-state clients. With your sister joining the team soon, it's all coming together. Gray Construction is growing."

I hate that I'm upset he doesn't ask how I'm doing too. "That's great, Dad."

"Sure is. Everyone's excited for you to join us this summer. I can't believe your internship is finally here."

A knot forms in my throat, my words crackling on their way over it. "Wait. What?"

Theo leans over the table and picks up a puzzle piece, magically placing it in its spot. "Don't tell me you forgot. The Gray tradition. Everything you've been working so hard for."

Since I was a kid, my father has been attempting to control my future by forcing me to join the family business. It's exactly what he did to my siblings. It's exactly what my grandfather did to him.

The summer before senior year, every Gray spends ten weeks completing an internship to prepare them for the job they'll begin after their college graduation.

"I mean... Is it necessary?" I ask, dropping my eyes to the table.

"The internship? Of course it is."

"No, I meant..." I wet my lips before trying again. "Is it necessary for me to do it? You already have—"

"Don't be dense. It's every Gray, Kenneth. Not just your siblings."

"What about my degree? I changed it—"

"To spite me," he bites, cutting me off again. His tone may be measured, but his nostrils flare as he glares over the dining table. "Your mother asked me to be patient with you, and I tried, but I think it's time for a little reminder of what's ahead. I'm glad your hasty change of major didn't mess up the plan. I didn't spend thousands of dollars putting you through school for you to not join Gray Construction. Can you imagine what that would do to me?"

There it is. The only thing that truly matters to him. Not his family or the happiness of his children. Nope. His image. To the world, Theo Gray runs one of the most successful construction companies in North Carolina and is a doting father with a beautiful and happy family.

To me, it's all perfectly curated bullshit.

He wasn't pleased when he found out I had changed my major from finance to biostatistics at the beginning of freshman year. With the switch, I assumed I'd be free of this tradition crap and be able to chase my own passions.

All this time, I thought I escaped, but I was caught in his trap and didn't even know it.

I open my mouth to speak, but he holds a hand up to stop me. "I'd advise you to think before you speak. You need to remember where you came from and who takes care of you. You're a Gray, first and foremost. Forgetting that will lead to losing everything."

Theo turns and his fancy shoes clack against the vinyl flooring as he storms out of the dining room. The door is open by the time I make it around the corner, with his megawatt smile plastered across his face.

"Welcome to the family business, son. Don't disappoint me."

Then he's gone.

I make my way into the living room and sink onto the ground, yanking my hair until my scalp screams to be released. This has to be a nightmare. What does he mean I'll lose *everything* if I don't follow him?

When I open my eyes, Cade is standing over me. For a giant, he sure does move stealthily. "Why do you look like you lost a puzzle piece and can't finish it?"

That reminds me. I lean over to retrieve the piece I threw at him earlier. Losing the final puzzle piece is a reoccurring nightmare of mine.

"What did he want this time?" Cade continues, sinking onto the ground beside me.

I roll the piece between my fingers, tracing its smooth curves. Puzzles have always been able to calm me, but it's not helping right now. Nothing can counteract the way my skin is crawling.

After checking the clock and realizing there isn't enough time to fully discuss how screwed I am, I opt for a half truth. "He just stopped by to say hello."

Cade's jaw sets, already frustrated. "Your dad never comes by without needing something from you. The last time he dropped by was in July, demanding you go home for a photo opportunity for a news article."

Damn him for knowing my dysfunctional family so well. I must have forgotten he has had a front row seat since we were five.

"Fine." I sigh. "He said—"

The shrill doorbell cuts me off, but Cade's eyes don't leave mine. I'm certain that no matter how many times they knock, if I asked, he would sit here and talk with me until Mallory kicked the door down. He's so loyal. I'm still not sure what I did to deserve a friend like him.

"Rain check?" I ask, because I can't handle a shitty dad and a broken door tonight.

Uncertainty weaves into his features as he stands and helps me up. “Fine. Rain check, but you know I have a terrible memory, so you better remind me. Now, go get ready because you look terrible.”

This time when he smiles, I mirror it.

After that shit-show, I need a distraction and a win.

Chapter Three

"I'm revoking your gamekeeper status, Cade. I'm serious this time. You're finished."

"MalPal," he soothes. "I literally picked out of a hat. What was I supposed to do? Pick again?"

"Duh."

The crisp five-dollar bill in my pocket crinkles as I slink beside Mallory, draping an arm over her orange-clad shoulders. I can't lie. My deflated spirits were lifted the moment she strolled in wearing a bright orange sweater and colorful striped shorts, as if it isn't thirty degrees outside.

I know exactly why she's upset. We haven't played table tennis for the Brain Bowl since freshman year, which is lucky considering she couldn't win a single set. I think it's because she holds the paddle like she's trying to squeeze the living daylights out of it. I've watched the woman in the goal, gracefully stopping penalty kicks and goal attempts, which requires impeccable hand-eye coordination. But the moment there's a paddle in her hand, she's like a cat in a bathtub.

All claws and chaos.

Mallory shakes my arm off and slides to the opposite side of the couch like I've got the flu. "Actually, I blame you, Gray. What did you do? Bribe him with a cookie? Cade's a weakling. That sugar fiend would give up his own little sister for a treat."

"Would not!" Cade argues, but considering there are three brownies jammed into his cheeks, nobody believes him.

I scoff. "Dude, you licked an icicle on Christmas for the last piece of your mom's fudge. It took half an hour to free your tongue."

"He did what?" Mallory gasps. "No fucking way."

"Language!" Cade shouts, even though his warnings do nothing for the potty-mouth beside me. "Plus, Mom's fudge is worth the pain!"

There's no arguing with that. Billie Owens makes the best desserts.

The soft upcurve of Mallory's lips is revealed as she wrestles dark, tight springs of hair at the base of her neck. Then she looks at me, and it turns into a grimace. "You watching me, Gray?"

I shrug, waving a hand at her outfit. "It's hard not to when you look like a walking Skittles advertisement."

She leans over the cushion that separates us to pinch my faded black T-shirt. "Just because you wouldn't know style if it crawled up your ass and introduced itself to your brain, doesn't mean you have to dress so dreary."

Feigning hurt, I grab my chest. My outfit isn't *dreary*. It's neutral. Black, gray, brown, white, and beige are my favorite colors.

In that order.

Leaning back, I use my only trump card. "Regardless, I'm currently leading the Brain Bowl, so maybe there's something beneficial about not being a rainbow twenty-four-seven? Might want to think about the foolproof logic behind that."

As if she had been waiting all night, Mallory snatches a grape from the bowl on the coffee table and pulls her arm back, but before she can chuck it at my forehead, Shay clears her throat.

"Enough."

The single word is laden with exhaustion, exaggerated by a stony glare. Cade stands beside her, towering over her tiny frame. Still, she's way more terrifying than the gentle giant beside her. I've seen her play soccer. She's a ranked defender for a reason.

"Let's get started. You guys know the rules," Shay continues. "No violence. Best-of-five sets and sets go to eleven. As a reminder, Kenneth has nine points, and Mallory has eight points in the Brain Bowl."

I grin at the side of Mallory's face, and I'm sure she can feel it burning into her skin because she leaps up and pulls Shay to the opposite side of the room. Cade drops beside me, massaging my shoulders like I'm preparing for a boxing match.

"Feeling good?" he asks.

I nod. "If it's anything like last time, we'll be done in half an hour."

Once settled on my side, I tap the paddle against my leg and watch the woman across from me. A few curls have escaped from their ponytail jail and hang around her face. There's a ferocity in Mallory's honeyed gaze, narrowed to study the table. Determination furrows her brow as a sliver of pink drags across her full bottom lip.

Mallory doesn't play to win. She plays to dominate.

"You look cute when you concentrate, Ed."

Her head pops up and she flashes me a wicked grin. "No way. Fake flirting won't work tonight. There's no getting under my skin when I'm in the zone, buddy. My serve."

Buddy? No thanks. I prefer Gray.

I toss the ball over the net. "Remember when you serve, the ball has to hit your side of the table before—"

"Gray," she stops me, tapping the table. "If you keep talking to me like I'm a child, I'm going to walk over there and bitch slap you with this paddle. Understood?"

Cade jumps out of his seat. "MalPal! What's rule number one? No violence! Don't make me get the timeout chair."

Mallory's eyes never leave mine, even as Cade screams about sportsmanship and respect.

My grip on the paddle tightens because *this* is why I play our game. When I'm with her, I feel free. No responsibilities. No family obligations. No stress. Only a bone-crushing want to win and compete with the most competitive person I know.

"You're on, Eddie."

She tosses the ball into the air and yanks her arm back. I'm prepared to return whatever wild smack she sends my way, but her confident smile wipes the smirk right off my face. With a swift flick of her wrist, a flash of white whizzes across the table, and the ball's harsh smack against the back corner echoes.

"What the..." I trail off, my eyes following the ball as it rolls under the couch. Mallory could barely get the ball over the net last time we played, and her serves were true comedy. Sometimes they landed on the table. Most of the time they smacked the wall.

"Where did you learn that?" I ask.

She pulls a ball from her pocket, savoring every second of my confusion. "After getting my ass kicked freshman year, I decided I'd never let that happen again and joined the rec center's table tennis league. Ruined my sleep schedule for a semester, but it clearly paid off."

I glare at the gamekeepers. "Did you guys know about this?"

Shay nods, which I expected, and Cade shakes his head. "No way, Kent. I was expecting MalPal to get creamed by you."

Mallory gags. "Phrasing."

I set my feet. This time, I won't focus on the ball. I'll follow the movement of her body, which is angled just enough to give me a slight hint. I shift to my right, ready to return it, but when it hits the left side of the table, my mouth falls open.

"Kent, you're getting creamed now. MalPal might actually win tonight!" Cade laughs, rushing over to give Mallory a high-five.

Glaring at him and pull a ball from my pocket. It's my turn now, and I doubt her receiving improved as much as her serving.

I toss the ball into the air, aiming for the back right corner, and a flash of shock rocks me when she shuffles to the side and returns it with ease. It's short, so I slam it back to her side.

Then everything goes dark, a shadow falling over me. When I lift my eyes, all I see is Mallory's blinding grin, shifting from excitement to pure fear. Full lips shape into an 'o' as the ball smacks me right between the eyes, and the hollow plastic feels like a golf ball to the face.

"Shit!" Mallory bites down on her lip to keep from smiling, failing spectacularly. She lifts her hand and points to her forehead. "You've got a little something... right there."

Cade stands and sighs. "I'm sure that was an accident. Just in case there's any retaliation, I'm going to get the timeout chair."

A bead of sweat drips from my brow as I smash the ball over the net. The ball is a blur of white as we volley back and forth.

"Wow, Gray," Mallory chuckles. "I expected more from you. Looks like you may have underestimated me this time."

"The game isn't over, Edwards," I bite out, spiking the ball toward the right corner.

Despite my best efforts, she only needs one more point to win the whole thing.

We've been at this for what feels like hours, and she's right. I did underestimate her. After years of knowing exactly how smart, talented, and driven she is, I should have known better than to make that mistake.

I'll never do it again.

With a small smile, Mallory pulls her arm back. The one plus to tonight is that I've gotten better at reading her, so I'm sure she's going for a long shot. Adrenaline shoots through me as I take a half step back, but the professional she's morphed into tricks me and barely nudges the ball over the net.

I leap forward to reach it, slamming my thighs against the table, but after the second bounce, I've officially been bested.

"Victory is mine! Suck it, Gray!" Mallory shouts.

Cade and Shay clap as she marches around the room, jabbing me in the chest with her paddle every time she passes me. The temptation to wrap my arms around her to stop the assault to my sternum is high. Instead, I swallow my need and head into the kitchen for a glass of cold water and a pity party.

My eyes wander into the dining room, spotting the unfinished puzzle scattered across the table. I'll probably never finish it. My father's negative energy and the confusion he brought ruined it.

I didn't lose once today. I lost twice.

Sneakers squeak on the tile behind me and the heat of Mallory's stare warms the back of my neck. I press the frosty glass to my cheek and realize that even ice isn't enough to counteract her intensity.

"Did you come in here to brag?" I ask.

"Yes, then Shay reminded me that I smacked the absolute hell out of you and told me I should check on you." She clears her throat, and I feel her hesitate. "Are you okay?"

Oh. I catch myself smiling at her softened tone. It's not one I'm usually on the receiving side of.

"I'm fine, Eddie. Not many people could survive a power smash from you, so I'm considering myself lucky to be one of the few."

Instead of laughing at my joke, which she never does, she makes a command.

"Turn around, Gray."

The smell of warm vanilla fills my nose when I do. She's closer than I expect, and my breath hitches when her chest grazes mine as she leans in to inspect the sore spot between my eyes.

"Ouch. That looks painful. You should put some ice on it."

I swallow hard and force my eyes away from her. "It'll be red for the next three to five business days. Remember, pale as a vampire." Another desperate attempt to make her laugh, but all humor is sucked out of the kitchen when her finger brushes over the sore spot. Every morsel of pain somehow disappears too.

"I'm sorry," she says. "I know I can get a little... intense."

Mallory's cutthroat energy is one of my favorite things about her. I consider myself fortunate to see it up close, even at the expense of my own safety.

"While I'm here," she continues, stepping back to grab an icepack from the freezer before handing it over. "I might as well brag since I did win. We're tied again, 9-9. I'm one point closer to junior year being mine."

"Relax, Eddie. We've got an entire semester ahead of us," I huff out, pressing the icepack to my forehead. "Five months is a long time. Anything could happen."

Like losing everything I've worked so hard for. Like losing her.

I follow the comet of color to the front door. Mallory's head falls back at something Cade says, and a sliver of jealousy tugs at the knot in my stomach. That type of joy is never aimed at me.

"See you at the next point opportunity, Gray!" she calls over her shoulder, and the words remind me of my place in her life. My time with Mallory has always been limited to the game and the game only.

And it makes me sadder than usual this time.

Chapter Four

I'm jinxed. Doomed. Cursed. Whatever you want to call it. My parents gifted me this bad omen on the day I was born, and I've been rolling with the punches ever since.

The name Mallory *literally* means unlucky.

I've coped with my poor fate by meticulously planning my entire life in my sparkly teal planner. Every appointment, meeting, class, hangout, practice, game, and goal is written inside. Color-coded too. I treat the expensive stack of paper like a source of good luck to keep misfortune away. However, no amount of planning will help if the goddess of fortune is not on your side.

And Fortuna is hardly on mine.

I was reminded of this cruel reality when I walked outside for class this morning to find my car's tire flat against the sidewalk. It isn't even eight in the morning, and the first day of class is already going downhill.

Hooking my backpack over my shoulders, I blow Shay a wet kiss for driving me to class before I dash into the public health building and climb four flights of stairs in record time. Standing outside the classroom, I check my watch. Three minutes to spare.

Being late is not a part of my brand. My motto is to show up on time or don't even bother showing up at all.

Relief swells as I notice familiar faces in the small science lab. Beverly from sophomore organic chemistry waves. Gerald from freshman business management lifts his chin. Debra from last semester's microbiology lab gives me a shy smile. Sadly, all of them are already sitting with other people.

Great. I may not be late, but I'm the last to arrive.

When an empty seat in the middle of the room catches my eye, I shuffle toward it, thankful nobody is watching my almost-late walk of shame.

I slip onto the tailbone-bruising seat and pull out my planner, forcing myself to take deep and slow breaths. My endocrinologist, Dr. Morand, should be proud of me for doing my morning breathing exercises, considering he calls me a ball of stress.

Today's agenda is already stacked: two classes, practice, grocery shopping, research summer internships, pick up my insulin, change my glucose monitor sensor, and prepare for the first week of school. I scribble *fix tire* in purple ink.

I take another deep inhale and freeze, suddenly more on edge than I was earlier. My skin crawls as each hair takes its time standing upright, my nose stinging at the assault on my nostrils.

Clean soap.

Citrus.

Chlorine.

Fuck.

"Gray?" I whisper, dread filling me as he swivels around.

The second his tired eyes meet mine, the enormous orange between his hands falls to the floor, and he has the audacity to gawk at me as if I slapped it down.

In our time in the Hilliard School of Public Health, we've never had a class together. While we have overlap in our studies, I prefer morning classes while he chooses afternoon ones. Now he has screwed up our foolproof system.

"Happy Tuesday, class!"

I straighten, forcing my eyes to stay on the professor's leopard print tie and not the man beside me. After a moment of hesitation, Kenneth follows my lead and faces the front.

"Welcome to Public Health Professions 301. I'm Dr. Andres Martin. Many of you may remember me from Intro to Epidemiology." He takes a moment to smile at each table, and I return it. I loved his class sophomore year. "The Hilliard School of Public Health has four undergraduate programs, so let's see what our mix is. How many of you are with nutrition?"

Six hands including mine go up.

"Environmental?" Nine hands go up.

"Biostatistics?" Kenneth's hand raises with two others.

"And health administration and policy?" My hand goes up alone.

"Perfect." Dr. Martin claps. "If you're sitting with someone in the same program as you, please switch tables."

Dr. Martin is well known for forcing students to mingle, but I won't let that keep me from my number one mission: avoid Kenneth Gray.

Gathering my belongings, I stand and sprint toward a seat with an environmental student. Her brunette braid whips back and forth as she waves me over.

"Wait," Dr. Martin says. He might as well be pointing at me because everyone's eyes jump to me. "You're health admin and nutrition, and your tablemate is biostats, which means you're good to stay."

I nod, swallowing a groan as I trudge back to my seat and plop onto the lab stool.

"Causing trouble on the first day?" Kenneth lets out a low whistle. "Atta girl."

When Dr. Martin looks away to stop another switch attempt, I push my middle finger into Kenneth's smug face to shut him up. There's no way I'm going to survive sitting beside him all semester. With the Brain Bowl, sharing a best friend, and being student-athletes, our lives are intertwined enough.

The volume of the room skyrockets as everyone dives into introductions. Well, everyone except us. I already know everything I need to know about my tablemate. He's spontaneous, untroubled, and mind-achingly relaxed all the time.

The complete opposite of me.

My moment of peace takes a nosedive straight to hell when Dr. Martin's gaze lands on our table. He encourages us to speak, opening and closing his hands like a chicken's beak. Fine.

"Mallory Edwards. Better than you."

"Kenneth Gray. Over my dead body."

As if hearing our exchange, the professor chuckles. "Now that you're acquainted, let's get into the syllabus. This elective is meant to be full of work and fun. We've got weekly quizzes, a final exam, and a project. Your project is an application for a summer internship for the Hilliard School of Public Health. While you aren't required to apply for the internship, every part of the process will be graded. The winner will choose a mentor from the specialty of their choosing and work beside them for ten weeks."

My spine straightens. Unlike everyone else in the room, my health administration and policy major requires a completed internship prior to the first day of senior year. Without it, I'll be put on academic probation.

Sure, it would be kind of funny, and terribly sad, to be a 4.0 student on probation. What isn't funny is how the required make-up internship class adds an extra semester to my degree plan and isn't offered in the summer. Which means everything I've been planning for years, graduation and my graduate school aspirations, would have to wait until the *next* fall.

After a rejection letter from my dream internship in Seattle, I've done nothing but panic. Even with five months until summer, most positions are already filled. I can't handle another email raving about my stellar application and not offering a position.

Internships are meant for learning, an opportunity to challenge myself and peek into my future. I wanted to be picky to avoid wasting my time and not getting a lick of hands-on experience, but now I'm cutting it too close for comfort.

Thankfully, the perfect opportunity is here.

"The best part is that you'll be working with a partner!"

Confused, I raise my hand and wait for him to call on me. "If there's only one winner, why do we have a partner?"

Dr. Martin snaps his fingers. "Great question. Partnerships and teamwork are the backbone of public health. I believe that working together will help push you all to new heights."

I glance over my shoulder to find a suitable partner. This decision could truly make or break my chances of winning.

"Slow down, everyone," Dr. Martin chuckles. "Your partners have already been chosen." All the air leaves my lungs like a deflated balloon when he seals my fate for the world's worst semester and most difficult elective. "Your partner is sitting right beside you."

Whereas most of the class celebrates, I feel like I've been hit by a bus and a train. At the same damn time.

Kenneth's eyes bore into the side of my head so harshly it burns, surely thinking the same thing I am: *fuck fuck fuckity fuck.*

What kind of sick joke is the universe playing on me?

The rest of class flies by in a blur because before I know it, I'm slinging my backpack over my shoulder to leave. I feel like shit, but Kenneth looks even worse. Frozen like a statue, he grips the table with such intensity it might crumble.

Whatever. He can stay here and whine. I need to fix this.

"Hi, Dr. Martin," I say when I reach the podium. "I'm Mallory Edwards. Do you have a moment?"

He's shorter than I remember, considering instead of looking up at him, he tilts his head back to look up at me. "Ah, yes. I remember you from epidemiology. I didn't realize you're a double major student. Impressive. What can I do for you?"

Kenneth appears beside me, and Dr. Martin tilts his head even further back to meet his eyes.

"I—" Waving a hand between us, I start over. "*We* were wondering if there's any way we could switch partners."

"Is there any particular reason you don't want to work with..." he trails off.

"Kenneth Gray, sir."

I wait an extra beat for Kenneth to continue and give him one of the millions of reasons we shouldn't *ever* work together, but he's uncharacteristically silent beside me.

"We don't get along," I explain simply. I doubt Dr. Martin has time to listen to years of grievances. I barely have time to deal with it.

"Well, a blind man could see that." He taps his chin before pointing at us. "Are you exes?"

"No!" I yell, taking a half step away from Kenneth. How could he possibly think that?

"Then I see no reason you two can't make it through a semester. Five months. Groups were chosen by fate, and part of your final grade is determined by how you interact with each other. Working with people you don't like is sadly part of the real world. While it's not fun, it's life." He leans back against the podium. "Do you think you two can handle it?"

No. Absolutely not. Partnering with Kenneth sounds like my own personal hell with no escape until May. I don't think we can work together for one day, let alone an entire semester. We're rivals. We compete *against* each other. Working together isn't in our vocabulary.

I start to answer, and my stomach drops when Kenneth clearly says, "Yes. We will be fine."

Dr. Martin waits patiently for my confirmation, so against my better judgement, I nod.

"Great! You might even be able to fix," he waves his hands in the air, "all of this." Gathering his belongings, he looks at me over his shoulder. "Any particular reason for your choice of majors?"

I shake off my annoyance, excited to finally use my perfectly crafted elevator pitch. "I chose health administration and policy because of the endless career choices. Nutrition started off as a selfish choice. Then I was diagnosed with type 1 diabetes and found a way to tie my degrees together."

"Sometimes those selfish choices end up being the most beneficial." He laughs heartily. "I remember the paper you wrote for epidemiology about the diabetes camp in your hometown. You did a lot of work with their donation letters, right?"

"Yes sir." I can't believe he remembers that. I did get a perfect grade, but still.

"I'd love to chat with you sometime about your experiences and the camp." His gaze drops to my chest, and for a second, I'm incredibly offended. Then I remember my CLU Soccer long-sleeve. "And you're a student-athlete! Do you have some time next week?"

I anchor my heels into the ground to keep from bouncing. "Of course!"

We stand silently as Dr. Martin gives us one last encouraging word about how teamwork makes the dream work before exiting the room, leaving my new partner and I standing side by side.

Heat fills me when his shoulder brushes mine. "We should talk, Ed—"

I jump when my back pocket starts to screech, wincing when I pull out my phone. Even though the name that flashes across the screen makes me feel more uneasy than this new partnership does, I use the excuse to get away.

"Later. Bye," I say, heading for the stairs before he can respond. The moment I'm a safe distance away, I click the green button and pull it to my ear. "Good morning, Mama."

Blaring car horns assault my eardrums, which lets me know she stepped out of her classroom for this call. The first sign this won't be a good conversation.

"Did you eat breakfast this morning?" she asks.

"Good morning to you too," I mumble. Stepping into the sun, the breeze whips around me as I head across campus for biochemistry. "Yes."

"What did you eat?"

I stitch my lips together to keep from snapping. This isn't what I need today. I was looking for an escape from Kenneth and ran smack dab into another problem.

"Can we do this later? It's been a rough morning, and I need to get going for—"

She cuts me off. "I get it. You're busy. I am too, which is why it's absurd that I had to walk out of class to make sure you're taking care of business like you're supposed to."

"You didn't need to do that," I remind her as I open the app and scroll through my blood sugar data from the past hour. "I've been in range all morning, so what's the problem?"

"In range doesn't mean good. Again, what did you eat?"

"Please stop," I whisper, taking a seat on a bench. "I know you're worried and I appreciate it—"

"Someone has to care, Mallory, and I'm sorry, but it doesn't seem like you do."

I feel like I've been slapped across the face, shame making my cheeks hot. Is she kidding? All I do is care. Too much, all the time. School, soccer, my future, my health. It's not like I can flip a switch and turn off my ability to care. If I could, things would be a whole lot easier.

Her sharp words wrap themselves around my throat, pricking my skin as my chest tightens. I've lived with anxiety long enough to identify when an anxiety attack is on the horizon. With the flat tire, my new partnership with Kenneth, and now my mom, I feel it hovering.

Which is why my tingling fingers press the red button without a goodbye. I power my phone off and shove it back into my pocket.

These are the days I could use a hug from my dad.

"Breathe," I say to myself. "You're doing your best." I continue this mantra on my way to class, forcing myself to not say what I'm really thinking.

You're a failure, Mallory.

Chapter Five

"Your bad juju is getting worse," Shay huffs from the grass, struggling to catch her breath. "It's barely Thursday of week one and you've already had a flat tire, struggled to fix said tire, got partnered with Kenneth, and slipped on ice on the way to practice. Maybe you should change your name."

"How do you guys feel about Melanie?" I ask, rubbing my sore elbow. "Seems a little less unlucky."

"No way. I went to high school with a girl named Melanie, and she was the worst," Adri, our center forward says. "If you know one bad Melanie, you know them all."

"Fair." I'll give them my other name options later. I'm too winded from that conditioning session from hell. Off-season is in full swing, and Coach Sumner is a big fan of cardio.

"Hey! My cousin's name is Melanie," Jo, our right midfielder, says between drinks of Gatorade.

"Exactly. She's an actual nightmare, and you know it," Adri counters.

I hold my hand up. "If we're talking about mean girl names, I think Adrienne is pretty high on the list."

"Agreed," Shay and Jo say together.

Adri bats her eyes innocently, but little horns replace her halo when she pops our thighs with a towel.

The stitch in my side resurfaces, but from laughter instead of burpees. Even though Jo and Adri are sophomores, they round out The Quartet. I can always count on these three to turn my days around.

Ending our too short break, Coach Sumner yells my name from the water cooler and points at the goal. I pull Shay up with a grunt, grab my goalkeeper gloves, and head to my home. Every day at the end of practice, the team lines up to take their best shot on goal, while I analyze and perfect my craft. Reading their eyes. Following their body language. Dissecting their approach. Covering all twenty-four by eight feet of the goal. Reacting not too early, but not too late.

It's a science.

"Mally!" a cheery voice calls out.

Once in the goal box, I turn to find Bex, the athletic department's registered dietitian, jogging toward me. As much as I adore the woman, her presence is never a good sign.

"Hey, Bex." I slide on my gloves. "To what do I owe the pleasure?"

She leans against the goal and sucks in air. "Michaela said you're on edge today. More than usual, which is worrisome. I think we all expected the next step to be off the cliff and into the abyss."

I drag a gloved fingertip across my neck at Michaela, the soccer team's athletic trainer, who gives herself a high-five.

"Don't be mad. I texted her first." Bex's face transforms from friend to dietitian-friend. "What's going on? You've got major stress waves radiating off you. I can't tell if your hair is extra poofy from that or the humidity."

I might as well be wearing a neon sign that says *I'm totally NOT okay!*

Slapping on a fake smile, I force my tone to stay casual. "Coach Sumner won't be happy with precious practice time being used to talk."

As expected, Bex sees right through my excuse. Holding five fingers up to Coach Sumner, she gets the approval she needs and stares at me. "Is it your mom?"

Shit. Am I that easy to read?

Word vomit crawls up my throat and I'm suddenly relieved to let it out. "Of course it is. We fought all break, Bex. Over the stupidest things too. I wanted ice cream, and she asked me if I thought it was a good idea. Five times. I went for a run, and she accused me of prioritizing soccer over my health. And she keeps texting screenshots of my blood sugar, as if I'm not getting the same notifications."

"I'm so sorry to hear that," Bex says. "You've been doing so well—"

I shake my head, cutting her off. "Don't patronize me, please. I'm not a child who needs to be soothed with lies."

She winces, and I regret the words immediately. High emotions don't mean I can go off on people for no reason. Especially when all she's trying to do is help.

"I'm sorry," I say. "I just don't feel like I'm doing well, so how can you be so sure that I am?"

Bex's face softens, her never-ending patience making me feel even guiltier. "I'm sure because I know *you*. There's nothing you half-ass. That word isn't even in your vocabulary. Your data keeps getting better and better." When she opens the app that rules my life, my stomach rolls instinctively. My blood sugar level pops up, and I have to look away.

"Speaking of numbers," she continues, "are you still happy with your game plan?"

I give her a *so-so* hand movement.

"It's okay for plans to change, you know? We could circle back on our insulin pump discussion."

That's the last thing I need right now. I'm tired of change. To me, change and failure are the same, and I'm not sure how much more I can handle before I break.

"I'm thinking about it," I lie through my teeth.

Bex's eyes narrow, but she doesn't push the subject any further. "Just so you know, your blood sugar was trending up. There's no need to pull you out right now. I wanted to give you a quick break."

Breathe.

My eyes burn as frustrated tears threaten to fall. My brain tries to remind me that diabetes is complex, but that does little to quell the frustration buried deep in my gut as shame fills my vision.

Dammit. Breathe, Mallory.

I can't lose soccer too. It's the last thing I have connecting me with my dad. My first coach. The person who took me to get goalie gloves so I could try out for the club team. The only parent who never missed a game, always screaming in the stands. Even on the hard days.

"Hey." Bex's sharp tone slaps me out of my spiraling thoughts. "Don't shut down on me. I tell you this every time we meet. You can strive for perfection, but I promise you, it will *never* come. Today you're high, sure. Do you remember yesterday? Yesterday was one of those great days! And the practice before break? You were lower than I'd seen in months. The trainers asked if it was within their job description to force feed you gummy bears."

I chuckle and the shame seems a little less blinding.

"This journey is not a straight shot." Her finger wiggles like a worm. "It's a roller coaster. You've got to strap in and give yourself grace or you'll never be happy. Failure is okay." I start to refute her last sentence, but she beats me to it. "Failure *has* to be okay, Mally."

Over Bex's shoulder, my teammates are gathered outside the penalty box. Laughter and labored breathing overpower the blood pumping in my ears. This team has been incredibly patient over the past year, giving me an extra minute to scarf down applesauce or rehydrate.

The only way I know how to repay them is to do my job and stop goals.

It hasn't been the easiest transition. The uneasy looks, endless check-ins, and constant worry from my friends, teammates, and family. Soccer is the only thing right now that makes me feel like me.

I take a deep breath, exhaling slowly. "I want to finish practice." It might not be physiologically possible, but as my shoulders fall, I feel my blood sugar do the same. "I need to."

"Good. Finish strong." Bex pats my shoulder. "Forget about everything that isn't on this field and play."

With renewed energy, I stare down the familiar black-and-white ball and take my position: a few steps in front of the goal line, feet shoulder width apart, knees slightly bent, hands ready, and eyes on the prize.

"There she is," Coach Sumner yells, blowing his whistle twice. "Adri! You're up!"

"Yes sir!" Adri steps up to the ball and winks. "Kick some ass, Cap."

I push open the front door, letting the heater wrap me with warmth as I slip off my tennis shoes. Shay heads to her bedroom to shower, and I shuffle into the kitchen. Standing over the sink, I spy a deep red lipstick mark in my reflection. Only Jane, Sunshine Junction's best waitress, kisses my cheek hard enough to leave a mark.

During midterms freshman year, I fell asleep in a bright yellow booth at Sunshine Junction with my head in a textbook. Instead of kicking me out, Jane threatened to ban anyone who disturbed me. Since then, she comes to every home game, memorizes my class schedule, and brings over warm meals and big hugs on bad days. In exchange for her kindness, I babysit her seven-year-old twins, Jaxon and Julie.

Behind me, Shay steps out of the bathroom and lets out a long yawn commingled with a scream. "Morning classes should be a crime. I'm thinking about skipping sports marketing at ten."

"Ten is hardly considered a morning class. Don't make me storm in at nine with bells and whistles."

Thanks to the reflection in the window over the sink, I'm able to dodge the cat toy she launches at my head. "Not everyone can get up at the ass crack of dawn like you, Mal."

"Nine is not the ass crack of dawn, you whiny crybaby."

While Shay drones on about morning people being vile, I admire our little home. Pale blue walls are adorned with photos and records of my favorite albums, with a plant in every corner. Winry, my black cat, snores quietly on the large sectional. I drag a finger across the kitchen's textured, floral wallpaper that I can't seem to hate no matter how much I try.

"Wow. Ignoring me? You know how to make a girl feel special," Shay deadpans. "If I don't skip class, do you want to meet for brunch after?"

I pop a pod into the dishwasher. "I've heard your morning-people rant too many times and didn't feel like being judged for being able to wake up before the sun is out. And yes, brunch sounds great. Sunshine Junction?"

"Sunshine Junction," she says, turning off the lights.

The thunderous ringtone I set for The Quartet group message stops me from heading to my room. I look at Shay, whose stank face is already illuminated with white light as she stares at the screen.

"Stop holding in your farts or you'll explode, Shaylene."

"Shut up and check your phone."

I click the lights back on and scroll to the first text from Adri in our group message.

Adri Da Pest

Guess who showed up looking for Mally after practice. I told him to eat shit.

Jo Momma

Witnessed it. It was pretty cool. Jordan practically ran away from her.

Adri Da Pest

Are you finally admitting I'm cool, Jojo? You hide it well, but I know you love me.

Jo Momma

This is why I don't compliment you.

Shayzilla

She is reading the texts now. Slowly.

Adri Da Pest

Slow as hell. Hurry up, Cap.

Me

This is why I keep our chat muted.

Adri Da Pest

You wound me </3

When I look up, Shay's eyes are narrowed. "Why is Jordan looking for you?" she asks, voice dripping with animosity.

Hell if I know. We've spent the better part of a year avoiding each other since our breakup, but I will never miss an opportunity to mess with my best friend.

"I didn't tell you? We're getting back together! Wanna be my maid of honor?"

Shay crosses her arms. "Don't start."

"No, *you* don't start. You know damn well you'd be my first call if I heard from him."

It's not like Jordan can get in touch with me anyway. He's been blocked since the day we broke up a year and one month ago and will stay that way until kingdom come.

"That's a relief. Now you can start dating again. It's about time you start searching for your happily ever after."

Winry pads across the hardwood floor, and I crouch down to rub the soft black fur between her pointy, oversized ears. "Shay, come on. You already know how I feel about this. I don't want to date right now."

Or ever again.

Honestly, I would like happily ever after to leave me the hell alone.

Long ago, I realized it's easier to be alone than to feel like a burden to the person I care about. Love puts my heart in someone else's hands, giving them control of the most vulnerable part of me. If I tried to explain that to Shay, she would insist Jordan was a bad apple and promise there are better ones out there. She would insult him and tear him to shreds, making me laugh until the tears ran dry and my stomach was in stitches.

But after the moment ends, I'd be left to wonder for the millionth time why loving me is so hard.

Plus, I don't need a boyfriend. I need a copilot, and Shay currently holds that title. I'm in the driver's seat, and she helps me get to the final destination, sitting with me through endocrinologist appointments, picking up my insulin when I can't, approaching me with care, and forfeiting all judgment to tackle the problem with me.

I need someone who won't treat me as a burden like Jordan did or smother me like my mom does.

While I appreciate Shay's concern, my dating life should be the least of her worries.

"Fine. I'll drop it." Fuzzy, pink slippers squeak as she shuffles to me, and I wince when she juts her chin into my sternum. "Can I sleep with you? I think we need cuddles and cartoons."

"You just don't want to deal with that mess you call a bedroom," I counter. "Eventually you'll have to deal with the laundry on your bed. You can't avoid it forever."

My best friend gives me a knowing glare as she grabs Winry. After a quick shower and skincare, I wrap my hair and join them in bed. Sleepovers are our love language. From pushing our twin beds together in the dorm to moving into this house, Shay will always take up three-quarters of the mattress. Her knee finds my hip bone, and Winry curls herself into my armpit.

While I'm sure there's no significant other out there for me, I know I've found my person.

Chapter Six

Kenneth

Anyone need a grandma? Because mine is for sale.

Hell. Free to a good home if you take her off my hands right now.

My grandmother's airy laugh fills the donut shop, pulling tired eyes to our table. I specifically chose the booth in the back to not bring attention to us, but it's no use. I'd join in if she wasn't laughing *at* me.

"Nan, it's twenty-three degrees out. I could get a cold. Or worse! Pneumonia! Don't you care about your grandson's health?" I cross my arms, but not because I have an attitude. The AC is on full blast, and the two towels wrapped around me aren't helping fight the chills.

"You've been swimming in that lake since you were born. A little cold weather hasn't stopped you before! Remember when you lost that bet to Cade in seventh grade and skinny dipped in the snow?" She shivers. "Because I do. I saw three *very* bright, *very* white half-moons that night."

My cheeks warm when the man in the booth behind Nan chokes on his coffee and buries his head behind a newspaper.

"Nan!" I hiss, smacking her hand. "I was thirteen!"

"And? Next time, don't stride butt naked across the dock with your grandmother in the kitchen." She rubs a pale pink mark on her hand, a permanent reminder of seeing my bare ass and dropping a scalding pot of tomato soup. "Anyway, I don't want to hear any more whining. You're the one who prioritized saving your phone rather than reaching for the ladder."

Somehow that ladder is in even worse shape than the dock, but I'm not going to push that today considering I was supposed to fix it this morning.

"How is it?" Nan asks. "How's home?"

It's been eight months since Nan moved into Eberly Assisted Living and three years since she left our home, Lake Anita.

Every visit with Nan goes the same. I watch the sunrise at Lake Anita, my feet dangling over the dock's edge as light peeks through the dense cedar trees, splaying shards of red, orange, and yellow across the black surface. Then I dust and water the plants. Right before I leave, I grab oranges from the sunroom. The orange trees Cade and I potted in tenth grade are still going strong. His trees are taller, but my harvest is kicking his harvest's butt.

The difference between this morning and every other morning is that I fell in the lake. Hence the possible pneumonia.

"Good. We got a little bit of snow last night, so it looks like a Hallmark postcard." I slide my phone across the table, and Nan takes it happily, scrolling through the photos with a wistful smile. "Cade and I will replace the ladder next weekend before coming to get you. And I refilled the bird feeders."

A shaky hand rests on top of mine. "I missed you this week, Fishie."

My cheeks burn at the nickname. It used to be embarrassing, especially when amplified through a megaphone at swim meets, but it grew on me over time.

"I missed you too, Nan. Now tell me how you convinced Dr. Hope to let you go on a walk after being on bed rest."

Nan was ready to go when I arrived. Her coat was zipped up over a teal CLU Swim hoodie and instead of her usual Birkenstocks, heavy boots were laced tightly.

"I asked nicely and told her my precious grandson was looking forward to our walk, and that she didn't want to disappoint you by forcing me to stay in bed."

"So, you guilted her into it." I push away my hot tea that tastes like soapy bath water.

"I wouldn't say that," she shrugs, finishing off her chocolate donut with sprinkles. "She only agreed because I promised to walk slowly and use that damned thing." Nan snarls at the cane leaning against the table. When she picked it a year ago, she loved it because it reminded her of Gandalf's staff. Within a month, the novelty had worn off.

"Good. Nobody needs to see you splayed out on the sidewalk like spilled milk."

Nan flicks my hand. "Watch your mouth. Just because I have MS doesn't mean I can't whoop your butt."

I laugh, loving that she always makes light of every situation. Even on her worst days, the only reason I didn't fall apart was because of her warm smile and can-do attitude.

Multiple sclerosis is one of those tricky conditions. My father was five when he found her with slurred speech and unable to stand. After many tests, at age twenty-three, she was told she had relapsing-remitting multiple sclerosis. As a kid I never noticed the pain she was in, but as I got older, I noticed everything. She always waved off my worries with a smile.

Then things took a turn, and I moved to Lake Anita to become her caregiver when I was fifteen.

That was when I realized her diagnosis was more than words on a page. I immersed myself in her world, researching and memorizing everything from symptoms and prognosis to treatments and medications. I quoted the work of biostatisticians and epidemiologists, making sense of every piece of data I could get my hands on.

It's the reason I changed my major before freshman year.

Stealing a bite of my cinnamon roll, she leans back. "So, what's new?"

Nan acts as if I don't see her every weekend, call her every day, and text her updates hourly. Even then, I indulge the nosy woman.

"Cade says hi." If you ask Nan, she has four grandchildren. My siblings, me, and Cade. Growing up, we spent every moment at Lake Anita. His only flaw in her eyes is that he chose baseball over swimming. "He would've come today, but he has plans with a girl he's seeing."

"Seeing or sleeping with?" She wiggles her brows suggestively.

I stick my tongue out, fighting a gag. "You're a grandma, you know? *My* grandma."

"How do you think you got here, boy?" Nan is crass and knows it. "Now tell me about you. How was your first week back?"

"Busy. I'm excited about my public health elective." For a multitude of reasons. "It'll be a lot of work, and there's an internship opportunity. A lead scientist for MS is on the mentor list."

Studying MS isn't just my dream. It's ours, and Nan has supported me every step of the way. That's why I'm confused when her pale green eyes narrow, staring at me like I've grown two heads.

"Kenny Boy. You look... weird. What are you not telling me about this class?"

Shaking my head, I rub away the goosebumps that appear every time she uses that nickname. It's the equivalent of being called your full name by a parent.

"If you must know, you nosy woman, I got paired with Mallory for the internship application project."

Nan pushes the curtain of red bangs from her eyes. "Mallory? The pretty girl you're always fighting with?"

It's impossible to not laugh as I crumple my cinnamon roll wrapper and toss it at her head. "Your memory must be failing you. I never said she's pretty. I said she's pretty *annoying*. Big difference."

"My memory is perfect, boy. I distinctly remember you spending every other visit talking about your little game. Mallory won this. You won that. She's gotta be pretty to keep playing for so long."

Ignoring her comment, I slide out of the booth and gather our trash. Dropping it into the bin, we exit the donut shop with Nan's hand wrapped securely around my elbow. I beg the gusts of wind to take the persisting thought that plagues my mind every time I see Mallory along with it.

Pretty is an understatement.

The walk from Cade's and my dorm to the freshman student-athlete welcome dinner was my own personal hell. I chose that as the perfect moment to tell my father I changed my major, which infuriated him because it wasn't part of *his* plan for my life.

On edge and pissed off, I had the misfortune of running into the most stunning woman I had ever seen.

Mallory was a rainbow blob in a room of muted colors at the bottom of the staircase. A multicolored cardigan hung loose over a cropped tank. Long and strong legs poked out of denim shorts, with yellow sneakers to seal the deal, but I couldn't take my eyes off her hair. A mesmerizing, dark cloud of coils framed her face. Each one tight as springs and thick as wool.

I watched as she and Cade talked easily, as if they had known each other for years and hadn't met only seconds before. I wanted that too. To be the reason for the loudest, most energized laugh I've ever heard. As if she was pushing all her happiness into the boisterous sound.

Comparing her outfit to *rainbow vomit* didn't get the reaction I was hoping for.

But what stole the show was her brain. Did my stupid comment about her wardrobe make her list every synonym for the words prick and pretentious? Sure did, and I smiled the whole time.

I keep my eyes on the ground, maneuvering Nan around uneven surfaces and rocks. "It's fine, Nan. We have our game and that's enough."

If I want her to stick around, it has to be enough. Freshman year, it was as if we silently agreed to play the Brain Bowl, compete, and nothing more. Which means if there's no game, there's no Mallory.

Nan sighs. "Forced companionship may be your saving grace, Fishie. I swore I'd never take Titus out of the friendzone. Then my ladies shoved us together for a dominoes tournament, and look at us now."

I refrain from rolling my eyes at her lovey-dovey tone because I don't want the back of my head smacked. Instead, I kiss the top of her head as we make our way back to Eberly Assisted Living.

Once Nan eats treats from the gift basket that was by her door when we returned, she falls fast asleep. I slink out of the room and into the hallway and run straight into Dr. Hope and her entourage of nurses.

"Kenneth!" she shouts. "How's our rock star doing today?"

"She's thrilled to be off bed rest. Thanks for letting her get out and walk. Any clue when she'll be able to go home?"

The doctor shakes her head. "It's too soon to tell. She's been here for eight months, and the average time patients stay here is around two years. We must be—"

"Cautious. Yeah." I hate that word.

She pats my arm. "It's nice to see you. She loves having you here."

The group glides past me, and I can't help but ask the question I ask every week. "Did my parents come by?"

Her thin lips purse. "No. Billie Owens came by on Wednesday at her usual time, but I didn't see your parents."

Guilt gnaws at my insides. Nan should be with me. I've offered multiple times to live at Lake Anita with her, but she pushed me to Clear Lake for college and swimming, opting to live with my parents for two years. I'm glad she's here now. Eberly Assisted Living is safe, and Nan's happy, which is the most important thing to me.

"Thanks, Dr. Hope. Call me anytime. I can be here in thirty minutes."

After checking on Nan again, I make my way outside, desperate for a distraction. As if on cue, my phone chimes. The ominous, yet bubbly tone alerts me to the sender before I pull it from my pocket.

Edwards Schmedwards

Are you free tomorrow to start?

I stare at the screen. With the way she ran away from me on Tuesday and ignored me in class on Thursday, I thought she would find a way out of this partnership.

Me

Not going to drop the class after all? Color me shocked.

She doesn't respond as quickly, and a pang of something I interpret as regret hits my chest. Then three dots appear on the screen.

Edwards Schmedwards

Mama didn't raise no bitch.

Me

Must you be so vulgar all the time?

Edwards Schmedwards

What you call vulgar, I call tasteful.

Edwards Schmedwards

So tomorrow? We both know you have nothing to do, so just say yes. The quicker we start, the quicker we're done.

Me

For being rude, I get to pick where we meet. Tomorrow at Claude's Cafe. 10am. Don't be late.

I send off another message before she can respond.

Me

Again…

My scowl shifts into a full-blown grin when my phone chimes. Riling up Mallory is my full-time job.

Edwards Schmedwards

I! Was! Not! Late! I was three minutes early and sadly ended up beside you. I'm cursed.

Cursed or not, we're stuck together.

CHAPTER SEVEN

"CAN I SEE THE nutrition facts, please?" I ask the employee behind the counter. Smaller restaurants like Claude's Cafe don't often post their nutrition information online.

"Of course," the woman chirps. Libby, a real-life angel with a blonde, braided halo, returns with a stack of papers and a big smile.

After ordering, I snag a booth by the window facing campus that's perfect for people watching. "Apologize" by OneRepublic pauses when I yank out my earbuds to start my breathing exercises. I need them more than ever because once Kenneth arrives, he will spend the whole hour driving me up the wall.

Although he was somehow early to our first class, Kenneth is notorious for being at least five minutes late. He thrives on nothing but freedom and doing whatever he wants, whenever he wants. Something that feels like jealousy pulses in my chest, and I shove it away when his large frame moves past the window.

Seven minutes late, might I add.

The bell above the door chimes, and Kenneth ducks to avoid running into it. His eyes crawl from the ground to my exposed stomach, catching me in the process of preparing for my breakfast insulin injection. I can almost hear the annoying tilt of his lips as he closes the distance, pretending to scribble on his open palm.

"Adding public indecency to your list of crimes. I put it at number two on the list. Nothing will ever beat peeing in a church parking lot."

"It was *next* to the church parking lot!" I counter, my cheeks warm. I'll never forgive Cade for calling Kenneth to pick us up that night. I was tipsy and there was no way I was going to survive the ten-minute drive home. Sue me.

"Yeah, yeah. Potato tomato, Ed."

"That's not the saying and you know it," I grumble.

His leg grazes mine when he falls into the booth, and I cross my legs under my butt. Warmth exudes off him like squiggles on a cartoon sun, and as nice as it feels, I'd rather freeze.

"Get here extra early to prove a point?" he asks.

"Get here extra *late* to prove a point?"

Kenneth rolls his eyes, perking up to wave at something behind me. "Morning, Libby. I'll have the usual, please."

Libby responds with a chipper agreement before the back door slams shut behind her.

"The usual?" I ask.

"Yup. I come here every day. Once you try a Claude's cinnamon roll, you'll never be the same."

I think of the sweet woman I met five minutes ago and wonder how she became acquainted with the most annoying human I know. "That doesn't explain why she was so nice to you. I should probably warn her to steer clear of you."

Kenneth chuckles, leaning in so close that I can smell the citrus on his breath and clean soap on his skin. "I didn't take you for a jealous woman, Eddie. I think I like this side of you."

Oh hell. This is why we don't talk about non-Brain Bowl things. I grab my planner and laptop from my bag, effectively ending the conversation.

"I'm kidding!" he says and leans back. "I avoid the line and pay with cash. In return, she and her girlfriend get free math tutoring from me. Win win."

I look over my shoulder at the empty cafe. "There's no line."

"Still." The table rocks as he leans against it, curiously eyeing the insulin pen in my hands. "Insulin?"

The tiny needle pricks my stomach. "No. Bleach."

"How does it work?" he asks, undeterred by my sarcasm.

"How does insulin work? Come on, Gray. I feel like that was explained in Bio 101 or something. It lowers—"

"Edwards," he interrupts me. A grin brightens his face, and red tufts flop as he shakes his head. "I know *how* insulin works in the sense of the definition. I want to know how it works for you. I bet you have an individualized plan."

I cock my head at the freckled man across from me. Not once has he even acknowledged my diabetes. Even when I was getting awkward questions and confused looks, he kept the normalcy I craved, and I'm still thankful.

"Well. It's a lot," I stammer, unsure where to start unpacking that question. I don't think anyone has ever asked about it.

"Sorry. That's a pretty loaded question. And a bit weird." He points at the soccer-ball fanny pack in front of me. "Can I take a look?"

I wait a beat before nodding and push it toward him. Wide eyed, he inspects and touches everything inside my diabetes kit. Everything but the needles.

He holds up an old medicine bottle. "Lactose pills?"

A surprised laugh slips out, so I cough to hide it. "Good guess, but no. Glucose tablets." I pop the used needle into my sharps container.

"Back to your question, the short answer is that I use my prescribed insulin-to-carb ratio before meals and snacks."

Kenneth hums. "Now I'm curious to hear the long answer."

While most people assume it's only carbohydrates to think about, there's so much at play. Timing, type of food, adjustments for my current blood sugar, corrections, and more. Plus, you can't forget about hormones. My time of the month is the worst.

I shake my head. We need to get back on track. "Actually, let's focus on the project. I doubt you came here to listen to me talk about myself for an hour."

Kenneth runs a hand through damp, scarlet waves. A soft smile tugs at the corners of his lips when he meets my eye. "Maybe next time then," he says quietly.

I don't have a clue how to respond to that, so I keep my mouth closed and reach for the saltshaker to keep my hands busy. It's terrifying how Kenneth can sound so genuine. Pretending to be interested in my care plan seems like a bit much. Even for him.

The worst part is that my lips almost betrayed me and smiled. My brain must have malfunctioned.

"Here you go!" Libby sings, startling me with her sudden appearance. A flurry of white granules scatter across the table. I apologize for the mess and mindlessly play in the salt until she drops off our food and drinks and heads back to the counter.

"Maybe you *are* cursed," Kenneth says, flattening the pad of his forefinger against the salt. "Pinch some between your fingers and toss it over your left shoulder."

I pause. That's exactly what I was about to do. "You're superstitious?"

"I'm not, but for someone who claims to be so unlucky, I assume you are."

He's right. I am superstitious. I avoid ladders like the plague. Flocks of birds are a big no-no. Splitting poles is my worst nightmare. Friday the 13th is my least favorite day, and I won't leave the house if possible. Then Shay brought home a black cat from the shelter, and I decided to test fate. Winry was too cute to turn away.

I toss salt over my left shoulder, and the aura of bad juju disappears instantly.

After cleaning up the salty mess, I reach into my backpack, pull out two thick folders, and slide one across the table. "Here you go. I printed off everything we need to ace this project."

And get me an internship to secure my future.

"Let me guess." Kenneth holds the folder beside his head. "A gray folder for Gray?"

"Ding ding ding," I chant.

A slip of gold paper falls onto the floor when he opens the folder. Using his insanely long swimmer arms, he reaches down to retrieve it and looks at me through the single punched hole. "A golden ticket? Eddie... Are you taking me to the Chocolate Factory?"

"You know I'd take Cade over you in a heartbeat," I say. "And no. This will count down the meetings until we are free of each other."

According to Dr. Martin's rubric, partners must meet three times for the project. Instead of wallowing about my predicament, I used those feelings to do something productive. The ticket in his hand is an hour of crafting.

Some people use sex to burn energy. My celibate ass crafts.

He studies it for a moment. "You act like you won't have to see me after we punch three holes, Edwards. Are you that excited to get rid of me?"

I don't answer, and thankfully he doesn't push. I'm not looking for a fight. I would like to enjoy my hot chocolate and egg bites in peace. I open my lime green folder and jot the due dates into my planner.

I'm blessed with only a few moments of silence and rich chocolate before the booth dips, Kenneth bouncing closer to my side.

"Care to make this project more interesting?" he asks.

"Not really."

"Hmm. That doesn't sound like the Edwards I know."

My molars clash. I hate the way he says my last name, like a threat and a challenge wrapped into one word. Just like a kid who learned their first curse word and can't wait to use it in every other sentence.

"Your first mistake is thinking you know me."

"Hear me out, Ed," he begs, holding up his hands. "If I proposed a game that puts the winner of junior year completely in the hands of this project, what would you say?"

I close my planner, distracted by the competitive spirit burning a hole in my chest. "We've never done that before. Why would we do it now?"

Kenneth grins, as if the fire inside of me is warming him too. "Shaking things up, I guess. Win the internship. Win junior year."

"What happens if neither of us get it? You heard Dr. Martin. It's competitive as hell."

"Then we'll go off our usual rules. We're still counting points all semester, so a Brain Bowl winner will be chosen regardless."

Kenneth is answering these questions too quickly. Is this something he's been thinking about?

"If you're okay with that," he continues, "let's discuss punishments."

When Kenneth lost freshman year, he had to attend every home soccer game in a soccer-ball onesie with a sign that read, "I Love Balls." He was a social media sensation and burned it when the season ended. When I lost sophomore year, he confiscated my planner for a month. If I was caught using my phone calendar or bought another, he added an extra week.

I got caught three times.

"Nothing will ever beat losing my planner, asshole."

"I'm glad to hear that because when I win," Kenneth taps his chin, "you have to go to the gala with me. Color coordinated and all."

My stomach rolls, hot chocolate threatening to make a reappearance on the table. "I stand corrected because that's a million times worse!"

"I guess you'll have to win."

Trust me. I will. "Fine, Gray. When I win, you'll be my errand boy at the gala. Getting my drinks and fetching those little quiches I love." His smug face falls when I land the final blow. "And you have to attend karaoke. Three songs of my choosing, and I get to record them all."

His throat bobs nervously. After freshman year's student-athlete gala, Cade pulled him on stage and forced him to duet "Promiscuous." Much to his dismay, I was quick enough to record the whole thing. Kenneth hasn't been to a single karaoke night since.

But for some strange reason, he agrees with my terms. After scribbling down the rules on a sheet of notebook paper, we sign our contract.

With his hand outstretched, he grins. "You seem at peace with the fact you'll be going to the gala as my *date.* Makes me think you might want this, Eddie."

"Don't be so sure that you'll be the one winning." I fight the urge to vomit and grip his hand. "And it's *so* not a date, Gray."

"That is *so* a date!" Shay's face is a mix of intrigue and disgust. Mostly disgust.

Giving Shay a rundown of my meeting with Kenneth is making me tired. After setting the rules, he sent cringey prom photos of couples in matching fuchsia outfits while I tried to keep hold of my sanity and finish the preparation questions that are due on Tuesday. In an hour, I got through two questions.

One punch down. Two to go.

"Look, I get it," Shay says, fixing her pink eyeshadow. "The game is meant to embarrass the loser, but have you really thought about how weird it'll be when you win? Kenneth following you around all night like a red-haired puppy dog."

"I would rather have him follow me around than be his date."

She weighs the options in her head before slamming the vanity mirror closed. "Valid."

Flintstone, my ancient, red Honda, goes over a hard bump, and I pray the new tire is more resilient than the last. The carnival is in town, which is our favorite bestie date. Icy weather disappeared overnight, leaving behind a beautiful evening to be enjoyed without the risk of frostbite.

Ten minutes later, we pull into the parking lot. Shay flings her door open dangerously close to a BMW and drops to the ground, searching for her phone that slipped under the seat during "Can't Touch This."

"Uh oh," Shay whispers when she stands back up.

"Turn your brightness down. You're going to ruin your eyesight." I close my door and walk around the car to nuzzle my chin into her neck. "What's wrong?"

"Cade texted me like five times."

"And? He's a chronic multi-texter. What did he say?"

She glances around the lot. "He's here. I told him we were coming, and I guess he didn't realize it wasn't an open invitation. I'll tell him—"

"Don't! Maybe we can try to convince him to ride the roller coasters with us."

Shay lets out a tiny sigh of relief, her eyes darting past me. That's when the soft curve of her mouth contorts slightly. I turn around and my stomach drops.

Kenneth is standing beside Cade's red minivan.

"Did Cade say *he* was coming?" I spit.

"Nope. He managed to leave that part out." She scowls as Cade jogs toward us, leaving Kenneth behind with his phone to his ear.

The look of dejection on his face sends panic whizzing through my body. Everything about this situation is wrong. Kenneth is easy-going, without a single care in the world. Not this.

Red strands are the victim of his frustration as he yanks them. "No—" he blurts, cut off by the person on the other side. "Okay," he says after a long silence. It's a simple response, but by the slump of his shoulders, the situation seems to be anything but simple.

Hanging up, he makes our triangle into an awkward square.

"You good?" Cade asks, carefully eyeing his best friend.

Kenneth nods, and the smile on his face is as fake as a three-dollar bill. "I knew guys night was too good to be true. I could've been at home finishing my puzzle."

"Don't say that, Grandpa. Now it's a party!" Cade slaps his back and ushers us to the entrance.

The comforting mix of colorful lights and the decadent smell of fried sweets and powdered sugar hit me as I scan the short roller coaster lines. I turn to grab Shay but end up watching her braided ponytail disappear into the crowd with Cade beside her, leaving me alone with a sea of strangers.

While part of me knew this would happen, I didn't expect it so soon. I pull my phone out and mash the question mark key ten times before pressing send.

At least he went with th—

Kenneth clears his throat. I whirl around quickly, taking in his dark blue flannel and slouched shoulders. He looks as disappointed as I feel, and I can't tell if it's from his phone call or from being left alone with me.

"You can follow them, Gray." I turn away from him. "I don't care."

He laughs, but there's no humor in the hollow sound. "I know you don't care. You've made that abundantly clear."

What the hell does that mean?

I shrug off the sentences that feel like a burn and make my way to a game. These poor moles don't deserve the beating they're about to get.

How dare they (*whack!*) leave me with him (*whack!*) and not even warn me (*whack!*) that they were going to ditch me (*whack!*).

Kenneth snatches the mallet from my hand and holds it hostage in the air. "Relax. The moles don't deserve that kind of beating."

"*Relax*?" I glare at him. "You're the one who's pissed off, so tell me whatever the person on the phone did so I can be even worse. That way you can go back to smiling like normal, because I like this version of you even less than your regular self."

He freezes, and when his hardened features relax slightly, I realize I've said too much. It almost sounds like I *want* him to smile, and I don't. I swear. But my slip up is enough to zap life back into his eyes, no longer empty. Dark green glimmers under the colorful lights.

"I didn't know you could get any worse, Eddie." If the mallet was in my hands, I'd smash it against his forehead. He sighs and the hint of a smile vanishes. "It's just family stuff. Nothing I can't handle."

Well, this is surprising. Mr. Mellow does have problems.

"That stinks. If it helps, you can tell them the position of 'Gray's pain in the ass' is filled and to find another job."

This time, his lips split into a full grin. Stepping beside me, he whacks the moles much softer than I was. "Our friends are definitely making out somewhere. Want to end the night now and split up?"

I'm this close to hightailing it to my car to wait for Shay when I get a genius idea. "Actually, I see a point opportunity." I gesture at the basketball game with hoops twice the height of Kenneth. "Dare to play?"

He looks behind him as if I was speaking to someone else, but the dangerous glint in his eye isn't missed. It's the spark that keeps what we have alive.

"You're on, Ed. Best three out of five. Gotta give me time to warm up."

I skip toward the nice man at the booth with Kenneth trailing close behind. "Sounds like you already know you're going to lose."

Chapter Eight

Kenneth

I lost. Again.

When I said whoever won the most games got a point, I wasn't planning to get destroyed. She wiped the floor with me at basketball, ring toss, the dunk tank, darts, bean bag toss, milk bottle knockdown, and the donut on a string challenge.

I'm losing the Brain Bowl 9-10. I know this because Mallory has repeated the score like a parrot, but I'm not thinking about the game. Right now, as I watch Mallory celebrate in her seat, I'm thinking about what the game has given me.

It's both the bane of my existence and the fire beneath me.

The sky has transitioned from the pale blue of her sweater to the deep blue of my flannel, her excitement glowing like a night light. Pointing at a stuffed frog the size of her torso, she looks right at me. Instead of calling me out for watching her she asks, "What do you think? Should I get the frog?"

I'm pretty sure I nod, but I'm too in my own head to tell. She squeals as the stocky man hands the frog over the counter. We've already made two trips to the car to drop off the other winnings—a giant banana, a bright pink pig, a boba plushie, and a cow with a cowboy hat.

Although her smile isn't directly aimed at me, I feel like I'm drowning in it. Mallory's bliss has slowly chipped away at the anger I started the evening with.

Even though I should have declined my father's call, I hoped it would be different. That he would ask how I'm doing or ask for my swim meet schedule.

Wrong. Father dearest has been calling and texting nonstop about the internship this summer, ideas for my office, my daily schedule, and plans for senior year, such as moving back into his house to be closer to him. There's even been talk about my contract already, but this phone call was specifically to degrade my decision of major, reiterating how I should have stuck with finance. Researching MS is pointless in his words, even though it's his mother who lives with it.

The Gray family. Royally screwed up.

There's possibly a new expiration date on my game with Mallory. I expected it to be graduation, where one of us would win and she would avoid me like the plague the moment the diploma touches her hand. We would cross paths at events like Cade's birthday parties and Cade's wedding and Cade's funeral, and that's all I would get.

But it could all end at the end of junior year. Now I have five months to find a way to build something with Mallory outside of our game. The Brain Bowl has always been my way in with her, but when it's over, what will I do?

My mind has been plagued by this question since my dad stopped by because there's no guarantee I'll be able to play our game senior year. If I go with my dad, I'll spend every free moment in Bryan, preparing for my future job like my siblings. If I go with my dream, I'll spend all my free time working to afford a life of freedom. Theo already paid for this semester's tuition, but what about senior year? My PhD aspirations may be covered by the school if I'm accepted into the biostatistics program, and it's clear my father won't be helping with anything else.

No matter what I choose, the Brain Bowl could end early, and I'm not ready to lose Mallory.

A scream from an unhappy toddler pulls me from my slump. I shield my eyes from the blinding lights and look to my left. "Eddie..."

The seat is empty. Well, the massive frog is staring at me.

I pick up the plushie and turn to the guy behind the booth. "Did you see where the girl who won this went? Blue sweater. Big, poofy ponytail. Gorgeous smile with a hyena laugh."

The man shakes his head. "Sorry buddy, and good luck next time. She's a beast."

He has no clue.

With the stuffed frog in hand, I follow the flow of people until I'm near the food trucks. My stomach grumbles at the prospect of sugar-filled, greasy food, but I make my way to the restroom. A line of women stand along the wall, and after a quick scan, I don't find the one I'm looking for.

As I'm walking away, the door creaks, and warm vanilla and coconut invade my nose. The intoxicating scent I smell every time Mallory is within five feet of me.

"Why did you do that? You can't just run off and disappear." I barely recognize my own voice, full of worry and frustration as I turn to face her.

And there she is. Blue sweater. Big, poofy ponytail. The only thing missing right now is her gorgeous smile and laugh, and it's all because of me.

Mallory grips my wrist and yanks me away from the prying eyes. "Don't snap at me, Gray. I told you I needed insulin."

Her pretty brown eyes are usually lit with fire, and my frustration vanishes when I notice their softened glow. Flecks of gold and worry twinkle throughout, and my heart heaves at the sight.

"Are you okay?" she asks, releasing my wrist.

It truly seems like she cares about how I feel, and it's scary how badly I want her to.

"Yeah. I just..." I trail off, rubbing the tingling area where her fingers were. There's no way to explain what's going through my head without telling her about my dad, how the Brain Bowl could end, and how I want more than a win this semester.

"We should eat," she says, saving me from embarrassing myself. "You look pale and I'm starving."

I search for Cade and Shay in the crowd. This is the longest amount of time we've spent together alone, and for some reason we aren't fighting. We might even be having fun. I'm not going to mess this up.

"I saw you eyeing those kids' fried Oreos. Do you want some?"

"Sure do," she says, leading the way to the food trucks. "I almost snatched theirs."

Once in line, we stand silently beside each other. Mallory fiddles with the rainbow medical ID bracelet on her wrist while I pick at a seam on her stuffed animal. I want to break the silence and say something, but nothing seems right.

"Nice weather we're having."

"Do you want to see the puzzle I finished last night?"

"Can you see us being more than people who compete against each other?"

It's not until Mallory checks her phone for the fifth time that I finally think of something not stupid to say.

"Is everything okay?"

Even with our tense relationship, getting Mallory to talk has always been easy. She's a lot like my favorite puzzles. With a lot of patience, I can eventually crack even the most complex ones. My shoulders relax when she locks her phone and tucks it away.

"I guess I wasn't expecting to not see them tonight. Shay and I always start on the roller coasters and end the night with our fried feast and people watch."

The line moves forward without her noticing, so I place my hand on her upper back and guide her forward. "It's okay to be upset, Ed. You weren't expecting me to crash your fun."

"It's not that. I thought the three... well, four of us, would spend tonight together. Not split up. Them and us." She straightens, shaking the disappointment out of her voice with a laugh. "But it's fine. I love them both, and if they continue being friends with benefits, or whatever the hell they are, it could become a regular thing."

I hadn't even thought of that. How often would we end up pulled together and possibly isolated? While I may not mind it, she would.

She pulls on my sleeve, yanking me to the window and out of my head. "What do you want, Gray?"

Corn dog. "Why?"

"It's faster if we're on one ticket. And will you split an order of fried Oreos with me?"

Of course. "I can wait, Eddie."

"Jeez, you're so stubborn. Fine, I'll pick for you." She leans into the tiny window, not needing to get up on her tiptoes like the woman before her. "Hi! Can I please get a turkey leg, one order of fried Oreos, two large waters, and... a corn dog." Red and blue lights illuminate her smirk when she looks back at me.

Mind reader.

The employee reads out the total, and I push my arm through the window to set cash on top of Mallory's card. Worried eyes bounce between us before the woman at the register cautiously reaches for the bill and pushes Mallory's card back to her.

She whirls around, placing a hand on her hip. "Stop paying for my stuff, Gray."

"The corndog is for me, and we're splitting the Oreos, right?"

"Yeah, but still—"

Cade's hollering grabs Mallory's attention, forcing her irritation to shift into happiness as she waves. Instead of joining us in line, Shay searches for a table while Cade heads to a different food truck. I offer to wait for our food and watch as she runs to meet her best friend.

Once our order is ready, I weave through the crowd and take a seat on the sticky bench across from Mallory. Placing the food between us, I reach for an Oreo, but Shay's sour expression stops me.

"I'm gone for one night, and now *he's* your fried feast buddy?"

Mallory kisses her forehead, leaving behind a dusting of powdered sugar. "Consider it your friendship fee for leaving me alone with him all night."

I smile and push the plate toward Shay. "Jealousy isn't a good look on you. Eddie needed an upgrade, and I was beyond happy to be of service. Let me know if you want me to take over full-time."

Each girl in The Quartet is different. I've gotten a glimpse of them all, together and separate, during our time in Clear Lake. My research concluded Jo is mild and calm. Adri is wild and free. Mallory is... Mallory. And Shay is reserved and fierce, decked out head to toe in pink.

I jerk backwards when Shay leaps over the table to tackle me like I've seen her do on the soccer field. It's as if Mallory expects this reaction because she doesn't even flinch. With one hand holding her turkey leg, the other shoots across Shay's chest like a seat belt to anchor her back onto the wooden bench.

Prevented from throttling me, Shay grabs an Oreo and shoves the entire chocolate disc in her mouth with a grunt.

"Isn't she lovely?" Cade chuckles, leaning forward to wipe powdered sugar from her lips.

If I thought Mallory was loud before, I've been proved wrong. Her normal volume is nothing compared to the piercing screams she's letting out as she flies through the air. No sane person would ride roller coasters after eating, but once her mind is made up, she will see it through.

Cade drops onto the bench beside me and passes me a beer. "You good?"

"Yeah." Swallowing the fizzy liquid, I exhale. "Dad's the worst."

The Gray Construction summer internship isn't news to Cade. He was around when my siblings went through it. Like me, he assumed I was free of that expectation when I changed my major.

We still haven't talked about my father's reminder that I am far from free and how I'll be cut off for not following through with the internship, but the carnival isn't the right place to discuss that.

"Other than that," he continues, "how was your night?"

"Well, I was ditched for a girl again—"

"Dude, we were like thirteen. Are you ever going to forgive me?"

I laugh and take another drink. "Other than that, it's been fine. She hasn't been too bad." That's a lie. Mallory hasn't been bad at all. "She obliterated me tonight. It's 9-10 now."

"Yeah," Cade sighs. "MalPal is pretty good at that."

I drop my eyes to the last fried Oreo. As hard as I try, I can't get the memory out of my mind of her perfect smile fading because of our best friends.

And how I never want that to happen again.

"You guys ditched her tonight. I know you and Shay are... whatever you two are, and that's fine. I'm happy that you're happy, but this was supposed to be a group thing. If I had driven us here, you'd be finding your own ride home. Don't let it happen again, Cade."

His shoulders slump. "I'm sorry, Kent. We got caught up. Did she say anything to you about it?"

Mallory exits The Loophole and howls maniacally before getting back in line. Her rare moment of vulnerability will be taken to my grave.

"Not a word."

After seven more rides, Mallory's voice is hoarse as we head to the parking lot. I'm still carrying the plush frog, which she named Mr. Pibb. I toss him into the backseat, and my stomach turns when I catch Shay and Cade leaning in. I've seen and heard enough of them to last a lifetime.

I jog around the car to escape and run straight into Mallory.

"Sorry," she whispers. The roughness of her voice pulls at the corners of my mouth. "I guess we had the same idea."

"You'd think they would be tired. Didn't they get enough earlier?"

"Horny bastards." Mallory releases her ponytail and shakes her hair, sending a flurry of coconut into the space between us. "Hey, what day do you want to meet up next week?"

For a split second, I think she's asking to hang out. My excitement fades when I remember the real reason. The project. I only have two more punches on my golden ticket to convince Mallory to spend time with me outside of the game, and that's going to take some strategizing.

"I'm not sure," I lie. "Let me get back to you."

"Well, let me know soon. Next week is busy. I'm babysitting the twins for Jane on Monday and Friday and meeting Dr. Martin after class Tuesday."

Swiping a piece of chocolate cookie from my shirt I ask, "Why?"

"Why am I babysitting or why am I meeting Dr. Martin?"

"Neither. Why is busy your default?"

She looks over the car to make sure our friends are still busy and sighs. "I'm not really sure why I'm telling you this, but fine. Honestly? I think I'm wired this way. The idea of standing still, of being unproductive—it terrifies me. I've always found purpose in movement, whether that's soccer, being with friends, babysitting, or studying. If I'm not moving forward, what's the point?" A bittersweet smile appears. "I know people call me a workaholic or whatever, and they're not wrong. I hate feeling stuck."

"Do you ever take breaks? Aren't you worried you'll burnout?"

There's something about the way she laughs dryly that tells me everything. She's already burned out and likely has been for a very long time.

I clear my throat, desperate to find a lighter topic. "Speaking of productivity, is everything you do planned?"

"Yup." Our shoulders bump as she leans against the car. "I'll never understand why you're so against planning. It's weird."

"Wait, I never said I'm against planning, Ed. I said I don't get why planners are so complicated. Simplicity is key. What's the point of having three hundred pages?" I tap my temple twice. "Plus, I prefer to keep it all up here."

Mallory looks up at the night sky and sighs. "What a life you have, Gray. No planning. No stress. No worries. Honestly, I envy you."

The air goes stale between us, only the screams of enjoyment in the distance. For the first time since my dad's visit, I want to tell someone everything. The years I spent following a plan that I never wanted. The feeling of getting away, only to realize I was never free. The uncertainty surrounding two very important things to me.

My career and her.

Mallory has never shied away from speaking her mind, but when her eyes widen, I'm sure that's not something she meant to say out loud.

"Gray—"

Cade's head appears above the car, and I'm blinded by his *I just kissed a pretty girl* grin. "Kent! You ready?"

"Yeah. Give me a minute." I look back at Mallory. "Don't worry about it, Eddie. It's okay."

"No, it's not. Nothing about that is okay." Her eyes fall to the pavement. "I shouldn't have said that. I'm so sorry."

Add that to the running list of things I admire about this woman. While she's blunt, she's also quick to apologize and means every single word. Mallory Edwards is special.

"Apology accepted, but not needed. We're good. I promise. Get home safely, okay?"

I open her door and step back, but my body stills when her hand lands on my shoulder. Two layers have nothing on her touch, burning through the thick material as her fingers run down the front of my flannel before her hand pats my chest pocket.

"Good night, Gray," she whispers, closing the door before I can ask what the hell that was.

Cade slings an arm over my shoulder, turning us toward his car. "Even though it's cold, I could really go for some frozen yogurt. Let's stop on the way home. Race you to the car!"

He pats my chest, and I wince when something stabs my skin. I reach into the pocket and pull out a folded ten-dollar bill that could have only come from one person.

As her car disappears, I can't help the flicker of hope that blooms.

Chapter Nine

Third Thursday is my favorite day of the month.

Trivia Night at Big Mic's Brewery in downtown Clear Lake is a tradition for The Quartet. We've only missed one night in the last two years, and Adri is to blame for that. My superstar center forward decided it was a great idea to challenge drunk men to race in five-inch heels. We stupidly agreed and watched her win all evening.

Adri leans across the circular table. Dark, loose curls bounce down her back. A deep brown sweater dress clings to her body, cinched in the middle with a gold belt. Golden, unblemished skin gleams as she scans the room. No matter where we go or what we're doing, Adri will always be the best-dressed person in the room.

"What are you drinking tonight, Cap?" she asks.

"Water. Long night of studying and work after this."

I can tell her brain is reciting its usual response to my statement. *As usual, Cap.*

After meeting with Dr. Martin this afternoon, our third since the semester started, I've added another task to my never-ending list. It'll be nice assisting him by writing donation letters, something I did for years while working for the diabetes camp in my hometown, but my already limited free time is dwindling away.

Adri's lips pucker, her long lashes batting with disapproval. "Yeah right. One Coors coming up!" She kisses my cheek and sashays to the bar.

"Coors *Light*, Adrienne!" I shout at the back of her head, standing to follow her. "If you come back with a Coors, I'll shred your silk scarves one by one. One by one!"

A hand grips my shoulder and pushes me back into my seat. Jo pats my arm before sliding into her unassigned, assigned trivia seat. Her maroon tracksuit and white sneakers look incredibly cozy.

"She knows, Mally. This is why she picks on you. She loves easy prey, and you're the easiest of them all."

I roll my eyes. "Gross. Don't say it like that."

Adri's been my personal nightmare since she joined CLU's soccer team her freshman year. Within two weeks, I became Adri's favorite prank target after she put a fake cockroach in my locker. Even though I was a sophomore and her captain. Instead of letting it roll off my back, I chased her with a flip-flop until she collapsed. Now, I'm often on the wrong side of a salt-and-sugar switch, email lists for men with erectile dysfunction, or oatmeal raisin cookies advertised as chocolate chip.

"Wait." I sit up. "Adri can't buy alcohol. Does she forget she's only twenty?"

And I confiscated her fake ID.

"Who needs to be twenty-one when men will do anything for a smile from a pretty girl?" Jo points at the bar behind me.

Surrounded by patrons is Adri, giving them the smile that has convinced men to hand over their credit cards on numerous occasions.

I turn away from the hilarious scene and start to fill out the trivia scoresheet. Shay, Jo, Adri, and I make a solid trivia team. It started out as team bonding, but only we kept it up. We place in the top three every time. Adri knows everything about pop culture and fashion. Shay dominates sports. Jo rules all things medicine and history. I have a knack for random facts, science, and music.

A chair screeches and I look up. "Hey, Shay. How was the walk?"

"It's a nightmare out there. The sidewalks were packed with everyone heading to the hockey game," Shay huffs. She's usually the last to arrive because she spends most evenings at the animal shelter. She sheds her pink coat and looks around. "Where's Adri?"

"Getting men to buy drinks in the name of feminism," I say.

"Not surprised." Shay slides into her seat, her attention landing behind me. "Don't look now, Mally, but that guy over there is giving you major 'do-me' eyes. Jo, isn't he cute?" Jo gives him a quick once-over, shrugging her shoulder, which encourages Shay to keep talking. "Plus, he looks dateable."

I toss Shay a glare. I had hoped we put this whole dating thing to bed, but clearly we didn't.

Adri reappears before I can tell Shay to shove it, accompanied by an Idris Elba lookalike. Her voice is like velvet, thanking the tank of a man when he drops baskets of snacks and a Coors Light onto the table.

I pop a piping-hot tater tot into my mouth as he walks away. "Who was that?"

"No clue." Adri tucks what I assume is his phone number into her purse before continuing. "Are you seriously glossing over the fact that a man who looks like sex on a stick is staring at you and has been since he walked in?"

It's easy to find the guy they're giving me a hard time about. Tall, loose blonde curls, and a nice smile. He's attractive, but sex on a stick is pushing it.

I give him a polite smile before turning back to my friends. "I sure am."

"No surprise there," Jo mutters. "You're somehow more against dating men than I am, and I'm a lesbian."

I kick at Jo's leg beneath the table, and accidentally strike Adri, who retaliates by clobbering Shay with the heel of her boot. We're so caught up in our whirlwind of kicking and insults, that I'm only vaguely aware of a familiar presence in the room.

My head pops up to find the man I can't seem to escape standing beside our table, looking right at me.

"No, no, no," I say, hoping the redhead smiling at me is a figment of my imagination.

"Hi, ladies," Kenneth says, and my best friends don't ignore him like I mentally beg them to. When his attention returns to me, he smirks. "Eddie. Feel free to prove me wrong someday, but does everything you wear have to be so bright?"

His eyes glide over my newly thrifted sweater and bright green pants, and my cheeks heat. Being the center of Kenneth's attention is like having a spotlight shining on you.

An annoying spotlight with freckled cheeks that's hellbent on bothering the shit out of you.

"Just because your last name is the worst color doesn't mean you have to be dull, Gray. A little color never hurt anybody."

"Well, it's killing my retinas."

I groan, already exhausted. The Brain Bowl has nothing to do with trivia night. It's for me and the girls. Not Kenneth.

"Why are you here?" I ask.

"I like trivia. But it's my first time here, so I don't have a team."

I sip my beer. "And how does that affect us?"

"Knowing you, I'm sure you have the rules memorized, Ed."

He's not wrong, because I do. Teams can't have less than three people or more than six. However, there's no way in hell he will be joining us tonight.

"Find someone else to take you. We're not accepting applications for teammates currently." I turn to Shay for support, but the weird look on her face says it's clear she has already fallen for his bullshit misery.

"If we don't let him join us, he can't play," Shay says with a shrug. For someone who almost strangled the man over a fried Oreo, I assumed she would be on my side and send him hightailing it home.

I look at Jo, who is generally the voice of reason, but I'm betrayed by the uncharacteristic gentleness in her eyes. "At least he's smart. He could be useful."

"Oh my god," I breathe, pointing at them. "*Judas*. You're all Judas!"

"Alright, Cap. Let's make it fair and vote," Adri says diplomatically, sipping her pink concoction. The twinkle in her eye tells me she's ready to play trivia and play with me. "Those against Kenneth joining us, raise your hand."

My hand is alone in the air.

"Those for Kenneth joining the Goal Gals, raise your hand."

My three best friends raise their hands, followed by Kenneth's.

Son of a bitch. I'm surrounded by traitors.

He slinks onto the chair beside me before I can put my feet on it. I don't understand why he's so keen on hanging around. He could have sat anywhere or invited Cade and his teammates to play.

Nope. Like Adri, I'm also his favorite target.

Leaning in close, he drops his volume. "I really wanted to play tonight, so thanks for being okay with this. It means a lot."

I'm the total opposite of okay with this. I hate that everyone else is.

"Whatever. Since we can't use this as a point for the Brain Bowl, we better win as a team, or I'll shave your head to make myself feel better."

"So competitive." A rumble from his chest shakes me when he laughs. "And who said we can't play for a point? Just because we're on the same team doesn't mean there can't be a winner tonight."

Excitement creeps into my voice. "Whoever answers the most correctly and also the quickest?"

"You know it."

Instead of shaking his extended hand, I use the large man on stage tapping the microphone as my way out and slide my chair further away from Kenneth.

"Hello, trivia people! Welcome to Big Mic's Brewery. I'm Mic. Don't forget all food and drinks are half off tonight. As usual, there will be eight rounds with ten questions per round. Round one is logos. Question one. The Olympic symbol consists of five interlocking rings. What are the colors of the rings?"

By the end of the last round, Kenneth and I are tied. The Goal Gals are in second place as a team, and we're on fire. Not only is everyone contributing to the score, but the smiles on my teammate's faces are brilliant. Even Jo has managed to look like she's enjoying herself.

And it's all because of him.

I'm almost too aware of my ability to take something that's meant to be enjoyed and squeeze the life out of it. The phrase 'it's just a game' should be tattooed on my skin considering how many times it's been said to me. Fun has always been something to be earned. Growing up, if I wanted to do something that wasn't related to soccer or school, everything else had to be taken care of first. If I didn't take care of the house or my mom, who would?

Even now I justify my few nights out by spending every other moment being productive. Helping. Growing.

It's not like I don't try to enjoy things. I swear I do. My internal monologue is constantly reminding me to have fun. It just won't stick.

With Kenneth here, he fills in the gaps I can't. He makes jokes when we mess up. He hypes up Jo and Shay until they can't help but smile, and he victory screeches with Adri. He nudges my arm when I secure a point, and he fist pumps the air when he does.

I'd give anything to let loose for once.

"Alright nerds. This is the last question of the literature round and the last for the night." Mic waits for everyone to quiet down. "One of my favorite shows is *New Girl*, and my favorite character is Nick. I'm a lot like him because I consider myself to be a loft troll. What famous author does Nick Miller compare himself to?"

I smile proudly. Nobody at this table has watched my favorite show, even though I talk about it constantly. With this point, I'll secure my lead tonight and in our game.

"Hemingway!" Kenneth whispers, and Adri scribbles down the answer.

My mouth falls open because he's right, and I can't believe it.

"How did you... When the hell did you watch *New Girl*? Last I heard, you called it crap humor, which is false, and not worth your precious time." I add a tally mark to Kenneth's side, leaving him with a point.

10-10. *Damn.*

His freckled cheeks are dusted with pink. "Over holiday break. All you ever do is quote it and sing the little jingle. I wanted to see what all the hype was about," he admits with a little shrug.

"And?"

"If they ever need a replacement for Schmidt, you're a total shoo-in. That part was written for you. Dramatic and driven? That's my Eddie."

I shove him away, because Schmidt is my favorite character. "Shut up."

It's hard to fight the smile that comes to my lips, and it matches the one on his. We're only three weeks into the semester, and this one feels different from the rest. While Kenneth is still playing the game and giving it his all, he's hellbent on being civil. A year ago, you couldn't have paid me a million dollars to play trivia with Kenneth and enjoy it.

But here I am. Enjoying myself.

A grimace curves my lips downward. "I know what you're doing, Gray. Call off this nice guy act already. I'm not going to fall for it."

Draping his arm around the back of my chair, he leans in so close that I can see the individual freckles across his nose. "Who says it's an act?"

Of course it's an act. It has to be. The fake flirting. The incessant need to get under my skin. Showing up at my favorite places.

But there's a sincerity in his words that scares me, so I run.

The metal stool screeches across the ground as I bolt away from the table like it's on fire. I'm halfway to the restroom before I hear him call my name, but I don't look back. I slam the restroom door into the wall, startling Shay at the sink.

"Dammit, Mallory!" she shouts, grabbing her chest. "There better be a murderer coming after you. What's wrong?"

I sit on the counter. "Nothing. Everything. I don't know."

"Say the word and we'll go home." She hops up beside me and leans against my shoulder. "We might have to invite Kenneth again. Tonight wasn't that bad with him here, surprisingly. He even brought me Oreos."

The reminder of how fun and thoughtful Kenneth is makes me wince. I still haven't forgotten how I acted at the carnival. I was upset and overwhelmed, stupidly telling him that I'm jealous of him.

But that's not why I'm mad at myself. What right did I have to say he has no issues or worries in life? Sure, I can think that all I want. Saying it out loud crossed a line. And without hesitation, he forgave me.

Even though I didn't deserve it.

"Hey, Shay."

"Yeah?"

"Am I..." I clear my throat, trying to rid the shakiness from my voice. "Am I fun?"

"Fun?" she asks, her voice pitching higher.

It's too late to backtrack now. "Yeah. Like fun to be around. How Kenneth was tonight. I know I'm intense when it comes to trivia, and soccer, and school, and life in general."

The only noise in the bathroom is the buzz of the light as I wait for my best friend to speak. To tell me the truth like she always does. That I've never been fun. Always a burden. Too stressed and too rigid.

Too much.

Interlocking her fingers with mine, I'm reminded why Shay is my person.

"You are the most fun person I know. I mean, all I do is laugh when I'm with you. Our time together is special. Whether it's listening to the oldies or making grilled cheese with you at nine in the morning because you bought a new cookbook. Intense doesn't begin to describe you. You're a rubber band pulled so tight that I'm worried you'll snap. And that's just who you are. You're stressed, bubbly, hilarious, complex, and the best person I know. Sure, you work yourself too hard, but I've never questioned if Mallory Edwards is fun because I know you are."

I'm close to tears when she presses our foreheads together to slow my breathing. "I'm sorry he won tonight," Shay continues. "You'll get him next time."

I groan. "I don't know how I'm going to make it through this semester. He's insufferable, Shay."

"And hot. Don't forget hot."

"Don't make me get Cade."

We laugh, our foreheads still pressed together. Neither of us flinch when the restroom door swings open and clangs against the wall. We both know who it is by the heeled boots clicking against the tile.

"Ugh!" Adri stomps her foot. "Why can't you love me like that, Jo? It's not fair!"

Adri tries in vain to pull Jo's forehead to hers. Without much effort, Jo keeps Adri at a safe distance. Keeping the amusement off her face proves to be more difficult.

"You're so clingy," Jo groans. "Don't make me pawn you off on the Hulk from earlier."

Adri smooths her dress and holds her hand out to me. "Fine, but I'm over all this lovey-dovey nonsense. Kenneth is buying the last round. He asked us to come get you, Cap, so get moving."

We exit the bathroom in a line. Adri's hand in mine, my hand in Shay's, and Shay's in Jo's.

"I love us," Adri sings.

Me too.

CHAPTER TEN

Kenneth

"SWIMMERS TAKE YOUR MARKS."

At Coach Brown's command, I bend down, hooking my fingers around the block. Squeezing my toes around the edge, I stare out over the water. It's calm and still, but it won't be for much longer. The shrill shriek of a whistle rings out, and I leap forward, palm over hand, elbows locked, and my head tucked between my arms. I pierce the cool, blue surface and welcome the comforting silence.

Keeping my head neutral, I kick hard and find my groove. The pace I've chosen seems safe. Fast enough to keep Coach from yelling at me, but not so fast that I'll feel like jelly.

Stroke, stroke, stroke, breathe. Stroke, stroke, stroke, breathe.

When I make it to the opposite end of the pool, I flip and push hard off the wall. Every time I come up for a breath, I listen closely to Coach Brown's reminders to keep heads neutral, relax the hands, and smooth out each stroke. I assess my form, relieved to know he's not yelling at me.

For once.

Water rushes across my skin as I slice through it, keeping my eyes forward. I don't need to know where my teammates are. I'm sure I'm somewhere in the middle of the group, which isn't exactly where I want to be, but my brain and my body won't let me go any faster than this.

After completing the last flip turn, I increase my speed and propel myself to the opposite side of the pool. Even with a slower pace for ninety percent of practice, lactic acid threatens to cramp my legs. I used to love the burn when swimming. Now it terrifies me.

My fingertips slap the pool's edge, and I rip off my goggles, tossing them onto the tile. As my eyes adjust, blue tennis shoes step into my vision. I look up to find Coach Brown looking about as happy as I feel, and I know exactly why.

"You're sandbagging, Kenneth. Care to tell me why?"

I yank the cap off my head and shake my hair. Not this today. "I'm not sandbagging. I'm negative splitting, which is exactly what you trained me to do. Dominique does it and it's fine."

"No. What you and Dom are doing are two completely different things, and you know it." His voice is tired. This isn't the first time we've had this conversation. And it probably won't be the last.

I pull myself out of the water, and my mood darkens like the fabric of coach's shoes I soaked. Mumbling an apology, I straighten. Coach Brown is six inches shorter than me, but two feet wider. There's no getting around him.

"You're swimming scared. Negative splitting is a technique that can be used to improve performance, but that's not the way you're using it. You're half-assing. *Sandbagging*. Trying to avoid hurting, and you know damn well that 1650 yards is a long way to go with no pain. You've got to let that one bad race go, because it's dictating the rest of them and ruining you."

Years of club swimming is what put me on Coach Brown's radar, giving me a partial scholarship for Clear Lake University's Swimming and Diving team. Freshman year was a dream, improving race after race until I made it all the way to the top and qualified for the National Championship meet. I was on top of the world, surrounded by the best collegiate swimmers in the country.

Until I took off too fast, and my body turned to stone halfway through the race. I went from third, to fifth, to eighth.

"Are you not upset about last week's race?" he continues. "You've got conference in two weeks, and I'm starting to think you don't even want to move forward."

"I do, Coach. I'm just—"

"Scared," he finishes for me.

I nod, because I've been scared since the moment Coach pulled me out of the pool after the race that changed everything.

"I get it," he says, his voice more gentle than earlier. "But we both know that swimming scared isn't going to get you back to the big stage for redemption. The only place it'll get you is watching from home, and you've only got a few more meets to get it together. The fear will pass, Kenneth."

While I know what he's saying is true, forcing myself to believe it is the hard part.

"Fear doesn't win championships. Confidence does. The Kenneth Gray I signed years ago wasn't afraid of anything. That kid swam to the beat of his own drum, even if it meant he didn't win. I need him to make a reappearance."

My throat tightens. "Coach, I'm—"

He raises a hand to stop me. "I know you're trying. I know, but I need the captain of this team to get it together. I believe in bad races, bad days, and bad seasons. What I don't believe in is letting it hold you back forever. Physically, you're ready to win it all. Mentally, I'm worried. I made you an appointment for tomorrow with Dr. Jacobs. He said you haven't been going to your sessions. If you miss this one, you won't be traveling to the meet this weekend."

His sneakers squeak along the wet tile as he marches away, the lecture ringing loudly in my head.

Of course I've been skipping my sports counseling sessions. There's something truly terrifying about being back in the headspace of the moment I lost myself.

"Ouch," a country accent drawls behind me. Grant hands over a towel and my bag. "I'm sorry, man. You know he means well, even though it sounds rough."

People who don't know Coach Brown might call him mean, which is far from the truth. He may act and sound like a drill sergeant, but if you listen carefully, each word is laced with a nurturing softness. Still, it feels like a punch to the jaw.

"I'm in a major slump, G."

Grant slips into the hot tub and stretches his legs out. "You could always switch to a sprint."

Flinging water at him, I laugh. "No thanks. I just need to find a way out of this. It's like the moment I touch the water, my brain revolts. It knows that slow is safe."

"What are you going to do?"

I sink down until my shoulders are below the surface, a jet massaging my right shoulder. "No clue. Hope I don't suck this weekend."

We sit in silence, letting the steamy water rejuvenate our sore muscles. The pool door opens, and a familiar voice breaks the calm. The baseball team uses the smaller pool for recovery once a week. Cade loves it because he gets to show off the skills Nan taught him years ago. Even though the guys give him crap, he still uses his swim cap.

"Kent!" Cade yells.

"Hey, Cade."

I close my eyes as Cade carries the conversation, as usual. Bits and pieces garner my attention. A party this weekend. New walk-out song ideas. If the mole on Carlos's back looks cancerous. Then it shifts, now discussing plans for the upcoming holiday.

"Don't even think about asking Shay out for Valentine's Day," Cade says, and a warning lies beneath his laugh.

"What about her best friend? I heard she's still single," Zeke, another baseball player, says.

"Not for long."

I don't recognize this voice and quirk my head toward the small pool.

"Yeah right, D." Cade's lighthearted tone sharpens. "Lay off MalPal. I'm serious."

"Chill out, Cade. You know that uptight girls aren't my type," Darin laughs. "I'm just saying that I heard Jordan is going to stop by the soccer field today and try to get her back. I bet they'll kiss and make up in no time."

The practice pool goes silent. Even Cade's splashing stops.

I sit up, desperate for someone to speak. Anybody. Because the thought of Mallory saying yes to Jordan makes my stomach flip.

"Uptight? Shut up, Darin," Cade finally responds. If there's one thing Cade hates, it's anybody talking about Mallory. "And she will never take him back. Not after what he did. He has no chance." The other thing Cade hates is Jordan Hill, her ex-boyfriend.

"That's fine," Darin says. "Jordan has always liked a challenge."

Mallory isn't something to be won. A challenge to be accomplished. She deserves someone infinitely better than Jordan. The year they spent together was hell for me. I was forced to watch a man who never deserved her get to be loved by her.

I'm positive there isn't a single person deserving of her.

"Seriously? Shut the fu—"

Coach Brown blows his whistle three times, cutting Cade off from his burst of anger and forces them to start their recovery day exercises.

"What time is it?" I ask Grant, rubbing my eyes to get rid of the red rage fogging my vision.

He brings his wrist to his face. "4:23. Why?"

I answer by jumping out of the hot tub, and the cold air chills my skin. I yank sweatpants over my damp legs, ignoring the nasty feeling of wet socks and jog to the door.

"Where are you going?" Grant yells.

I push open the door and turn back. "To see about a girl."

Chapter Eleven

"Hey! Watch it!" I yell at the driver of a blue Subaru who thinks stopping for pedestrians is optional.

For four thirty on a Tuesday afternoon, campus is lively. Every parking spot is filled for tonight's basketball game. Even I'm going, although I'd rather go home and wallow about how crappy today was. I'm running on three hours of sleep. Muscles I didn't even know existed hurt like hell. It took fifteen minutes to find my keys after Adri hid them in a basket of jerseys. And worst of all, I've been dodging Mama's calls all day.

I am one bad thing away from a full-fledged freak-out.

"Rory!"

My body freezes as the nickname I despise more than anything rings out, the wind carrying it. The choice alerts me to who is calling for me. Even though I can't see him, my spine straightens, preparing for the worst possible thing that could happen to me today.

I knew splitting that pole would come back to bite me in the ass.

"Hey, wait up!"

This time, the tenor voice is much closer and coming from behind me. I turn around, and my heart falls into the pit of my stomach as he appears, jogging through the vehicles with a smile on his face.

It's been a year since the last time I heard Jordan's voice, and it wasn't even really him. It was his voicemail message after declining my fifth call.

"Rory." His breathing is labored, leaning against the black Mustang parked beside Flintstone. "I've been calling your name for like three minutes. Could've waited for me, you know?"

Other than the lack of loose black curls that used to bounce in the wind, Jordan looks the same. Deep-brown skin glitters in the sunlight. His eyes are so dark that they sparkle. I used to think it was beauty. Now I know it's arrogance.

"Wait for you?" Flintstone beeps as the doors unlock. "I wouldn't have waited if I had heard you."

From three feet away, I'm already choking on the sour smell of his cologne. When he steps forward, I reel backwards and press myself against my car. He holds his hands up in a way that tells me to chill out. To relax.

Absolutely not.

"I just want to talk, Rory."

"Stop calling me that," I bite through clenched teeth. I hate it even more than Edwards. "You can't just pop up and corner me into a conversation."

"But I miss you," he coos, using that sweet voice that used to make me melt. It makes my skin crawl now. "I've been trying to talk to you, but you blocked me over something so small. It was one night, Rory! A once-in-a-lifetime opportunity to see my favorite band. I thought you would understand that."

I scoff. "Once in a... are you kidding me? You've seen them live four times, Jordan! *Four*!" I drop my voice to a whisper. "I begged you to skip the concert to stay with me, and you wouldn't."

I had known something was wrong for a while. I was sleeping more, drinking more water, and using the restroom more often. The only thing trending down was my weight.

Fast.

For a year I fought to forget what happened the night we broke up, and it all comes rushing back to me like it was yesterday. Each wave is more nauseating and painful than the last.

"I told you I needed to get to the hospital, and you told me to drive. I was scared, sick as hell, and couldn't even depend on my own boyfriend. The one time you didn't forward my call, you told me to stop being insane and hung up on me."

After sending me to voicemail for the fifth time I knew it was over between us.

Like I'm a pet, he claps to stop me from talking. "Come on. You're making this a bigger deal than it was. You ended a great relationship over nothing. One minor issue and you ran for the hills."

"I could have died!" The wind carries my voice through the parking lot, the seriousness of that night ringing in the air. I bet the people in the training room can hear me, and I don't care. "You really have the nerve to call that *nothing*? You promised you'd always be there for me and disappeared the second I needed you!"

He frowns, as if he's just now realizing how serious that night was. "Okay, but it's been over a year! Can't you move past this? I love you, Rory, and I know you still love me."

Even now he can't apologize. Taking ownership of his actions has never been his strong suit.

When we started dating, Shay called him Mr. Perfect. There wasn't a single thing he seemed to do wrong. He brought me flowers, stayed up with me while I studied, charmed the pants off everyone we met, and came to every game like a supportive boyfriend.

The cracks in his perfect exterior started to appear after eight months together. No matter what happened, it was never his fault. He forgot to pick up dinner? I didn't remind him. He overslept and missed class? I should have woken him up. He didn't pass a test? I shouldn't have distracted him.

I was the one who apologized. The one who mended fences that should have been left to rot.

As scary as that night was, it saved me from wasting any more time in that relationship. I should've left earlier, and I have my diabetes diagnosis to thank for giving me the wake up call I needed to leave him and his shitty behavior behind.

"I don't love you, Jordan."

"You do," the delusional asshole says. "That's why you're upset with me after all this time. You want to hate me so badly, but I know you, Rory. Better than you know yourself. You still love me."

The taste of vomit touches my tongue when he grins. It's ugly and mean and twisted. And it's so close to me now, filling my vision with only him. In my blind rage, I must have missed when he closed the gap. There's almost no space between us.

Move, I think, but nothing happens.

I'm absolutely sure it's not love or missing him that's keeping me grounded. It's fear. Fear that this won't be the last time he corners me. Fear that this is only the beginning of Jordan trying to re-enter my life.

He thinks one night was the reason I broke up with him, but he's wrong. It was the nail in the coffin. Jordan went from Mr. Perfect to Mr. Absent in those last few months. Missing my games. Forgetting my birthday. Postponing date nights until I stopped planning them completely. Giving me the silent treatment when things didn't go his way. Calling me crazy when I tried to explain my feelings. Being jealous when I spent time with Cade. Losing his shit when I competed against Kenneth for the Brain Bowl.

Then he left me alone with no way to the hospital.

My vision staggers through each frame when he reaches for me, trying to slap away four blurred hands when I'm only supposed to see two. Static rings in my ears as dread sends my chest into overdrive.

His condescending tone tries to convince me that I asked for this, and I'm starting to believe that maybe I did. I should have gotten into my car and driven over his feet as I sped away. Instead, I let him invade my space.

He finally catches my wrist and my knees buckle, but I don't hit the ground.

Instead, something grabs my other wrist, and I'm yanked out of Jordan's grip so roughly that my backpack falls to the ground. My body is pressed against what feels like a wall, trembling as it holds me close. I blink hard, focusing on the blurry face of the person holding me up.

Even with the sun blinding me and the unfamiliar twist of anger in his normally mellow features, I know exactly who it is. Kenneth looks down and his whole face relaxes.

"I'm so sorry I'm late, Eddie." Shifting his attention away from me, his voice turns rough and unrecognizable. "What the hell are you doing, Jordan?"

CHAPTER TWELVE

Kenneth

"I SAID," I REPEAT when Jordan doesn't answer me fast enough, "what the hell are you doing?"

After hearing about Jordan's plan from Darin, I had to go. I didn't have the slightest idea what I would say when I found her, but I knew I couldn't stay at the pool any longer. Part of me only wanted to make sure she got into her car and drove off without Jordan in tow. Then I arrived at the parking lot and saw the person who let her down when she needed him the most.

The reason I got a call from Mallory asking for a ride to the hospital a year ago.

Jordan puffs his broad chest out, eyes empty and dark, contrasting the bright grin across his face. "Kenneth Gray! Nice to see you're still showing up unwanted and uninvited. I guess some things never change."

My molars clash. "You're out here harassing Eddie in broad daylight, and you want to be upset about something that happened over a year ago? It's your own fault that you refused to help."

"*Eddie*. Damn, I still hate that stupid nickname." Misplaced confidence radiates from the shorter man as he steps forward. "You've always been readily available when it comes to her, and everyone knows you were waiting for us to break up so you could swoop in and save the day. Tell me. Have things changed between you two? Any reward for your loyalty?"

My cheeks burn at the implication of his words, growing hotter when Mallory shakes out of my grip and takes a half-step away from me.

"I'll take that as a no, and let me tell you why, Gray." His smirk grows. "Rory hates you. She always has and she always will. No amount of showing up will ever change that. She will never be *your* Eddie, and it's pretty pathetic that you thought your little nice-guy stunt of taking her to the hospital would change everything."

My mouth goes dry. A little over a year ago, I was heading back to Bryan for the holiday break when my phone started ringing. The name that flashed across my screen was shocking enough. Then she took a broken, wobbly breath, and before she even spoke, I was speeding back to Clear Lake.

At one point, I hoped that night would be a turning point for us. We could play the Brain Bowl *and* be friends. But when the new semester started, we fell back into our usual routine. Rivals and nothing more.

Part of me hopes she forgot everything that happened. It would hurt less than pretending it never happened.

I'm about to respond when a firm voice beats me to it.

"I know you're an asshole, but shut up, Jordan. Don't ever talk to him like that again."

Jordan's fiery gaze leaves mine, calming for her. "Don't defend *him*. I'm here to fix things and get us back on track. You and me. I love you, Rory."

He's good. It would be easy to fall for the perfected tremble of emotion and practiced honesty in his voice.

The one thing that's noticeably absent from this spew of bullshit is an actual apology. No ownership is taken as he works to twist the past into something smaller than it was.

"There's no getting us back on track, Jordan. We're done. We've been done, so leave me alone," she begs, emphasizing every word.

His callous smile crumples. "You're clearly not feeling well, and it's making you say things you don't mean. Let's talk it out over dinner." His glare cuts to me. "Alone."

"What don't you understand? No. Never," Mallory spits, vocalizing my thoughts. Slender fingers wrap around my elbow. "Gray, let's go."

Jordan's voice is like the buzz of an annoying fly that won't go away, talking at our backs as I bend over to grab her backpack. Then he utters the words that make fury rush to my fist.

The same fist that's about to find a home against his nose.

"Whatever. I wouldn't want to deal with your baggage anyway."

"My baggage?" she chokes out.

When we turn around, the perfected softness of his face is long gone, finally showing the real Jordan. "Yeah," he laughs. "Good luck finding someone who can put up with you. You should be thankful I still wanted you. I spent a whole year dealing with that stupid game you play with Kenneth, your daddy issues, and your inability to have fun like a normal college kid. *Baggage.*"

I barrel forward, stopped by the grip on my forearm.

"No," she mutters. "Don't take the bait. This is what he does."

Mallory has never needed a hero to swoop in and save her. She's standing up for herself and taking the high road, although she deserves nothing more than to let hell loose and fight.

Taking her hand, I remove it from my arm and step forward. I revel in the way Jordan shrinks as I tower over him.

"I'm going to say this one time and one time only. Don't ever speak to her again. Do you hear me? Not a hello, goodbye, or how are you, because she is none of your business. You were lucky, Jordan, because she loved you, and you never deserved a second of it." I glance at Mallory, who is staring at her feet. "Let her go now, or I'll make sure you do."

His fist clenches. "Who do you think you are—"

"You're right," I say. "She's not mine, but whether you like it or not, I'll always be there for her. Try this again, Jordan. I dare you."

As his shoulders slump, the air of arrogance slips away. I didn't expect it to be this easy, so when he gives me a microscopic nod in agreement, I grab Mallory and hold her close as we walk to the soccer training room.

Once inside, she pulls me into an empty room and crawls onto the cushioned table. I look down the empty hallway, searching for a trainer. "I'm going to get Michaela."

"No!" Mallory practically screams. "Don't leave me! Please, stay."

My grip tightens on the knob. It's the same thing she said in the emergency room. I didn't leave her then, and I won't leave her now.

I pull up a chair, but I don't sit. "What's happening, Eddie? Let me get someone. With medical experience preferably."

"It's... an anxiety attack," she says through staggered breaths.

"Has this happened before?"

She nods.

"What helps?"

No answer.

"Eddie, this is serious. Let me go get—"

"No!" More quick and shallow breaths. "Nothing works. I can't... I just can't figure it out. I've tried." A tear leaks from beneath her trembling hands, streaking over a smooth, dark cheek.

"Five minutes." I sit down and thank the heavens she swipes away the tear before I can. "In five minutes, I'm going to get a trainer. Are you dizzy?"

"Sort of. There were two of you earlier," she hiccups. "Two Grays is my worst nightmare."

"Sounds like a dream come true if you ask me, but let's keep you horizontal. How are you feeling?"

"My head hurts. I'm cold. I'm scared. *Fuck*, why did he come back?" Her voice breaks on the last word. "He wasn't supposed to come back."

Pure adrenaline, anger, and what feels a lot like hatred course through my veins. I barely reign it in, trying to keep my voice steady for the woman shaking on the table. "He's gone. He's not going to bother you ever again. I promise."

She scoffs. "Why does everyone do that? Making promises they can't keep. You're no different, Gray."

I wrap my hand around hers. "I would never do that to you. About Jordan. About anything." Hardened eyes full of distrust cut to me, and I hook our pinkies in a silent promise. When she squeezes mine, I exhale. "Let's try something, okay? I want you to tell me five things you can see."

Mallory cranes her neck to scan the small room. "The anatomy poster on the wall. A container of tongue depressors. A box of tissues. A rolling stool. KT Tape."

"Four things you can feel."

"Callouses on your palm. The cushion. My shin guards. My head pounding."

"Good. You're doing so well," I say. "Take a deep breath and tell me three things you can hear."

The breath is slow and rattles the table. "The clock clicking. Cars honking. Our breathing."

"Two things you can smell."

A sniff. "Sunscreen and disinfectant spray."

"Last one and we're done. One positive thing about yourself."

Mallory's face contorts, and it takes her longer to answer this question. Her chest rises and falls at a steady pace, the fingers of her free hand playing invisible piano keys on her stomach as she thinks.

"I've got a really nice ass."

Laughter sputters between my pressed lips, surprising both of us. For a moment I'm able to forget what happened in the parking lot and enjoy our bubble of lunacy.

"True. Can you give me another one? Something real. Deep breath first."

Mallory sucks in a deep breath, speaking through the exhale. "I may not be fun, but I know that someday, my hard work will pay off. That's what I'm proud of."

This answer kick-starts my heart in its place. Mallory has always known exactly who she is and what she wants to do with her life. Taking control of every situation and turning it into an opportunity for success.

But how can she believe she's not fun? I don't care what Jordan said. I have the most fun when I'm with her.

"You did great, Eddie. How are you feeling?"

"Better. Much better," she says, releasing my hand to stretch her arms over her head. "What the hell was that?"

"A grounding method for anxiety and panic attacks. It can help bring a person back to reality and pull them out of their head."

Her smile is weak. "Where'd you learn it?"

"Counseling," I admit.

"You see a therapist?"

"Since I was twelve. Recently, I've been skipping appointments with my sports psych though, so...." I give her a moment to take in something that few people know about me. When I find no judgment, I push on. "If we're asking hard questions, how often do you have anxiety attacks?"

"Sometimes."

"How often is that?"

"Gray," she says, her voice sharp. "Stop. I'm fine. It's fine."

"Nothing about this is fine," I counter. "Thinking about you dealing with this on your own for god knows how long scares me, Ed. Especially because you haven't been able to find something that helps you through them."

Mallory's motto has always been to suck it up and push through. Headache? Push through it. Three tests in one day and running on no sleep? Push through it. Sick as a dog, but it's competition season? Push through it.

Sometimes people need something stronger than that.

She flips onto her side and faces the wall to end our conversation. Since her hair is bunched at the top of her head, taking away her ability to hide in it, she's done the next best thing.

I should stop talking, and I will. After I make her smile.

"For someone who feels your emotions so strongly, you sure do hate talking about them. What's up with that?"

"Me? Feelings? *Pshh*. Never." I hear the unmistakable hint of a smile in her voice. "Talking about them isn't fun. Never has been."

"It's not an easy thing, so thank you for telling me."

She lets out a heavy exhale, flipping onto her back with her eyes closed. Sitting on my hands does nothing to stop me from reaching out to stroke her cheek, and I smile when she doesn't pull away.

"You gave me a method that worked, so thank you." Exhaustion coats her voice, making it huskier than usual. It's always low and comforting, but it's making me feel dizzy.

"I didn't know," she says after a while. "I didn't remember you were there that night until I heard you guys talking about it in the parking lot. I must have blocked it out with all the stress and news and medicine. I'm sorry. I should have—"

For the second time today, I take her hand, interlocking our fingers. "Don't apologize to me. You did nothing wrong."

"But why didn't you say anything? You acted like nothing happened."

"Because I didn't do it for acknowledgment. I did it for you, Eddie."

Another promise is met with disbelieving eyes, searching mine for a lie or exaggeration. I can promise she won't find one. Not today. Not ever.

"I can't believe I stayed with him for so long. I feel so stupid." Mallory lets out a self-deprecating laugh. "How did I not see how terrible he was?"

I squeeze her hand. "You wanted to see the best in someone you cared about. There's nothing stupid about that. I know it's been over a year, but do you still—"

"Love him? Hell no."

The knot in my stomach releases. While I could've guessed from the way she acted today, hearing the words makes it feel so much more real.

"Good. He's pretty terrible," I say, and she nods in agreement.

"Thank you, Gray. For being there for me that night and today. There are a lot of things to be afraid of, but I'm not going to let something so small be the reason I can't move forward today."

Without another word, her eyes flutter shut, and the small room is filled with quiet snores that release the tension in my jaw, shoulders, and stomach.

It's been a few minutes since she fell asleep, and her words are still ringing in my head. Mallory isn't going to let her shitty ex-boyfriend ruin her day, so why can't I let one race go? I've raced more times than I can count, and while I can't remember them all, I know that nationals wasn't the first bad race I've ever had. And it definitely won't be the last.

If I keep letting fear run me, I'll never find out what's waiting for me on the other side. "Thank you, Eddie," I whisper.

When I'm sure she's okay, I half-heartedly untangle our hands, walk out of the room, and make my way to Michaela. Her forehead wrinkles when I step into her office's doorway.

"Mallory is in room two. She wasn't feeling well after practice. Just wanted to let you know."

Suspicion shifts into concern as she pushes past me and sprints down the hallway.

When I step outside, the sun is dipping low into the sky, and I pull my phone out.

Cade (sexiest man alive)

Where are you? The game is starting.

Me

Got caught up with something. Be there in 5.

After pressing send, I open another chat and my fingers fly across the keyboard, sending it before I can talk myself out of it.

Me

I won't be in class Thursday because I'll be traveling for a meet. Today stays between you and me. I promise, Eddie. Get home safely.

Chapter Thirteen

Kenneth

"You should have seen him, Fishie. He looked like Denzel Washington. Tall and handsome in that black suit. I wanted to eat him up."

I gag for what feels like the millionth time. "Nan, I love you, but I can't handle hearing about your date with Titus. Keep the raunchiness for the ladies at physical therapy." I glance at the microwave and check the time. "It's barely nine. Can't old people have dates that go any later?"

She blows a raspberry into the phone speaker. "Hush up. They stayed open an extra hour for us. It was very romantic."

I can hear the smile in her voice. As long as she's happy, I am too.

"That's great, Nan. What did you have for dinner?"

As Nan talks, I prepare for my evening at home. Even though Nan and Cade disagree, there's nothing wrong with staying home on Valentine's Day. It's not like I have a special someone to celebrate with. The last time I did was Emily Martin in seventh grade. My teenage heart was hers. Until it shattered when she gave my gift of chocolate kisses to *her* crush. Which happened to be my best friend, Cade.

He still feels bad for being the "other guy" after all these years, which is why every Valentine's Day he tries to make up for it. This year it's my favorite pizza from Sizzle and Slice Pizza and, as always, a giant bowl of chocolate kisses.

Cade Owens is the most thoughtful friend a guy could have.

I'm treating tonight like any other. Working on my current puzzle, the northern lights, and sitting on the living room floor surrounded by textbooks, my laptop, and the gray folder. The semi-finalists portion of our applications are due tomorrow. It should have been easy to print my transcript and jazz up my resume, but even after beefing it up, it still lacks the *oomph* I need to wow the judges.

"Kenny Boy! Are you even listening to me?"

I nod, closing the gray folder. "Yes. I heard you ate a steak way too rare for my liking. You had two glasses of wine, which is why you're yelling. There was red velvet cake and cheesecake, so you got both. And you had an amazing time with Titus."

I wish she would have video called, but she's underneath the duvet, tipsy and tired. "I'm not yelling," she mutters. "And don't tell me your plan is to work all night. Why didn't you go out with Cade? He told me he invited you."

"Of course he did," I murmur, shoving my hand inside a bag of potato chips. "One, it's a Monday. Two, we went out this past weekend. Three, bar hopping with Cade on Valentine's Day is a recipe for a set up. I'll pass on that."

"With your nonexistent love life, you could use a set up. And stop ruining your dinner with chips! I raised you better than that."

I drop the second handful back into the bag. "Fine, but not because you told me to."

Nan's tipsy giggles follow me to the pantry. I put the chips back, and my stomach groans with excitement when headlights peek through the living room window. Moments later, the doorbell rings.

"Yay!" Nan cheers, vocalizing my thoughts. "Make sure you have on a shirt. You don't want to scare the pizza boy."

I look down at my gray sweatpants and bare chest. The woman somehow knows everything. "It'll be quick. They won't even notice."

Running to the front door, I grab the ten-dollar tip from the counter. The door opens, and I immediately wish I had listened to Nan because the pizza delivery guy isn't standing on my porch.

I must miss seeing Mallory's face because I'm being haunted by the ghost of her. For an illusion, it sure does look real. From the impatient lifted brow to full lips curved into a wry smile. I reach for her hair, and when my fingers disappear into the softest cloud of curls, I exhale softly.

Nope. Not a dream. Mallory is standing on my doorstep looking like *that* while I look like *this*.

If there's one thing to know about her, it's that she loves a theme. Wearing an oversized red sweater vest, faded black denim that hugs her thighs, and black Doc Martens with red laces, she is the epitome of the day of love.

And for some reason, she's at my door.

Things have been quiet since the other day in the parking lot. We've been so busy with classes that we haven't been able to plan a point opportunity, which means I haven't seen much of her.

"Hello? Earth to Gray." Mallory lightly smacks my hand, reminding me it's still in her hair.

I cross my arms to protect my chest from the frigid air. "Are you lost?"

"Something like that," she grunts. "I was kicked out by our horn-dog best friends after Cade came over. Apparently playing the *Despicable Me* theme song on repeat was ruining the mood, so they kicked me out. He barely let me change out of my pajamas before dropping me outside the door with my backpack."

I hear Nan's muffled voice from my pocket and press the mute button.

Mallory must hear it too because her eyes dart around me and into the house. "Oh. I didn't know you had company. I'll go—"

"No!" I say quickly. "Nobody's here. I'm just surprised you are."

She gives me a look that says she's just as surprised as I am. "I know it's weird, but Adri is on a date. Jo is asleep. Jane and the kids are in bed because it's Monday. Every library on campus is closed for this stupid, fake holiday, and it's too cold to sit in my car." With a shrug, she sighs. "And that's the story of how I ended up here. The bright side is that I didn't come empty handed."

I follow her finger to the welcome mat. I was too busy staring at her to notice the biggest bag of popcorn I've ever seen at her feet, coming all the way up to her knee.

"For me?"

Mallory grins and hands it over. "My friend works at the drive-in. I use this trick to bribe the twins. I hope it's enough for you."

It is, but I don't need a bribe to let Mallory in.

I point toward the living room, telling her I'll meet her in a minute. Once she's around the corner and out of earshot, I reach into my pocket for my phone.

Great. The call wasn't muted. I sigh, bringing it to my ear. "How much of that did you hear, Nan?"

Her smile sounds even bigger. "I heard nothing. Good night, Fishie."

"How do you have jicama but not a regular household vegetable like green beans or broccoli?" The plate on her lap wobbles as she leans over to grab the Parmesan cheese. "I've never met anyone who has a whole jicama laying around."

Last week while trying to buy a potato, I grabbed a jicama, which has gone unused until tonight. With a little salt, pepper, and paprika, Mallory has created my new favorite way to eat vegetables.

Her original plan was to crash here for ten minutes before sneaking back in through her bedroom window. I convinced her to stay instead of possibly hurting herself and needing a trip to the hospital.

Promises of pizza had her thinking about it, and when I added that we could count this as our second required project meeting, she was on board.

In the thirty minutes she's been here, my knowledge about diabetes has increased exponentially, and I'm not even close to scratching the surface. With every meal, she prioritizes fiber. I sensed hesitation in her voice when she asked if I had any vegetables she could add to dinner. I was off the couch and halfway to the kitchen before she even finished her question and came back with a wannabe potato.

In true Mallory fashion, she made it work like she always does.

"It was an accident," I laugh. "But I'll be buying jicama every week for the foreseeable future. These are amazing."

I only see half of her proud smile as she heads toward the wall behind the television. She assesses each frame slowly before turning back to me. "How did I not realize these are puzzles? I thought they were paintings. You did these yourself?"

I nod, gathering our plates. Cade and Nan call me a grandpa because of my hobby, but it's rewarding. Each puzzle has been glued, framed, and displayed for everyone to see.

Once the pizza is in the fridge with plenty for Cade to snack on later, I gather my stuff and hook her heavy backpack over my shoulder. "Let's work in the dining room. There's more room over there."

Even though she's been here many times, Mallory's eyes are wide as she assesses the overly spacious living room and formal dining room.

The house is *big*. Much bigger than a place that normal college students can afford to rent in this town. Only Cade knows that my dad owns the house, which is why we're able to live here for free.

"Is the decoration up to your standards?" I ask.

In her hands is a photo of me and Cade from our high school graduation. "For two heterosexual men, it's not half bad."

A low laugh slips out as I set her backpack onto the table. No wonder it's so heavy. She pulls out a clunky laptop, the lime folder, a hole puncher, the soccer-ball fanny pack with her diabetes kit, her planner, an assortment of snacks, two notebooks, and a pencil bag.

Holding up my end of the deal, I hand over my ticket. With a loud crunch, she looks at me through a hole in the thick paper.

"Two meetings down. Only one more to go until we are done working together." Mallory is giddy as she slides it across the table, unaware of the way her words hit me square in the chest.

I wonder what would happen if I refused to take it back. Maybe this wouldn't have to end. I want so much more than three meetings and seeing each other at point opportunities. And the likelihood of that is slipping through my fingers.

I hum in acknowledgment, facing the other thing that is sending me into a tailspin. I'm not sure why I'm trying so hard to get this internship. Even if I win, who knows if I'll complete it, but if everything I've worked so hard for is going to be taken from me, I might as well go out with a bang.

"I need a favor," I say, breaking the long silence.

She slides a purple pen behind her ear, and it disappears into the curly cloud. "Yeah?"

"On my resume, most of my work experience is business related, minus math camp, tutoring, and one research opportunity. At this rate, I'm not going to make it through semi-finals."

Mallory's eyes fall to the paper I slid across the table. She drums her fingers against it as she scans the words.

"Okay," she says slowly. "What do you need from me?"

"Well, you're the most critical person I know—"

"Gee, you really know how to sweet talk a lady."

"It's a compliment, which is why I need your help. You're the only person I trust to tear into it." I nudge it closer to her. "I promise I won't get butt hurt. I need your painful honesty."

Helping each other is foreign for us. Well, at least discussing it is. We've always just done it and moved on without a word.

I wait for a scoff or outright refusal. Surprisingly, neither come.

"Sure. Why not?" The contents of her pencil bag spill onto the table, searching through the colorful pens and highlighters. "You must be freaking out if you're asking for my help. Feeling desperate, Gray?"

"And nervous. It's all coming up so fast. It'll be the end of the semester before we know it, and I don't want to mess up my opportunity."

If she catches the double meaning in my words, she doesn't show it.

Mallory opens her own folder and hands over two sheets of paper. "Here. If I'm doing this, then I might as well put you to work. Feel free to give me some feedback. I've been told I ramble."

I take the papers and scan a random section. "Eddie. Why is this bullet point six lines long?"

One bare shoulder rises and falls, and I swear she lets out a small giggle.

I savor the sound and continue reading. "'*Cabin two was comprised of two four-year-olds, six five-year-olds, and four three-year-olds.*' You really wrote out the demographics of the kids at camp. Race and ethnicities too. Are you advertising or bragging? Either way, it's working. Straight to the semifinals."

Mallory's *real* laugh takes me by surprise. Not because I don't hear it often, because any time she's around Cade, she's laughing.

This time it's because of me, and I'd do anything to hear it again and again on repeat for the rest of my life. Her wild, full-of-life cackle will forever be ingrained into my brain, along with this moment. There are many faces to Mallory, and I feel honored to get to be part of the one that's shown the least.

Relaxed.

An hour later, my resume is colorful and full of comments. Green highlighter means good, which is severely lacking. Yellow highlighter means expand on this topic. Red highlighter means delete.

The markings are supplemented with copious notes in her loopy handwriting. Only the ones in blue pen though. Purple pen dictates her random thoughts throughout our time of silence.

"Hamsters scare me" is written in the upper left corner and *"Math is the worst"* is scribbled at least thirteen times throughout my math-heavy resume.

In an hour, I've learned more about Mallory from her resume than she has allowed me to know in almost three years. Her middle name is Ella. She plays the saxophone. On top of school and soccer, she worked at a year-round camp for kids with diabetes, which is one of many reasons she's qualified to write and edit donation letters for a camp Dr. Martin is hoping to open. Hours and hours of volunteering line the page, each one a testament to her hard work.

Her words from the carnival replay in my head. She's never been one to stand still.

"Well, your resume is practically perfect," I say. "Everything on here is applicable and will make a big impact on the judges." Mallory beams until I add, "But you've got to slim down some of these sections."

I tap on a line that contains the definition of autoimmune disease. *"They already know this!"* is scribbled beside it.

"Okay, okay. I see what you mean," she concedes, scanning the rest of my notes. "Thanks for the help, *Adrian*." Mischief sparkles in those big brown eyes as she taps my middle name at the top of my resume. "Adri is going to love that you guys have the same name. Kenneth Adrian Gray. Makes you sound like a socialite."

"At least I don't have the middle name of an old white woman, Ella."

Mallory leans forward to rest on her elbows. "Who says I'm not an old white woman?"

We stare at each other for a moment, lips quirked and features mellow.

That is until her phone rings, stealing her eyes from me. Although I can't hear what Shay's saying on the other side, I'm sure our night is over because she hangs up with a promise to be home soon.

With her backpack zipped, we step into the darkness. I walk ahead to open her car door and close it once she's in.

When I make it back onto the sidewalk, the quiet whir of the window rolling down makes me turn back. The moonlight illuminates Mallory as she rests on the console. Waiting for me.

I poke my head through the window. "You watching me, Ed?"

"Shut up before I run over your toes." Her eye roll stops short, landing on the steering wheel. "Thanks for letting me crash your solo party. It was weird, but..." She trails off, and I already know what she's thinking.

Me too, Mallory. I had fun too.

I step onto the curb to keep my toes safe and wave. "Good night, Eddie."

"Save some of that popcorn for Cade and make those edits tonight. There's no way you'll wake up before class tomorrow morning to get them done."

Dim tail lights disappear into the darkness, and she's gone.

But only in the physical sense. The smell of vanilla and coconut burn stronger than the candle in the living room. The house even feels a bit brighter, as if the color she exudes has merged itself onto the walls.

Mallory is lingering.

CHAPTER FOURTEEN

"GOOD MORNING, MALLORY. How are you feeling today?"

I roll my neck, avoiding the all-knowing eyes of my counselor. "Like shit, but who cares about me. How are you, Sharon?"

Bright purple lips purse as she settles into her seat across from me. Her lipstick matches everything else in the office. The purple lamp in the corner fills the room with lavender light. My socked feet pull at the violet, fuzzy rug. Even her books are varying shades of purple.

"I care, and I'm doing well. Now, why don't you tell me why you feel like shit?"

I rub my eyes. "I hate spring."

Following my unpopular opinion are four harsh sneezes that make my eyes water. This stupid pollen-induced sinus headache assaulting me doesn't help.

Sharon hands over a, no surprise here, purple tissue box.

To be honest, I have Kenneth to thank for being here. Every time I find myself perched on Sharon's couch, I send up a silent thanks. Since the parking lot incident two weeks ago, I've had three counseling sessions.

"March is terrible for people like you, but is pollen the real reason you look like you haven't slept in ten days?"

I look down at my stained T-shirt and mismatched socks that remind me I have no room to fight back. "Can't a girl look terrible without being persecuted?"

"Of course they can, but you know I'll always give you crap. Want to talk about it?"

Snuggling my knees into my chest, I sigh. "Can I have the wheel?"

Her chair creaks as she leans up to grab my favorite tool from the wall, and she hands over the colorful emotion wheel. "Let's start with the core options. Which of these resonates most with you right now?"

Happiness, sadness, disgust, fear, surprise, and anger. I point at the word anger.

"Okay. What in that section best describes what you're feeling?"

I take a moment and toss around each word in my head, carefully selecting the one most accurate at this moment.

She follows my finger. "Insulted. What's making you feel insulted?"

I lean back, pulling a plum pillow with gold tassels against me. "I know I'm not stupid. I work hard every day to prove that I'm not stupid, but no matter what I do, I end up feeling stupid. Does that make sense?" Sharon nods at my nonsensical rambling, so I continue. "That's how I feel when I talk to my mom. She spent the ten minutes of freedom I had yesterday going over my blood sugar levels with me, mom-splaining my own care plan! Ruined my whole Tuesday. She acts like I'm incapable of caring for myself."

Sharon scribbles something on her notepad. "Do you think you're capable of caring for yourself?"

I hold tight to Bex's words that this journey is a roller coaster. "Yes, but I don't know if I'll ever truly feel great about it because it'll never be perfect."

"You know how I feel about that word in this room, ma'am."

"I know," I say, mimicking her counselor tone. "I'm working on it."

"Which is growth. How did you respond to your mom when she," Sharon checks the notepad, "mom-splained your care plan?"

"I hung up and we haven't spoken since." I groan into my palms. "The worst part is that I really do miss my mom. A lot. I was hoping we could have one conversation that didn't have to do with my diabetes."

Sharon moves to the edge of her chair. "I can tell that you miss her and in her own way, that may be how she is trying to show that she misses you, loves you, and wants to protect you. What she might not understand is that just because the intention is good, doesn't mean the actions are affecting you in a positive way. What matters is the outcome and how it makes you feel. Have things always been this way between you?"

"No. Everything changed after my dad passed away five years ago." I avert my eyes. "But it wasn't until my diagnosis that this started happening."

Sharon nods. "Tell me about life for you and your parents when you were young."

A brief smile touches my lips, the memories clear as day. "I was the kid who never went to sleepovers because I couldn't stand to be away from them for too long. We saw every new movie, tried every restaurant in town, and stayed up late dancing to records that they listened to as kids. It was the three of us against the world." My lips fall along with my heart. "When he passed, I had two people-sized holes in my chest. Even though Mama was only up the hall, it seemed harder to get to her, and he was literally gone from this world."

I watched as bills piled up, groceries dwindled, and the house went from my calm to my chaos. From that moment, taking care of my mom became my number one priority. My only eye of the storm was soccer and knocking things off my to-do list day after day. I only felt like I could breathe when I was working.

I look up at Sharon, ready to share something I've never said out loud.

"Even when she came back, I didn't trust her to take care of me. And even though I barely trust myself most days, I don't think I've trusted anyone to take care of me since."

Trusting someone means letting them in, which leads to mess ups, which leads to apologies, and I hate apologies. People mess up, sure, but I'm the one who ends up hurting the most when they do. I'd rather be alone than to feel that kind of pain ever again.

After a long pause, Sharon speaks. "If you don't mind me asking, what changed after your diagnosis? It sounds like things escalated quickly."

The next words get tangled in my throat. I swallow the hard lump and push through. "My dad died from type 2 diabetes complications, which is why she—"

I'm cut off by my own sobs. Sharon moves to sit on the small table in front of me and takes my hand. I can't hear her with all the blood in my ears, so I keep talking.

"Doctors called him non-compliant for years, which was bogus. He didn't have the means or help he needed to learn. By the time he found a team who supported him, his kidneys were already failing. I was thirteen when he started dialysis. All the anxiety my mom held onto for my dad was passed to me when I got my type 1 diabetes diagnosis. She spends every moment worrying I'll be taken away from her too."

My voice breaks, thinking of my mom. Stranded in my childhood home. Distanced from me because we struggle to communicate. Being forced to deal with her own fears all alone.

"It's not fair that she already lost the love of her life. She doesn't want to lose me too."

When I'm done talking, I look up expecting to see that fragile, pitiful look I'm used to when people hear the full story. Sharon doesn't look at me that way, and I'm thankful.

"I'm incredibly sorry for your loss, Mallory. You went through so much at a time in your life when you were learning about yourself and who you wanted to become." She hands over another tissue. "Have you talked to your mom about how her words and actions make you feel?"

"We have it out every now and then, but I don't want to hurt her any more than I already have. I just want us to be able to talk normally. Like we used to."

"I have something we should look at." Sharon leans over to open a drawer and pulls out a stack of papers. "Have you heard of setting boundaries?"

"On social media, yeah. Were these from your last session?"

"Nope." The stapled stack of paper falls heavily into my lap. "I had a feeling we would get onto this topic today."

I roll my eyes, thankful the crying part of this session is over. "Witch."

"Counselor," she winks, patting my knee. "We've got twenty-five minutes. Let's get started."

"*Mallllll*," Jaxon screams as if we are a football field apart rather than five feet. "Kick it harder! I can take it!"

I pull my leg back and kick the soccer ball a smidgen harder than before. He dives to the left, stopping it before it rolls into the net with a grunt just like I do.

"That's my boy! You're going to be an Olympic goalie with stops like that."

Jaxon grins, pushing his tongue through the gap in his teeth. The Tooth Fairy is not too happy about accidentally slipping a fifty-dollar bill under his pillow, instead of the five-dollar bill she meant to put there.

Behind the goal, Julie sits in the grass. Unlike her twin brother, soccer isn't her favorite sport. She prefers gymnastics, which explains why she's in a middle split instead of playing with us.

"Quit showing off, Jules!" I call out. "You're making me jealous."

She looks up from my phone and rolls steel gray eyes. My tiny twins share the same gorgeous color. Julie's eyes are calm and quiet, whereas Jaxon's are like a Category 5 hurricane.

"Stop skipping our stretch time. Then maybe you could do it too."

I stick my tongue out at the dig that's too sassy for a seven-year-old and hand Jaxon the goal bag. It takes a moment for him to wrestle the collapsible goal down, but he eventually packs it up and slings it over his shoulder.

Jaxon hobbles over, licking a grass stain on his sleeve. "Where are your glasses, Jules? Mom is gonna be pissed when she finds out you're on Mal's phone without them."

I crouch down, placing my hands on his ruddy cheeks. "Where did you learn that word?"

"Pissed?" He pulls an unwrapped lollipop from his pocket and stuffs it into his mouth. "You."

It's official. I'm going to lose my babysitting job.

"Don't worry, Mal," Julie says, flicking her brother's nose. "Mommy says worse."

Jane and I need to watch our mouths around these parrots.

Julie reaches for my outstretched hand and holds it tight. Her brother's hand is sticky and wet, but I clasp it as we make our way through town.

I never thought I'd find myself in Clear Lake, North Carolina. It's a college town that people seem to never leave, and I understand why. I don't want to leave either. The record stores Shay and I spend hours roaming on the weekends. The hole-in-the-wall restaurants I single-handedly keep in business. The karaoke bars I've watched Cade morph into Whitney Houston in. My tiny twins.

After stopping by the record store, we make it to Sunshine Junction. Every table is filled with rowdy college students except for the booth in the back corner by the sunflower mural that is reserved for us. Julie climbs in first, sliding thick glasses over her nose before reaching for my phone.

"One, nine, one, six," she mumbles, reciting my password. "Your mom and Cade texted."

Walking out of counseling this afternoon, I sent my mom a message asking to talk. I've never been good at sitting on something for too long.

I slide onto the seat across from her and ask, "Can you read them to me?"

Julie nods, excited to show me how much her reading has improved. "Your mom said I'm free to...morrow. And Cade said do black pants and... a brown shirt go to...ge...ther?"

I laugh, ruffling her hair. "Great job, Jules! I'll text them later."

Jaxon tumbles into the booth beside me and points out his mom's bright green hair. Jane drops off three steamy mugs, takes an order for a large party, and cleans up a spill in one trip, looking effortless as she does so. I've always admired that her hospitality voice and regular voice are the same.

"Mal, did you hear that?" Jaxon stands on the seat, his eyes trained on the table his mom is at. "I see Kenneth!" is the last thing he says before his stubby legs take off, heading toward the redhead he calls his second best friend. Jaxon is already across the room by the time I stand.

"Kenneth!" Jaxon shouts, leaping into Kenneth's lap. An experienced pro with the rowdiness of the twins, he manages to keep his drink from toppling over and hugs the child.

"Jax! Have you grown since the last time I saw you?"

"Yup! And look!" Jaxon smiles wide and points at the gap between his teeth. "I lost my second tooth!"

"A big one too! How much did the Tooth Fairy bring you for that?"

"Fifty bucks," I answer, stopping at the edge of the table. "The Tooth Fairy isn't happy."

A pang of hurt nips my skin at the miffed expression on Kenneth's face when his eyes finally make it to mine. I didn't assume he would be happy to see me, but I didn't expect displeasure either.

But nothing is more surprising than the never-ending, gorgeous waves of deep auburn that flow over the back of the chair opposite of Kenneth. Gorgeous blue eyes that remind me of summer are looking up at me.

Kenneth is on a date. A *date*!

"Oh..." My eyes dart between them before I extend my hand toward the beautiful woman. "I'm Mallory, and this is Jaxon. As you can see, he's a slippery one."

Jaxon wiggles in Kenneth's arms. "Slippery! S...l...i...p...pery!"

A laugh slips between her painted red lips. From the amount of awe in her expression, you would think she has known Jaxon all his life.

"I'm Karla. It's so nice to meet you, Mallory." Instead of pulling her hand back, it drifts up. Dainty, painted fingernails pinch my olive-green sweater. "I love this color on you. I've been on the hunt for sweaters and have had zero luck finding ones that aren't itchy. Where did you find this one?"

"I stole it from my mom years ago. I've had great luck with garage sales in town. And I love your dress!"

Karla beams, smoothing out sky-blue satin that makes her eyes pop, paired with a cream turtleneck underneath. Adri would love to raid her closet. "I found this baby at a discount store thirty minutes up the road. Three bucks!"

"No way!" I yell. This woman is thrifty and sweet. All the sourness I felt earlier vanishes when she shoos away the wayward glances being shot at me. I like Karla.

I turn back to Kenneth, who is staring at me like I'm some mythological creature with four heads that magically appeared.

"Eddie," he croaks out. "This is my—"

I pull Jaxon from his lap and plop him onto my hip. "Karla. We established that. I've got to get back to Jules, but it was nice meeting you, Karla!"

Without a second glance, I jog back to the booth in the corner. Placing Jaxon on the yellow seat, I point a warning finger at him to stay put, softening the command with a peck to his forehead. Squeezing beside Julie, I keep my eyes on the sunflower mural and focus on taking deep, slow breaths.

Throughout our time at CLU, Kenneth hasn't had a single girlfriend. It's obvious it isn't from a lack of opportunity. He has options. I've watched many girls try, and none have ever gotten what they want.

Now I know why.

A small hand on my jaw halts the grinding of my teeth into a fine powder. I drop my scowl and slap on a smile, smoothing Julie's ponytail. "What should we get for dessert? I'm thinking apple pie or chocolate ice cream. Will you pick for us?" I ask.

Ignoring me, she turns to look out over the restaurant. When she sits back down, she beckons me to her. "He's looking over here," she whispers.

I force myself not to check. "Why are you telling me this?"

Julie unlocks my phone and takes down a large yellow blob with a red bird before answering. "Mommy says you wear your heart on your sleeve. I don't know what that means, but you look sad." She nudges my arm up until she's cuddled against me. "I'm sorry your heart is sad, Mal."

I want to tell her that I'm not sad. To be honest, there are too many emotions rattling around in my head to pick just one. Happy that Kenneth isn't alone like I am. Confused that he never once mentioned a girlfriend. Possibly even mildly jealous. I bet he doesn't make Karla feel like a pawn in a game, which is partially my fault. The Brain Bowl is ours, and I've had years to stop it.

However, Julie is seven, so I pull her into my lap and watch her take down green pigs with colorful birds.

Thirty minutes later, Jane appears at the end of the table with her purse in hand, to-go boxes, and a tired smile.

"Ready for bed?" I ask.

"Hell yeah." Jane gives me a weird look. "I saw you met Karla."

Placing a sleeping Julie on my back, I dodge her mom's overly perceptive gaze. Showing Jane that I'm rattled will open a can of worms I might not be able to close. After a moment, she takes the hint and heads for the exit. Jane knows I'll talk when I'm ready.

Each step away from Kenneth and his date fills me with relief, until I hear something so quiet that I almost miss it.

"So that's her?" Karla whispers.

I grind my teeth, keeping my focus on Jane's back and the door. I'm not sure what Kenneth says about me, but I'm sure I never want to know.

Chapter Fifteen

Kenneth

I'VE DEVELOPED A BIT of a problem. You see, I am not a morning person. I wouldn't even consider myself an afternoon person, but this semester is different.

My eyes pop open with ease, and I don't curse at my alarm clock. My feet hit the floor, and I don't wish I could crawl back into bed. I pull on my clothes and don't hate that they're not my pajamas. It's a breeze to get out of the house, grab breakfast, and drive to campus.

Only on Tuesdays and Thursdays.

Somehow, I find myself sitting on my stool with a Claude's hot chocolate with extra whipped cream for Mallory, waiting for her to walk through the door and glare at me for arriving before her. If I knew that sitting next to Mallory in class would make me a person who can be on time and enjoy the early mornings, I would've made sure we had classes together years ago.

Dr. Martin started class by telling us he received the list of those who made it to the semi-finals, but as a man with a flair for dramatics, he dove into a lesson on epidemiologists and postponed the reveal until the end of class.

Mallory's fingers drum against the table, glancing at her watch every two minutes. As much as I enjoy seeing her fidget, I'm freaking out too. My foot hasn't stopped bouncing, and I kicked her twice. Luckily, she was too absorbed in the time to notice.

"He can't seriously make us wait any longer," she mutters. "I'm going to puke all over the table if we don't find out soon."

All I want to do is be supportive. Lay a hand on her shoulder and tell her she's got this in the bag because I'm certain she does. But that's not what she needs right now. Mallory needs a distraction.

I swipe a curl from her eyes and chuckle. "You're going to puke when you hear my name called, and not yours."

Mallory gasps and throws her foot at me, hitting the knot in my calf. My yelp of pain stops Dr. Martin's lecture, and he grins at our table and shakes his head.

"I see some of you are getting antsy, so let's do this." He pulls a sheet of paper from his bag, and orange highlighter bleeds through the white. "Over two hundred applications were submitted, and only twenty-five made it to the next round. I'm pleased to say four of you are moving forward. Mason Gowing. Alondra Thurman." His finger slides down the paper. "Mallory Edwards and Kenneth Gray."

Mallory rounds on me with her hand raised and a wild look in her eyes. She can't possibly be bold enough to smack me across the face in a room full of witnesses. When I flinch, she wiggles her fingers impatiently.

A high-five. Duh. Our hands collide with an accomplished clap.

"Class dismissed. I'll see you all after spring break. Enjoy your week off! Can you four stay back for a moment?" I nod and sink back onto my seat.

As the room empties, Mallory slumps against the desk, as if she's exhausted by the good news. "I guess we're stuck together for just a little while longer," she says.

The sarcastic tinge I was expecting to hear is missing. That's been happening a lot recently. We talk like people who don't hate each other. Like people who could one day be more than rivals.

"Congrats, you four," Dr. Martin beams, handing out a new set of instructions. I scan the sheets of paper for the next list of tasks. One personal statement, a cover letter for our dream job, and three letters of recommendation: two professional and one peer. And I have until the beginning of May to make it good enough to beat twenty-four other students.

"Do you have any advice on how to stand out?" Mallory asks, pulling me back into the conversation.

"Be yourself. The judges only glimpse into you as a person is through your personal statement. Tell them why you're the best person for this internship." Spreading his arms wide, he wiggles his fingers. "Give them everything they need to see that you're going to make a difference in the world."

While Mallory races over to congratulate Mason and Alondra, I let the news wash over me and bask in what feels like pride. It's been so long since I felt this kind of hope. Like I have a chance to chase my own dream.

"Hey," I say when Mallory returns for her bag. "Want to go by Claude's? We could work on our personal statements."

Her lips pucker. "What month is it?"

My eyebrow quirks. "March. Why?"

"What sport do you play?"

"Swimming. The 1650-yard freestyle."

"What's your favorite vegetable?"

"Jicama. What are you doing?" I ask.

She reaches up and thumps my forehead. "Just making sure your brain hasn't been taken over by aliens."

"That's a possibility," I chuckle, because here I am asking Mallory to hang out with me. School-related celebration or not, it's new. Maybe it is aliens. "Is that a yes?"

She heaves her bag over her shoulder. "I'm not hungry, but thanks for the offer."

Betrayed by her own body, her stomach growls its displeasure in her lie.

"Sounds like a cinnamon roll would be nice. Another hot chocolate too. My treat."

Mallory steps around me and heads for the door. "That's nice of you, Gray, but you probably have places to go and people to see."

Finally. An opportunity to set things straight. I'm sure Mallory couldn't have cared less that I was at dinner with a woman, but I don't want her to think I have a girlfriend.

Just in case.

"Nope. My sister is in town, and she knows I'm busy today. You met her last night."

"Karla..." Mallory's mouth gapes. "Karla is your sister?"

I nod. "Sadly."

Karla's been in town for a little over a week. After finishing graduate school, she's taking a short break before starting at Gray Construction as an architect. Which means she's running amok in my life, asking questions that are none of her business and begging to see Mallory again. She swears they would be the best of friends, which I can see being a real possibility.

Mallory wrings her hands, and her tiny smile makes me unreasonably excited.

"Fine, as long as I can get some caffeine to help me get through outlining my personal statement."

"You don't drink caffeine, Eddie. It gives you headaches and makes you jittery. I haven't forgotten what happened during finals sophomore year. You knocked over all those plates at Sunshine Junction."

"I was caffeinated and exhausted." She bumps my shoulder as we descend the stairs. "That wasn't one of my finest moments."

I chuckle. "And did you say outlining?"

"Gray. Please don't tell me you're one of those people who can raw dog essays and somehow make them perfect."

I scrunch up my face to hide the smile that peeks out. "Could you be more vulgar?"

"I absolutely fucking can," she sings.

Settled in our booth at Claude's Cafe, I pull up the email from Mallory. In less than twenty minutes, she created an outline that hits every target and mandatory criteria that Dr. Martin laid out for us.

I do, as Mallory so beautifully calls it, raw dog essays. I start typing and hope I find my footing along the way.

Out of two hundred people, I made it through to the next round. Having this tiny bit of hope feels both powerful and stupid. For the first time, I question if my dream doesn't have to be over.

I'll still have Nan, and I'm sure Karla won't care if I go against Dad. She might have been excited to join the family business, but I doubt she'll mind that I'm not.

My decision won't matter to Keaton, my older brother, considering we've never been close. We haven't spoken in years. Not since I told him I changed my major.

And my mother will do exactly what Dad says, cutting me off.

Life without my parents won't be any different than it is now. We already don't talk. The only thing that will change is my layer of security. Regardless, they're still my parents, and part of me still wants to make them proud.

I look over the table at Mallory, who's rummaging through her backpack. If she knew about my mental turmoil, she'd tell me this should be an easy decision. That no amount of security or family pressure should matter more than my dream. I'm sure she'd believe that giving it all up because of my father's threats is cowardly.

Every time he feels me slipping away, he tightens the reins and pulls me back in. I hate people like him. People that need to control everything in their lives and the lives of others.

All the courage I scrounged up on the walk to Claude's vanishes into thin air, my fingers freezing halfway through the message telling him I won't be completing my summer internship with Gray Construction. I shove my phone into my pocket as shame weasels its way through the pride, shattering my good mood into a million pieces on the table.

My fingers slam against the keyboard to distract myself with the outline. Each letter clashes harshly as I channel all my frustration into the wobbly keys, pushing me deeper into the depths of my own head until it's all I can hear. *Click, click, click.*

The only thing that manages to partially pull me out is a jar of peanut butter that knocks over my tea, sending a flood of brown across the table.

"Are you okay?" I ask, lifting my computer into the air.

Mallory hasn't a clue what happened, still pulling things out of her backpack.

"Eddie. What's going on?"

"My pen. I need to go home. Can you take me?"

Even though I only heard bits and pieces of what she said, I definitely heard the word pen. I reach into my backpack and place a black pen in front of her before looking at my computer. "Easy fix."

"What the hell?" Her knees knock against the table as she bolts up, stuffing everything back into her backpack. "I need to get home, Gray. I said I don't have my insulin—"

I sigh into the screen and cut her off. If I can get through this outline, I might be able to convince myself that it's a good idea to tell my father to shove his controlling and manipulative plans where the sun doesn't shine.

It's at this very moment I realize they're similar in this way, my father and Mallory.

I'm tired of people who are controlling.

"You needed a pen, so I gave you a pen. It's not a big deal. I know you have this aching need to be in charge of every single thing in your life, but that's impossible. Having complete control over a situation, person, or idea is not attainable. It's suffocating. You don't have to treat everything like it's life or death, and I can promise you that forgetting a pen is not that important. You can't control me."

I slam my laptop screen shut and look up, but it's not the eyes of the man I want to say those words to staring back at me.

Nope. It's not my father I yelled at in a quiet coffee shop.

Instead, caramel-like eyes glisten. Angry tears threaten to spill over and slide down those rounded cheeks. The realization splits straight through my anger.

"*Control* you? I'm not trying to control you. I stupidly asked you for help, so it's my fault for thinking you'd care. And not having my insulin pen *is* life or death." Looping her backpack over her shoulders, her face turns into an unreadable slate of stone. "It's nice to know things really don't change. Thanks for proving me right, Gray. Once an asshole, always an asshole."

Without another glance, she races out the door. I'm frozen to my spot, turning in time to watch her neon-green shoes disappear around the corner. Then everything falls into place.

Well, more like crashes and burns into place because I misheard her. She didn't say pen.

Mallory said *insulin* pen.

"What the hell are you waiting for?"

Libby's cold stare is harsh enough to give everyone in the cafe hypothermia. In her hands is a hot chocolate with extra whipped cream, a drink that was supposed to be enjoyed by the person I sent running out the door.

I so badly want to believe that I'm asleep and in the middle of a nightmare, but I'm wide awake and deeply regretful.

"I..." I stare out the window. "I have to go."

"Yeah, you do. Idiot. Go find her and un-fuck this. Quickly."

The wind whips against me as I round the building like Mallory did, but I find nothing. No neon sneakers. No bouncing hair. No Mallory.

People curse as I sprint down the sidewalk to my truck, bumping their shoulders roughly. She is running all the way home because I didn't think before I spoke and messed everything up.

Inside the truck, I dial Cade's number, and he answers on the first ring. "Hey! What's up, Kent?"

"Mallory..." The truck splutters to life, making me wait for my car to connect to Bluetooth. "I messed up, Cade. She left her insulin pen at home, and I wasn't paying attention. She's running. Last I saw, she turned on Chattanooga Street about five minutes ago."

I hear a plate shatter against the ground, and Cade hisses into the speaker. "Ouch! Okay. Hold on. Shay's here, so I'll let her know. Where are you?"

I pull onto Chattanooga Street, speeding down the route to her house. My eyes never leave the sidewalk, willing her to appear. "I'm headed there right now."

Cade covers the microphone, muffling his words to Shay, but her response is loud and clear. The front door slams, and I count eleven seconds before he comes back to the phone.

My shoulders slump as his sigh fills the truck's interior. "Kent. What the hell happened? How did you—"

"I'm an idiot. I'm sorry."

Brake lights blare crimson as the car in front of me screeches to a stop. I'm barely able to avoid slamming into its bumper, and a string of expletives leave my lips as I pull into a parking spot in front of a boutique. I kill the engine and throw open my door.

"Made it?" Cade asks, sounding hopeful.

"Traffic. Running. Talk soon."

It takes five minutes to make it to the red house on the corner. Every part of me aches when I make it to the front door, and my fist beats hard enough on the door to splinter it.

Fear scorches my throat as I scream, "Eddie? Ed! Answer the door!"

Silence.

I move to a window and peer through a gap in the kitchen curtains, pressing my face to the glass. Nothing is amiss other than the fridge door hanging open. I go back to the front door, continuing to knock as a car pulls into the driveway, followed by frustrated footsteps behind me. Shay shoves past me and unlocks the door, pushing it open.

"How could you?" she seethes, slamming the door in my face.

I have no clue, Shay.

Chapter Sixteen

SHARP PAIN STABS MY temples. Actually, my whole head feels like it's being blended up for a brain smoothie.

I reach for the cup of water on my nightstand and finish it in seconds, cool water dribbling down my chin. Two empty applesauce packets lie crumpled beside me, and a large grape juice stain bleeds through my pale purple comforter.

Low blood sugar is the scariest thing I've ever felt. It's an out-of-body experience. While the world seemingly moves around me normally, I'm stuck in slow-motion. It felt as if the sidewalk had turned to quicksand, my feet sinking deeper into the concrete with every step. Beads of sweat gathered above my lip as I ran, ignoring the honking cars and stop signs that stood between me and the house.

Running wasn't my best idea ever, but I had to get home. I need my insulin to be with me at all times. It literally keeps me alive.

I smack myself in the head three times. On the fourth, I remember Claude's, and a sharp pain of dejection stabs at my heart when the memories of Kenneth appear. The way his eyes clouded, nearly unrecognizable as they shifted into something that looked so much like hatred when he looked at me.

He's never been upset with me like that. The words he said may have been directed at me, but they were loaded enough to make me assume I'm not the only person he can't stand.

Couldn't he see the fear in my eyes? Hear the terror in my voice?

Still, I'm the one who forgot my insulin. That's the first time it's ever happened. Being distracted won't be a valid excuse when I end up in the hospital with hypoglycemia or in diabetic ketoacidosis.

Or worse.

My brain feels like it's being split in half with a meat cleaver when my head turns too quickly, catching Shay push the door open with her foot. "Good. You're awake. I'll text your mom," she says, crossing the room with two pieces of toast on a plate. "I called Bex. She said to eat this."

"Thanks." I nibble on a corner. "What else did she say?"

Shay is visibly shaken. Lines crease her blemish-free forehead as she paces back and forth at the edge of the bed. "That it happens, and I need to not come in here and freak out when you wake up, but that's impossible. How am I *not* supposed to freak out when I've spent the last two hours making sure I didn't need to force feed you gummy worms?"

I bite my nail cuticle until it bleeds, trying to keep back my tears. I'm so tired of disappointing the people I love and being a burden to them. "I'm sorry, Shay. I'm so sorry. I know you were with Cade, and I ruined—"

"Don't you dare finish that sentence, Mal." She's no longer pacing, standing right in front of me. "You didn't ruin anything. I'm here because you are my best friend, and I love you. What happened? I was out of the door before Cade could tell me."

I push the plate of toast aside. "I was going to drive to campus this morning and made a last-minute decision to walk. My kit was already in the car when I changed my mind, and by the time I was at Claude's and ready to dose insulin, it was too late, and I panicked."

Shay cradles my head into her chest, her floral perfume wrapping me with love. "I'm so glad Kenneth called Cade when he did. You were already asleep when I got home."

"What?" I look up. "He called Cade?"

"Yeah. He was at the door when I got here. I didn't have time to feel bad about being an asshole, but now I do. He somehow looked even worse than you do right now, and you look rough."

I find my reflection in the mirror and grimace. My hair is flat against the back of my head. Dark circles are settled beneath my eyes. White, chapped lips rub painfully against each other.

"Thanks, bestie," I grumble, forgiving her the moment she presses our foreheads together. We chuckle for a second before the weight of this afternoon comes crashing down again. "I don't know how to face him now. He acted like I was insane. I asked for help, and he lost it on me. Rivals or not, it hurt."

I thought I'd be angry that he pushed me aside after promising he would always be there for me, but that's not the emotion I'm struggling to understand.

It's sadness.

"I know, and Cade laid into him for it." Shay rubs large circles on my back. "Kenneth blames himself for the whole thing. He said he didn't even hear the word insulin at first."

With a dismissive snort, I pull away from her. "He shouldn't blame himself. I'm the one who screwed up. I failed today. *Me*, Shay. Nobody else is at fault."

Sadly, it doesn't make the sting of his reaction hurt any less.

"I hate when you say that," she sighs. "You're human. You're bound to mess up."

"Yeah, but it's literally the one thing I can't afford to mess up. I was lucky today. What happens if—"

"No." Shay holds up her hand and cuts me off. Her features contort at my unspoken words, with unshed tears gleaming in the light. "Don't say it. I can't... I can't think about that."

I want to roll my eyes, fight, and scream that it *needs* to be discussed. Scary or not, it's my reality. I don't have the luxury of ignoring it.

"I'm not trying to minimize it," she promises. "I just want to think about your next steps. We can talk about ways to move forward."

"Like what? Strapping my diabetes kit around my neck so I never forget it again?"

"Relax, Ms. Drama." Shay urges me to take another bite before continuing. "Maybe it's time for an insulin pump? I saw you researching them the other day."

I cuddle my knees into my chest. "Are you saying this as my friend?"

"I'm saying this as your copilot and best friend. We promised to tell each other the truth, and I think it's time. I can't lose you, Mally. Not now. Not ever."

Part of me wants to protest. Then I remember I ran home in a pure panic to get my lifeline. Having it with me at all times could be better.

She drops my phone in my lap. "I think he's expecting your call."

Unlocking it, I scan the messages lined up against my wallpaper. All from Kenneth. Each one is more worried than the last. The last one sent twelve minutes ago is only two words.

The Worst Color Ever

Please, Eddie.

I swipe them away and open Dr. Morand's contact card.

Here goes nothing.

Chapter Seventeen

THIS HAS BEEN THE worst spring break to date.

It's been one whole week without a word from Mallory. With every message I send, I'm taunted by the read receipt and no response. I forced myself to stop texting her three days ago. Even though I'm not sending them, I keep drafting ten-page apologies before deleting the message moments later. I would settle for a middle finger emoji as a response.

But as much as I deserve it, she deserves space even more.

Turning onto the road to the pool, I adjust my rear-view mirror. Practice today should be short considering the meet tomorrow is important.

Well, all of them are, but this is my last chance to qualify for the National Championship meet in two weeks. Last season, I missed the qualifying standard by nine seconds. I stood behind the podium, looking longingly at the group of proud athletes who had qualified.

Year one I made it. Year two I was scared. Year three is the year I turn it all around.

Since my not-so-pep-talk with Coach Brown, my weekly counseling sessions and Mallory's reminder have helped me not completely suck in my last three races. Although I didn't place at the conference meet, I feel like I'm finally on an upward trajectory now that I'm making a real effort to fight my fears.

The thought of using a championship win as a point in the Brain Bowl flits across my mind for a second, vanishing the moment I spot neon-green tennis shoes.

With legs bare against the wind, turquoise KT tape runs down her hamstrings. Her laugh dances through my open windows, drowning the Paramore song blaring from the stadium speakers with something even more nostalgic.

Mallory is okay. Happy. Safe.

My brain begs me to stop and think, but I ignore it. I turn on my hazard lights, park my truck, throw open the door, and take off running straight toward the woman who has every reason to hate me.

By the time Cade's warning to let her come to me flashes in my head, it's too late. I'm a yard away, and the scent of sunscreen, grass, and vanilla keeps pulling me in.

Even if she tells me to leave, I need to apologize.

"Hi."

Mallory freezes, and the smile I've missed slips off her face as she takes me in. It feels like a punch to the groin, but at least it's from her.

"What do you want, Gray?"

I rub the back of my neck and begin to regret my impulsivity. She's still mad, and she has every right to be. "I saw you on my way to the pool, and I wanted to make sure you're okay. Can we—"

"No. I'm busy."

"Okay." I force myself to smile, swallowing down sadness. "Can you let me know when you're ready to talk, Eddie? Please."

At the nickname, a flash of something I can't decipher flits over her face before snapping back to stone. She checks her watch before letting out a slow breath. "You've got one minute."

This time my smile is real, because that's all I need.

"I was wrong. Incredibly wrong. Stupidly wrong. Even though I wasn't paying attention, it doesn't excuse how I acted or spoke to you. I should have taken you home the moment you asked because there's nothing more important to me than making sure you're safe and happy. I promised I'd be there for you and ended up doing the exact opposite. It's my number one priority, and I did a terrible job of showing you that the other day."

When I made it back to my car that day, I realized I had grossly assumed something about Mallory. She's nothing like my father. His controlling tendencies are manipulative, cunning, and egotistical.

She is none of those things. Not even close.

To call Mallory controlling is a disservice to the work she puts in.

"I have no idea how it feels to live with a chronic condition or the terrifying feeling of realizing that something you need to survive is missing. You're not controlling. You're so much more than that. In the best way possible. You're diligent and driven. Cautious and careful. And I'm sorry, Eddie. It will never happen again."

The wind dies abruptly when I finish, giving me the opportunity to hear her shock. It's as if all the air is pushed out of her lungs, the exhale relaxing her entire body.

"You're... sorry?"

"Yes. I'm so sorry."

"You're sorry that my feelings got hurt?" she asks, her voice pitching higher.

I shake my head. "No. I'm sorry that I acted poorly and hurt you. For being an idiot and not listening. For not being there for you."

"You're sorry." This time it's not a question. She actually believes me.

Her features take on the Mallory I missed over the past week. An eye roll replaces the apathetic glare and my favorite half-smile, half-scowl takes over her lips, as if she doesn't know which to grace me with.

She's back.

"Maybe I should run away more often if it leads to apologies."

I take a step toward her, testing the waters. "Yeah right. Even you aren't that petty."

"You don't think so?" Her laugh is light and airy, like the way I feel in this moment. "Is there anything else you want to apologize for while we're here?" Mallory pushes a strong leg out, setting up like she's ready to race. "If not, I'll be going now."

I freeze. This is it. My opportunity to finally bring up the silent agreement we made to play the game and nothing more. The chance to move into something more than rivals. I don't know what exactly, but I'm certain I want so much more with Mallory Edwards.

I'm even more desperate to know if she does too.

"I'm kidding, Gray. There's no need to open that can of worms. With our history, we would be standing out here all weekend. Apology accepted, but not needed." Mallory shrugs, but I don't miss the pained look in her eyes. "Plus, I'm the one who forgot my insulin. I'm sorry for putting you in that position."

"Apology accepted, but not needed," I repeat back. "And I never want you to apologize for something so human. I forget things all the time."

My cheeks burn as I look down at her, sorely lucky that she's here right now, and even better, the half-scowl is gone. I'm getting a *real* Mallory smile. One that's not a byproduct of something Cade said or a successful win at a Brain Bowl point opportunity.

It's because of me and for me.

"Hey, Kenneth. How are you?"

Mallory jumps at the new voice, and I force myself to look at her friend. "Hey, Jo. I'm doing much better now. You?"

"I'm alright." Jo gives us a funny look and bumps Mallory's hip as she strolls past us. "We're heading to the pool. Let me know how yoga is, Mal."

Now that I think about it, I've never seen Mallory swim. Sure, she's been *at* a pool. Never *in* it. A good chunk of college parties take place at pools, but she's never floated in the water, battled it out during chicken fights, or sat on the pool's edge with chlorine-saturated hair hanging over her shoulders.

There's so much I don't know about this woman, and now that I've gotten a taste of Mallory outside of the game, I can't get enough.

"Why don't you swim?"

Her nose crinkles. "Why would I need to? I prefer land."

"All I'm hearing is that you can't swim. There have been so many parties and recovery days, and never once have I seen you in the water. You're always sitting in a chair listening to music or being nosy."

She smirks. "You watching me, Gray?"

We both know the answer to that question.

"Avoiding the topic only makes you look more suspicious. Just admit it. You can't swim."

"I can swim! I just don't. I'd rather not frolic around in water that's full of pee and poop. I prefer my water filtered, with a little bit of fluoride in it."

I push a finger into my ear and clean it out. I must have misheard her. "Excuse me?"

The hilarious part is that she has the audacity to look at me as if I'm insane. "Are you telling me you've never thought about the disgusting shit floating around in pool water?" she shrieks. "I bet you've swallowed so much gunk! Urine. Feces. Hair! Pools are disgusting, and I don't care what anyone says. Chlorine can't be *that* good."

A burst of laughter explodes so hard from my chest that I have to bend over, my body shaking from the wild turn of our conversation. It takes a moment to catch my breath, which gives my brain just enough time to produce a thought.

"I want to take you somewhere."

"For the project? It could be our third punch—"

"Nope." I shake my head. "Non-project and non-school related. If you get there and you hate it, you don't have to swim, I promise. Would you at least come?"

"To a pool? Hell no."

"Not a pool. A lake, which is even better."

She fakes a gag. "All bodies of water are gross, Gray. At least pools have chlorine, even if it isn't perfect. Animals take care of their business in the water. Plus, there's bacteria and algae, and if I can't see the bottom—"

"Do you think I'd take you somewhere dangerous?"

"Possibly!" she shouts, throwing her hands up. "And our applications are due soon. There's too much going on."

"We have two months until May."

"A little over a month and a half," she corrects me. "What about the cold front that's supposed to hit next week? Swimming in the cold? Never ever."

"Perfect! Let's go this weekend. The weather will be perfect."

I'm saying the word perfect a lot, but if she agrees, this weekend has the potential of being just that.

"I don't—"

I press my hands together and beg. "I know you don't like water, but I promise I'll make it the best day. And if you hate it, I'll reimburse your time with something comparable of your choosing."

"Anything I want?" she asks, her smile turning mischievous.

I feel her resolve cracking. I'd do karaoke a million times if she said yes. "Anything."

"Fine," she finally says, and my stomach splits with surprise. "But if you take me to a pool, I will literally drown you in it."

"I wouldn't dare." I look over at my illegally parked car. If I don't leave now, I'll be late for practice. "My meet is all day tomorrow, so let's plan for Sunday. I'll bring the towels."

She chews on her bottom lip nervously. "Do you think the lake monsters are more likely to eat a girl in a bikini or a one piece? I want to keep my chances as low as possible."

Thoughts of Mallory in a swimsuit have my mind racing, so I force my brain to focus on something much less attractive. Like the dent on my truck or the way I'm about to get screamed at by Coach Brown for being late.

"The monsters will be on their best behavior," I promise. Her mouth opens, probably ready with another excuse, so I keep talking. "And no, I won't be too tired after the meet."

If anything, being with her will be rejuvenating.

There's a little extra pep in my step as I rush back to the truck. I grip the steering wheel, but Mallory waving in the mirror halts my celebration.

I poke my head out of the window. "Miss me already, Eddie?"

"One day you're going to choke on all that ego, Gray." Her smile is glorious. "Good luck tomorrow, and don't open your mouth under water!"

"Good swimmers never do. See you Sunday!"

My face burns, likely close to the color of my hair as I peel down the road because Mallory just agreed to hang out with me outside of the allotted three punches, and I'm going to make every second count.

Chapter Eighteen

Kenneth Gray apologized to me. Without prompting, bribing, or sarcasm.

I'm so used to the *"I'm sorry that your feelings got hurt"* bullshit ones, which was what I fully expected when he stopped me.

I've always thought of apologies as band-aids, used to fix an issue over and over until they're no longer sticky, making them completely worthless. With every half-assed apology I've gotten over the years, my belief in those two words withered away, leaving me with zero trust in them.

Until Kenneth said them.

I thought his proposition was a weird dream, but here I am in the passenger seat of his navy pickup. His promise to take me to a lake is in motion, and I'm anxious.

And sure, I'm always anxious, but this is different.

I also have a tiny confession to make. A solo watch party for his race took place in my bedroom during a study break. The starting beep went off, and he dove quickly and expertly into the water, his arms propelling him with speed I'm sure makes many jealous. Hell, it made me jealous. My breath synced with every graceful stroke, and I couldn't take my eyes off the screen. When the announcer screamed that Kenneth met the standard, solidifying his spot at the National Championship meet, I yelped loud enough to wake Winry from her nap.

This morning when I opened the front door for him, I was so excited that I leapt right into his arms. Kenneth finally had his first real breakthrough since freshman year, and the only way I knew how to express my excitement was hugging the man I've never hugged.

It was clear I had crossed a line when he froze like a block of ice, the tips of his ears fuming red. I stepped back, ran past him, jumped into the passenger seat, and have been pretending to be asleep for the last twenty-five minutes.

I sit up and sigh, giving up on Operation Fake Sleep and roll down my window to let the cool breeze lick my skin. After a bit of research over the past week, I found out that my assumption was correct. Lakes are even nastier than pools. But even with that newfound, terrifying knowledge, I'm fully prepared to get in the water.

I know. I'm not sure who I am anymore.

It felt like a gift to have Kenneth smile at me like that when I agreed to come. After almost three years, I thought I had seen all his smiles. The kind smile. The polite smile. The smug smile. The photographed smile.

Standing there on that sidewalk, he showed me one I had never seen, and it was just for me. A bit crooked and shy, lopsided and perfect. The plaster around my heart cracked at the sight, and I hated every second.

"Are we almost there?" I say, dragging out the last word like a child.

Kenneth takes one hand off the wheel and scribbles on his forearm. "Adding impatient to your running list of crimes."

"I would've bet big money it was already on there."

"I can be kind sometimes." There's a glint in his eye when he looks at me, but his attention returns to the road.

"Why are you smiling like you're plotting a crime?" I ask. "I didn't tell anyone where I was going today."

I slap a hand over my mouth. Every true crime podcast host would shame me for that slip up. Now I regret not telling The Quartet or my mom. I was afraid they would try to make this a big deal.

I don't even know what this is to be honest.

"Don't worry, Ed. No crimes will be committed today." His soft chuckle evaporates the remaining tension between us from the awkward hug, making it easier to breathe. "Look, we're here."

Slowing down, he clicks the blinker on and turns onto a lone road that leads to a forest of trees. Pushing my face out of the open window, I inhale deeply, taking in this random slice of heaven he's brought me to.

"That smell… What kind of trees are those?"

"Cedar. My favorite."

The ignition shuts off, but I don't move. The prettiest shades of blue and green have me starry-eyed and distracted.

Kenneth taps my forehead through the open window before the passenger door swings open. With an extended hand, he nudges his head in the direction of the water. "Want to look around? The view is even better from over there."

I stare at his freckled hand. Before today, there's no way I'd take his hand without trying to snap his wrist. But my legs feel wobbly at the idea of swimming, so I take it for support.

Kenneth leads me through the lush grass and onto a rickety dock. Lights hang between the dock's wooden beams, probably gorgeous at night, like fireflies floating above the water. The deep green trees that loom over us smell way better than any air freshener. As if amplified by speakers, every note from the birds above float in the air.

A dizzying feeling hits my head as I peer over the edge. Nope. Can't see the bottom.

I scramble backwards, running into Kenneth behind me. He checks in silently with a raised brow. After a moment of deep breaths, I finally nod, telling him I'm okay.

"Where are we?"

"Lake Anita," Kenneth breathes. "Welcome to my home, Eddie."

"This…" I crouch down to drag my finger over Kenneth's and Cade's names carved into the wood. "This is your childhood home?"

"Basically. My parents have a house in town, but we don't have the best relationship. I started living here with my grandmother when I was fifteen, which was a dream come true. I guess I was what you could call an angsty teen, and I wanted to take care of her."

I'm about to ask him if he was one of those who listened to Pierce the Veil and sobbed over the lyrics, but when he pulls his shirt over his head, I'm thrown by the sight. Freckles cover every inch of his strong shoulders and wide chest. His stomach is surprisingly unmarked, and a trail of red disappears into his shorts. It's as vivid as the hair on his head.

My mouth goes dry. When did he stop looking annoying and start looking like *this*?

I force my eyes to the ground, but clearly not fast enough because he clicks his tongue.

"You watching me, Eddie?"

Smug bastard. I remove my own cover-up and toss it to the ground, leaving me in a teal bikini.

"In your dreams," I grumble.

I sit on the edge of the dock and rip open a package of tape for my new insulin pump. It has been a week since I got it, and I'm still getting used to having another little machine on me.

"How do you know what I dream about?" he teases, eyes flickering between the two taped areas on me. "You got something new?"

I rub the black tape to make sure it won't fall off in the water. "An insulin pump."

He nods, and I can see all the questions he wants to ask. Instead, he hands me a pair of red goggles. "No more procrastinating. It's time to prove you can swim." When I finally situate them over my hair, he wipes the lenses with his thumb and grins. "You ready?"

I peer over the edge again. The lake is liquid black, hiding everything that could be lurking beneath the surface. There could be an animal or a fallen branch or a lake monster. Something could grab my foot and drag me down.

"No," I answer honestly. "Not being able to see what's in the water terrifies me."

"I know it looks scary, but I'd never put you in harm's way."

Kenneth holds out his hand again, and I stare at it. My brain must be playing tricks on me. Somehow, the bane of my existence is making me rethink everything I thought I knew about him, because I *want* to hold his hand right now.

As if holding it will make facing my fears a bit easier.

"Don't let me get eaten by a gator," I beg, letting our palms brush. "I don't want to be their afternoon snack."

He crosses his free hand over his heart. "On three."

"One," we say at the same time.

"Two."

A shudder of guilt rips through my body, and the final number gets stuck in my throat.

I shouldn't be here. I don't do things like this. I should be at home studying for my biochemistry exam and writing a personal statement that will knock the judges' socks off. Being at Lake Anita isn't productive. Now I'll have to stay up all night to make up for the lost time.

How could I have been so careless and stup–

"Hey, Ed," Kenneth says, and my eyes shift from the water to his sharp, freckled jaw. "It means a lot to me that you came today. I know it's weird that I asked you to come do something you hate. This is my favorite place in the world, and I'm happy I get to share it with you." My heartbeat slows as he meets my eye. "I know there are so many other things you could be doing instead, so I'm glad you're here with me."

The shame of not working slips away as he tangles our fingers.

For extra security of course.

He's right. I do have so many other things I should be doing, but I'm happy to be here too.

Standing next to Kenneth, my shoulders fall. Not even when falling asleep do I feel this at peace. A mellow state hangs over Lake Anita, and I feel it radiating off the man beside me and deep into my bones.

Relaxed is a feeling that I never expected to associate with Kenneth Gray, but here it is, and today I'm not going to fight it.

Fuck it.

"Three!"

My fingers are shriveled like raisins, and I'm struggling to open a package of crackers and cheese. Kenneth floats on his back, and his eyes flutter open when I finally rip into the snack. He opens his mouth, cheering when he catches the piece of cheese I toss.

I swipe crumbs from my legs onto the dock. "How long has Lake Anita been in your family?"

"Forever. My grandmother grew up here, and it's been passed down for generations."

He points to a cozy, charming house I hadn't noticed until now. The home gleams a pristine white, blinding against the backdrop of the surrounding forest with its own private lake. A cobblestone path leads to the front porch, adorned with rocking chairs and draped in sunlight. The space is full of love and memories that I can feel from here.

"Where is she now?" I ask, but then I realize how personal that question is and cover my mouth. "Never mind. I'm sorry. I shouldn't have asked that."

His floating falters for a moment, and he flips over to tread water. "No worries. She lives at the assisted living facility up the road. Nan has multiple sclerosis."

Kenneth answers every question I ask. Nan was a swimmer who started a family with her high school sweetheart. She's the person who taught Kenneth how to swim and never missed a meet. Since moving into the assisted living facility, she has only been able to watch them on the television.

"I wish I could do more for her," he says, guilt weighing his words down to an almost-whisper. "She's given me so much support over the years, and I barely manage to visit her once a week."

I cross my legs, keeping my eyes everywhere except on Kenneth's face. "From the outside looking in, I think you're being a little hard on yourself. You're a student-athlete with a difficult major that I assume was inspired by your grandmother. You come every weekend to take care of your home and see her. You walk out of class when her doctor calls. You're her right-hand man when it comes to decisions about her health. I think what you're doing is pretty amazing, Gray."

And because I can't have another soft moment with this man today, I stand abruptly before he can speak. I don't think my heart can handle it.

"Break's over, Gray. I didn't come out here to float. I came to show you I can swim and possibly get eaten by a lake monster." I turn and backflip off the dock, rejuvenated by the cool water.

Kenneth lets out a sharp whistle when I resurface, holding up nine fingers. "It was a little wobbly at the end. Try again."

I crawl up the ladder and curtsy. "As you wish," I say, but follow up with a cannonball that covers him with a water.

I don't know how long we've been out here, and I don't care either. I'm going to enjoy this time of laughing and everything else I had no idea I could have with Kenneth Gray.

The sun is lazy in its descent, as if it's not ready for the day to end. Truthfully, I don't want it to end either. I see why Kenneth loves this place so much. Thirty seconds after he parked, I decided I wouldn't mind coming back here again.

With him.

I smile at the photo I secretly snapped. Freckles are dotted across the wide expanse of his back, and the sun rests like a halo above his head. Just in case I never come back, I want to take a piece of Lake Anita with me.

The smile on my face grows when a text from Shay comes in. The seventh since I left the house this morning.

Shayzilla

If you don't tell me where you are right now, I'm calling the police.

I desperately need to come clean to my best friend. We can order takeout, and I'll tell her the honest-to-god truth.

That I have no clue what's going on.

I shoot Shay a brief proof of life message and silence my phone as we head toward the truck, warmed by the sun and the presence beside me.

My eyes narrow when Kenneth rushes to reach my door before I can.

"No matter how many stank eyes you give me, I won't stop opening them," he promises.

Keeping up the thoughtfulness, he waits until I'm buckled to push the truck into drive. Instead of turning on his blinker and heading home, he looks in the opposite direction of Clear Lake.

"Do you mind if I stop by and see Nan? I couldn't swing by yesterday. I know you've got a lot going on, so feel free to say no. I can come back after I take you home."

My talk with Shay can wait. "I don't mind one bit."

"Would you like to come in and meet her?"

Oh god. Why do I want to say yes?

My head shakes quickly in protest. "Nan needs to hear all about your big win. I'll walk around and find something to do." I pull my tote into my lap before looking back at him. "Maybe next time?"

His smile splits wide, and my heart flips because it's the one that's just for me.

"Next time, Eddie."

Chapter Nineteen

Kenneth

"Why are you running off already?" Nan asks, holding onto my arm as we head into the dining hall. "You should stick around for supper. Titus is going to be sad he missed you."

"You know I love a good pot roast, but I need to get back to Clear Lake." I check the window one more time to make sure Mallory isn't waiting in the heat and unlock the truck. "I've got a passenger that has been a real trooper being spontaneous for a few hours."

Nan spent our forty-five minutes together bragging to anyone who would listen about the race, her arms slicing through the air to act out my form for the crowd.

Dr. Hope even agreed to let Nan come watch the National Championship meet in person, but I made her promise to leave the megaphone.

"A passenger?" she asks as we pass Lucinda, who bats a heavily shadowed eye at me. "Wait. Did you bring Mallory home, Fishie?"

"Maybe."

Nan digs her heels into the ground until I stop walking and pulls me in for a hug. "Tell her I say hello. I would love to meet her next time."

I barely refrain from telling her Mallory already agreed, but getting both of our hopes up isn't something I want to do.

As much as I want Mallory to come back, I know today is an anomaly for us.

The truck is empty when I make it back outside. I lean against the passenger door and check my texts. There are none from Mallory, but there are three from Grant asking if he can get a blow up of my head for the meet in two weeks. I respond with a middle finger emoji as she rounds the corner.

"Looks like you found some goodies," I say, opening her door.

"Gray, this town is adorable! How long has that bookstore been there? They had the cutest kitten running around. I ate way too many samples at the bakery, and I bought fudge. I got a few for the girls, cookies and cream for Cade, and rocky road for me. Do you remember when they brought those mini cakes to the football field during freshman year?"

I nod. "I ate like seven of the German chocolate ones and was sick for days."

"Well," she says, holding out a small container of German chocolate fudge to me. "I hope this doesn't bring back any bad memories."

"Thank you, Eddie," I choke out. Even if it makes me sick, I'm eating the whole thing.

The gesture is so kind that my hands shake as I take the fudge, and I'm thankful that she doesn't notice. Mallory's distracted by the small town I grew up in. A town I never cared for outside of Lake Anita, Nan, and Cade's family. With her beside me, I'm reminded of its beauty.

"Did you have a good day?" I ask, clocking her deepening frown as we drive further away from Bryan.

A sleepy smile spreads across her lips when she looks at me. "Surprisingly, yes. It was a very good day."

The drive home looks like it will be a lot less tense than the drive up, which was completely my fault. Who knew something as simple as a hug from Mallory would make me panic? She closed the space between us so easily, and instead of enjoying it, I froze like I had been caught doing something wrong.

Even though it felt so right.

"I wanted to talk about earlier. The hu—"

A loud pop cuts me off, followed by a hissing sound that reminds me of deflating balloons. Mallory sits up as the wheel spins out of my hands, veering us to the right side of the road and straight toward a cluster of trees.

"Shit, shit, shit!" Mallory screams.

She reaches for the handle above the door but it's too late. A sickening thud echoes in the interior when her shoulder slams against the door, and the whimper of pain she lets out pierces my ears. My arm shoots across her chest to assist her seatbelt with anchoring her into the seat.

Nails dig into my forearm as I regain control of the truck. I release a shaky exhale when it finally bumps and groans to a stop in the grass.

The moment we're stopped, my hand flies from her hip to her cheek, letting the other get tangled in her hair as I bring her face to mine. "Breathe, Eddie. Take a deep breath for me. In and out, real slow."

After the seventeenth shaky breath, her eyes flutter open.

This is so not the time, but I take a brief moment to really look at Mallory. It's crazy how beautiful this woman is. I've never had the pleasure of seeing her this close. Only an inch separates our noses from touching, and her body tenses as the realization hits her.

But she doesn't pull back.

"Are you okay?" I ask, rubbing a pale scar beneath her eye.

She nods hard, as if trying to convince herself. "You?"

"I'm fine, but your shoulder. God, Eddie. That sounded so bad. Can you move it?"

Giving my hand a squeeze, she removes it from her cheek and winces when she rolls her shoulder. "It'll be sore, which I can live with. It could've been so much worse." She gives me a small smile before unbuckling her seatbelt. "We should go check the damage."

I follow her lead and round the lopsided vehicle to the passenger side. The front tire is flat to the ground.

"Cursed," she mumbles. "I'm totally cursed."

Grabbing my phone, I dial the number for roadside assistance. Although my father was too busy running a business to teach me the basic life skill of how to change a tire, he has never forgotten to pay the annual fee for emergency help.

Just as the perky voice answers, Mallory presses the red button. "No, we don't need them." She holds out her hand. "Keys, please."

My matching keychain from Cade jingles as she moves to the backseat. Folding the seats down, she pulls out a black pouch and a wonky tool that I've never seen before. "What the hell is that?"

She gives me a bizarre look. "A jack. Have you never seen one?"

I shake my head, likely unnoticed because Mallory is in problem-solving mode, moving to the next task on her mental agenda. Metal tools from the pouch clang against each other as she puts the pieces together in a way that looks wrong but somehow seems right. After a few minutes, the spare tire lands on the ground from beneath the truck with a thud.

When she moves for it, I step in front of her. "Wait. Are you sure you're feeling okay?"

"I'm good, Gray, I promise. Thanks for asking. I promise I'll tell you if I'm hurting."

I nod and move for the spare tire. "Fine, but at least let me help. You've been showing me up for the past five minutes. I can't have you hurting your shoulder *and* my ego." I drop the spare and my crappy toolbox to the ground and look at the mess scattered around us. "Do you mind telling me why we pulled all of this out when I have roadside assistance? Which is free and easy. *This* doesn't look easy."

"Free and easy doesn't mean quick. They won't show up for at least an hour, and I can change it in half that." Mallory pushes her phone into my hands. "Text Cade and ask him to come and follow us home. The tire will make the trip, but it'll be dark soon."

I look at Cade's contact card warily. I didn't exactly tell him about today. If I had, he would have gotten way too excited, and considering there's nothing to be excited about, I kept it to myself.

Still, I send the message like she asks and leave out the fact that it's from me.

I take a seat on the ground beside her to watch her work. "How did you learn to do this?"

"Remember the first day of class?"

"How can I forget? The day we became partners."

She nods, digging through the toolbox. "When I was headed to class, my tire was flat, which is why I got to class much later than I wanted to." She places a tool around what she calls a lug nut and steps on it, bouncing to loosen each one. "So, I watched a few videos until I felt ready, and then I changed the tire before practice."

"Wait. You learned this from watching strangers on the Internet?"

She gives me a grunt that I take as a yes.

"You look like a pro."

Mallory turns to face me, the light in her eyes dimmed. "No, but I wish. My dad was actually the car pro. When I got my license, he wouldn't let me drive until we had a lesson on how to change a tire. It was a safety thing for him."

My brow furrows. "Did the videos give you a refresher?"

"No. I was a stupid teenager, and instead of listening to my dad, I spent the entire hour scrolling social media and messaging my friends. By the time he finished, I hadn't heard a single word and learned nothing. It sucks because I'd do anything to go back and actually pay attention."

Jordan's words from the parking lot sit heavily between us. *Daddy issues.* What a terrible way to describe someone who's dealing with the loss of a parent.

"I'm sorry, Eddie."

Mallory wipes her face with her arm. Sweat or tears, I don't know, but the tremble in her voice gives me a hint. "I thought it would get easier to talk about him, but it hasn't. It hurts just as much as it did when I was sixteen."

I plant my feet firmly on the ground and shift my weight forward until I'm kneeling beside her. As much as I want to hug her, I know that putting my hand on her shoulder is safe, so I do that instead.

"Only you get to dictate your grief. There's no timeline or rules to follow. Thank you for telling me."

"Thank you for listening to me. It means a lot." She stands, dusting gravel and grass off her knees. "Can you gather the lug nuts so I can lift the truck?" I nod, watching as the muscles in her arm flex as she works. "So, why didn't your dad teach you how to change a tire? Isn't it one of the tests of manhood?"

"Talking to me has never been his priority, which means teaching me things was pretty much out of the question too."

I expect silence or sympathy like everyone else gives, some iteration of an apology for something they can't control. Apologizing for the way my father has always shoved me aside until I'm of use to him.

Relief swells when she snorts. "Sounds like he's a real piece of shit."

It's the perfect response. Vulgar and validating. Incredibly Mallory.

With the car in the air, I pull off the flat tire and put on the spare. "I guess it won't hurt to learn something from you today since I did teach you how great swimming is."

As if we didn't have a random heart-to-heart, Mallory throws her head back and laughs, the boisterous sound warming me from the inside out.

The sun and her smile battle it out for which is the most brilliant, and she wins by a landslide.

"Don't get all cocky, Gray. All I said was that I didn't hate it. I still prefer life without infections or diseases from nasty water."

It doesn't take long to lower the truck and retighten the lug nuts. Pride radiates off her in happy squiggles, humming as she rechecks her steps to make sure she didn't miss one.

Of course she didn't. She's Mallory Edwards.

"And you finished four minutes faster than you expected. If you weren't here, I'd be stranded for a half hour or more, so thank you."

"No problem. Did you learn anything?" she asks, leaning against me to catch her breath, which effectively makes me lose mine.

I sure did. I learned I'm falling for Mallory Edwards.

"Yup. I learned you're a slow, but decent swimmer, and your tire changing skills beat mine, which doesn't mean much."

She rolls her eyes. "At least I know how to change a tire. I passed the man test. Did you?"

I grin and rip into the applesauce packet she hands me. "Are you ever anything except a smart aleck?"

And gorgeous.

"Nope!"

The familiar sound of Cade's car horn pierces the air. The moment he arrives, the easiness between the two of us will be gone, ending our good day as we shift back into our routine.

This has never been our normal.

"Kent? You're here too?" Popping a U-turn, Cade pulls up behind the truck. I can see the questions bouncing around in his head, but he bites his tongue and says, "MalPal changed the tire, huh?"

"Why ask when you already know?" I grumble.

Mallory jogs to Cade's open window and hugs him. Surprise colors his features when she moves back to my truck and jumps inside. He stares at me through the glass, clearly immune to my silent plea to keep quiet. Poking his head through the sunroof, I pray Mallory can't hear him.

"Me and you. Talking. Tonight!" The seriousness of his tone contradicts the overly excited smile on his face.

Waving him away, I make my way to the driver's side window. "Eddie, I won't be offended if you go with Cade. I'm sure you've hit your Gray limit for the week."

She buckles her seatbelt and starts turning the knobs until she finds a radio station she likes. "No, it's okay. I'm good right here. I started my day with you, which means I'll finish it with you."

I open my door and beg my breathing to slow. It's nearly impossible to keep my heart from beating out of my chest as I slide into my seat and buckle up. Does she know that it sounds like she's enjoying her time with me? And if she did, would she stop saying these things?

I turn up the volume, letting an old Rihanna song play. "I knew you liked me a little bit, Eddie."

Mallory laughs, copying the lyrics. "Shut up and drive."

Before I know it, we're at her house. Last time I was here wasn't under the best circumstances, but this time is so much better.

I lean over and push her door open because she made it clear about five minutes from the house that she wasn't waiting for me to get out of the truck and jog around to open it.

Mallory dips out of frame to admire the spare tire, and when she comes back into view, her eyes narrow. "Why are you looking at me like that? Is there something on my face?"

I'm grateful that a blade of grass rests on her cheek so I can say, "Yup," and reach across the console. I roll the fleck of green between my fingers. "The price of hard work."

Mallory doesn't mumble. If she's speaking, you're sure of every word leaving her mouth. That's why the whispered sentence she mutters makes me unbuckle.

I reach through the open window and grab her bag strap before she can escape up the sidewalk.

"Wait," I beg, releasing her. "I didn't hear you. What did you say?"

With a huff, Mallory stops and turns around. Every emotion on her face is clear. Drained from the sun. Excited about the spare tire. Annoyed that I asked her to repeat herself because we both know I heard her the first time.

It all makes my head spin.

"Liar," she huffs out, and her gaze shifts to the ground. "I said I had fun, and going back to Lake Anita with you wouldn't be the worst thing in the world. But if you tell anyone I said that I'll deny it and never swim again."

"I'm happy to hear that because I'm already planning our next trip." More time with Mallory at my favorite place? I can't think of anything better than that. "By the way, you get a point for the tire. In a competition of who is handier, you win."

"11-10. God, I love winning." She taps the frame and steps back. "Promise me you won't drive on the spare for too long and you'll drive slower than usual. No highways either."

"I promise. Thanks for today, Eddie."

Mallory jogs to Cade's car and gives him a quick hug before heading into her house. I hoped Cade would leave when we pulled up, but of course he wouldn't. He's too busy grinning at me like the Cheshire Cat.

I smile back, but this is something I need to figure out on my own. Cade with his big heart will only try to help. If I'm going to turn Mallory from rival-enemy to rival-something-more, it's going to be done by me and me alone.

No meddling or good-intentioned assistance from my best friend is allowed.

Chapter Twenty

Bending my knees, I jump toward the upper left corner of the goal, successfully knocking the ball over the post with a grunt. Jo slaps her thigh and gives me a thumbs up before moving back to midfield.

Adri's next, making her way down the field to me. Her movements are fluid, as if she's dancing rather than dribbling. She twists and glides around Shay, our best defender, with skilled touches and her signature smirk. Once she's right in front of me, she pulls a strong leg back and rockets the ball toward the bottom right corner.

I drop down and slide across the grass with my hands open. When I try to grab the ball, it bounces off my fingertips and rolls away.

"Keep going, Adri!" Coach Sumner shouts, and she races forward to recover the ball. I use the millisecond to reset and stand.

Her second kick is even faster, like lightning aimed at the top left corner. I leap into the air and catch it between gloved hands. With a deep sigh, I secure the ball into my chest.

Adri groans and blows me a kiss before jumping on Shay's back, likely giving her hell for not stopping her.

My teammates have a love-hate relationship with me in the goal. They love it when I stop our opponents' shots but hate when I stop theirs.

"Mally!" Bex's ponytail bobs from the sideline, and I instinctively cringe, preparing myself for bad news.

Sliding off my gloves, I tuck them into the band of my shorts and meet her by the water cooler. "What's wrong this time?"

My negativity bounces off her like she's made of rubber. "Nope! Today, I am not the bearer of bad news. I come with good news. No! Great news!" She stops bouncing up and down to pull a sheet of paper from her back pocket and unfolds it. "You hit seventy percent time-in-range this morning."

"Y-You're joking," I stutter, taking the paper. Bex has highlighted the number for me with a smiley face and note scribbled beside it.

"This is only the beginning. Remember this journey is a roller coaster and enjoy the ride. – Bex and Dr. Morand."

The memory of setting this goal in Dr. Morand's office with Bex and Shay one month after my diagnosis brings along a sudden appearance of tears. After a year, I thought I'd never reach my goal, but today I can say that seventy percent of the time, my blood sugar is in range.

I did it.

"All because of the pump?" I choke out.

Bex rubs my arms, blinking away her own rush of emotion. "The pump may help, but your daily efforts and working on your anxiety have been a real game changer. I'm so proud of you for stepping out of your comfort zone. You look good, Mally."

I soak up the praise like a sponge, loving the way being proud of myself feels. For so long, my diabetes seemed like something I would never be able to get a handle on. The bad days always seem to stick with me longer.

I'll make sure this day outlasts them all.

Sharon deserves a bonus for the time and effort she puts into our sessions. She has given me the tools to find my safe place in my head. My first answer was a soccer field, the place I've spent my whole life.

Then out of nowhere, it changed to a place that smells of cedar, intensified by the wind. Where the sun is warm and comforting as it dries my damp skin. Where crickets and cicadas never stop chattering. And the redhead I can't stop thinking about waves at me from the dock at Lake Anita.

I smile. "I feel good."

Bex's lips form a not-so-nice word when I pinch her shoulder. When she tries to retaliate, I block her hands. "Ow! What was that for?"

"No green for Saint Patrick's Day!" I answer, showing her why she can't pinch me back. My socks, shorts, and sports bra are all green to celebrate the holiday. I even wore my green goalkeeper gloves.

"Crap. No wonder I've gotten pinched five times today."

I pat her head and swing my bag over my shoulder. "See ya, Bex!"

"Enjoy your night! Drink some green beer for me!"

I give her a thumbs up even though I've decided I'm not going to tonight's St. Patrick's Day party that Kenneth and Cade throw every year. Shay won't be happy I'm bailing, but she will understand.

"You really thought I was going to let you miss the party of the year?" A glimpse of green eyeshadow glitters as Shay reverses out of our driveway. "Dumbass."

I'm the driver in our friendship. I'm not even sure why Shay even has a car considering she walks everywhere and only drives once a week. So the fact that she's in the driver's seat is wrong on every level.

After I attempted to bail on tonight's party, Shay picked my outfit, changed me, dragged me through the front door, and tossed me into the backseat of her baby-blue convertible. I try the door handle, but as expected, she child-locked them.

Dammit.

"This is a crime, you know? Kidnapping is a felony." I whine, jamming my knees into the back of her seat. Shay keeps her eyes ahead, turns up the volume, and leaves me with my own thoughts.

My heart and brain are good-for-nothing traitors. I can't figure out how I went from wanting to crush Kenneth Gray under my shoe like a bug, to having what feels like a crush on him. A *crush.*

How old am I? Thirteen?

On Tuesday morning, his truck with a brand-new tire sat in my driveway, Kenneth insisting on driving us to class. On Wednesday he dropped off my favorite candy before my gala planning meeting. And this morning, Cade arrived for our bestie breakfast with sunshine-yellow tape from Kenneth to cover my insulin pump.

And I liked the way it felt to have him there, showing up, and smiling at me. I must be losing my mind.

"*Shaaaay,*" I whine. "Stop ignoring me. If we go home, we can have a girls' night. I'll order those dumplings you love."

"Don't tempt me with food, woman. You're not missing tonight, and I'm going to give you three reasons why. One, you look amazing in green. Look at you right now. Those emerald pants on you is god's gift to men." I chuckle, looking at my pants and white corset. "Two, it's a themed party, which is your favorite kind of party. And three, you can't miss the scavenger hunt!"

I blow a raspberry. "But I don't want to go."

She adjusts the mirror and looks at me. "You're avoiding him, aren't you?"

My eyes dart to the window. "Nope."

"You know, it's okay if you want to be friends with him, Mally. You spent a whole afternoon with him at a lake and didn't even tell me about it until after. You *swam* with Kenneth after years of avoiding swimming! That's huge!"

"See!" I yell. "This is why I didn't tell you before. You're making it a bigger deal than it is. It was his way of apologizing and nothing more."

"You're so full of crap. Kenneth Gray apologized, and you accepted it. That's a *huge* deal." Shay rolls through a stop sign. "When is the last time he apologized to you?"

"Well—"

"Trick question," she interrupts. "Never."

She's right. Even when Kenneth bumped into me at last year's St. Patty's party, he ran away before I could blow up on him for spilling green beer all over me.

To be fair, I probably looked homicidal.

My seatbelt chokes me as we jerk to a stop, barely avoiding a group as they stumble across the road. It's not even dark out and the festivities have already begun.

"Promise me you'll try to have fun tonight," she pleads, pulling into the guys' driveway.

Thankfully, she's out of the car before I have to lie to her. I yank the door handle a few times until she remembers she imprisoned me in the back seat.

Festive as hell in a green baseball jersey, Cade waves us down as we walk to the front door. "Wow, MalPal. You look good in green, girl. That's definitely your color."

Shay nods. "I told her the exact same thing."

He grins, reaching for my perfectly styled twist-out before remembering he needs his hands to play baseball.

Cade looks down at Shay before speaking again. "Tonight is going to be perfect."

She looks at him and smiles. "So perfect."

My eyes dart between them both. "You guys are acting weird. Cut it out before I walk home."

Cade presses a quick kiss to my forehead before draping his arm over Shay's shoulder. "Hey, Shay. Can you help me out with something in the kitchen?" His voice sounds robotic, as if he's reading off a script, but Shay doesn't seem to notice and lets him lead her into the house.

I make a beeline for the couch, and as soon as my butt hits the cushion, a body drops heavily into my lap.

"You're late, Cap." Adri hiccups, curling around me like a koala. "What's up with that?"

Jo settles beside me, holding six fingers in the air over Adri's head before pretending to strangle herself.

"I'm not late, babe. You've just been pregaming since practice ended," I laugh, pulling a piece of curly hair from her pouty, glossed lips.

"Yup. I needed to get ready to kick your ass at the scavenger hunt."

"Please be serious, Adrienne," Jo yells over the music. "You'll be asleep before it even starts."

Adri doesn't fight back because she can't. Her head falls into the crook of my neck, warming the skin with soft, rum-scented breaths.

"She's something else," I chuckle, rubbing her back. "I have no idea how she's sleeping through this."

My eyes rake over the crowd of bodies dancing to Akon, but the one I'm searching for doesn't appear. I turn to chat with Jo, but she's already watching me.

I would say looking at me, but Jo is just as observant as I am, which means I'm being watched.

"Looking for anyone in particular?" she asks.

"Nope," I lie.

She leans back, keeping her gaze on the butterfly puzzle hanging on the wall. "Okay, Mal. Whatever you say. And just in case you *did* want to know, I also haven't seen him."

Note to self: no more updates for the girls because all they do is give me shit.

The volume of the room drops, giving my ears a much-needed moment of relief. The dining table creaks as Cade climbs on top of it with Shay holding onto his leg.

"Hello, party people!" he hollers. The room hoots, and red cups of green beer are held toward the ceiling. "Thanks for coming to K.C.'s St. Patty's Day Bash! After three years, you guys know the rules, but here's a reminder. Get in your own bed if you want to get freaky, treat the house with respect, and no peeing in the grass, which means you better find a toilet."

"Hey!" someone shouts, clearly offended by the last rule.

"The scavenger hunt will start in thirty minutes, and we're mixing it up this year. First, the gift card for the winner is doubled and was gifted to us by our favorite bar, Roddy's Place. Last year's winner had a little too much fun and spent five times more than the amount of the gift card. Isn't that right, Kent?"

Accented by slaps to his back, a familiar laugh stands out in the crowd. I perk up slightly at the sound. He's here.

"The second change is... drum roll, please," Cade sings. Everyone pats their laps obediently, smiling up at the man who controls every room.

"We..."

A wicked grin splits across Cade's lips.

"Have..."

Shay winks at me, and I know. My fate is sealed.

"Partners! Check the sheets on the walls to find your partner. Discuss a game plan and get ready to have some fun."

I offer my best friends a one finger salute, but they're intentionally avoiding me and rapping "Still Fly" by Big Tymers. How dare they ignore me with my own party playlist?

As if sensing my jitters, Jo pulls Adri off my lap so I can stand. "Even though we already know exactly who they paired you with, I know you need to see it."

Adri's head pops up just enough to give me a tipsy smile. "Go kick ass for me, Cap."

I nod my appreciation before running out of the living room. Using my shoulders, I push through the crowd of people until I make it to the foyer.

My finger runs down the sheet until I find Edwards, and I follow the arrow that connects me and my partner for the evening. Hovering over his name, my mood plummets.

Kenneth Gray.

"Oh fuck me," I mutter. Is it possible to be *this* unlucky?

"Language, Eddie."

I jump at Kenneth's deep voice behind me, and my heart pounds loudly in my chest. He's way too close, even though the foyer is empty. Only we decided to check the paper on this side of the house.

After collecting myself, I whirl around and jam my finger into his chest. "*You*. Did you do this on purpose?"

Kenneth holds his hands up in surrender. "No, I swear I found out when you did. Cade is always in charge of the scavenger hunt so I can play, but I had a feeling he'd pull something considering how weird he has been since seeing us together. As you know, our best friend is a meddler."

There's nothing Cade loves more than to be in other people's business.

At this rate, I'll never escape Kenneth. How am I supposed to not think about him when I'm about to spend my favorite party of the year by his side?

"So... partners." Strangely, the word doesn't irritate me as much as it did at the beginning of the semester. "Again."

"Looks like it. And we can't use tonight as a point for the Brain Bowl. On my way to find you, Cade told me that we either take the night off from the game, or we're banned from next year's party."

I groan at another lost point opportunity.

Then I smile. Kenneth and I paired up means only one thing.

"Since we can't beat each other..."

The excitement in his voice matches mine. "I guess we've got to beat everyone else."

K.C.'s St. Patty's Day Bash

RULES:

No driving allowed!

All tasks must be photographed and sent to Cade as proof!

Do <u>**NOT**</u> leave your partner!!!!!!

1. Find Guinness beer
2. Kiss Me I'm Irish shirt — ASK FOR CONSENT FIRST
3. It's orange, green, and white, and flies in the air
4. I spy a fellow with a green top hat and suspenders
5. Take a photo with someone Irish
6. Red hair, don't care (Kenneth, you cannot take a selfie)
7. See green beer, chug green beer
8. What's an Irishman's favorite cereal?
9. Would it kill ya to find a kilt?
10. Find a pot of gold

Chapter Twenty-One

Kenneth

I'm going to do something stupid tonight.

Scratch that. It may be simultaneously the smartest and dumbest thing I've ever done. I'm going to tell Mallory how I feel.

Even if my feelings aren't reciprocated, being friends would be more than I ever thought I'd have with her. I can and will sit on this crush for however long I have to.

Forever if necessary.

Part of me thinks there's a chance she may feel the same way. It doesn't feel logical or realistic, but living delusionally hasn't failed me yet.

The gas station on the corner checks off number one, and I send the photo of me in front of the walk-in cooler filled with Guinness beer to Cade as proof. The reason Mallory and I are always winner and runner up is because we don't hang back after the game begins. We strategize on the move.

When we make it to Eastgate Bar District, it's as if the sun never set on this sliver of town. Lights from bars and clubs brighten the sidewalks, which are filled with people in varying shades of green.

Mallory grumbles about the disgusting number of people on the sidewalks, bouncing around to avoid them while I fall behind.

I'm a slow walker. If Cade isn't calling me a grandpa, he's calling me a zombie. All I can see is dark curls and green pants that look too damn good on her getting further and further away, until she finally disappears.

It's clear Mallory has no patience for me tonight.

With a deep exhale, I pull out my phone to text her. Partners have to stay together, or our points won't count. We can't afford a loss tonight.

"Gray."

I jump, and my eyes fly to meet the prettiest shade of brown I've ever seen. "When did you—"

"We don't have time for lollygagging tonight. I—We need to win, dammit."

My green flannel's sleeve is yanked, her hand wrapped around my wrist to pull me off the curb and into the crosswalk. I can't even fight because I'm too busy focusing on the slight contact between her fingers and my wrist.

"Where are we going?" I sputter.

"Green beer. Since you have nationals next weekend, I've got this one."

Relief washes over me as we step into Roddy's Bar, and when she releases my wrist, I feel a loss of warmth.

Roddy, the owner of the best bar in Clear Lake, almost jumps over the counter when he spots us. "If it isn't my favorite rivals. Cade told me to expect you together. I thought he was pulling my leg, but here you both are."

Mallory rolls her eyes. I'm sure she will punish Cade for this until the end of time.

Roddy curls his finger and beckons her closer. "Mal, I made something special for you. Give me a second."

Jogging to the back, he returns with a green beer that's just a little lighter than usual. Mallory lets out an adorable gasp, and I grin at Roddy for making her so happy.

"You made me a lite green beer, Rod?"

"Sure did, my dear! Gotta make sure my favorite girl has a good night too. On the house."

"You're the best," she says to Roddy. Picking up the pint, she faces me. "Start taking pictures, Gray. This won't take long."

And she's right. Less than four seconds later, the cup is drained, leaving behind a soft green foam on her upper lip. Adoration bubbles in my chest at the photo of Mallory, eyes closed and the glass in the air.

After texting Cade the photo, we step out of the bar, and Mallory leans against the wall and scans the list. "That was way too easy," she laughs. "Next we should look for the—"

"Leprechaun! Number four!" I blurt, pointing at a man in a green suit by the crosswalk.

Mallory follows my finger and takes off, screaming for him to wait.

By the time I catch up, they're deep in a conversation about why St. Patrick's Day is the best holiday for college kids, followed by Halloween.

I'm a bit disappointed to find out he's not leprechaun-sized, only a couple of inches taller than Mallory. What bothers me the most is that he's staring at her like *she's* the prize at the end of the rainbow.

I mean, she is. But I don't like it.

"Jake agreed to a picture!" she beams, and I thaw slightly at her excitement.

Hands in a double peace sign, she poses beside *Jake.* I lift my phone, and a sliver of white cloth catches my eye, hovering a little too close to Mallory's ass for my liking.

"Watch it, Lucky," I say. "That's your first and only warning."

Catching my drift, Mallory steps away from the guilty-looking man. The camera flash floods their bodies just as she flips him off, creating the perfect photo. I reach out, thankful she takes my hand, and tug her to me.

Not behind me, because Mallory can and will protect herself, but just close enough.

"What a creep. Can't a girl ask for a photo without the risk of being touched?" She screams excitedly as Jake trips over his own shoelaces and stumbles.

"You okay?"

"Very okay," Mallory smiles sweetly, which makes my scowl vanish.

A few more people from the party are finally out, but none seem to be paying attention to the list.

I place a hand on Mallory's back, guiding her through the busy sidewalk as she sends a warning text to the soccer team about the leprechaun.

"Hey," I say, patting her shoulder. In line for a new club, Jane waits with a green beer in each hand and matching hair. "Jane's outfit fulfills number two."

I stick my arm out for her before she can take off, which makes her lips tick upward. "Wow, Gray. I'm starting to think you like being pulled around."

"Yeah, yeah," I say as nonchalantly as possible, but it's pointless. She knows just as well as I do that I'm loving every second of this.

Jane squeals when she spots us, wrapping her arms around Mallory without spilling a drop of beer. "Sweetie! Goodness, you look gorgeous. I remember when I had a body like this. I was too hot to trot."

For the first time ever, I hear an accent when she speaks. Scottish maybe?

"And Kenneth!" Her eyes dart to Mallory's hand gripping my wrist, but she doesn't let me go. "I like that green on you, kiddo. How's Karla?"

"Thanks, Ms. Jane. And Karla is getting on my nerves, as usual. How are Jaxon and Julie?"

"They're good. Dropped them off with my parents since my favorite babysitter is out having some fun, which makes me one happy lady." Intrigued eyes shift between us. "How nice to see you together and not trying to strangle each other."

"It's a new development we're working on," I chuckle. "There's still a fifty-fifty chance."

Mallory checks her watch. "I'm sorry to cut this short, Jane, but can we take a picture? It's for the scavenger hunt."

Jane laughs. "Get over here and kiss my cheek already!"

I snap the photo of Jane grinning like she won the lottery and tuck my phone away to give Jane a hug, but her grip on my arms tightens when she pulls back.

"You better not drop green beer on my girl this year. You hear me?"

I nod silently. Of course Mallory told her about that. It wasn't one of my finer moments.

"She's pretty scary," I shiver, as Jane disappears into the club.

"And Irish, so we knocked off numbers two and five."

I click my tongue, finally able to place the accent. After sending the photo to Cade, I jog to catch up to Mallory who is already on the hunt.

"You're really good at this, Eddie. Now I know why you demolished me during the scavenger hunt freshman year. How did I beat you last year?"

"The green beer challenge got me. One turned into five with Adri, which took me out. Then you dropped your beer on me, and I called it a night."

I grab her wrist and pull us to a stop in the middle of the sidewalk. "Hey, I'm sorry for spilling beer on you. And I'm sorry for waiting an entire year to say that. There are so many times I wanted to apologize. I'm an idiot for not doing it sooner."

Mallory looks up and her eyes flitter with something I thought I'd never see when she looks at me.

Trust. She believes the words I say.

"Apology accepted, but not needed. And I'm sorry for calling you a spoiled brat living off daddy's money."

My brows knit together. "You never said that."

"Not to your face," she sings.

I grunt to stifle my laugh as she takes my wrist, leading me through the crosswalk toward a man in a kilt.

Maybe it is my lucky night.

It's been forty-two minutes, and we only have one left.

Mallory convinced a mother to hand over her child in an Irish flag onesie. A girl from her recipe development class with red hair walked out of a bar, and they took a selfie. Her earrings counted too since they're the marshmallows in Lucky Charms, an Irishman's favorite cereal.

I'm not sure how Mallory could ever believe she isn't fun. The woman is so full of life that I feel like every second with her etches itself onto my brain. I'm sure I'll never be able to go back to a life that isn't full of hearing her laugh, watching her multitask, seeing her succeed, or being by her side. This is my new normal, and I'll never be the same.

"What did you do for the pot of gold last year?" she asks.

"The vinyl store had a gold record hanging in the window, so I put a black flowerpot beneath it. What about you?"

"A black bowl filled with goldfish. I was sadly one of the drunks eating from the communal bowl of cheesy goodness. It was the last task I did before the beer incident."

She shoots me a glare when I laugh, and I'm thankful we're alone. I can actually hear myself think now that we're on the quieter side of Eastgate. We've been stuck for over ten minutes with no luck, and people are finally starting to take the scavenger hunt seriously.

Mallory tilts her head back, and a sudden bolt of inspiration rocks me as a streetlight ignites her eyes. I rush forward, grab her shoulders, and move her around until I find the perfect position.

"What are you doing, Gray?"

I reach for my phone. "Stay still."

My camera focuses on her dark irises, swimming in a pool of the most gorgeous shade of gold. Curiosity deepens the color as she stares at me through the lens.

When the shutter goes off, I step back and hand over my phone. "I think we should use that for number ten. A pot of gold."

She studies the photo, shaking her head. "I'm not sure if I'd call this gold. Maybe gold that's been heated for too long and slightly burned." Zooming in, a soft laugh leaves her lips. "I've always thought my eyes look like mud. Chocolate if I want to give it a prettier comparison. Green eyes are unique. Blue eyes are beautiful. Brown eyes are so... normal. Boring sometimes."

The urge is strong to tell her exactly how beautiful they are. To tell her how many times I've found myself lost in her eyes before she catches me.

Brown doesn't do them justice. They're the color of the Earth after a good rain. Sunlight through a bottle of whiskey. A honeyed glow that adds sweetness to her gaze, even when sharp and focused. They're gingerbread men that remind me of Christmas with Nan, and more comforting than a mug of Claude's hot chocolate.

"Out of all the words someone could use to describe you, Eddie, not a single one would ever be normal or boring."

I wince when Mallory takes a step back. I've gone too far.

"This is weird."

"What is?" I ask.

"You. This." She waves her arms between us. "Everything about this semester is so different. I mean, am I just supposed to gloss over the fact that we went from hating each other to whatever the hell this is?"

I blink hard. "Hate? I've never hated you, Ed. Not for a second."

Pretty brown lips part and let out an exasperated gargle of sound, but no words come out. Just a blank, confused stare, and I'm suddenly desperate to explain.

"I know we've had some not-so-great moments over the last few years, but I'm positive that it's impossible to hate you. It's just weird because up until this semester our interactions were strictly limited to the game."

"I thought that was a mutual agreement!" she says, finally finding her words. "That we were going to play the Brain Bowl and leave it at that. A competition."

The Brain Bowl. I think back on my time with Mallory. The fun moments spent playing for point opportunities, only to spend the next week watching her from a distance because that was the silent agreement we made when we started our game.

To compete and play. Nothing more.

It wasn't enough then, and it will never be enough now.

"You already said that this semester has been different, and I agree. But not only is it different, it's also been nice." I pause and wait for her to look at me. "A lot has changed in a couple of months, but I'm not opposed to it. Haven't you enjoyed how it's been between us?"

There's no way she can't feel this too. Right?

"Gray, come on. What will admitting that do for us?"

"I don't know. It could help us move forward. Move past whatever all of this is into something else."

"To what?" A nervous chuckle slips out. "Being friends?"

My heart cracks on the word, but my disappointment is overshadowed by my eagerness to agree. Friendship with Mallory is more than I could ask for. All I wanted was a real reason to be with her outside of the game, and here it is. I won't pass up this opportunity.

"Exactly. Friends." I bite the inside of my cheek until it's tender as I await her answer.

"Healthy competition," she finally murmurs. As if electricity jolts through her, she sticks her hand out to me. "Healthy competition between two people who don't dislike each other."

"Friends," I correct her.

"Friends," she concedes with an eye roll. "We should get going before someone beats us back to the house. I don't want to lose tonight."

"You never want to lose, Eddie. That's nothing new."

Mallory's smile returns, but only for a moment. Her body slams against mine roughly, almost sending us both to the ground.

Clearly drunk out of his mind, the man who ran into her sprints away, leaving an empty cup behind. I look down and cringe. Her white top is now dark green and soaked.

"Watch where you're going!" she yells, wiping beer from her face.

I rip off my flannel and wrap it around her shoulders. Without any direction, she sticks her arms through the arm holes and lets it fall around her. I pull it tight, hoping it stops her teeth from chattering.

"What an asshole," I mutter.

Mallory gasps. "Kenneth Gray. Did you just cuss?"

It takes a moment for my brain to process the fact that Mallory just said my first name for the very first time. The singular word was almost enough to make me combust on the spot. I drop my eyes, but it's nearly impossible to button the flannel because all I can think about is the way my name sounded like pure ecstasy coming from her lips. And how I'd do anything to hear it again.

"I am capable of cursing, Ed. Just not around you. You do that enough for the both of us."

She stays quiet, watching my fingers work with an adorable smile.

"So as my friend," I continue, "do you think you would be able to make it to my meet this weekend?"

Another gasp. "First you cuss, and now you want me at your meet? Is this real?"

"Very real." I finish the final button and lift her chin to meet my eyes. "It's a total ego boost for me. Having my rival that I convinced to be my friend act as my cheerleader? That's a dream come true."

Her eyes flash with a challenge, but the ferocity shifts into something shyer when she nods. "I'll be there."

God. I need to hug her. I sorely messed up my opportunity before the lake, but I won't this time. Looping my arms around her waist, I keep a loose hold on her in case she wants to slip out.

But rejection doesn't come. Mallory rests her cheek against my collar bone and snakes her arms around my waist. The heat from her body sends flames down my front when I pull her tight against me.

"Edwards."

She looks up and our eyes meet. "Yeah?"

This might be the only time to tell her that I want more. Hell, I want *her.* That I need to kiss her more than I need air.

"I—"

Another body crashing into us stops my confession. Not hard enough to send us to the ground, but enough for Mallory to let out a surprised yelp. I manage to keep us upright and whip around, ready to lay into whatever idiot just ruined my chance to tell her how I feel.

"My bad," Grant chirps before I can speak. With one of his boots in his hands, he lifts his cowboy hat up to get a good look at Mallory beside me. His lips split into a devious grin when his eyes dip down, likely spotting her hand holding my wrist. "Mal, that Kenneth-sized flannel looks damn good on you. Y'all are looking real cozy tonight."

I shake my head. "Really, G? You've got to be more careful—"

"Can't stay and chat. While y'all are sitting around wasting time, I'm going to take the win and claim the gift card. Let's go Mark!"

My chest seizes as I watch Grant and his scavenger hunt partner for the night take off. We can't lose tonight. Mallory would never forgive me for distracting her.

I reach for her arm, but she's long gone.

A flash of emerald passes up Grant and Mark like it's nothing. The three race down the dark street, shouting and laughing as they weave through drunk people. I shake my head at them, shove my hands into my pockets, and start the walk home. There's no need to run.

I have no doubt that Mallory will win.

Chapter Twenty-Two

Kenneth

"What are you doing here, Gray? Go home."

Mallory's gaze is like bullets from her seat in our booth at Claude's Cafe. My backpack thuds against the floor. "I have some schoolwork to do."

"No!" Her volume increases as I try to slip into the booth. "Are you listening to me? I said no. You should be at home practicing your breathing or whatever people do before a big race."

Ever since I invited her to tomorrow's race, she's been oddly strict about reminding me to hydrate and fuel my body. It's made the week leading up to nationals more bearable. I feel less like a nervous mess, and more like the unshakable competitor I aspire to be.

Like the woman refusing my entry into the booth.

"This is how I relax, Eddie. Working on something else."

That's only a partial truth. After pacing back and forth in front of the television, Cade kicked me out to walk off my nerves. And I knew exactly where I'd find Mallory.

"And bothering me," she mutters, but moves her foot. "Don't blame me if you can't focus tomorrow afternoon."

Little does she know I blame everything on her nowadays. For filling my brain with a constant need to be around her. For being the person I seek out for comfort. As if seeing those wild curls and vivid outfits can somehow slow my heart rate. Today's rainbow cardigan feels like home.

I slide into the seat across from her, and my stress shrinks slightly.

Mallory holds out her hand. "Ticket."

"No way," I say, pushing her hand away. "This isn't project related."

And there's no way I'm wasting our last punch on a meeting like this.

This isn't the answer she wanted, so she blows a raspberry at me and pulls her computer in tight. With our final project due in a little over a month, her pinched brow tells me she's writing her personal statement.

Which is another reason I'm here.

"I want to ask you something," I begin, pausing when her head pops up. Honeyed eyes are wide with... hope?

There are a million non-project related questions I'd rather ask.

Would you have kissed me the other night?

Do you have any idea how much of my brain you occupy?

Is this happening to you too?

Sadly, those must wait.

Her shock turns to smugness when I say, "I need your critical brain again. Would you look over my personal statement? I used your outline and want your opinion."

She twirls an orange pen between slender fingers. "My outline, huh? I'm sure it was about a million times easier than raw dogging it like a heathen."

I bite back a laugh. "Someone should wash your mouth out with a bar of soap."

Mallory grins. "Email it and I'll take a look after your race. I don't want you thinking about it while you're trying to win tomorrow. Speaking of, how are you feeling?"

For once, it doesn't feel like a lie to answer this question. The fear of dying mid-race has turned into fear of not doing my best, which makes me never want to half-ass again. Giving up before the race even starts is no longer an option.

"I feel good. Ready to give it my all."

She hums, bringing the mug of mostly whipped cream to her lips.

Actually, I do have one more question.

"Are you..." I clear my throat, not liking the hesitation in my tone. "You're still coming tomorrow, right?"

Mallory's face softens, and I'm taken back to the St. Patty's party. It's the same look she gave me while we stood under the streetlight. The moment I thought that maybe I'm not the only one who wants more.

Warmth spreads through me when she covers my hand with hers.

"I wouldn't miss it for the world, Gray. I'll be the loudest one there."

CHAPTER TWENTY-THREE

"ALRIGHT." OLYMPIAN GREGORY KECKNER'S voice booms through the speakers. "Let's take a look at our lane assignments for the last heat of the timed finals for the Men's 1650-yard Freestyle. In lane one, we've got Malachi Livingston from Texas. Boone Brokaw from Florida in two. Creed McLaughlin from Arkansas in three..."

Goosebumps run up my arms as the announcer goes through each elite swimmer from all over the country. They're all so impressive it's scary.

"Kenneth Gray from Clear Lake University is in lane five," Gregory says.

"Woohoo! Kick some ass, Gray!" I yell, drowned by the roar of cheers from the stands. There's an amplified sound that catches my attention too.

Is that a megaphone?

A tiny smile flutters past his lips before stretching into a serious line. Up on the platform, Kenneth bends slightly at the hips. The automated voice commands them to take their marks, and when a beep rings out, they're in the air. Kenneth's response to the sound is Pavlovian. With his elbows locked and arms strong, he disappears beneath the surface with a splash, sending ripples through the clear blue water.

I move to the edge of my seat and hold my breath until he reappears with hard kicks and fast strokes. Stress makes me squeeze the hands intertwined with mine.

"Ouch!" Shay and Cade yelp, but neither pull away. If anything, they squeeze even harder. We're all on pins and needles as the guy in lane two reaches the end of the pool first and flips smoothly, pushing off the wall and heading to the other side.

Shay slumps against me. "I'm already freaking out. I hate this."

I kiss her forehead, not taking my eyes off lane five. "Me too, but it's okay."

"How many times do they go back and forth?"

"Sixty-six. Thirty-three laps total," I say.

A whole mile of this. Swim. Turn. Push hard. Repeat.

Cade's cheek hardens against my shoulder. "Look who did their research. Nice pants, by the way."

My skin warms, and I blame it on nerves and not the fact that I painted custom pants for today. The '*KG*' on my front and back pockets taunt me, but they're cute.

When Kenneth said he felt good again, I didn't know what to expect. I've watched him race before, and today seems different. It's as if he's stronger mentally and physically.

"Looks like Brokaw in two and Gray in five have broken away from the field," Gregory announces. "They're neck and neck, ladies and gentlemen, and it looks like they're speeding up too."

Holy shit. He's right. It's as if they've shifted into another gear, flipping at the exact same time.

My body starts to sway, and I rip open an applesauce and down the entire packet. I know exactly what Kenneth would say if he could see me right now.

"Relax, Eddie. Breathe and watch me tie our game."

The thought of his low, cocky voice releases a bit of the tension in my shoulders.

Come on, Gray, I think. *Win.*

Swimming displays the strength and agility Kenneth has been honing for years, each muscle rippling as he fluidly moves through the water with deliberate and smooth strokes. It's a beautiful sport, but he's the most beautiful part of it all.

It's an honor to watch him do what he loves.

"Gray has moved out to the front, and it's a race to the finish. Brokaw is trying to make up the distance. I think..." Gregory goes silent, and everyone jumps to their feet to watch the final stretch.

Cade, Shay, and I are already screaming before Gregory can make the declaration that sends the crowd into a frenzy.

"Kenneth Gray is the 1650-yard freestyle National Champion!"

Kenneth rips off his goggles and stares up at the big screen, where his name sits at the top. Long gone is the solemn face of the man who felt like a failure freshman year. Now shines a smile brighter than the trophy he will be holding soon.

Ripped from the pool by his coach, Kenneth is pulled into a bear hug before being ushered to the other side for the award ceremony. From the top of the podium, Kenneth waves to the crowd as we recite CLU's chant.

Cade's mom, Billie, Cade's little sister, Violet, Shay, Cade, and I cheer until he disappears into the locker room.

I'm not sure how long I've been staring at my shaky hands when Cade nudges me and points at the stairs.

"Hey, MalPal. Let's meet him by the concession stand."

I nod wordlessly and follow my friends. The same jittery energy I felt at the St. Patty's party whizzes through me, and I know it's because I'll have to see him soon. How am I supposed to react as a friend? Are we allowed to hug again?

Things were so much easier when I didn't like him.

"Mallory!"

The moment I step off the stairs, my face is buried in auburn waves that smell like strawberries and cream. The cinnamon freckles on her shoulders are so similar to her brother's, except he has significantly more. "Hi, Karla!"

Karla releases me and her smile flits over to Shay. "You must be the Shaylene Turner I've heard so much about." She ruffles Cade's locs. "She's a cutie, Cade. What'd you do to convince her to hang out with you?"

Cade flicks her forehead with a hard *thwack.* Considering Cade and Kenneth are essentially brothers, it's no surprise these two also act like siblings.

If she's here, I bet she brought—

"Nan!" Karla waves her over. "Come meet Kenneth's friends!"

A soft clicking sound makes its way to us, accompanied by the sweet smell of orange that is so familiar I almost trip.

The short, red-haired woman pats Cade's cheek, shakes Shay's hand, and kisses Cade's mom and sister before turning to me.

"Mallory. Goodness gracious you're tall." Nan uses my handshake as an opportunity to wrap me in a hug. "It's nice to finally put a beautiful face to the beautiful name. I'm Sandy, but call me Nan."

"Hello, Nan," I say, warmed by her affectionate welcome. "It's so nice to meet you."

I'm not sure how to navigate being around Kenneth's family considering we've been friends for one measly week, but Nan doesn't care. Within seconds, she pulls me into the concession line and starts asking rapid-fire questions about my family and my childhood.

I adore her already.

Karla joins us in line, protectively stepping between us. "Stop grilling her, Nan. You don't need to know her zip code or mother's maiden name. You're not a hacker."

Nan smacks Karla's leg with her cane. "While I won't apologize for being nosy, I will apologize for my granddaughter being a turd. I hope that's not a deal breaker, Mallory. I promise she can be sweet."

I wink at Karla before turning back to Nan. "I'm pretty nosy myself, so no worries."

"Good to hear. So, why don't you tell me what's going on between you and my grandson?"

Karla gives me a look that says *I told you so* and skips away, leaving me alone in the hole I dug myself.

Nan holds onto me with a careful smile, looking so kind and open that it makes me want to spill my guts about the confusing turmoil her grandson is putting me through.

Thankfully, Kenneth's arrival saves me from embarrassing myself.

I stay in line so Nan can go to him, promising to bring back popcorn with extra butter.

A few minutes later, with popped perfection in hand, I make my way back to the group. Kenneth's head lifts before I've even made it halfway across the room. His lips shape into the smile that's just for me, sending those stupid butterflies in my belly into overdrive.

Nan reaches up and pats his cheek. "I can't wait to tell the ladies in PT that my grandson is the National Champion. My Fishie!"

Kenneth's eyes cut to me when I giggle, narrowed in a way that should be threatening. Too bad it's downright adorable.

After more congratulate hugs, Shay, Cade, and Cade's mom and sister head back into the stands to watch another race. I'm right behind them until Kenneth grabs my wrist and asks me to stay. I should feel like an outsider watching the Grays interact, but I don't. All three of them make me feel like part of their family, filling me in on inside jokes and telling me embarrassing stories about Kenneth. With every groan and grumble, I'm more and more convinced he's loving every second of this.

"Crap," Nan mutters.

"What's up?" Kenneth asks.

"I left my purse upstairs. Karla, let's go look for it." She nudges her granddaughter, who is saving her number in my phone for our thrifting day.

Nan links their arms, and as they disappear up the stairs, I spot a poorly hidden leather purse behind Nan's back.

Kenneth must catch it too because he's shaking his head when I turn back to him. "They feed off each other's energy. Always have. The funny part is that I'll put up with their sneakiness if it means they're here."

"I'm so glad they were both able to watch you today. You were amazing out there, Gray."

Kenneth brushes our hands together, sending a zap of electricity through my fingers. "All I know is that I'm one point away from you having to be my date to the gala. 11-11, Eddie. I'll break the tie soon."

I shove him away. "You always have to ruin the moment, huh?"

He gives me a once over, assessing my outfit. When his eyes finally meet mine again, I take a moment to memorize the exact shade of green that looks back at me. Have they always been like this? So soft and beautiful?

"Thank you, Mallory."

All the air leaves my lungs. My first name sounds foreign coming from his mouth, pleasant and dizzying at the same time. For almost three years, I've been Eddie, Ed, or Edwards.

"For?" I choke out.

"For being the loudest one out there, just like you promised, and for helping me realize I can't let fear hold me back." He swallows hard, dropping his eyes to focus on the tiny *KG* on my front pocket. "Last season was rough, and I was so scared this one would be the same. But when I looked in the stands and saw you, I knew I had to keep my side of the promise. To do my best."

Genuine Kenneth smiles aimed at me are a rarity. Well, *were* a rarity. Now it's like he can't keep himself from gracing me with them.

Long gone are the hard glares and smug grins, and I'm not sure why that doesn't worry me.

Kenneth opens his arms and even though hugging him is all I want to do, I stop him with a hand to his hard chest.

"What do you think you're doing?"

He freezes, cheeks tinted crimson. "Hugging you?"

"I think not. Your skin is contaminated."

Even though my tone is deadly serious, his hurt expression is replaced by one that makes me think he isn't taking me seriously at all. His heart pulses rapidly against my palm.

"So, you would hug me if I wasn't contaminated?"

The weight of his chest makes my elbow bend slightly. "Quit it. I'm warning you, Gray."

"Answer the question. Would you?"

My arm shakes against the pressure as I admit, "Yes. I would."

The moment the words leave my lips, he grabs my forearm, pushes my arm down, and wraps himself around me. Kenneth Gray is hugging me. In public. And I'm willingly hugging him back.

Just like I remember, we fit together so perfectly. My head in the crook of his neck, his chin in my hair, and my arms looped around his waist.

I inhale, and the seriousness of this moment sets in. The smell of chlorine is nonexistent. Only clean soap and detergent fills my nose.

"You showered?" I ask, leaning deeper into him.

"Of course. I knew there was no way you'd come close to me if I didn't, and I wanted nothing more than to hug you. It's all I've been able to think about since the race ended."

In his arms, I finally can put words to how I feel about the man I swore I'd never care for. And I have no clue what to do with this new knowledge.

"Congrats, Kenneth."

Chapter Twenty-Four

Kenneth

I've been able to avoid our third and final punch for a while, but I can't push it back anymore. I need feedback on my personal statement, and I know that comes with a final hole being punched in my golden ticket.

Gravel crunches loudly as Flintstone creaks to a stop in my driveway. Jogging to the front door, I stop and check my reflection in the mirror. I push a hand through my hair, which looks violently red today, and smile to check my teeth.

Let's do this.

I swing open the door, and a purple bowl is where Mallory's head should be.

"Surprise!" she chirps.

"Is the surprise that you went grocery shopping?" I laugh, looking at the bulging grocery bags on the welcome mat. The smell of flour hits me when I peek beneath the white towel covering the bowl.

"More or less. I brought stuff for a pizza party. I hope you didn't already have dinner plans." She leans over to grab the grocery bags, but I reach down to take them before she can.

I step aside and usher her in. "Nope. No plans."

We drop the items on the kitchen counter, and I notice the massive amount of dough in the bowl. "How many people did you invite? This could feed the whole block. Did you invite the whole swim team?"

She rolls her lips to keep the smile away. "The girls and I got a little excited, so we made a bit more than we expected. You and Cade can freeze the leftovers. My freezer is already full of dough." Mallory lines up jars of marinara, bags of cheese, and toppings on the counter. "I didn't want to ruin the surprise by asking what toppings you wanted, so I bought them all. Nothing spicy because you hate spicy foods. I got ricotta, roasted garlic, spinach, sausage, pepperoni, and more, but there's no pineapple if you're one of *those* people."

"Ed." The sweet gesture wraps itself around my vocal cords, making my voice crack. "This is too much. How much do I owe you?"

"Not a thing. Yesterday you kicked ass and today we celebrate."

My neck burns. Yesterday felt like something straight out of a movie. I'm a National Champion, my favorite people were there to watch, and I feel like I'm getting somewhere with Mallory.

Although she wore teal like everyone else in the CLU section, Mallory always adds a little bit of color. I knew she was crafty, but I had no clue she would show up to the meet looking like that. Vibrant flowers decorated the denim, with *'CLU SWIM'* down the leg and *'KG'* on the pockets. She waved wildly from her seat, trying her hardest to make sure I could see her.

In any room or crowd, I'll always find her.

"Thank you, Eddie."

She gives me a soft smile before turning back to the groceries. "Can you turn on some music? Cooking without music is like movies without popcorn. Just plain wrong."

I head into the living room and connect my phone to Bluetooth. Instead of choosing one of my songs, I select the playlist she shared with me last week. "Party All the Time" by Eddie Murphy blasts through the speakers, and Mallory lets out an excited whoop.

Once on the couch, I open Cade's text thread and start typing.

Me

What is considered a date?

I don't have to wait long for an answer.

Cade (sexiest man alive)

The only person who can answer that is the woman who spent hours shopping and planning to celebrate you tonight. Have fun, Kent :)

I'm about to ask him what he knows when glass shatters in the kitchen.

I turn down the volume and stand up. "Eddie?"

A pause. "No biggie, but there's marinara sauce everywhere."

Locking my phone, I grin. "Too much dancing. Not enough paying attention," I yell back, heading to the closet for a towel.

Tonight's going to be special.

"You seriously didn't eat pizza for that long after your diagnosis?" I ask, squeezing a dollop of ranch onto my plate.

"Nope. I was terrified of my favorite foods. I ate chicken and broccoli every day for breakfast, lunch, and dinner for three months. Bex was terrified I was never going to move past it."

Mallory's whole grain, high fiber dough is perfect. It was created for her recipe development project, and I'm always down to be a guinea pig. My pizza is half pepperoni, bacon, sausage, and spinach and half

BBQ chicken, while hers is filled with bell peppers, spinach, mushrooms, tomatoes, ricotta, grilled chicken, and bacon.

I was in charge of the jicama fries this time.

"What made you open up your food choices?"

She stares at a bubble of cheese. "Honestly, I missed going out with friends and eating tacos and Thai food. The fun feeling of dirtying a million dishes to make a meal in my own kitchen." Mallory pauses and the table creaks. "Are you taking notes?"

I look up to find her halfway over the table, staring at what I've been typing as she talks. A list of foods she likes, dislikes, and how they affect her blood sugar. There will always be things I don't know, but I want to remember everything she goes out of her way to tell me.

"Yes," I admit. "I don't want to forget anything you say."

The look on her face is one of surprise. "You're something else, Gray." Before I can ask what she means, she stands and picks up my empty plate. "Come on. We've got work to do."

After the dishes are done, leftovers are stored away, and the mountain of extra dough is stuffed in the freezer, I take a seat at the dining table while Mallory digs through her backpack for the sheets of paper that contain my hopes and dreams.

My personal statement.

With a sigh, she sits beside me and sets the papers down.

I cover my eyes. "How bad is it?"

She doesn't answer me, which makes me worry even more. I take a quick peek through my fingers, but my hands fall away from my face when I reach for the papers. Mallory still doesn't speak as I flip through each page, but now I'm sure something is very wrong. There isn't a speck of color on them. Each sheet is as clean as it was when she printed it.

"Why are the pages blank? No highlighter, or notes, or suggestions. Not even your random thoughts! Did you not have time to read it? Did it suck so badly that you just…" I'm starting to feel sick. "I knew you hated it."

Mallory lets out a laugh. "Breathe, Gray. There are no notes because it's perfect, and you know I don't throw that word around lightly. It's authentic and raw and beautiful. Exactly what the judges need to see. It's clear that researching MS is your dream."

The sweetness of her praise sours almost immediately. Working as a biostatistician is all I want to do, and it's being ripped away by my father and his stupid expectations.

After the meet, I received a text from him. It wasn't like the ones I've been getting from friends, old coaches, and teammates. Nope.

"Finally."

I reach for my glass of water and swallow my disappointment. "So, how did you figure out your passion in life? Was it after your diagnosis?"

She drums her fingers against the table. "No. It was right around the time my dad started dialysis. I knew I wanted to work in healthcare, but I didn't have any specific plans. My dad's endocrinologist let me shadow her, which was how I learned about a camp for kids with diabetes. I expected my counselor application to be ignored since I was only thirteen, but the director, Saul, offered me a position working with him. He was the local health department's community health worker, acting as a liaison between healthcare providers and the community."

I nod. "You told Dr. Martin that choosing nutrition as a major was a selfish choice. Why is that?"

"Because it was just supposed to be a transcript booster." A dreamy smile brightens her face. "Then I met Bex, who showed me another way to help people, the way I wish someone would have helped my dad before it was too late. It's all I've ever wanted to do. Help people."

I take a deep breath, taking in all the information I'm learning. Mallory's motivations are so similar to mine. Wanting to help people, driven by the people that we love.

"You're going to do amazing things, Eddie."

"It's exactly what you're going to do for people with MS. I bet Nan is so proud of you."

Being reminded of Nan and the fact that I haven't told her about my dad's threat makes me choke on the guilt I've worked hard to bury over the last few months. Nan would be so disappointed in me.

"And what would you do if the plan you've created and worked hard for suddenly changed?"

Her lips pucker as if she's eaten something rancid. "Honestly, I'd cry and scream into my pillow for hours. But then I'd fight like hell and bet on myself to make sure that it doesn't happen."

"Bet on yourself?" I ask. "What do you mean?"

"My dad used to say it a lot when I was younger. I never knew what he meant, but it all clicked this semester, because there are no backup plans when it comes to my dreams. It's why I need to win this internship. If I don't..." She trails off, and the fear in her face melts away when she looks at me. "Hey, are you okay? You don't look so good."

I look away before I tell her everything about my dad. I can't. Tonight is supposed to be about us, and that will ruin everything.

Reaching into my backpack, I grab my ticket and slide it to her. "Thanks for sharing that with me. I'm sure that betting on yourself will always be the right decision."

With a loud crunch, the third and final punch is made. My three mandatory meetings with Mallory are up, but for some reason, she doesn't look happy. If anything, she looks disappointed. Maybe even a little restless as she stares at the ticket.

"Hey, Gray. Can I ask you a question?"

"You already did," I tease, leaning in at her hushed tone. "Of course."

"If you could go back, would you play the Brain Bowl again?"

I was worried it was going to be a hard question, but this one is easy. "Without a doubt."

I don't miss the one-word question she whispers.

"Why? Because everything has always been decided for me by my father. Before I came to CLU, I felt numb. I was just going through the motions of life. I didn't think coming to Clear Lake would change anything, but then I met you, Eddie. And although our first conversation wasn't pleasant, being with you made me feel something. Two weeks later, I'm bragging about getting the higher Bio 101 quiz grade. Three days later, you demolished me at tic-tac-toe in a study room. A week later, I beat you at Monopoly, and you threw the thimble at my head. Honestly, I wouldn't change a thing."

Mallory is going places. When she leaves CLU, I don't want to be left behind. I want to watch Mallory soar and excel, all while standing right beside her. Rooting for her, celebrating her highs, and holding her during the lows.

As expected, she avoids my kindness with humor. "Not even when I threw a dodgeball at your face, and you punched Cade because you thought it was him?"

"Not even then," I laugh. "Well, I do regret one thing. I'm sorry—"

"No!" The chair screeches against the floor as she leaps up, slapping her palm over my mouth. "Are you going to apologize again? I can't handle any more of your perfect apologies."

I move her hand but keep ahold of it. "Listen to me, Ed. I shouldn't have let us go on for years only playing the game. I should've spoken up and said that's not what I want. And I'm sorry for calling you rainbow vomit thirty seconds after meeting you. You didn't look like rainbow vomit. You looked perfect. I was upset with my dad and took it out on you, which was wrong of me. Truthfully, I was intimidated."

"By me?" She scoffs. "Why? You were the six-foot-three, hot swimmer everyone on campus was obsessed with."

My smile slants into a smirk. "You thought I was hot?"

She slugs my shoulder. "As I was saying, why?"

I meet her eyes, hoping she knows I mean every word, and I plan to spend every day proving it to her.

"Because you were the spark that changed it all, Eddie. I met you and knew everything would change."

Her breath hitches at my confession. I watch as fear and doubt dance across her face, but I spot a tiny glimmer of hope sitting in those golden pools. It's small, but it's all I need.

I will wait as long as she needs.

I'm not ready for our night to end, so when the perfect idea pops into my head, I push away from the table and stand.

"Hey, Ed. Want to do something crazy?"

Chapter Twenty-Five

"Excuse me?" I scream. "You want me to do The Dip with you?"

The Dip is a Clear Lake University tradition. The lake that runs through campus has been used by athletes to celebrate championship wins for years. When the soccer team won the National Championship last year, I barely did my own dip. I submerged myself for half a second before running for the shower.

Most people invite their significant other or best friend to do it with them. Someone special the champion believes helped them get there.

That's why I'm baffled Kenneth wants *me* to do his dip with him.

If Mama was here, she'd tell me to live a little. Before coming to Kenneth's tonight, we had some time to chat. Since our boundaries conversation, we've been talking more often. Our code word "lollipop" lets her know when I'm feeling uncomfortable, and we move to a safe topic.

Annoyingly, her favorite safe topic is Kenneth.

When she asked about my day, I told her that Shay, Jo, and Adri spent the afternoon with me grocery shopping, making pizza dough, and destroying the kitchen. I explained the golden ticket I made for the project and how I was going to Kenneth's for our final hole punch.

"You know," she started, her face glitching on the screen as she made her way from her bedroom into the kitchen, "I don't think I've seen you have this much fun during the school year."

My eyes rolled, preparing for the 'you're too young to be so worried about life' conversation.

"What are you talking about? I may not do a lot, but I'm almost always with the girls or Cade. Probably too much if I think about it."

"Exactly!" she laughed. "And you know I love hearing about the girls and silly Cade, but they won't be there tonight, right?"

I shook my head. "It's for our class, Ma. Just us."

"So, you're throwing a homemade pizza party? For a class meeting?" A humorous snort slipped out. "You're doing something special for Kenneth. You do see that, right?"

I saw it, even though I was trying very hard not to. If tonight's meeting was normal, there would've been no need to spend the whole day planning and preparing for it.

I wanted tonight to be special. I wanted to celebrate his big win.

Groaning, I put the phone down and tied my silk top. "Okay, fine. I see it. What about it?"

"Nothing at all. It's just new. And I must say, it's nice to see you like this."

I shifted my glare from the mirror to the camera. "Like what, Mama?"

Her coils, so similar to mine, bounced as she laughed. "Like you're alive, baby girl."

Kenneth clears his throat, pulling me back to the present. His eyes are black right now, dilated with excitement.

I should say no, but the word dies on my tongue. I've done everything in my power for the last two and a half years to keep Kenneth out. Walls so high that it should have taken decades to climb over.

Did I leave a gap? A place for him to sneak through?

This wasn't part of my plan. The game has always been something I could control, and now I feel it slipping as my heart moves into the driver's seat. Even when I lost, I knew the game would go on. It was a constant in the midst of fighting with my mom, stressing through classes, and feeling like a failure in my own body. And if I really think about it, the Brain Bowl hasn't been my constant.

Kenneth has.

My eyes refocus on the eager man kneeling in front of me. "Fine," I sigh, trying to sound like I'm not excited. "When? Campus should be empty tomorrow."

"Eddie, Eddie, Eddie." Red tufts of hair flop as he vibrates with excitement. "I was thinking we could go right now."

I'm swaddled in Kenneth's clothes. His T-shirt hangs down to my knees, and the pair of shorts he let me borrow are loose around my waist. Submerging myself in a lake in my favorite silk top was not happening, and I'm actually enjoying being enveloped in the familiar smell of Kenneth.

I point at a warning sign. "See this? It clearly says not to swim in the lake unless you have a pass."

He slips his shoes and socks off, placing them beside my sandals. "You're such a stickler for the rules. I'm guessing you made sure to get a pass when you dipped with your team?"

"Yup. My dip was sanctioned by campus."

"Well, I have a pass. It's called the 'don't get caught' pass. Don't worry though, Eddie. I made sure you're covered too." He winks, barely managing to dodge the sandal I toss at his head.

When was the last time I spent a Sunday night not studying? Actually, I can't remember the last time I did something fun with someone other than Cade or the girls. Babysitting the twins doesn't count because they're forced to spend time with me. And now I'm spending time with Kenneth. Outside of our three required meetings. Outside of the Brain Bowl.

And it might end with me being arrested for breaking campus rules.

The last bit of worry I have about this situation slips away as Kenneth threads our fingers and leads me to the edge of the lake.

"If you don't want to do this, I understand. I can do it by myself, and we can go back to working, or I'll take you home. Whatever you want."

His grip on my hand loosens, and I find myself tightening it for the both of us. "No, it's okay. I want to do this," I promise. "I'm weirdly honored and mildly freaked out that you picked me."

His smile lights up the darkness around us. "There's nobody else I'd rather do this with, Eddie."

Although we should be quiet to avoid getting caught, we're already here. In honor of our school spirit, we chant together, our voices loud and proud.

"Victory is ours. We're number one. Get a CLU because we're second to none!"

With that, I leap off the grassy bank and icy water engulfs my body. Pushing soaked curls out of my eyes, I find Kenneth's already on me. A blast of laughter leaves my chest from the goofy smile on his face. I cover my mouth, but it doesn't stop the sound of joy from leaking between my fingers. His concerned expression relaxes as he joins me with his velvety laugh. It's insane to be so happy because we know if we're caught, we're in big trouble.

But I couldn't care less anymore.

"I can't believe that in two months, I've willingly swam in *two* lakes. I feel like I missed out on so many pool parties and recovery days."

"And chicken fights." Kenneth grins. "I'll make sure to remind you how much you enjoy swimming from here on out. Hopefully you'll come back to Lake Anita soon, yeah?"

"Yeah." I smile back at him. "Soon."

He is so handsome. Just looking at him is making my stomach flip, and it's not from the lake water I accidentally swallowed.

Hair sticks to his forehead, crimson and curled at the ends. Freckles glow in the moonlight against his tanned skin. Cade was right. He just needed a little bit of sunlight.

Trying to rid his beautiful face from my vision, I send a wave of water at it and try to get away, but my efforts are in vain. A large hand wraps around my ankle and drags me back to him. The stitch in my side returns with a vengeance as he promises payback will not be sweet.

I don't even recognize the noises coming from my own mouth, and they get louder when he spins me to face him. These gasps of air sound like freedom and feel like true comfort.

It's not until Kenneth cups my cheeks that I fall silent.

Green eyes drop down to my lips and rise. *Painfully* slowly.

Even in this icy lake, my body floods with heat. Like the night of the St. Patty's party, I'm struck with the thought that Kenneth looks like he wants to kiss me. And if he did, would I be okay with it?

My eyes flicker down to his lips, and a nervous laugh slips out at the words my brain is literally screaming.

Yes. Hell yes. Please kiss me already.

My breath catches when something presses softly against my lips.

Sadly, it's his finger.

"Dammit, Eddie." His voice is tight and gruff with something I haven't heard from him before. "I love your laugh. God, I love it so much that it's probably a little unhealthy, but right now I need you to hold it in before we get caught."

I follow his worried eyes and find white light gliding across the grass.

"You promised we wouldn't get caught!"

Kenneth grips my hips and lifts me out of the water before pulling himself out. I focus on the beam of light getting closer, rather than the way his muscles bulge as he slips on his shorts and shirt.

"The worst punishment we'll get is a strict lecture."

"That's a bold assumption to make," I say, squeezing the water from my shirt and shorts. "What if they tase us?"

A laugh pushes through his tightly pulled lips. "It's a campus police officer. Not a kidnapper."

"You don't know that!"

"Do you trust me, Ed?"

He asks it so easily, as if it isn't the most loaded question I've been asked this week, and I took a biochemistry exam the other day.

But unlike biochemistry, where every question Dr. Lila asks makes me doubt everything I've ever known, I know the answer to this question. It's as easy as breathing. I trust Kenneth so much that I'm sure if my old self could see me now, she would explode on the spot. Trust isn't just a word or a feeling. It's an action that is earned daily with effort and hard work.

Kenneth has been showing me I can trust him long before tonight.

His eyes crinkle at the corners when I nod and pull his hoodie over my wet shirt. We both fail spectacularly at hiding our goofy smiles as we slip on our shoes and prepare to escape.

Until my phone lights up, reminding me to take my birth control with a screeching alarm. Kenneth yelps at the sudden sound, which makes my jittery ass scream even louder.

"Hey!" a burly voice calls out. The flashlight beam finally makes it around the wall of trees and whips to us, showering us with light. "You kids know you aren't supposed to be in the lake."

I shield my eyes from the light and shout, "Don't tase us!"

"Tase you? I wouldn't do that—" The officer steps forward and drops the beam to the ground. "Well, I'll be damned. Kenneth Gray, is that you?"

Are you kidding me?

"Hey, Officer Dylan," Kenneth says so nonchalantly that I want to punch him. "Haven't seen you in a while. Have you been able to golf with my dad lately?"

"Nope. Been too busy catching kids doing things they're not supposed to be doing on campus." They both crack a smile, but it does absolutely nothing for my stress level.

Who cares that they know each other? I knew we shouldn't have come out here without a permit. I'm now a campus criminal, and I'll take my punishment like a champ.

"I'm so sorry," I say, holding my hands up. "I don't think an arrest is warranted for this situation considering we were celebrating, but I also understand we have no permit." I shoot an ugly look at Kenneth. "Whatever the punishment is, I'll take—"

The collar of my shirt chokes me as I'm pulled backwards.

"No way," Kenneth whispers in my ear. "I promised I wouldn't get you in trouble." When he turns me around and forces me to look him in the eye, I know he's about to say something stupid.

"Run, Eddie."

"What?" I hiss.

"Run!" he repeats.

I look over my shoulder at the man with the taser on his hip and a big smile on his face. He doesn't even look shocked by Kenneth's command.

When Officer Dylan chokes on a laugh, I take off toward the parking lot with a wild cackle. In less than ten steps, Kenneth catches up to me with my sandal that fell off in his hand.

"Stay out of the lake!" Officer Dylan yells at our backs. "And congrats, Kenneth! I'm proud of you, kid!"

Kenneth yells back his appreciation before lacing his fingers with mine as we race down the hill and toward his truck.

Shivering, I realize this is how it feels to be alive.

Chapter Twenty-Six

Kenneth's golden ticket is mocking me.

I spent so much time on that piece of paper, and now it's calling me a hypocrite because all three punches have been made, but I find myself still sitting across from him at Claude's Cafe. I tried to convince myself that this could be extra credit since we're meeting more than the required amount, but even I know that's a bunch of bull.

The truth is, being with Kenneth in our booth has become my new normal. Studying doesn't feel the same if he isn't sitting across from me, talking himself through some complex math problem that I understand about ten percent of.

The look of concentration on his face paired with his tongue pushing past his lips tells me he's in the zone. In this state, he's so unaware of his surroundings. A mug shattered moments ago, but his gaze never left his notebook and calculator.

Just as the timer on his phone goes off, I saddle up for my first joke.

"Why do omelets enjoy April Fools' Day?" I ask, leaning on my elbows.

Kenneth closes his spiral notebook. "I have a feeling you're going to tell me no matter what. Why?"

"Because they enjoy practical yolks."

When his face doesn't change, I nudge him with my foot. "That one was so good, Kenneth! Come on. It deserved a laugh."

His lips quirk, but not at the joke. He loves that I alternate between his first name and last name now. It's small, but it almost feels as if we're letting go of our old routines and habits, creating a new path.

"I know you've got better. Try again."

The perfect joke comes to mind, and I grin. "Why do squirrels swim on their backs?"

His forehead wrinkles. "Because it's fun?"

"Nope. So they don't get their nuts wet."

Holy shit. If you had told me that making Kenneth laugh would give me the same feeling as acing a test or stopping a goal, I would've made it my life's mission years ago. It starts off quiet, with a jump of his shoulders, and when it really gets going, it's a thing of beauty. Crinkled eyes and rosy cheeks.

He wipes his eyes and leans back. "I think the purpose of the holiday is to prank each other, but I prefer your jokes, Eddie."

After making me promise to have more jokes ready later, he reopens his notebook and sets another timer. I like this little routine we have. It helps him be productive and forces me to take breaks.

I've been on edge since my harsh phone call with my advisor yesterday. For thirty minutes, she constantly reminded me that I still don't have an internship lined up for the summer.

As if I had somehow forgotten.

I haven't liked my advisor, Ms. Silva, since she called me childish for rejecting an internship opportunity last semester, but it's not my fault the interviewer described the position to me as someone to take notes and look pretty.

Discussing my motivations for my degree and career choices with Kenneth the other night reminded me of the reason I work hard day after day. As much as I want to win the Brain Bowl, being able to truly help people like my dad is what I'm chasing after. I won't settle for an internship that won't help me get there.

Which is why I have to secure the internship.

My screen is split between Kenneth's personal statement and a donation letter I'm working on for Dr. Martin, but I keep rereading his personal statement. It's perfect in every sense of the word. Every sentence does nothing but solidify what I've known for years, even though I fought to ignore it.

Kenneth is a great competitor and an even better person. The way he speaks about his passion for MS research and his grandmother makes my heart swell.

I've come to terms about my feelings for him. I like Kenneth Gray.

Even then, I can't let it go any further than this. I'm not even sure what it is that he wants. Sure, he admitted some things, but there was never an outright confession. And if he had confessed, I still don't know what I'd do. I have no clue how to tell him what I would need from him as a partner. Someone who won't smother me like my mom or treat me like a burden like Jordan.

The tiny part of me that wants to be an optimist is curious. What if I tell him exactly what I need and he exceeds my expectations? Kenneth could become a Guardian of the Blood Sugar. He could sit at my games and use the app to follow my blood sugar from the stands. We could sneak turkey roll-ups and cheese sticks into the movie theater so I can enjoy popcorn without worrying about a spike in my blood sugar. He could be the person that I turn to on the good and bad days.

But I don't know if I can bring myself to find out. I can't risk losing control of my heart again.

Alarm vibrations shake my glass of water until Kenneth presses the screen to stop it.

He rubs his eyes, fighting back a yawn. "Did you finish the donation letter for Dr. Martin?"

I look down at my screen. The cursor clicks judgmentally right where I left it fifteen minutes ago.

"Yeah," I wince, closing my computer. "Actually, I was wondering if you would write my peer recommendation letter?"

Kenneth crumples a piece of paper and tosses it at my head. "Not cool. I'm not falling for that."

It takes me a minute to understand what he's talking about, and when I do, I shake my head. "No! This isn't a prank. I'm being serious. You know more about my grades and achievements than anyone else I know. You're the best person to write it for me."

The smile I think about constantly appears. "I would love to."

"April—" His eyes narrow and I laugh. "Just kidding."

"Would you write one for me too?" he asks.

I pull out the rubric to look for any rules against writing letters for each other. "I don't see where it says we can't, but wouldn't it be weird if we did?"

"Nope. We're partners, Eddie," he says confidently. "It'll be fine. What do you say?"

"Okay, but you better make mine good, or I'll destroy you in yours."

He grins, but it falters as I stand. My insulin pump has to be changed every two to three days, and since I'm not getting any work done here across from him, I might as well walk home, change it, and finish Dr. Martin's letter.

"I'm going to head home. Feel free to stay—"

Kenneth's notebook slams shut, followed by two textbooks and a journal. He ignores the wary glances from other patrons and continues to shove it all into his backpack.

"What are you doing?" I ask.

"You need to go home, so I'm taking you home."

I shake my head in protest, but I can't keep myself from smiling. "No. I mean, that's kind of you, but you don't have to, Gray. I'm not running away this time."

"I don't care." He stands and slings my backpack over his shoulder. "I'll never make that mistake again, Eddie."

Chapter Twenty-Seven

Kenneth

"Roll up the windows and come inside," Mallory says as I pull into her driveway. "The least I can do is invite you in for lunch."

While it's normal to come home and see her on my couch with Cade or around for parties, there's never been a reason for me to go inside her house. I can't pass up this once-in-a-lifetime opportunity.

Everything in the cozy space is incredibly Mallory. Potted plants hang from the ceiling in front of large windows, covered by buttery yellow curtains. The off-white couch is littered with multicolored quilts and her winnings from the carnival. There are so many photos and records on the walls, I can barely see the paint.

"Is curry okay? I've been wanting to try these frozen meals and bought every kind."

I look at a picture of The Quartet smiling on the soccer field. "Sounds great. I'll take any of them."

"Perfect." The oven beeps, and she walks into the living room. "While it's preheating, I need to change my insulin pump, so make yourself at home. Don't be nosy, and stay out of Shay's room."

"Me? Nosy? That's definitely more up your alley." I spot the foreign objects in her hand. "Can I watch? I'd like to learn."

"For what?"

For you.

"Because I care," is what I say instead. Not a lie, but not enough to scare her away.

A pained expression takes over her face. I don't even want to know what thought just flittered across her brain. Mallory assesses me as if she's searching for an ulterior motive, but my reasons are pure. I care about her more than she will ever know.

"Sure," she finally says, turning to march down the hallway. "Hurry before I change my mind."

I jog after her into the hallway bathroom and open my list of notes. "What's step one?"

"Before I do anything, I need to check my blood sugar." She opens an app on her phone and pauses. After a few seconds she says, "All good."

Lifting her shirt, a white insulin pump rests on her lower back. She tugs at it for a second, but it holds on tight. With a sharp inhale, it finally comes off. She rubs a goop of antibiotic ointment on the spot. "This is mandatory because infections are no fun."

"Do they happen often?"

"Like three times, and I'd love if it never happened again." She swabs her stomach with what smells like an alcohol pad. "I'm switching the pump to my stomach. I prefer my insulin pump on my stomach or lower back. It doesn't work well on my arms, and I can't stand it on my outer thighs."

I type on my phone quickly, keeping my eyes on her. "Got it."

"Any questions?"

"Why do you switch spots?"

Forgoing words, she takes my hand and places it on her stomach, slowly moving it across the skin. "Feel that?"

I swallow hard. All I feel is admiration and heat crawling up my neck.

Oh, and a bump.

"That's what happens when I don't rotate the site," she says. "That little bump can decrease the absorption of insulin, which increases the risk of high blood sugar. I need that risk to stay as low as possible."

I nod, my eyes bouncing between the notes on my phone and her, watching as she fills the insulin pump. In one fluid motion, she places it on her stomach with a loud click, and the needle sinks into her skin. She doesn't flinch like I would.

With a relieved sigh, she looks at me through the bathroom mirror. "And that's it."

When the oven timer beeps, I offer to clean up so she can put our meals in the oven. She gives me a grateful smile and rushes out of the bathroom.

I swipe everything into the trash can and drop to my knees, reaching for a box that fell. When I stand up, I'm face to face with a black cat that is sitting on the counter. Its yellow eyes bore directly into my soul.

The most superstitious person I know has a black cat?

Without warning, Mallory grabs my wrist, pulls me to the couch, and hands me a smelly treat. "That's Winry. She's sweet, but cautious around new people. Don't scream, don't jump, and leave the treat in your palm. She's a finger nibbler."

Nudging her shoulder, I smirk. "I didn't realize I was at the pet-meeting stage."

"Don't get cocky. If Winry doesn't like you, we can't be friends."

I glare at the small cat. *You better like me because I'm not going anywhere.*

Winry meows her own menacing threat.

Cautious eyes fall to the treat in my palm, and she stalks across the rug. Her whiskers tickle my palm as she sniffs me, then the treat, then me again.

"I think she likes me Ed–Ouch!" I scream, yanking my fingers away from sharp teeth. Tiny little holes mock me.

Mallory scratches the cat's ears. "I warned you."

With a full stomach, I lean back and pet Winry, who has made herself at home on my lap.

Mallory plops down on the opposite side of the couch, clicking through every streaming service. "What do you want to watch?"

"Movie or show?" I ask.

"Depends on when you need to leave."

She's in no rush to kick me out? Sweet.

"Movie. Emperor's New Groove." I shudder. "I had a dream about Yzma last night."

"That's hot." Mallory tosses a blanket onto my cat-occupied lap, which sends Winry to the ground and prancing out of the living room.

My phone buzzes in my pocket as the opening credits begin. I assume it's Cade asking me about dinner plans, but my peaceful afternoon shatters when I read the message waiting for me.

Mom

Nationals celebration in two weeks. Saturday at 6. Are you bringing Cade?

I somehow forgot that even though my parents won't celebrate *with* me, they'll always use the success of their children to further the superiority of the Gray family. When Keaton graduated from business school, they celebrated with a massive party. When Karla graduated and was accepted into a prestigious master's program, she got the same treatment.

This celebration will be no different. They'll brag and pretend we're a loving family for two to three hours, and the moment the last guest leaves, they'll go back to being poor excuses for parents.

"Hello!" The movie pauses. "You're missing the best part, albeit every part is the best part. Do you need to take care of something?"

"No, I'm good." I lock my phone and sigh. "Sorry, Ed. My mom texted and told me there's a mandatory family thing I have to attend."

"Gross. What for?"

"Apparently they want to celebrate my win." Even though they didn't come watch.

Mallory crosses her arms. "So, my pizza party wasn't good enough for you? Ouch."

The phony hurt in her voice makes me feel a little better. "Nothing will ever top homemade pizza and running away from a security guard. That's a night I'll never forget." Suddenly feeling overheated, I push the quilt off my legs. "It's not really a party for me. It's for my parents. They'll invite all their friends and coworkers and spend the whole time telling everyone how proud of me they are, when the truth is they couldn't care less about swimming."

Or me.

"Double ouch." Mallory sucks in a sharp breath. "Why would they even call that a party? It sounds like hell."

"Hell is the perfect way to describe it, which is why I usually take Cade to these things. He's good with people and boring conversations, but he's got a meeting with an agent."

"That's two Saturdays from now," she says, because of course she knows Cade's schedule too. "I've got an idea. What if I go as your buffer in place of Cade?"

"Okay, enough with the jokes, Eddie."

Mallory crosses her legs beneath her and faces me. "I'm not joking or pranking you. This is a real offer. You don't go alone, and I get to people watch and eat free hors d'oeuvres. Win win."

I inch toward her. "No. That's not a win win. It won't be fun for you."

"Will Nan and Karla be there?"

"Yes," I answer. I'm sure her mind was made up already, so this is just icing on the cake.

"Great, then it's settled." A carrot magically appears, and it crunches loudly between her teeth. "Growing up, my parents were my only family, so I never got to experience a big family dinner. Based on television, I'm expecting a few wine glasses to be thrown and at least one arrest."

I almost laugh, but the fear of bringing Mallory into my mess of a family is too much. "I can't let you do this."

"Let me," she pleads. "This party should be to celebrate you and your accomplishments. You're not supposed to hide in the corner feeling suffocated, so it's decided. I'll postpone my Saturday pad Thai for an awkward dinner party with the Grays."

I scoot closer until there's half a cushion between us. "My parents aren't good people, and I don't want to drag you into that. Nothing good comes from them."

She tilts her head to the side. "What do you mean nothing good comes from them? You did, and I think you're pretty great, Kenneth."

This woman. I wonder if she realizes how good her words make me feel. I've always heard such amazing things about the girls and Cade, but I love it most when she says these things about me.

"And Karla," she teases. "She's even better than you."

Finally, the laugh she's working hard to get out of me tumbles out.

Feeling oddly confident, I lean over and pull her into my lap. With a yelp, she wraps her arms around me as I shift our bodies downward until my head is propped up by the arm rest and her head is on my chest.

Mallory Edwards is in my arms and I'm in heaven.

"Is this okay?" I ask, trying to slow my heartbeat.

"Yeah. Totally fine." She clears her throat, sounding totally not fine. "How mad would you be if I told you this was all part of some elaborate prank right now?"

I bury my face in her hair and smile as she presses play on the television. "Furious."

CHAPTER TWENTY-EIGHT

EVEN THE MOST SOLID teams have issues. Which explains why I'm two hours away from Clear Lake in the middle of nowhere with mine.

After a fight between two freshmen during practice, Coach Sumner shipped us off for the long weekend to his vacation home. No ifs, ands, or buts. Coach doesn't do drama, and as captain, it's my job to make sure there's none before we head home Sunday afternoon.

I've got three days to get this team together.

My teammates lounge on the beige, shaggy carpet, their eyes scanning the colorful three-day itinerary I made. Every event I chose for this weekend has been selected to encourage team bonding and communication, which is good because the two reasons we're here are shooting daggers at each other from opposite sides of the room.

Adri's hand shoots up like we're in a classroom. "Why are we waking up at six tomorrow morning? I sleep until noon on Fridays. You're taking away my beauty sleep on this wonderful, long weekend, Cap."

I pop a cracker into my mouth. "It's called *sunrise* yoga. Not afternoon yoga. Coffee and tea will be ready before, and breakfast will be served right after. And yes, I got the peppermint coffee creamer you're obsessed with."

"I knew you loved me," Adri says. She jabs a finger in Shay's direction. If looks could kill, Shay would be on death row. "What are you going to do about this one?"

Everyone shivers, remembering how cranky Shay is in the morning.

"Don't worry. I'll deal with her. I brought a spray bottle and my foam sword, so don't mess with me, Shaylene," I warn her, and her murderous expression fades.

The other night when I stopped by Cade's to pick up his speaker, Kenneth and Cade were busy chasing each other around the house and beating the hell out of each other with foam swords. Neither noticed me standing at the door, watching them for over five minutes. The photo I took of Kenneth sitting on Cade's back still makes me laugh.

Shay and I bought our own this morning.

"Why would you pair me with *her* for the three-legged race?" Gemma, reason number one we're here, yells.

Ivy, reason number two, rolls her eyes. "Stop acting dense. We're here because your feelings got hurt about not starting in the last scrimmage."

Ah, so this is the reason why we were banished by Coach Sumner. Damn him for making me babysit.

"You two, stop it," I say. "Everybody except for Gemma and Ivy, out. Feel free to explore the property. Don't forget your phones and a flashlight, and I mean a *real* flashlight. Not just the one on your phone. Grab one from the bucket by the door, and remember we are in the middle of the woods. No broken ankles. No falling in the creek. Come back by six for dinner."

My teammates scatter quickly. It's clear they'd like to avoid drama.

Once we're alone in the house, I put on my captain hat. "You guys do realize that we're all spending our long weekend in the middle of nowhere because of you two, right?"

They nod. "Sorry, Mally."

"No need to apologize for that. I'll never complain about team time, but I need you guys to work this out. You have an opportunity to move forward this weekend. While you might be competitors in a way, you're also teammates. I'm not saying you need to be besties, but teammates have a special bond too." I walk to the cooler and grab a water bottle. Gemma and Ivy both start to speak, and I shake my head. "Take the weekend to figure it out. If my bonding activities don't work, then we can talk. But I would advise you fix this soon, because if Coach has to get involved, it won't be pretty."

Without another word, I exit the living room. Instead of walking to the bedroom to finish unpacking, I press my back against the wall and wait.

After an agonizing silence, Gemma finally speaks. "If you make us lose the three-legged race, I'm going to hate you forever."

Ivy snorts. "Me? Worry about yourself. I'm going to wipe the floor with you."

I rub my temples as the front door slams, both girls going to explore with the rest of the team. This is going to be a long weekend.

The first day was a total success. Shay managed to crawl out of bed for sunrise yoga, even though she glared at me from her mat with a piece of bacon hanging out of her mouth. Jo led us through an hour of yoga, managing to keep it together even though Adri kept calling it downward doggy style.

After a late dinner and finishing my recommendation letter for Kenneth, I fall face first into the leather couch.

I'd fall asleep right here if it wasn't so loud from the party going on around me. My game day playlist blares through the speakers, "Imma Be" taking everyone back to junior high.

I flip onto my back, surprised to find Jo holding out a beer to me.

"You look like you need this," she says. "Great job today, Mal. It's only Friday, and Gemma and Ivy aren't trying to strangle each other anymore. Pairing them up for the three-legged race was genius."

I move my leg, and the couch shifts as she sits beside me. "I'm glad. I hope the next two days go as smoothly as today did."

When I rub my pulsing temples, Jo asks, "You good?"

"Meh. I'm exhausted, so I have no clue how they still have so much energy. I was sure my itinerary would have them all in bed by now. We've been going since the sun came up."

I glance around the room. Adri is playing Twister, her body contorted in ways I didn't know were possible. The dining table is a battlefield as Monopoly proves to be friendship ending. Near the kitchen, wooden blocks topple to the ground, followed by, *"Ha! I told you not to pick that one!"*

"Well, it doesn't help that they're all drunk. I think you're the only sober one here."

I gasp and grab Jo's cheeks, which are flushed and warm against my palms. "Jo! You're drunk too?"

"Maybe a little tipsy." She hiccups. "Figured I might as well join the craziness. Adri promised she would teach me the difference between good vodka and bad vodka."

"If you love yourself, don't do that." I shake my head and glare at Adri's back. "That's how she tricks you into going shot for shot, and no vodka is good. Take my advice and steer clear of that hellish game. Plus, we've got our two-on-two soccer games tomorrow."

"Since you're team mom *and* team captain, maybe you can write me a pass to skip tomorrow's activities? For your best friend."

Although she and Adri are a year below Shay and I, they're incredible members of this team and even better friends. The Quartet began when Adri called me for a ride home after a frat party got busted. Shay and I crawled out of bed, took them to Sunshine Junction, and the rest was history.

"So, do you want to finally tell me what's going on between you and Kenneth?" she asks.

I pop open my can of beer, but don't bring it to my lips. "We're friends, Jo. Working on our project. Nothing more."

"You swear?"

"Swear." I'm telling the truth. We are friends.

Regardless of how I feel about him.

She leans against my arm, always a bit more touchy when she gets a little bit of alcohol in her system. "I never thought I'd hear those words come out of your mouth, Mal. Friends with Kenneth. It's funny how things change."

Before I can agree, Adri bursts into the living room. Her drunk talent is being able to do gymnastic moves and the entire "Rasputin" dance without breaking a sweat. Completing a wobbly back walkover, she slides into the splits with her arms in the air. "Ta-da!"

"Holy shit, you're wasted," I laugh. "Are you going to be okay tomorrow? I told Jo that getting sick on the field is not allowed."

Adri stands and pops her hip as if I've offended her. "Puking is for bitches and losers, and I am neither of those." Grabbing Jo, she pulls her up from beside me. "Want to join us, Cap? I'm going to show Jo the wonderful world of vodka."

I look at Jo, who lets out an intoxicated giggle at my worried expression.

Waving them away, I lean back into the couch. "I'd rather make it through the night. You guys go kill your livers, but don't forget that we have lots of activities planned for tomorrow."

After I finish my beer, I grab my fanny pack and head into the bathroom. Glass clangs against the counter as I pull the small bottles from my bag. For this mini-vacation, Dr. Morand and Bex recommended it could be a good time for an insulin pump break, restarting insulin injections.

I'm actually looking forward to putting my pump back on when I get home.

I open the app, which alerts me that it's time to change my continuous glucose monitor's sensor. Thankfully, I knew it needed to be replaced and came prepared. I place the new sensor on the counter, peel the monitor off the back of my right arm, and dive in. After separating the transmitter and sensor, I toss the old sensor into the trash. Once everything is prepped, I swipe the back of my left arm with an alcohol pad and snap it on.

I re-open the app to make sure everything paired properly, and my mouth falls open at the notification.

"What? Pair a new transmitter?" I refresh the app and shake off my worry. When it reloads, everything will be fine.

Then the same message pops up and my chest aches.

"No. No, no, no. Please not tonight."

Even though I'm already sure there isn't one in there, I dump my fanny pack onto the counter and search through the contents. Of course I didn't pack a second transmitter. They're supposed to last up to three months and this one has only been on for six days.

Shit shit shit.

I reach into the bag to find my blood sugar test strips for manual checks, but the pocket is empty.

During the water balloon fight, Shay very kindly moved my bag out of the splash zone. But because it wasn't zipped, the strips fell into a puddle and were ruined.

A quick Google search tells me that the closest pharmacy and urgent care are almost forty minutes away, and they're either closed or closing in the next fifteen minutes.

"Fuck!" I whisper, panic sharpening the word.

I rush into the bedroom for my keys, but I know I can't leave. Driving without knowing my current blood sugar is too dangerous. Blood sugar levels become even more unpredictable after drinking, and I don't even have the tools to monitor it.

Not a single person in this house is sober enough to drive me to Clear Lake tonight. Hell, there's no way they will be awake and sober before noon tomorrow at the rate they're going.

Everything is blurred by tears as I grab my phone and make a call. Tears stream down my cheeks as I give instructions to the kind voice on the other side. For all I know I could be yelling, but the calm cadence of his voice soothes me.

"I'll be there soon, Eddie. I'm on my way."

I hang up and slide down the door until I'm on the ground. Closing my eyes, I search for my safe place like Sharon would tell me to do.

I listen for sounds of birds lost in the trees and rub my arms to simulate the warmth of the sun on my skin. I imagine the dock's splintering wood digging into the back of my legs. I visualize the guy I'm falling for holding my hand as we sit on the dock.

"Kenneth will be here soon. Breathe." I repeat this over and over until a memory resurfaces, giving me an idea.

"Five things I can see. The floral comforter..."

Chapter Twenty-Nine

Kenneth

My fist bangs against the front door of the cabin in the middle of nowhere. As the minutes tick by, it gets noticeably harder to not kick the door down. The two-hour drive felt like an eternity on the winding roads and narrow one-way streets to this hidden place.

This cabin is massive enough to house the whole football team. Who knows if any of the girls can even hear me from their bedrooms.

Cade and I were in the middle of a FIFA tournament when my phone started ringing. When Cade saw Mallory's name, he answered it with his voice in its usual silly state. Then he shoved the phone into my hands and ran to his bedroom, returning moments later with her spare house key.

Her words were hushed and rushed, giving instructions that I committed to memory. At her house, I gathered test strips, three sensors, and three transmitters from her bathroom before speeding to the address she sent. Since then, she hasn't answered her phone.

I call again, and it goes straight to voicemail.

Again.

Someone better open this door in the next thirty seconds or I'm kicking it in. I pull up Shay's number that Cade sent me, but right as I'm about to click the call button, the front door swings open.

"Kenneth?" She steps into the dim light, rubbing tired eyes. "You're here?"

Without waiting for an answer, Mallory steps forward and throws her arms around my neck. Damp skin cools my collarbone as I pull her against me. The familiar scent of coconut does a better job of calming my racing heart than the grounding method I tried in the car.

This is all I thought about the entire drive. I think I might need this hug more than she does.

"I'll always come when you call, Eddie. Every single time."

When I finally get the strength to release her, I follow her into the house. I hold back a laugh as I step over a player whose face is covered in permanent marker. The living room looks like a cannonball of board game pieces exploded, scattered over every inch of shaggy carpet. From here, I count seven bodies on the ground, one on the couch, three curled in front of the fireplace, two on top of the dining room table, and one in the corner.

Mallory leads me into the kitchen and clicks on the light before dropping into a chair. She fiddles with the drawstrings of my black CLU Swim hoodie, which I haven't seen since The Dip.

It looks so good on her. I don't ever want it back if it means she will wear it forever.

I lean on the wall across from her. "Sorry for pounding on the door. I called and couldn't get through. I was worried you decided you couldn't wait and started driving back to Clear Lake."

She drags her hands down her face. "Shit. My phone must have died. I almost made it through three things I could smell and fell asleep on the floor. I'm sorry."

"All that matters is that you're okay." I give her a quick smile before wrinkling my nose. "Do you remember what the three things you could smell were? Because all I smell is—"

"Puke? Yeah." She rolls her eyes. "They're deep cleaning the whole house before we leave. I don't know what Coach thought would happen when he banished twenty-seven college students to the middle of nowhere with nothing to do after dark. Of course they're going to drink."

The laugh that follows is not normal, but it's her eyes that scare me. The sadness is suffocating.

"Did you have an anxiety attack?"

"No," she sighs, reaching for a water bottle on the counter. "But I felt it coming. It sat there, like it was waiting for me to fall down the hole and spiral. I remembered the grounding method thing that we did together in the training room, and it worked again."

I grin. "That's a win, Ed. That's a freaking win right there."

"Maybe, but this shouldn't have happened in the first place." She slams her palm against her forehead, voice choked with anger which I realize is aimed at herself. "I ruined your Friday night because I can't get my shit together. I forgot to zip my bag, so my test strips got wet and were ruined. Somehow, I can pack nine pairs of underwear for a three-day trip, but don't come prepared to manage my own condition."

"Hey, you can't beat yourself up. Accidents happen. Bags don't get zipped, and things fall out. Technology malfunctions—"

She throws her hands up. "None of that matters! I should have brought ten transmitters and sensors because I know exactly how unpredictable diabetes can be. Over a year later, and I still haven't learned my lesson. How is that not my fault?"

"Because you won't ever be prepared for every little thing in life. I know that's not what you want to hear, but things are going to happen that even you, the most prepared person I know, aren't ready for. You only planned to change the sensor. You had no idea the transmitter would malfunction only a few days into its three-month limit. How is that your fault?"

Mallory deflates, slumping back into the chair. "Just forget I said anything. Okay? You don't get it."

"I will never get it, Ed." I take a single tentative step forward. "I'll never understand exactly what you go through or how you feel. It's not my place to try to tell you either. All I can do is be here for you and tell you the truth."

"And what's that?"

The distance between us feels so much farther than five feet. The wall she's putting up is so high, and I'm not sure if what I want to say will bring it down or make it impossible to crawl over again. But I have to try.

"That you aren't stupid or forgetful or ill-prepared. That you live in a world where things happen and it's nobody's fault. That having the memory of a goldfish is necessary at times like this. That your brain is being mean as hell to you, and I'd do anything to make it stop."

I blink back a rush of relief when her shoulders relax, and the wall that was so close to shutting me out crumbles to the ground.

"I'm sorry, Kenneth. I'm tired and grumpy and... I'm so sorry for snapping at you."

"Apology accepted, but not needed," I recite. Our thing.

She pushes herself up and grabs the grocery bag of supplies I brought. "How did you know the limit is three months on the transmitter?"

My cheeks burn and I scratch the back of my neck. "I did some research."

"So, you take notes when I talk, and you do research on your own?" I nod, and she finally looks at me. "You keep on surprising me, Gray. Thanks for bringing this. I'll be back in a minute."

"Eddie." I swallow hard. "How would you feel if I put it on for you?"

Puffy eyes make her look even more surprised. “What?”

Diabetes videos are all I watch on YouTube nowadays. After searching her specific brand of insulin pump and continuous glucose monitor, videos were bookmarked and studied until I had the step-by-step instructions and other pertinent information memorized.

“I know how to do it. I mean... In theory I know how to do it. I haven’t done it in real life, but I watched a ton of videos that talked me through the process. I can do it for you.”

My chest deflates when she gifts me the smile I’ve been waiting for. “I would love that.”

“What in the hell happened while I was asleep?” Mallory hisses.

We maneuver carefully over scattered bodies, empty bottles, and crushed cans that cover the living room floor. Adri is fast asleep, using the Twister mat as a blanket. Her face is shoved into the corner as if she fell asleep while put in a time-out.

“I had no idea your teammates could trash a place like this.”

“They’re animals. Goddamn animals. Tomorrow is going to be their worst nightmare. We’re not just doing two-on-two. I’m taking these dumbasses on a hike at seven in the morning. That’ll show them.”

She moves toward Jo, who is star-fished in the middle of the floor with a half-eaten graham cracker on her forehead. I reach for Jo’s arm to help her, but Mallory stops me.

“No way. The moment one of these drunk idiots sees you, they’ll be screaming bloody murder, and I can’t handle any more craziness.” She points down the hallway. “I’m staying in the second room on the right with Shay, but I'm leaving her on the couch tonight. Wait for me in there?"

I nod and head for the bedroom. I'm about to shut the bedroom door when a voice pierces the quiet.

"Are you okay?" Jo slurs. "Did I hear Kenneth, or am I just *reaaaaally* drunk right now?"

Mallory shushes her. "Keep your voice down, babe. There was a small hiccup, but don't worry about me. Let's focus on making sure you don't hate yourself in the morning."

"Too late. I regret everything. I should have listened when you told me not to listen to Adri. Do you think I can sue her for damaging my liver?"

"Sadly, no." A pause. "We need to get you to bed. What are you looking for?"

I almost laugh when Jo's sniffles. "I think Adri ate my graham crackers. That's stealing. I'm gonna sue her so hard."

Closing the door behind me, I send Mallory all the patience I can muster. She's going to need it.

Thirty minutes later, Mallory walks into the bedroom and locks the door behind her. She buries her face in her hands to muffle the scream she lets out. "That was terrible. Shay thought it was morning and tried to run away, Jo ate half a pack of crackers before passing out, and Adri thought I was a kidnapper and started throwing Jenga blocks at me."

Dropping the itinerary I was reading, I stand. "Looks like your morning hike might need to be pushed. They'll need to sleep it off."

"Hell no. They can sweat out their hangovers." She scans the floor. "Why is this room suddenly giving me less anxiety?"

"I shoved all of Shay's clothes that were on the ground into her suitcase and put it on the highest shelf in the closet. That'll teach her a lesson."

I hold the sheets up and wait for Mallory to slip beneath the floral bedspread. The moment her head hits the pillow she bolts back up, but I already have her scarf in my other hand. Cade refuses to sleep without his, so I grabbed hers from the dresser just in case.

The mattress groans as I take a seat beside her. "How are you feeling?"

"Like I could sleep for a whole day." After securing the scarf around her head, she covers her face. "I'm sorry for ruining your night. I already feel like a burden, and I never wanted to be that to you—"

I cut her off. "You? A burden? What are you talking about, Ed? Why would you ever think you're a burden to me? Or anyone for that matter?"

She bites down on her bottom lip. "You drove two hours to the middle of nowhere, and now you're here dealing with the smell of puke and my inebriated teammates."

"And?" I hate that she's apologizing for needing help. For asking for help. "You are not a burden to me. You never have been, and you never will be. Getting to be there for you is all that matters. It doesn't matter the day of the week, time of day, where you are, or where I am, I will be there when you call."

Although she's looking at me, it feels like she's looking *through* me, but I don't look away. I wait patiently for Mallory to kick me out and tell me I crossed a friendship boundary.

But her next words take me by surprise.

"I had my first anxiety attack the day of my dad's funeral. The second one came two weeks later. My mom was asleep at the kitchen table, which was odd, but I was happy because it was the first time she had left her room since the funeral. Earlier that day, she told me she was going to grocery shop, but the fridge and pantry were still empty when I got home. I woke her up and she told me that seeing my dad's car in the garage was another reminder that he was really gone, and she cried until she fell asleep."

She takes a deep breath before continuing. "It took a while to get her in bed. I needed air, so I started walking to the grocery store. Next thing I knew, I was kneeling on the sidewalk, trying not to pass out."

My heart seizes. "Eddie. It's okay. You don't have to tell me—"

"But I want to tell you." Each word is said with such force that I shut up and nod for her to continue.

"Sometimes I want to blame my mom, even now that we're finally moving past everything. Let her be the person I'm angry at instead of myself for a change. But I never will be able to. I know she left me alone, but we were both drowning at that point. Our grief just consumed us in different ways. As much as I wanted to hide, I knew that would only make her life more difficult than it already was. Mama needed to grieve, and I needed to be perfect so she could."

She looks down at her hands, the feeling of guilt weighing heavily around her. "I took control at sixteen and haven't learned how to let go of it."

Suddenly everything clicks into place. The way she takes care of everyone around her. It's something that makes her such a great friend, daughter, and captain. She puts everyone before herself, like the caring, selfless woman she is.

Even when it means she has to hurt.

Mallory gasps, and the sound shatters my heart. I do the only thing I can think of and press my forehead to hers.

During finals sophomore year, I watched Shay slam their heads together while studying at the library. I expected a painful yelp, but relief bloomed in Mallory's features when she looked up at Shay.

"Eddie, I need you to breathe for me."

She nods twice in quick succession, giving me ten breaths before opening her eyes.

Her hand moves to my face, rubbing gingerly beneath my eye.

"Shay does that for me when I feel like I can't breathe, so thank you." She pulls away and looks at the door. "Did you know that Shay wanted nothing to do with me when we first met?"

I chuckle at the change of topic. "No way."

"Yup. We were assigned as roommates during early freshman soccer training, and I tried everything to make our roommate situation turn into a friendship. I invited her to dinner, bought us movie tickets, planned trips to the bookstore, but she turned me down every time. That went on for three months. She made it very clear that we were roommates, teammates, and nothing more."

"So, what changed?"

"It was my dad's remembrance day. One minute I was tying my shoes so I could head to class, and the next I was hyperventilating. I didn't even know she was still in the dorm. She heard me from her room, ran over, and smashed our foreheads together. She said the pain would distract my brain, which it did. Then she swore I'd never be alone again." Mallory's smile is small, but her joy is palpable. "Thanks for doing that for me."

"I'll always be here for you, Ed. Ready for bed?"

"Yeah," she mumbles. "Will you stay with me?"

I poke my thumb toward the living room. "Won't Shay be upset if she wakes up and I'm in her spot? I'd rather not get mauled."

"She won't wake up anytime soon, and just in case she does, I tied a bell around her wrist."

Tapping her temple, I crawl beneath the sheets beside her. "You're a genius."

I outstretch an arm, and she curls into my side. Her feet are like ice as she pushes her legs between mine. She wraps a hand around the back of my neck, brushing my hair in slow strokes.

"Comfortable?" I ask.

"Very." Her eyelashes flutter against my jawline. "I'm starting to think you like saving me. You just keep showing up when I need you."

I look down at the woman in my arms, swallowed by my hoodie and more vulnerable than I've ever seen her.

I have no clue how to tell her that even though I preach nothing is perfect, that *she* is perfect to me. I have no clue how to make her believe just because her shithead of an ex made her feel like a burden, it doesn't mean I'll ever feel that way. I have no clue how to tell her she's the strongest, best person I know.

I'll show her with my actions.

"You've never needed saving, Eddie." I press my lips against her forehead. "But I do like *you.*"

She swats my chest. "Wow. You almost sounded serious for a second."

I shake my head, fixing my eyes on the ceiling fan. "There's nothing in this world I'm more serious about than you."

Even if she doesn't reciprocate my feelings, I'm proud of myself for finally admitting it out loud. I close my eyes, ready for sleep to take me.

Then she speaks, and my whole world flips.

"You know what, Gray? It's a good thing I like you too."

Chapter Thirty

Kenneth

"No way." Cade's voice is nearly a whisper, which is unlike the rowdy guy I've known since childhood.

He should be getting ready for his important meeting with an agent. Instead, he's got one dress shoe on and his white button-up hangs open, while he's staring at me like I'm an idiot. And I probably am, because asking, "*Hey, would you think I'm an idiot if I say goodbye to the plan I've worked so hard for because I'm worried about going against my father?*" wasn't the smartest.

"Is that what he came over here for at the beginning of the semester?" Cade asks, guilt swimming in his eyes. It's not his fault. He tried to talk about it, but I wanted to avoid this conversation.

I glance through the window by the front door. Any minute now, Mallory will arrive to drive us to the party at my parents' house. We haven't talked about our confessions from last weekend, and I was hoping to do that on the drive, but I know this talk with Cade will haunt me for the rest of the night.

I walk into his bedroom, hoping it will encourage him to get ready. "Yes. I needed to think on it and figure out what to do."

"Think on it?" he erupts. "Think about what, Kent? Giving up on the plans you made for yourself? For Nan? You were supposed to be free!"

"I know, Cade, but I'm not. He made it clear that I'm stuck. They're already discussing my salary."

"Fuck your salary! I don't care about that!" His chest heaves, and I know he's pissed. Not *at* me, but *for* me.

One perk of being best friends for so long is that I can read Cade's mind, so when his eyes dart to his keys on the bedside table, I move between him and the door.

"Cade—" I try, but it's too late.

With keys in hand, he pushes me aside and darts out of his room. If he gets out of this house, Cade can kiss goodbye his dreams of playing in the MLB and say hello to getting arrested for punching my dad in the face. He's practically been begging to fight him since we were kids.

"Hitting him won't help!" I yell at his back.

"We won't know that until I try!" he counters, but the smugness in his voice fades when the rug he swears brings the house together ends up being his downfall. He trips over the corner and stumbles, giving me a chance to slip past him and block the doorknob before he can recover.

I hold my hands up. "Just listen, Cade."

"Move, Kent. I'm not playing around." He stands and smooths out his dress pants, lips pulled into a straight line. "Just because your dad is a total asshole doesn't mean you have to play his stupid game. And now you're going to give up, all because he said so?"

"I might have to—"

"But you've worked too hard!" His fist slams against the wall as regret slams against my chest. Cade is fun and agreeable. He has laugh lines at twenty-two and smiles more in one hour than I do in a day, but right now he's unrecognizable.

"I'm only going to tell you one more time. *Move.* If you can't tell your dad no, I will."

I don't budge. He will have to physically move me if he wants to get past me.

"They're my family," I say.

Cade scoffs, his body vibrating with rage. "Family? You've got to be kidding. They're people who want to control you. Your dad only cares because it affects him. And your mom? She's practically non-existent."

My mother. Up until I was five, she always protected me, Keaton, and Karla from our father's crap. Then she bought into the family image bullshit and stopped standing up for us, allowing him to say and do whatever terrible thing he wants, whenever he wants.

"I know they aren't the best, but they're all I have."

Cade flinches as if I slapped him across the face. That's the worst possible thing I could've said.

"All you have?" he asks, emphasizing each word.

"I didn't mean it like that, Cade."

He turns away from me, showing off the sharp line of his clenched jaw. Hurt radiates off his body like daggers, each one pricking my skin, and I deserve every jab of pain.

"I didn't mean it like that," I repeat, desperate to explain. "I meant that no matter how shitty or terrible they are, they're always going to be my parents. Even after twenty-two years of their crap, part of me still wants everything to be okay between us."

The crease between his brows loosens. We both know all too well what it's like to have an absent parent, something that bonded us further when Cade's dad left his family.

Finally surrendering, his shoulders slump. "I hate him so much. It's not fair. We're going to get this figured out. Okay?"

"It's either him or my dream, Cade. No matter what, everything will change. If I pick my dream, I'll be completely cut off."

"And if you pick your dad?" he asks.

"I'll lose my freedom."

I've always been able to depend on my parents. It once was a privilege I never took for granted. Now I wish I had never been stupid enough to believe Theo Gray gave out of love.

Cade rubs a hand over his face. "Have you told her?"

"I can't, man. I need a little more time to figure out what's going on between us. The game is what brought us together, and I don't know how she will feel if I tell her the Brain Bowl is at risk. I can't lose her."

With Mallory I feel like I can do anything. Be who I want, when I want, however I want. I'm not ready for her to see that I'm a coward.

A sliver of faded red catches my eye, pulling to a stop behind my truck. Cade catches it too and starts to button the rest of his shirt. I check the clock, frustrated that Cade will be late because of me.

"It's fine. This is more important to me than any meeting," he says, giving me an award-winning smile. Nobody would know that only moments ago he was debating how best to tackle me to get to my father.

I pull him in for a hug, letting go when the doorbell rings.

"Your dad better be on his best behavior," Cade mumbles, swapping our positions. "Go finish getting ready, and I'll let her in. But I think you should tell her soon, Kent. MalPal might surprise you."

A bump in the road jolts me from my seat, and I realize I've been silent for the entire thirty-minute drive.

With a deep breath, I prepare for the next three hours of hell. This will be the longest amount of time I've been in this house since moving to Lake Anita when I was fifteen. Even on holidays, I give myself half an hour before escaping to Cade's house or Nan's facility.

The street is lined with guests' expensive cars, everyone already gathered inside the largest house in the most affluent neighborhood in Bryan. Flintstone stands out as we drive down the road in search of a parking spot, but compared to him, the other cars lack character.

Mallory lets out a low whistle. "I thought you said this was a family get-together. I don't know if I can be around this many Grays for hours. I'm barely making it with you."

"Stop making me want to laugh. I'm supposed to be in suffering mode," I say. "And family get-together for my parents is code for massive party with people I don't know, yet they know everything about me."

Celebrations at the Gray house are for show. My parents invite everyone over to their perfect home and put on their rehearsed family faces. Father and mother of the year. Husband and wife of the year. The people who supposedly love their kids all the time and not only when they need something from them.

Yeah right.

Once parked, Mallory opens the vanity mirror to apply a layer of gloss to her lips. Her hair is done differently tonight. Instead of free, it's braided into a halo around her head. A few loose curls framing her face beautifully. My eyes trail down her exposed neck, wishing it could be my fingers.

Or lips.

She slams the mirror shut and faces me. "Are you okay?"

I look at the massive white house and take a deep breath. "I will be when this is over."

She takes my hand in hers and rubs a splatter of freckles. "You don't have to do this alone. I'm your backup tonight. I'll clock someone over the head with my heel. I wasn't expecting a fight, but I'm always ready."

I give her hand a squeeze and exit the car, thankful that she waits for me to open her door. "My own personal bodyguard? Lucky me."

Mallory leads the way to the front door with long and confident steps that compensate for my nervous ones. A yellow sundress clings to her fluid frame, pulling me in like I'm a plant that's desperate for a little bit of sunshine.

Before we make it up the steps, I swap our positions. Ellen Gray will be in host mode, meaning she's likely watching us through the peephole.

The second my feet touch the welcome mat, the door swings open, but it's not my mother.

"Kenneth!" My father's voice is pitched with calculated enthusiasm. "Nice of you to finally show up to your own party. Only," he checks his watch, "twelve minutes late. It's great to see you're finally growing up a little, considering you were thirty-seven minutes late to your high school graduation party."

Starting with the snide comments already, I see.

He winks, and I can tell he's already trying to find a way around the promise he made hours ago. Tonight will have no discussion of the summer internship or a future career at Gray Construction.

My mother appears beside him, matching the door in a pristine white pants suit. She's silent as usual, giving me a quick head nod as a greeting. Their eyes dart over my shoulder, likely at the flash of yellow fidgeting nervously behind me.

"And who is this?" Theo asks.

Mallory moves to my side and holds out her hand. "I'm Mallory Edwards. It's nice to meet you both."

"Oh. The soccer player," he coos, holding her hand for a second too long. "I'm Theo, and this is my wife, Ellen." When he finally drags his attention away from her, his lips curl into a smirk. "Very pretty, Kenneth."

Every part of me goes rigid, and I reach for her hand as if holding onto her will make my father less of an asshole.

"I'm aware, Dad."

Theo waves me away like an annoying fly he can't get rid of and continues grinning at Mallory. "Excuse the stick up my son's behind. Mallory, we're glad to have you here with us today. It's nice to see our little Kenneth is finally making more friends than Cade." This time it's Mallory who stiffens. She goes to respond, but thankfully she's cut off by someone yelling from inside.

My mother finally speaks, not really looking at either of us. "We've got to get back to our guests. Please enjoy the party." Without another word, they usher us inside, turn on their heels, and leave us alone in the foyer.

"Well, aren't they... something," Mallory sighs. She tips her head back to the high ceilings, likely estimating how much this house is worth. "Where are the posed, awkward family photos? Doesn't every rich family have at least one?"

"Theo and Ellen Gray wouldn't be caught dead with photos on the wall. Family photos are not an elegant decoration to them. Only expensive pieces of artwork that look like the ones Cade's sister gives me for my birthday every year."

Mallory grabs her chest. "Violet gets you birthday cards? Is it bad to say I'm jealous?"

"You may be Cade's favorite, but I'm Violet's and that won't ever change, Eddie."

As if told about my arrival, the string quartet my parents always invite starts to play the most doom and gloom song I've ever heard. Every muscle in my body tenses as the music crescendos, until the beautiful, yet terrifying sound dwindles into silence.

Hands are covering my ears, but they're not mine. My focus shifts to the woman holding my face, filling my vision with yellow. I can see nothing but her.

"Kenneth. I'm right here, and I'm not going anywhere."

At Mallory's reminder, I grab her hands. I'm glad she lets me hold them, because it's the only thing keeping me from bolting out the door.

"You look beautiful tonight, Mallory. Thank you for being here."

A shy smile breaks across her lips. "There's nowhere I'd rather be. Just say the word and we can go."

I look at the door longingly. "Now?"

"We have to go in and say hi at least. Even if your parents aren't going to celebrate you properly, Nan and Karla will." She squeezes my hand. "Also, I was thinking we could stop by the lake after. I've got a surprise."

"For me?"

"No. For Nan." She jabs me with her elbow. "Duh for you."

Without waiting for an answer, she marches us down the hallway toward the party. "Let's go party, Gray. I've got rich-people food to eat and people to watch."

As long as she's here, I know tonight won't be so bad.

Chapter Thirty-One

How was Kenneth raised by this narcissistic asshole?

There's no way the man who talks me down from anxiety attacks, drives hours in the middle of the night to help me, laughs at my dad jokes, and gives love so freely has a father like *this*.

What disgusts me even more is that nobody will speak up. Instead, a laugh track from some terrible sitcom rings out every time Theo Gray speaks, desperate to kiss the asshole's ass. Ellen Gray hides behind her wine glass, and Keaton Gray, the brother I found out existed today, keeps opening his mouth as if he wants to speak up, but can't bring himself to.

Theo is smart enough to not be cruel to Kenneth around Nan or Karla, but he doesn't know me.

I love all of Kenneth's smiles so much. All of them except this one. The one he has plastered on tonight makes me sick to my stomach. It's tight and forced, letting the comments roll off his back when he deserves to rage and scream.

When he pulled me aside to warn me about his dad, I knew tonight would be rough, but I didn't expect this. I vehemently disagreed when he asked me not to react to a single thing Theo says about him.

Honestly, I'm proud of myself for already letting two of Theo's passive-aggressive comments past me without clawing at him for hurting Kenneth.

But once he hits three strikes, he's out.

"It's about time," Theo says, holding his champagne flute in the air. "You all know Ellen and I spent *way* too much money on Kenneth's swimming career. Thousands of dollars over the years. Private lessons, competitive swim team fees and meets, and an endless amount of gear. We're so glad he made our money and time worth it. Finally, a return on our investment."

The room breaks out in another loud laugh, and I flinch. My heart splinters into a million pieces as Kenneth's grip on the stem of his champagne flute tightens, that fake smile pulling at his lips. The reins on my control slip as another piece of him breaks away, shattered by the words of the man who is supposed to love him.

Strike three, Theo.

"Why would you say that?"

Every eye in the room jumps to me, but I keep my eyes trained on the man with cold, green eyes. When Kenneth wraps his hand around my elbow, I shake my head. I'm not going to back down. This was supposed to be Kenneth's night. A night to honor his accomplishments, yet Theo has done everything in his power to tear his own son down at every turn.

"Is there a problem, dear?" Theo asks, his voice lifted as if we're sharing an inside joke. "Did I say something wrong?"

"Yeah, you did. The whole purpose of this party is to celebrate Kenneth's win, and that's not what's happening here. For the last three years I have watched Kenneth fight to get where he is today. I know he appreciates every dollar you spent in his pursuit of swimming, but to equate all his hard work to being something he owed you in return for your sacrifice is low."

Ellen chokes loudly on her wine, and Theo's cleft chin finally drops for the first time all night. He doesn't look so powerful now with his mouth gaping like a fish. Rendering a narcissistic asshole into silence isn't easy, but I've successfully done so.

"Now if you'll excuse us, I have a National Champion to celebrate."

Without another word, I grab Kenneth's hand and pull him out of the dining room and toward the kitchen, where I know Nan, Karla, and a bottle of champagne await us. When I turn back to see the dirty looks being shot my way, all I see is him. Green eyes, so soft and kind, crinkled at the edges. The smile that I'd do anything to see is aimed at me. Genuine, a little lopsided, and absolutely perfect.

This is Kenneth.

The true epitome of joy.

Blades of dewy grass scrunch beneath my heels as I walk toward the dock. The wind whistles through the trees to welcome me back to Lake Anita.

The lake looks even prettier as the moonlight illuminates the dark surface and casts a comfortable glow over us. Our legs dangle over the dock's edge, and the twinkling lights add to the allure of the night. I'm so happy to be back here.

"Have you ever seen anything more beautiful?" he asks, looking over the lake.

"Nope," I say, but while his eyes are on nature, mine are on him, taking in every inch of the man beside me.

His light blue button-up clings to his broad shoulders and is tucked into jeans, because of course Kenneth would wear denim to an important party. His sleeves are rolled to his elbow. I'm sure that before today,

I've never found forearms attractive. And here I am, ogling his. Red hair flops lazily across his forehead and it takes everything in me to not run my fingers through it.

Maybe I went a little further than providing a buffer tonight, but nobody will treat Kenneth that way while I'm around.

The surprises hidden in my bag sit heavily on my lap. I'm a gift bag kind of girl. Wrapping paper brings on full-blown freak-outs over jagged lines and wonky corners, but for Kenneth, I tried.

Embarrassingly hard.

Friends get each other gifts. *Friends* celebrate each other. *This is totally normal,* I try to convince myself, but my shaky hands disagree.

"Has your dad always been like that?" I ask, putting aside the surprise for now.

"Yup. He loves to say terrible things under the guise of humor. Even as a kid, he never hesitated to hurt me. Swimming was my way of taking control back. I assumed that when I was in the water, I was in charge, and tonight reminded me I've never been in control. He wrote the checks, waiting for me to pay off a debt I didn't even know about." Kenneth pauses to swallow. "Theo Gray eventually always gets what he wants."

I look up, catching the tightness of his jaw. It's in this moment I realize he's not sad about his dad's disgusting actions.

He's scared.

"I know they're shit," he continues, "but I've never needed for anything. Never wanted for anything."

Except love, I think. I don't dare say it out loud.

"I didn't know you had a brother," is what I say instead, hoping this is an easier topic, and I'm certain it's not when he lets out an even deeper sigh.

"We're not close. Keaton's four years older and moved out of state for our dad's company right after graduation. This is the first time he's been home since, and nothing has changed. I was lucky to have Nan, Karla, and Cade when I was growing up. Billie and Violet too. I wouldn't have made it without them."

I wring my hands together. "I can't imagine you going through that all alone. I'm glad you had them."

"Me too." Placing his palms on the dock, he finally looks at me. "Thank you for tonight, Eddie. For standing up for me and making tonight special."

I rest my hand on top of his. "I'm sorry you had to deal with that. It was supposed to be your night."

"With you there, it was perfect. You know, Ed, from the moment I saw you freshman year, I knew I wanted to be close to you. I meant it when I told you I've been following that feeling you gave me since day one. Things between us may have started off ugly, but it feels different now. It feels good."

I look up at the starry sky. "Fortunate misfortune."

"Huh?"

"It's the phenomenon that bad things happen but somehow something good eventually comes out of the situation. Even though it once looked bleak and impossible."

Like Kenneth fighting with me on my first day of college, and now we're friends. Or my flat tire at the beginning of the semester, which lead to us becoming partners. I used to think he was the reason I was cursed, but I'm realizing he's the best strike of luck I've ever had.

He presses his shoulder to mine. "I think that's a great way to describe us."

We stand, but before he can head for my car, I pull out the two wrapped gifts. The corners aren't perfect, and the edges aren't even close to being straight, but he still stares at them in awe.

"Congrats on your win, Kenneth. I know tonight wasn't easy, but you deserve to be celebrated."

"Those are... for me?"

I hand him the smaller gift. "Who else would I get gray wrapping paper for? Don't mind the messy edges. I don't usually wrap presents."

"It's perfect," he says quickly. "Absolutely perfect."

Kenneth's face transforms from shock to confusion to horror as he peels the paper off the present. "A planner?" There's no trace of that phony laugh from earlier as he flips through the pages. "Of course you would get me a planner."

"I know you hate when they're too complex, so I found the simplest one on the market. It's less than fifty pages and only has the basics. No water trackers, mood trackers, or habit trackers."

He drags his finger over the beige cover. "I'll use it every day."

He unwraps the second gift just as carefully, and a jolt of something that feels like pure pleasure zaps through my toes when his breath catches and looks at me.

"Is this..." Kenneth's eyes glaze in the moonlight.

"Yup. Your favorite place in the world. You've got so many puzzles of cool places. I thought you needed one that reminds you of home."

The photo I snapped during our first trip to Lake Anita made the perfect custom puzzle. Cedar trees cascade high into the sky, providing shade over the water. Kenneth's red hair steals the show though, glowing on the edge of the dock with his back to the camera.

The silence is so long and heavy that I feel the urge to look away, but Kenneth is too fast, capturing my cheeks before I can, forcing me to meet his eye.

"You got me a puzzle. Of my home. And a planner. That doesn't make me want to hate planners." I watch as his throat bobs, searching my face. "Why, Eddie?

I smile. "Because I'm proud of you, Kenneth."

His features go slack, as if my words don't make sense. Saying them feels weird, but it's the truth. Kenneth is the best rival and friend I could have asked for, and he deserves to know it.

"I was sure we were going to kill each other when Dr. Martin paired us together, and we still might kill each other depending on the results, but this partnership has been the biggest surprise to me. I originally wanted it to crash and burn, but it's done the exact opposite.

"Competing with you is the most fun part of my life. Honestly, being with you is special, no matter what we're doing. Every day you get better, and I thought I'd feel threatened by that. Instead, I'm glad I've been given a front row seat to watch you shine. In the pool. In class. Everywhere." My voice breaks slightly, but I push forward. "I finally feel like I know the real Kenneth Gray. Long story short, I'm sorry. I wish I could take all my bullshit back, and I hope you'll forgive me."

Shit. I didn't apologize. I went on a full-blown tangent, and by the way he's speechless, I'm sure I went too far.

As someone who never truly trusted apologies, I've always overcompensated by apologizing for every little thing, usually going overboard.

"Hey," Kenneth finally whispers. "Can I tell you something?"

"Not if it's that you don't forgive me..."

He chuckles in that low way that makes me feel dizzy. "I'm not going to tell you that, because you never needed my forgiveness. I have loved every moment with you. Cherished every second we've spent together. Moving forward and making new memories is all that matters to me now. Seeing you with my grandma and sister. Swimming here with you. Seeing you every day, even when there's no reason to be together."

"I want that too," I admit. "Friends is—"

"No," he cuts me off, his voice barely audible. "Friends don't make each other feel like *this*."

The hairs along my arms rise. "Feel like what?"

Kenneth takes my hands in his, and my legs turn to gelatin when he says the words I'm sure will change us forever.

"Like losing you would feel like losing part of myself."

The honesty in his voice flips my whole world upside down. I look away, staring at our linked hands. His freckled thumb rubs mine gently, each stroke another silent reminder that he's serious.

No words come, even though everything inside me wants to agree because I feel the same way. Friends don't make each other feel like this. I know that much is true.

Because I've only ever felt this way with him.

"You don't have to say anything," he says, releasing me. "Tonight was a lot. The party, these amazing gifts, watching you make my dad speechless for the first time ever. Everything about today was so special." Kenneth runs a hand through his hair. "Forget everything I said. Please. Being friends with you is everything to me. As long as I get to be around you, I'm happy."

"Kenneth." I wring my hands, trying to replicate the warmth of his fingers intertwined with mine. "Do you really want me to forget what you said, or can I answer?"

He winces. "It depends on what you're going to say."

My mind screams at me to not speak. To let the conversation die now. To stay nothing more than friends who compete. But my heart longs for him. Every inch of the kind, thoughtful, and intelligent man standing before me.

"Disliking each other was safe. Rivals was safe. Friends felt safe at first. Now it feels like we're moving toward something I didn't plan on feeling ever again."

"Is that a bad thing?" he asks, and I shrug. "What do you know then, Eddie?"

"That you were going to kiss me during the scavenger hunt," I say. "And again during The Dip."

"And every moment in between to be honest," he confesses, making all the air leave my lungs. "All I do is think about you. Being with you. Making sure you're happy. And if it's not clear, I like you, Mallory. So much. I find myself talking about you to anyone who will listen. It's painfully obvious how I feel about you." He drags his thumb over my bottom lip. "It's always been you."

I lean into his touch, even though I shouldn't. We haven't had the talk. Kenneth doesn't know I need a copilot. Not just another guy who promises me the world but can't back it up when life gets hard.

Every coherent thought vanishes when he leans down, and my back arches slightly as his fingertips graze my spine. I track the slow drag of his tongue over his bottom lip, desperate to know if they're as soft as they look.

"We can walk away right now and go back to being friends, Eddie. Whatever you want is what I'll do. You're in control here."

Once again, my comfort is his main priority, and it solidifies my next action.

I kiss him.

I kiss him because I want to. Because I need to. Because it's all I think about. Because I like him too.

Hell, I can't even put into words how I feel about him.

A hint of sweetness lights my palette as his lips graze mine carefully. His hands slide to my hips, fisting the yellow fabric as if he needs something to anchor him to the ground. I pull at the thick strands of red that have plagued my every waking moment, and in this moment, I feel nothing but him.

This kiss is good. No, it's better than good. It's perfect.

Life altering.

Who am I and what the hell is happening to me? Kisses have never been this sweet.

Kenneth pulls back, his eyes never leaving mine as he tucks a hair behind my ear. "I'd wait forever if it meant I got to kiss you again, Eddie."

"I don't think you'll have to wait that long. Just give me a minute," I laugh, struggling to catch my breath. "What the hell are we going to do now?"

He closes his eyes, and I'm glad I'm not the only one struggling to breathe after that. "Let's figure it out tomorrow. I'm enjoying this moment a little too much to worry about what's coming next."

"I hate you and your lack of crippling anxiety so much," I mutter.

But all my worries are forgotten when his lips meet mine again.

Chapter Thirty-Two

I'm a confrontational person. People often think confrontational people enjoy arguing, which isn't necessarily true. Confrontation allows for honesty and transparency in relationships, which is necessary.

But today? I can't handle being honest or transparent, which is why I'm in bed and ignoring my alarm to get ready for my first official date with Kenneth.

Yes. I said date.

Two knocks on my door send Winry to the floor, trotting to greet the person on the other side.

"Mally?" Shay says, pushing the door open. "You better get up and start getting ready. There's no way you're going on a first date with your hair looking like that."

I pull my hood over my head and pull the strings tight. "I'm not going."

"What do you mean you're not going?" Cade shrieks, loud enough to burst my eardrums. Heavy footsteps race down the hallway toward my room, and he pops his head over Shay's. "MalPal, don't listen to her. I think you're *totally* date ready. Go just like that."

"Shove it, dickweed," I hiss, hurling my stress ball at his head.

Shay pulls him down by his neck to whisper in his ear. With a pat on her head, Cade blows me a kiss before leaving us alone.

She closes the door behind her and leans down to grab the stress ball. "Spiraling about the kiss, huh?"

I scream into my pillow as a response.

"Thought so. Adri and Jo are planning an emergency sleepover and movie night, so be ready to give all the details. Were you threatened?"

I want to say yes, but that would be a lie. "No. I kissed the man I spent years hating willingly. *Willingly,* Shaylene!"

"Was it good at least?"

She doesn't want to know the things I have to say about that. Not a single one is even remotely appropriate.

Dammit. I want to kiss him again. It's all I've been able to think about since last night.

"Mallory Ella Edwards! You're literally thinking about kissing him right now!"

"Am not!" *I so am.* "Okay fine, but it doesn't matter. Relationships are and will continue to be a sore spot for me. It's probably best to end it now."

"Bullshit," Shay mutters, squeezing the hell out of the stress ball. "I'm calling bullshit. Stand up and start getting ready right now. I'm not playing around."

"Oh god, I can't handle this right now. Let me go back to sleep."

"No! You're basing this belief off one failed relationship with someone you don't care about and your relationship with your mom, which has improved drastically. You are allowed to trust and be happy, Mally. The person for you is going to stand by your side on the good, the bad, and the ugly days. They're going to be the copilot that you deserve."

"But I don't want another copilot! *You* are my copilot."

"Duh, babe. I'm your best friend, and I'll always be your copilot. However, do you think the guy you're attempting to bail on would be a good copilot?"

I want to nod so badly. Kenneth would be an incredible copilot. Over the last few months, he has shown up for me in ways that opened my heart and mind to the possibility of a relationship. In many ways we're still the same, competitive and full of life, but now my heart is involved which scares the shit out of me.

"What if he messes up, Shay? Worse than letting me run home and not paying attention. An apology can only go so far."

Shay crosses the room and sits on the edge of the bed. "Do you remember our first fight after your diagnosis?"

I shake my head. I have a great memory, so why don't I remember this?

"You were at a party with some friends from class, and I got a notification that your blood sugar was super high. I freaked out. I blew up your phone, got dressed, and was about to drive myself to the party to get answers. Minutes later you got home, and I lost it on you."

It all comes rushing back to me. Our worst fight to date.

"You told me if I wasn't going to take this seriously, I needed to find a new copilot."

She winces as if the memory is painful. "Yeah. You tried so hard to explain, and I wouldn't listen. I let my worry dictate that conversation, and it could've ruined us. With the way I acted, I would've understood if you never wanted to talk to me again."

"Damn," I mutter, tears pricking my eyes. "How did I forget that?"

"Because you love me. I apologized like crazy, and the next day we sat down to set rules and discuss how we should approach each other."

I finally get where she's going with this.

"We wouldn't be here right now if it wasn't for the problem and the conversation that followed," I say.

"Exactly. You can't expect Kenneth to know how to be your copilot without talking, creating plans, and setting boundaries. Just like you did with me. Just like you did with your mom. There's a great guy asking you for a real chance." Pressing our foreheads together, she sighs. "You know I love you big, but you're overthinking this."

"I love you big, and I'm always overthinking."

As the door closes behind her, I roll over and stare at the text Kenneth sent this morning. It's a photo Karla took of us last night. His hand rests on my lower back, holding me steady as I laugh at whatever hilarious thing Nan said about Theo.

Kenneth's eyes are on me though, filled with the same adoration I'm sure I look at him with.

Cuddling my pillow, I send off a quick text and let my phone fall to the ground. Here in my bed, I can't fall harder for the one person I was never supposed to have.

Here in my bed, I can't get smothered or be a burden.

Chapter Thirty-Three

Kenneth

Showing up on Mallory's doorstep with a bag of Chinese food is a risk, but it's one I'm willing to take.

After asking for a rain check on our date, she hasn't answered a single message. I meant it when I said I would do anything to make her happy, and if that's leaving her alone forever, so be it. I just need to hear it from her.

After my fifth knock, the door swings open.

"Dammit," Shay mutters. "I'm going to strangle her."

I walk into the house, but I don't see Mallory. Cade's long limbs are sprawled across the couch, with his locs laying messily down his forehead. "Hey, Kent," he says. "Look at you showing up to get your girl. Did you bring me lunch too?"

I flip him my middle finger and drop the bag of food onto the kitchen table before turning back to the person who knows Mallory better than anyone. "Got any advice for me?"

Shay bites her fingernail, dropping her voice to a whisper. "Listen, I'm really glad you're here, but I need to know that you're not just putting in effort for now. You're going to continue showing up for her, right?"

I nod. "Every single day. I want to be with her."

Pleased with my answer, she leads me down the hallway. "Be patient, let her talk, be clear about your intentions, and I know you two like to play games, but this isn't a game. She's scared, and she needs to know that you're serious. And most importantly, don't make promises you can't keep. She doesn't deserve that."

She stops abruptly outside of what I assume is Mallory's bedroom door and awkwardly pats my shoulder. "Good luck, Kenneth."

Once she's gone, I gather the courage to push open the door and step inside the spacious room. My eyes scan the walls briefly before landing on the bed. Her pale purple comforter is wrapped around her body like a cocoon.

Closing the door, I take a steadying breath. "Hi, Eddie."

A groan leaks from beneath the comforter. "Son of a *bitch*! I'm not even safe in my own bed."

I'm not sure what that means, but her dramatics pull at the corner of my lips effortlessly.

"I know you asked for a rain check, but I wanted to check on you. I didn't mean to push you last night, but it's clear that I did, and I'm sorry. I had been thinking about kissing you for a really long time."

Two years and eight months to be exact.

"Why are you sorry?" She sniffles. "I'm the one who kissed you."

I wish she would stop hiding her face so I can read her and know exactly what's going on in that complex, beautiful brain of hers. Is it doubt? Worry? Fear? How can I fix it if I don't know?

"Do you want to eat lunch? We could talk after—"

"Not hungry," she says a little too quickly.

"Okay." I glance around the room. "Do you want me to leave, Ed? I don't want to push you—"

"No!" Mallory bolts up, finally letting me see her beautiful face. It's definitely worry creased into her forehead.

"Okay," I say, taking a seat at her desk.

She looks down at her hands and picks nervously at her nails. "I want to tell you something, and there's a chance it might not make sense. Just please hear me out before making a decision."

"Of course. What is it?"

She sighs. "I need a copilot."

A what?

As if reading my mind, she continues. "A copilot is the person who will be my partner. My teammate. As independent as I am, I'm human, and there are days I need someone I can trust to lean on. It's not always going to be sunshine and rainbows, and there will be times when there are more bad days than good days. Sometimes that goes on for months."

"Isn't that normal for everyone?" I ask with a smile.

"Yes," she almost laughs, "but I don't want it to happen again. To be smothered or treated as a burden. I care about you, and you deserve a burden-free life. Someone you don't need to worry about. Someone easy and fun. Anything with me won't be that."

"A burden-free life? Eddie, life will never be easy. I didn't have an easy life before you, and I don't expect one with you either. Living with diabetes doesn't make you any more difficult of a person or partner."

Her eyes are filled with worry when she looks at me. "I know that, but what happens if you decide this is too much? I'm too much. Do we go back to how we were before? Become strangers? Never speak again?"

"None of the above, because that won't happen. My days aren't complete if you're not a part of them." I wish I could hold her hand, press it against my chest, and promise her the world, but I know that won't help. "I want to be there for you like you are for me. Like you are for everyone in your life. Everything that comes with you, I want to be part of."

"You make it sound so easy." She turns away from me to look at the wall. "Your optimism and hopefulness could be nothing more than a fleeting emotion."

I try not to take her words personally. Mallory's distrust and fears aren't about me. They're about the pain she has experienced. The things she has gone through have shaped her life in ways I'll never be able to understand. As a realist, she clings to the most probable scenario, which is that I'll be the same as those who have hurt her, so I stick to the truth.

"Okay," I concede. "These things take time, so take all the time you need. We can go as slow as you want. You're the one in control here."

"I'm always in control," she jokes. "Being a partner to someone with a chronic condition isn't a walk in the park, you know?"

"Good. I hate walks in the park. They're boring. I prefer life at a much faster pace."

A glorious laugh slips from between her lips, and it cracks the tension in the air. I breathe a little bit easier, preparing myself for her next reason we shouldn't give this a shot.

"Right now, I feel uncharacteristically cranky, and I know if I check my blood sugar, it'll be low." After checking her phone, she pops a few gummy bears into her mouth and gives me a look that says *I told you so*. "It's an alarm waking you up in the middle of the night because my blood sugar is dropping. Or vomiting and ruining bed sheets or your clothes. It's having to stop driving because I spiked and suddenly feel dizzy."

She pauses to eat another gummy. "It's a lot, but truthfully, I love every single part of this journey. The good days. The bad days. Even the ugly ones. Each day is different, and I'm finally starting to feel comfortable with that. But with that comes boundaries I have to set, and I can't be with someone who smothers me or treats me as a burden."

She has said that twice now. Now I know what she's scared of.

I swallow hard, weighing her words. "You need a happy medium."

Mallory nods. "Exactly. And you don't have to be that, Gray."

"Don't do that," I beg.

The issue isn't that she called me Gray. That's normal nowadays, the alternating between my first and last name. This time, I'm sure she's using it as a wall to keep me out.

"Please don't go backwards, Ed. We've come so far over the last few months. Do you not want me to try?"

"I do," she says quickly. "I'm sorry. I just want to be completely honest with you because I'm scared."

"How can I make it less scary?"

She shrugs. "Communication is important. I need you to be honest with me. When it gets to be too much, tell me. Don't lie to preserve my feelings. Without trust and transparency, there's no future for us."

For *us*.

My mouth goes dry at the possibility of a future being spoken into existence, and she's the one who said it.

Mallory is just as scared as I am. There's a chance she could hurt me too. The conditional love I'm so used to could be right around the corner, but I know I can trust her to give me the kind of love I've always wanted.

"Done and done," I say, and even though her eyes roll at my promise, she opens her arms.

Like a magnet, I'm pulled toward the stunning, vulnerable woman I'm lucky enough to be trusted by. I practically sprint across the room and drag her onto my lap, drawing lazy circles on her back as she counts the freckles on my forearm.

"I'm really scared, but I'm also really excited. I like you a lot, Gray," she whispers, and the quiet confession makes my heart pound even harder.

"I like you even more, Eddie."

I'm about to kiss her when the door swings open, revealing Cade's silly grin. "Hey lovebirds, I don't mean to ruin the moment or anything, but all of this food Kent brought over is about to get demolished if you guys don't hurry up."

Mallory's head pops up. "Lunch?"

"Chinese," Cade and I say at the same time.

"Egg rolls?"

I loosen my hold on her hips. "Of course. Can't forget your favorite food group—"

She's up and out the door before I can finish. Cade gives me a quick thumbs up and takes off after her. The sound of my two best friends fighting like siblings makes me smile until a body hits the ground. I jump up, but my body relaxes when Mallory let's out a celebratory hoot, which means it's Cade laid out. Shay yells at them to calm down before three chairs screech across the ground.

"Hurry up, Gray!" Mallory yells. "I can't fight him off for much longer! No, Cade! That's mine!"

I follow the voice of the woman I'm in love with. For once, everything is going right.

Chapter Thirty-Four

"I DON'T LIKE BEING blindfolded and I don't like surprises, so this first date isn't off to a great start."

Even though everything is black, it's too easy to picture the slow, gorgeous smile taking over Kenneth's face. He gives me one of those low chuckles that makes my skin tingle and turns the radio off.

"Considering you've said that twelve times in the last fifteen minutes, I think I'm well aware of your aversion to letting me surprise you."

I groan, reaching blindly for his hand and frown when I can't find it. "You're being sneaky. Are you taking me somewhere crazy like Nobu?"

"There's not one in Clear Lake. Do you want to go there instead?"

"No."

"Good." His hand slides into my lap, callouses sliding over my skin before he laces our fingers. The thrill that surges through me from something as simple as his touch leaves me lightheaded. "Because I think you're going to love what I planned."

I roll my lips together to keep myself from smiling. There's no doubt in my mind that whatever he has planned is going to be perfect.

Quite frankly anything would be fun with him. I'd pick up trash on the side of the highway during a thunderstorm without an umbrella if it meant I might get a little more time with Kenneth Gray.

Even with his hand in mine, I can't sit still, smoothing my outfit for the umpteenth time.

With little guidance on dress code, I went with my trusty frayed denim shorts and a violet knit top. Per Adri's suggestion, it's unbuttoned low enough to see the lace tank beneath.

He looked like a dream in dark gray and black when I swung the door open, his eyes devouring me like I was a purple Skittle.

"How many first dates have you planned?" I ask. "I can't imagine you've had many if blindfolding someone is your idea of a good time. Wait, I take that back."

By the chuckle he lets out, I know my innuendo lands, but he doesn't answer my question, and without fail, my brain shifts into worst-case-scenario mode.

Does that mean he's been on a lot of dates? How many is a lot? Ten? Twenty? One hundred?

I rip my hand out of his grip to cover my face. "On second thought, don't tell me. I don't want to know the number of women you've wooed."

"*Wooed?* Are you sure you aren't an ancient old woman?"

"Excuse me. You're the one who puzzles for fun."

He takes my hand again and presses a soft kiss to each knuckle, his breath tickling my skin. "Would you believe me if I told you this is the *first* first date I've ever planned?"

I almost ask if he's joking, but there's no tremble of humor in his voice. Instead, there's a shyness that makes me want to wrap my arms around him and never let go.

"Why does that make me feel incredibly special?" I ask, squeezing his hand a little harder.

Finally, the car slows with the rhythmic click of the blinker, leading us into what I assume is the parking lot of a restaurant or movie theater. The usual first date locations.

When the car shifts into park, I reach for the blindfold, but he stops me with his voice.

"Not yet, beautiful," Kenneth says, and his door creaks open.

I smile at the thought of him jogging around the truck. I'm not sure I'll ever get over him opening my door when we're together.

The April breeze cools my bare legs as he helps me out of the truck, and as if I'm not already discombobulated, he spins me around a few times.

When his heavy hands rest on my shoulders to steady me, he leans down, his breath warming the shell of my ear. "You are incredibly special. And I'll make sure you never forget that."

Then the fabric falls off my eyes.

I blink a few times, shielding my eyes as they adjust to the real world again. It takes a moment, and once they do, the checkered flag that whips in the wind makes my stomach do a somersault.

"Go karts!" I shriek, inhaling the smell of burned rubber and gasoline. "I haven't done this since I was a kid."

Kenneth wraps his arms around my waist. "I've seen the way you speed in Flintstone and thought you'd love this. I originally was thinking about taking you to play paintball, but I remembered you called it—"

"Unsanitary," I finish with a grin.

Now I'm glad I didn't wear the miniskirt Adri tried to force me into.

Once through the gate, shrill screams of excitement shatter my eardrums, hitting notes I thought only Mariah Carey was capable of. The energy of the arena buzzes with electricity as the current racing group returns, whipping off their helmets with wild smiles and even wilder hair.

"So much better than Nobu," I breathe.

"Are you sure?" he laughs, pointing at the concession stand over his shoulder. "The menu is much more limited, but if you're lucky, you'll go home with a milkshake at the end of the night."

"Well, I am feeling pretty lucky."

He presses his lips to my temple, and I melt into it. Hell, I melt into him.

"Me too, Eddie."

The man at the counter beckons us to him, looking as tired as I'd expect from someone who corrals overenthusiastic children and adults all day. "Well, don't you two look happy." He takes Kenneth's cash and hands over two tickets. With a scowl, he grunts. "It'll pass."

I choke on a laugh right as the gate swings open, yanking Kenneth through it and toward the wall of helmets. That guy may be perpetually grumpy, but he isn't wrong. This kind of happiness often does pass and fade away.

But I have a sneaking suspicion that it won't this time.

Reaching into my tote, I grab my travel-sized bottle of disinfectant spray and give the inside of the helmet a good spritz. Kenneth hands his over, and I do the same.

"Lice?" he asks.

"Lice."

Kenneth taps my temple before pulling me against him. "This brain of yours is a masterpiece, Eddie."

I expect Kenneth to let me go when the safety instructor, Linda, walks up in her khaki pants and reflective green vest, but he doesn't. Apparently, we're *those* people now.

PDA people.

The rules are simple. Hands and feet must stay inside the kart. Helmets stay on. No bumping or rough driving. Obey the officials. Watch the road. No texting and driving. Stay buckled.

After I'm securely strapped into the bright orange kart, I look to my left and admire my date. Kenneth must have struck a deal with the sun because the evening glow dusts his freckles with gold, the precious dots begging to be counted one by one.

I check to make sure Linda isn't watching me and pull out my phone. Screw the rules. I need to capture this moment.

The camera shutter makes his gaze skate to me, staring through the camera's lens. I expect him to ask our question. Instead, he says, "You are so beautiful."

My face heats as I tuck my phone away. "I was just thinking the same about you."

The starting light turns red. *Ready.*

I look at Kenneth. "Be careful please."

His lips curl into a smile. "No warning about kicking my ass?"

"That was implied, but since you asked for it..." The second red light appears. *Set.* "Eat my dust, Gray."

The last thing I hear is a burst of laughter, drowned by the roar of engines as the light turns green. I mash the gas pedal and the engine sputters as I take off, whipping around the other racers with an excited squeal.

Not even in my wildest dreams did I think Kenneth would bring me here for our first date. It goes to show how well he knows me. To bring me somewhere where I can feel the wind in my hair, scream as loud as I want, and compete against him.

We didn't need to sit across from each other and discuss our favorite colors, television shows, or our majors because we're already ingrained into each other's lives.

He knows me, and I know him.

A blur of crimson hair in a crimson cart speeds past me, and my smile widens. My cheeks are going to be sore as hell after this.

"Having fun?" Kenneth screams.

"Hell yeah," I call out, keeping my eyes on the track.

I'm having the best time.

Smooth chocolate coats my tongue, the milkshake chilling my frazzled vocal cords from screaming for three hours.

We've been parked outside of my house for the last hour, chatting about everything and nothing with my legs thrown across the center console and resting on his lap.

"I can't believe you caught a charley horse in the middle of a race," he laughs, pushing his strong fingers into the tight muscle of my calf. "And I can't believe that guy pushed me out of the way to check on you."

I whimper when he finds the knot. "You were a little jealous, weren't you?"

"A little? I was way more than a *little* jealous. I wanted to be the one to carry you away and kiss it all better, but Mr. Firefighter had to swoop in and steal my opportunity."

"You're so dramatic. Brian might have bridal carried me to a table, which was sweet, but you know I wouldn't have let him kiss it all better."

Kenneth's smile grows. "*I* wouldn't have let him, Eddie. I did love hearing you tell him you were on a date with me. I had to pinch myself a few times while we were out tonight. Part of me wasn't sure if I had conjured up the whole thing as one big daydream. I kept expecting to look to my left and suddenly see Cade sitting beside me, but nope. It's you."

I pull my legs back to my side so I can lean forward. His hand instinctively reaches for the back of my neck, and he tugs me to him until our lips meet. Not tentatively like our first one. It's sure and certain and makes my body tingle as his lips move against mine.

My hands find his cheeks, because even I need to make sure I'm not dreaming.

"Before I get too excited and tell my mom," I whisper against his lips, "are you sure you still want this?"

Kenneth chuckles, never taking his eyes off me. "I want it all, Eddie. As long as it comes with you, it's all I'll ever need."

Every validation he offers mends my fears piece by piece. It didn't bother him when I needed to break after four races for a snack, or when my insulin pump fell off and I had to put it back on.

Nope. He stood on the other side of the door, making me laugh until I forgot I was in a dingy bathroom.

Things almost seem too easy for us. Our conversations flow as if the pipe from my brain to my mouth is left open, wanting to share every thought that crosses my mind with him. How my favorite color has always been amber, but emerald, the color of his eyes is quickly taking the lead. How I've had "Right Down the Line" stuck in my head all evening because he told me it makes him think of me. How I've never had a first date like this, and I never want another first date with anyone else.

I want all the dates with Kenneth.

"I don't want tonight to end," I admit, looking over my shoulder at the house. Jo's car is in the driveway because we planned a sleep-over so I can tell them everything about the date.

"Me neither, but it's late. I can't have you blaming me for your lack of sleep or falling asleep in class. Dr. Martin is always looking for a reason to mess with us."

I wait for him to open my door and tangle our fingers the second I can. The walk up the sidewalk seems too fast, and I know it's because in a few moments, I'm going to have to let go of him and go inside.

For so long, I wasted time fighting with him and missed out on so many good things. I'll never make that mistake again.

"I had a great time," he says, dragging a finger along my jawline. "I'd love to take you on a second—"

"Yes," I say quickly, probably looking a little too eager. I don't care. "Tomorrow?"

He leans down to press a quick kiss to my lips. "I hoped you'd say that."

I'm deprived of kissing him again when the porch is bathed in light as the front door swings open behind me, and the sharp chill of air conditioning nips the back of my legs.

"Kenneth. Is there a reason you're back nine minutes earlier than the time we agreed on?"

I turn around to find Shay in her pink pajamas and fuzzy slippers with her arms crossed. Her smile is small, but I've known her long enough to know this is the equivalent of a full-blown grin.

Kenneth wraps his arms around my waist and pulls me in until my back hits his chest. "I didn't want to get on your bad side already, Shay. I thought having her back early would give me a better chance of stealing her tomorrow night too."

Shay shrugs. "What do you have planned for my best friend? And if you say Netflix and chill, I will physically harm you."

I glare at her. We agreed to a second date only minutes ago. There's no way he's going to have an answer without lying.

"I made reservations at Tandoori Tales for dinner. I've got tickets for *Up* at the park, and then we'll likely spend the rest of the evening on your couch where I'll quiz her on the material for her biochemistry exam that's on Thursday."

My gaze jumps to Kenneth. "Wait. When did you make those reservations? And how do you know I have a test?"

"Three days ago, and I've been using my planner. Duh." He winks at me before looking back to Shay, with Adri and Jo now standing behind her.

Kenneth leans over and picks up a grocery bag I hadn't noticed until now. Boxes of our favorite candy fill the plastic bag, the perfect addition to our post-date recap.

"Thanks for letting me steal her for a little bit before girl time," he says.

"Look at you bribing us with sweets," Adri beams, taking the bag. She digs around for a moment before pulling out a bag of peach rings. "I see you wore your favorite colors tonight, Kenneth. Two stars for creativity, but I'll add an extra because you're cute."

Jo rips open a bag of jellybeans. "Five stars for consistency."

I glare at my friends, pulling Kenneth's head down to face me. "Ignore them. Tomorrow sounds great. See you."

Kenneth gives me one last kiss before bidding my friends goodbye. My chest heaves from excitement, already thinking about what I'm going to wear for our second date.

Tomorrow.

Shit. I need to call my mom.

I slip off my shoes and flip both of my middle fingers at my three best friends. "You guys are the worst. Giving me a curfew like I'm your child, when in reality, I'm the mother of this group."

"You're just mad that we interrupted your makeout session on the porch," Adri cackles, dragging me to the couch. "Jo! Grab the vodka!"

"Hell no! It's a Monday!" I shriek, trying to slip out of her hold and escape to my bedroom. "I have class in the morning!"

"So do I, but we have a post-date recap tradition for a reason," Jo reminds me, walking into the living room with a bottle of tequila in her hand. "Plus, you're the one who bailed on your original date and had to reschedule for tonight."

"So, if you really think about it, it's your fault we're drinking on a weekday, Cap." Adri tosses me onto the couch and gives Jo a nasty look. "Gross! I know you heard me say vodka!"

As if the word vodka makes her physically ill, Jo grabs her stomach. "There's no way in hell I'm drinking vodka with you ever again."

All three of them take a seat on the rug. Jo crosses her arms impatiently, Adri bounces excitedly on her butt, and Shay pours tequila into four small cups.

Three pairs of eyes look up at me expectantly before we tilt our heads back and swallow the clear, bitter liquid.

"Alright." Shay's smile is bigger than I've ever seen. "Tell us everything."

Chapter Thirty-Five

Kenneth

My voice is hoarse from screaming at Mallory all afternoon.

Well, *for* Mallory.

With one minute left, CLU is up by one against Wyland University in the last off-season scrimmage. Wyland's best kicker stands to the left of the ball, preparing for a penalty kick.

Mallory's eyes are glistening, scanning the kicker with an intensity that would make anyone feel violated. It's almost unseen, but the corner of Mallory's lip ticks upward at the challenge before her. It's amazing how composed she looks. Zen almost. Even with the roar of the crowd, the intimidating kicker, and all that space to protect, she's calm in the eye of the storm.

The kicker dashes forward, and I have no clue how goalies decide which way to jump. A thump echoes as the ball flies to the lower right corner of the goal with incredible speed. The crowd gasps, but not because she scores.

It's because of Mallory's immediate response.

She leaps to the ground with her arms over her head. Everything moves in slow motion as the ball makes contact with the tip of her goalie gloves, only speeding back up when she knocks the ball around the goalpost and successfully keeps Wyland University from tying the game.

I'm on my feet like everyone else in the stands, cheering as she gets tackled to the ground by her teammates.

"And there you have it folks!" the announcer screams. "Thank you for spending your Saturday with us in Clear Lake!"

Mallory wiggles out of the pile and scans the stands. I follow her smile, only to find a carbon copy of Mallory in the section over. If I didn't know she was an only child, I'd assume the woman was her sister. Their grins are identical, pushing the boundaries of their faces.

The team jogs to the edge of the bleachers, tossing their towels into the stands. Mallory heads for her mom's section, but winks at me when she passes my seat.

"Never expect to get your girl's towel," Cade says, waving at Shay as she jogs by. "They always give them to the kids on the front row or to their parents."

My girl.

We haven't had the official talk, but after three dates, it'll happen soon. Still, she's my girl, and I've been hers since the moment I met her.

"Shay's your girl now?" I ask, knowing it'll piss him off.

"Why does nobody understand friends with benefits?" He grunts and points at the gate. "There's MalPal. Stop messing around and just ask her to be your girlfriend already, okay? It's been almost three years. I can't wait another day."

"Almost three years of what?"

He grins at Mallory before turning his smile to me. "Of watching you be completely in love with her. Do something about it already."

I jab him in the side with my elbow and stand. He's right and knows he's right. He's my best friend for a reason.

Waving goodbye to Cade, I make my way down the bleachers. Too many people stand between me and the woman I'm trying to get to, clogging the aisles and hugging their players tight.

I'm ready to hug mine.

"Great game," I say when I reach her, pulling Mallory into my arms. Her skin smells like grass and sunscreen. The scent of hard work. "That last stop was amazing, Eddie. She really thought she could score on my girl."

She smacks my chest with her glove. "You're getting way too comfortable being all cozy and cute with me in public."

"Do you want me to stop?"

"Nope," she smiles. "Just acknowledging it."

We walk out of the stadium hand-in-hand, with Mallory's eyes on a swivel once we reach the sidewalk. "Did you see my mom?"

"If by mom you mean twin, then yes. She was your second biggest fan out there today."

"Oh really? Who's number one? Cade?" she teases, unbraiding her hair. "Would you like to meet her?"

I blink hard. "You want me to meet your mom. Is that—"

"Normal this soon? Probably not, but I'm okay with that. Only if you want to though."

Meeting the parents is something I haven't done before. Dating was out of the picture in high school, my limited free time spent working at Gray Construction and working for a swimming scholarship. Not a single person has caught my eye since meeting Mallory on the first day of freshman year, so I don't care if it's too soon.

I would be honored to meet the woman who raised the woman of my dreams.

When I nod, her eyes blow wide. "Are you sure? This is your last chance to back out."

"Eddie, I'm not going anywhere. This, you, is all I've ever wanted." I pull her to me and kiss her like there's nobody around, even though there are people all around. When I finally pull away, I say, "Plus, I need to see if the high level of energy is genetic."

"It absolutely is. You'll see."

The sound of her name makes us jump, and we turn around to find a woman running straight at us.

"Mama!"

Mallory sprints down the sidewalk, leaping into muscular arms. The woman's hair is buzzed to her scalp and gray. Bulging biceps pop out of her tank as she lifts Mallory off the ground, her eyes shining with pride.

"Great game, baby girl. They ain't got nothing on you and your skills in the goal." Bouncing side to side, she mimics Mallory's goalie shuffle.

Suddenly, she freezes, her smile somehow growing when her attention shifts to me.

"Hello," I say, extending my hand. "I'm—"

"Oh, I know who you are. You're Kenneth Gray." She captures my hand, shaking it with both of hers. "My daughter and your CLU Swim profile didn't mention you're practically a giant."

"Mother," Mallory hisses.

"What? I had to stalk the boy my baby girl wouldn't shut up about. Plus, I never got to thank you for taking her to the hospital when she needed you, so thank you."

Warmth floods my cheeks. "I'd do anything for her."

"I'm Riley," she says, releasing my hand.

Mallory makes a strangled noise from deep in her throat. "You still make Cade call you Mrs. Riley!"

"That's because I like messing with Cade. He always gets so flustered."

Mallory shoves a hand into her mom's face, yelping when she licks straight up her palm. "And now you see why she isn't allowed to come here often. She's a hot mess of a woman."

"You think that was bad? I'll show you bad." Riley turns to me. Her eyes are darker than Mallory's, almost black and sparkling with intrigue. "I've heard a lot about you over the years, Kenneth, but I think that was a different guy. I don't know much about this new Kenneth that's taken my daughter on three dates, but I'd like to."

I speak up before Mallory tackles her. "The old Kenneth was an idiot. Don't get me wrong, I love competing with her, and I always will, but this is significantly better than what we were before."

Riley lets out a hearty laugh and drops her hand heavily on Mallory's shoulder, snapping her out of shock. As much as I want to keep this at a slow and safe pace for Mallory, it's hard to not spill my guts about her every time I have the opportunity.

"Okay, Ma. Time to stop being weird. I'm sure Kenneth is busy, and we have plans tonight. I need a shower before—"

"You should join us, Kenneth!" Riley suggests with a clap.

"It's a girls-only thing. You need to abide by the rules you created."

"Don't use big words with me, little girl."

"Abide is not a big word! You're an English teacher!"

I love their relationship.

"Shay's parents surprised her, Adri and Jo are busy, and all of our reservations are for three," Riley whines, pinching Mallory's shoulder. "Don't be rude."

"I'm not being rude! You're being pushy."

I catch the worried glint in Mallory's eyes and speak up. "Mrs. Riley—"

"Riley," she corrects me.

"Sorry. Riley, I appreciate the invite but—"

"Please don't say no! It's rare that I get to meet Mallory's friends."

"Cade wouldn't have been invited," Mallory grumbles.

"Not true! He was invited once and bailed because he's too ticklish," Riley counters.

Ticklish?

Riley looks at me expectantly, so I look to Mallory. As much as I don't want to intrude on her family time, my judgment is clouded. Part of me wants to spend as much time with her as I can, regardless of who is around.

I'm also fascinated by their dynamic. Growing up with parents who wanted to be around wasn't my reality, so when I see something beautiful, I gravitate toward it. They've been working hard for the past few months to rebuild their relationship.

After a moment, Mallory nods. I expect a look of defeat or worry, but her excitement is palpable.

"I'd love to join you," I finally say.

The words are barely out before Riley has my wrist in a death-grip and pulls me into the crosswalk. She doesn't even know what vehicle I drive, but she clearly isn't one to ask questions.

"So, Kenny Boy. Can I call you that? I need you to drive because I got a ride from the airport, and we need to get to the nail salon!"

"Sure, but my grandma calls me that when I'm on her last nerve, so if I jump, that's why," I say.

"Stop, that's so cute," Mallory gushes.

I almost trip over my feet when I finally process what Riley said. "Wait. Did you say nail salon?"

"Sure did!" Riley beams. "Pedicures and then dinner. The first person to laugh covers the dinner tab. This is the first time we've done this in over a year, so it's extra special."

"No!" I screech, unsuccessful in my attempt to free my wrist. "My feet are the most ticklish part of my body! I'll wait for you guys outside. Where my feet are safe and untouched."

"Too late, Gray. You already agreed, and she clearly wants to see this through." Mallory kisses my cheek and jogs to Riley, pointing at my truck. "Both of us have ticklish feet. That's what makes the game so much more fun."

"Fun? Sounds like torture," I grumble, fishing my keys from my back pocket.

Riley and Mallory look at me with the same cheeky smile, and I swallow the rest of my complaints. I make a mental note to never put Mallory, Riley, Nan, and Karla in the same room. Those four could convince me to do just about anything.

"Fine," I exhale. "But if I kick someone, I'm blaming you two."

I weasel my way between the two women and swing open the passenger door for Riley and the back door for Mallory.

"Handsome, smart, and a gentleman? I like you, Kenny Boy. Now, to the nail salon!" she hollers.

What have I gotten myself into?

"Kenneth!" Mallory wheezes. "I can't believe you screamed like that!"

I roll my eyes, holding her by the back of her shirt like she's a kitten. I learn something new about her every day. My current favorite is that when she finds something hilarious, her legs give out and she falls to the ground.

"It should be illegal to be that ticklish, son. You should get that checked out," Riley chokes through her laughter. "All she did was pull your feet out of the water and you laughed! Quickest loss we've seen so far!"

Finally recovered, Mallory straightens and ties the knot in her top. Riley barely let us stop by Mallory's house so she could take a quick shower and change. Stretched curls are pulled to the base of her neck in a tight bun, a few hanging free to frame her face. A pale green skirt hangs down to the middle of her shins, with an eye-catching slit on her left side all the way up. Sandals show off the tiny white flowers on her orange nails.

As if I need another reason to stare at her, the wind picks up and whips the fabric around her thighs. Mallory's body is a work of art. Every curve, dip, and line perfectly carved and curated.

I cough away a rising need from deep in my gut, refocusing on the next part of the night.

"Well, I guess dinner is on me," I say, forcing my lips into a frown. "A loss is a loss. Where are we going?"

"Ida's Kitchen," Mallory says. "Have you been there before?"

"Can't say I have."

"Good." Riley hooks her arm with mine and pulls me two doors down. The purple sign in the window tells me we're already here. "You're in for a treat. I hope you're ready for the best soul food of your life."

Not even two steps into the dimmed room, a crash of hellos bellow from all over the small building, aimed at the two women walking ahead of me. Before we're even seated, a woman with a white apron bounces over.

"My girls! Welcome back to Clear Lake, Riley!" The three women hug before her deep-set eyes shift to me. "And who is this fella?"

Mallory speaks before I can. "Pearl, this is Kenneth. He's a classmate of mine and swims for CLU."

"*The* National Champion," Riley corrects her with a proud grin.

I extend my hand. "Hi, Ms. Pearl. It's nice to meet you."

"Call me Pearl, sweetheart." She gives my hand a firm handshake and winks at Mallory. "Talented and respectful. Handsome too. Nice work, Mal."

Mallory crawls into the round booth and covers her face with the large menu. "Can you guys be any more embarrassing?"

"Don't hide from me, sweet girl! It's been too long since I saw your pretty face," Pearl teases. "What can I get y'all to drink?"

We all give our orders. Once Pearl disappears through the kitchen doors, Riley opens the menu and looks at me. "Any food allergies, Kenny Boy?

"Nope," I say.

"But he doesn't like spicy food," Mallory adds, peeking over the menu.

Riley gives me a disappointed look. "Everything here is spicy!"

"No it's not. The food is only spicy because you douse your plate in hot sauce, Ma." Mallory knocks away the hand trying to flick her. "Do you mind if we order for you, Gray? I'll make sure to get things you'll love."

"I don't mind at all," I say, pushing my menu aside.

"Perfect. We eat family style. Three meals, three sides, and one dessert split between us."

As if sensing we're ready, Pearl reappears and Mallory grins. "Can we please get an oxtail plate, fried catfish and chicken platter, and shrimp and grits. For sides, mac and cheese, collard greens, and sweet potato casserole. Andddd... banana pudding for dessert."

My mouth salivates at the order. The price doesn't even cross my mind. This will be the best meal I've had in years, and I'm in great company.

Riley pushes out her bottom lip. "No chitterlings? So rude."

I lean close to Mallory's ear. "What's a chitterling?"

A look of humor gleams in her eyes. "You wouldn't like them, I promise. Shrimp and grits are more up your alley. She'll get over it."

"Probably not," Riley grumbles.

Mallory downs her water glass, and I stand to let her out of the booth. "I've got to run to the restroom. Will you get me a refill if Pearl comes by?" I nod, and she turns to her mom. "Be good, Ma, and don't be too... you."

Mallory's flowy skirt barely makes it through the restroom door before Riley does exactly what her daughter told her not to do.

"So..." she says.

And it begins. "So..."

Mallory's reminder from earlier comes to the forefront of my mind. Riley is a lot like Nan, a bit nosy, but it's all with love. No beating around the bush. No easy questions.

"Is she teaching you how to be a copilot?" she asks.

"I'm currently in the trial period. It's going pretty well so far."

She laughs, twisting the wedding band on her finger. "She's her father's child, I'll tell you that. He would've loved to see the independent, strong woman she's become." Riley's face falls slightly. "I'm going to make this quick, Kenny Boy. I don't know how much you know about our relationship, nor is it my business to tell you, but I want to give you a bit of advice."

I reach for my glass. "I'd appreciate that."

"There are a lot of things I regret in my life, but the biggest would be pushing my baby girl away to the point of almost losing her." Her eyes dart to the dark hallway. "My advice is that patience is going to be your best friend. Think before you speak and approach her with love. It's so much harder to come back from a mistake than it is to pause before you make it."

Long gone is the silly woman who has neon-green aliens painted on her toenails. Now sits a mother with regret weighing heavily on her chest. From what Mallory has told me, I know Riley is doing everything in her power to move forward and make things right.

I swallow hard. My response is on the tip of my tongue. That with me, Mallory will be safe. Her heart, her mind, her trust. That I'll do my best to be the partner she deserves. The copilot she deserves.

Being Mallory's copilot would be the greatest honor of my life.

But footsteps from the hallway keep me from speaking. "Everything okay?" Mallory asks, putting a hand on my shoulder. She takes in our secretive expressions and sighs. "Mama, what did you say?"

The thick emotion in the air is slashed by Riley's normal smile. "Nothing! I didn't bully or interrogate him if that's what you're worried about. We had fun! Isn't that right, Kenny Boy?"

I'm not lying when I say, "So much fun." I let her into the booth and we sit down. "And now that Eddie is back from the restroom, are there any embarrassing stories you can tell me about her, Riley?"

Riley claps, bouncing up and down in her seat. "Oh, I have so many! Let's start with the time she dented my brand-new car with a soccer ball. The best part is that her dad tried to take the blame."

I drape my arm around Mallory's shoulders as Riley dives into the story. This right here is something I don't have. A relationship with my parents where we can joke and laugh with clear love for each other. I'm jealous, but not in a bad way. I may not have a good relationship with my parents, but Mallory sharing hers with me feels special.

Chapter Thirty-Six

Kenneth leans back into the seat, rubbing his stomach like it's a genie's bottle. "That might be the best meal I've ever eaten."

As if he can feel my eyes on him, he raises his head to look at me, a sleepy grin across his lips. It's so sweet that the banana pudding goes savory on my tongue.

Mom takes a final bite of grits before letting her spoon clang against the plate. "Told you, Kenny Boy. Best. Meal. Ever."

Kenneth attacked the meal like he approaches math problems, methodically. He started with something he knew he would enjoy, the shrimp and grits, moaning as butter and salt coated his tongue. Then he tried something he was a bit nervous about, the oxtail. Then the chicken and catfish, which he called the safest option. I tried to gauge which was his favorite, but he gave no hints. Every moan, slurp, and nod of approval was identical.

"What did you like most?" I ask.

Without hesitation, he answers, "Oxtail. I'll dream about it for the rest of my life." He pats his belly with one hand and covers mine with the other. "What about you? What did you like most?"

I look over at Mama, her eyes fluttering closed. The moment she heard about Kenneth freshman year, she immediately thought he was going to change my life. Our arguments were buffered with talks about school and Kenneth. She encouraged me to have patience and give him grace, even after hearing me bitch and moan about him for hours.

Although we haven't had the smoothest path, here she is, mending and repairing our past to change our future day by day.

"Being here with you guys."

He pulls me closer to him, and his lips are soft against my temple. "I meant about the meal, but that works too."

Mama's eyes pop open. "Trying to make a move on my daughter when I'm not paying attention?" She balls her hand into a fist and holds it out to him. "Good for you."

I slap her hand away. "You're a heathen."

"Don't call your mother that!" Pearl chastises me. "Even if it's true." She sets the bill down and plops onto the seat next to Mama, the old friends picking up right where they left off from their last three-hour phone call.

Kenneth reaches for the bill, but Mama snatches it first.

"Nope. I'm changing the rules tonight. Your presence here tonight was a treat. Thank you for joining us, Kenneth."

The way they smile at each other makes me feel secure. I like the way it feels with him here. It feels right.

When we step outside, Kenneth's truck sits alone in the parking lot. I guess we had too much fun, considering Ida's Kitchen will be closing any minute.

Mama yawns, stretching her arms over her head. "You kids head home. Pearl gets off soon, so we're going to Eastgate. I haven't been out in ages and want to stop by and see Roddy."

"What time will you be at the house tonight? I'll give you a key."

She shakes her head. "I'll stay at Pearl's place. Who knows what time we'll be done, and I don't want to wake you up."

I nod. "I'll pick you up for breakfast in the morning."

"Not too early in the morning, please." She hugs Kenneth so tight that he lets out a squeak. "See you soon, Kenny Boy! Let's all get together one more time before I leave."

"I'd love that," he says. Once a tentative plan is made, he kisses my cheek and heads to the truck to give us some time alone.

This is the first time I've seen Mama in person since Christmas, which wasn't a great time for us. Since then, we've done a lot to rebuild our relationship. Although there have been a lot of hard days, each day we get better and work on our relationship. I'm happy to have my mom back, and I know my dad would be proud if he could see us now.

Once the car door closes behind him, she whips to face me with that *I'm gonna say something stupid* face on.

"Marry that boy," she whispers.

I slap her arm. "Did you get a lobotomy you didn't tell me about?"

"I'm just saying I think he's a good one," she says quietly, taking my hands. "Forget about your brain for a moment, Mal. When you think about Kenneth, what does your heart say?"

I've never been one to think with my heart. My brain has always been the one to run the show, making logical, realistic, and cautious decisions. That's why I smile when my heart responds to her question by thumping loudly, but not in a frightened state. Instead, it's calm and steady, radiating nothing but comfort and certainty. My brain and my heart are on the same page for once.

"It says he's a good egg."

"A very good egg," she agrees.

She pulls me deep into her chest for a hug and wraps her arms around me. For a moment, I'm able to forget about securing an internship, the Brain Bowl, and my budding relationship with Kenneth.

It's just me and my mom.

"I'm so proud of you, Mal. It's an honor getting to watch you grow into the woman you are. The strong, beautiful woman I always knew you'd be."

She sniffles, and tears prick behind my eyes. Mama never cries. While cuddled between my parents as a kid, they'd tell me that I got her energy and my dad's emotional side. I've always been the perfect mix of them.

"Daddy would be so proud of you, baby girl."

And there it is. Tears slide down my cheeks as I bury my face in her shirt. I haven't cried like this since the day of his funeral. The day everything changed. But this time Mama is here. We aren't on opposite sides of the house, alone and drowning in a sea of grief. Nope. She is right here, holding me tight as we keep each other afloat.

Five years later, and we still miss him so much.

After a tearful goodbye, even though I'll see her tomorrow, I shuffle back to the truck and wipe my face to rid all evidence of sadness. Kenneth seeing me cry again is the last thing I need.

I may break and tell him I'm falling in love with him.

Chapter Thirty-Seven

"What are we?" I blurt.

During dinner with Mama, finalizing our internship applications, and settling onto the living room couch to watch *Lilo and Stitch*, I asked myself this question a million times.

"What do you want us to be?" he teases, looking away from the television with a silly smile, but it vanishes when he realizes I'm serious.

And I'm so serious. Kenneth is patient, kind, and thoughtful. Slow to frustration and anger. Because he's human, he messes up, but his apologies are genuine. The man I'm lying on top of is everything I've ever wanted in a best friend and copilot. I want to give this everything I have.

As the final stone from the wall around my heart falls, my voice drops to a whisper.

"More, Gray. I want to be yours."

As if struck by lightning, Kenneth bolts up, taking my body with him as he sits up. My legs straddle his hips, leaving my skirt hiked up around my thighs. He's seemingly unaware of the interesting position we're now in.

He doesn't answer me, his face frozen and mouth slightly open.

"If that's even what you want," I stutter, desperate to backtrack. "That was so random. I'm sorry. I was thinking about tonight and... Shit. I don't even know if you want to be mine—"

"I've been yours since the day I met you, Ed."

I choke on a gasp. "What?"

"It's the truth. You threw color into my sad, gray life. I know that sounds cheesy considering you were wearing every color under the sun the first time I met you, but you were the first jab of pure happiness I had felt in a very, very long time. I wanted to be around you all the time."

A laugh bubbles out of me. "This was just supposed to be a game. Nothing more. How did we get here?"

"You've never been a game to me. The Brain Bowl is separate from the way I feel about you. The game is temporary and will end someday, but this?" He gestures between our chests. "This has never felt temporary to me. *You* have never been temporary to me."

I hold my pinky out. "You promise?"

He looks down warily at it. "Of course, but I know you hate big promises. You don't have to do this."

I lift his hand and hook my pinky around his and squeeze. "I believe *your* big promises."

Without hesitation, he leans in, his lips so close to mine. "I'm so lucky," he whispers, slipping one hand into my hair, while the other fists the skirt he's been staring at all evening. His fingers trail up and down my thighs, leaving streaks of heat in their wake.

"You really are," I tease before our mouths collide.

This kiss is much less careful than the ones before. My body heats up quickly from roaming hands, nips, and nibbles.

Pushing my hips into his, I yank his shirt over his head in one fluid motion, tossing it onto the rug. My lips find his neck, placing bites along his jaw and collarbone. Each freckle gets some much-needed attention before I come back to his lips.

He meets every roll of my hips with precision, sending bouts of electricity through my body from the friction against me. His hands find my ass, roaming over the thin fabric, and he groans against my lips.

There are too many layers between us.

I need them off.

I need him *now*.

Cold air chills my lips when he suddenly pulls back, his full lips pink and swollen. Each individual freckle across his nose, cheeks, and chin glistens in the dim light. I search for an inkling of doubt in his features, but I find none.

"I know emotions are running high right now, but if you want to stop, say the word and it's done. I'm happy being here with you. On the couch, fully clothed, watching cartoons."

My grip on his arm tightens. "Holy shit. Why was that so hot?"

"Someone respecting your boundaries? Not sure, but I'm happy to be of service." He rubs his hands up and down my legs. "If you do want to continue, I have one rule. I want our first time to have time and space, and that's not going to be tonight."

I cross my arms over my chest. "Wait, why do you get to set rules? That seems unfair."

"Do you have any rules?"

"Well... no. I just like being in charge."

The deep chuckle he lets out when I crawl off his lap sends my arousal into overdrive. "You're always in charge here, Ed."

Once in my bedroom, I close the door behind me and click the lock as his weight falls onto the mattress. My eyes fall to his hand in his lap, adjusting himself as he waits. An aroused Kenneth is one I've never seen before, and one I won't ever forget. I rub my legs together at the sight of him and imagine him between them.

I'm *going* to put him between them.

I drop my skirt to the ground in a heap. "It's laundry day," I explain, overly serious for someone wearing *The Hulk* panties. "No judgment allowed. I didn't think this would happen tonight."

As if he can't wait any longer, he crosses the room and walks me to my bed. He sits down and pulls me in between his legs, peppering the sliver of skin between my tank and underwear with kisses.

"They're perfect. You're perfect."

Instead of the usual eye roll that would accompany such sweetness, I hide my embarrassment by unfastening his belt. Before I can unlatch it, he turns me around and pins my back to his chest.

"Eddie." His lips brush my ear, and I suck in a sharp breath. "As badly as I want you to touch me, tonight is all about you."

I shake my head in protest. Doesn't he know I can feel him against me? His body is practically begging to be touched as I grind against his lap, desperate to make him feel good. And to be honest, if he's worried about not lasting long, I think he will be surprised at how quickly I fall apart.

"Fine," I finally say, because I can't wait any longer. "But I'm not happy about it."

"By the time this is over, you won't even remember being annoyed with me. I promise."

My instinctive nature to fight back is halted when he tilts my chin up kisses me so hard that it wipes the scowl straight off my face.

"You're so beautiful. Even when you're pouting," he breathes, dragging a finger from my pouted bottom lip, over my chest, along my stomach, down my leg, and back up the inside of my thigh. "I can't believe you're real."

I take in his flushed cheeks, swollen lips, and messy hair. His heart thumps against my back, and I reach up and trace my finger along the sharp edge of his jaw, pulled tighter than the strings in my belly.

"You watching me, Eddie?"

Yes, and he would know how much he's affecting me if he would touch me already. I push his hand down until it finally reaches where I want him the most.

Need him the most.

He clicks his tongue. "Tell me what you want, Mallory. I want to hear you say it."

"Kenneth," I beg. "Touch me. *Please* touch me."

I release him, watching as he draws slow shapes on the outside of my underwear. A heart. A camel looking thing. The letters *M* and *K*.

"I thought you'd never ask, honey."

His hand disappears beneath the elastic band and fabric. It's almost embarrassing that one graze over my clit sends my knees knocking together.

Kenneth chuckles, pulling my legs apart. "I thought you wanted me to touch you." This voice, deep and cocky in my ear, is doing something to me. "Keep them open for me, okay?"

I nod and lift my hips to let him slide my underwear down my thighs and onto the floor. His lips infuse my neck with sweet praises while his thumb worships my clit with slow circles. Pressure is already building in my belly from the languid motion, but he doesn't stay long, sliding a finger inside.

"Mallory, you feel so good. Perfect." My head falls back against his shoulder, watching as his sly smile grows. "And I bet you taste even sweeter," he adds. "*Fuck*, I can't wait to taste you."

Oh my god.

"Kenneth, please—" I start, and the sound that leaves my mouth when he curls his finger forward is straight-up sinful.

For a man who hasn't been with a woman in the three years I've known him, he sure as shit knows what he's doing.

"You have no idea," he says, using his free hand to play with the hem of my shirt, "how much I adore you, Ed. I've dreamed of hearing you say my name like this for years. *Years*. And it was worth the wait. So worth it. Now, lift your shirt up for me."

I do as he says, arching my back in anticipation for him to touch even more of me. My nipples harden as he presses kisses to my neck, rolling one nipple between his fingers. He lets out a throaty hum in response to the whimper that leaves my lips. I'm sure he'd be smirking at the effect he has on me if his mouth wasn't occupied with my neck.

Slipping a second finger inside, he picks up speed, achingly perfect and hitting deeper and harder than before.

"That's my girl. Right here, yeah?" he grits out, making the strings in my belly pull tight, and my pussy flutters around his skilled fingers.

"Stay there. *Please*," I stammer, so very close to my release.

Kenneth does exactly as I ask, unchanging in his relentless tempo to let the pressure build and build until I'm ready to fall apart.

"There it is. Is this everything you dreamed of? Because it is for me. Everything and more. Oh, I feel you getting close. Come on my fingers, Mallory. Go ahead and come for me, honey."

The smug asshole has the audacity to smile as I come undone in his arms, but it's the sound of his laugh that sends me over the edge into the best orgasm of my life.

"*Kenneth*. Com... I'm com—"

His lips and tongue swallow my words. Back arched and thighs trembling, I ride out my high, whimpering into his mouth with a grateful whine. Kenneth keeps an unwavering, slow swirl on my clit until I'm limp with exhaustion.

My eyes widen when he removes his fingers, promptly placing them in his mouth. A flicker of desire ignites when he swirls his tongue around them.

"I'm ruined, Eddie. Officially ruined."

With wobbly legs and my head spinning, I barely manage to move off his lap, my back damp from being held against his chest. He lifts the comforter and I slip beneath it, trying to figure out what the hell just happened.

Now *that* is how you make a girl orgasm. I thought I was an anomaly. Adri and Shay always go on and on about how it's supposed to feel, and now I know for myself. I make another mental check to why Kenneth Gray is my dream guy.

Intelligent. Competitive. Too handsome for words. Damn good with his hands.

The sound of Kenneth moving around wakes me up, pleasure replaced with sadness. We've only slept together once, and it was the best night of rest I've gotten in years. Warmed by my own personal heater and safe in his arms.

I sit up. "Where are you go—"

Denim hits the ground with a cling of metal, leaving behind navy briefs that cling to his toned quads, showing off even more cinnamon-like specks traveling down his thighs.

"You're staying?" I ask.

Kenneth gives me a funny look. "I'd like to, if that's okay."

"Yes!" I say quickly, not caring how clingy I sound. "Stay with me."

My favorite smile lights up his face as he grabs my bonnet from the dresser and clicks off the lamp. I quickly tie my hair down and take my place beside him. Just like at the cabin, I bury my face in his neck and intertwine our legs.

"So, you're really not going to let me take care of you?" I ask. Even though I'm worn out, making him feel good is my priority.

"Nope. Like I said, tonight was all about you. We're taking baby steps here."

"Baby steps?" I scoff. "Giving me the hardest orgasm of my life is considered a baby step?"

"I'd say so, considering it's the first of many. We're barely getting started." He lifts my chin to look me in the eye, and I feel his heartbeat slow. "I wanted to ask you earlier, but this seems like the perfect time. Will you be my girlfriend, Edwards?"

I press my lips to his. "It's about time, Gray. I was starting to worry you never would ask."

He chuckles. "Is that a yes?"

"Yes." I squeeze him so tightly he could pop, resting my head on his chest. "Baby steps feel like leaps and bounds with you, Kenneth, but it's as if everything I've ever worried about was all for nothing."

Chapter Thirty-Eight

When I step onto the dimly lit porch, I'm met by a surgical mask and the suffocating smell of disinfectant.

"What took you so long?" Cade scolds me, shoving a mask into my hands.

I cough, waving my hand in the air. "What the hell is going on? You can't send someone with anxiety twelve cryptic messages right when they wake up and then not respond."

"My bad. I was a bit busy with that one." Cade jams his thumb over his shoulder. "I'm pretty sure it's food poisoning. I got back last night around midnight, and he was in the bathroom. Said he ate at a food truck for dinner. When I woke up thirty minutes ago, he was still in there."

"He was in the bathroom all night?" I scream.

"I think so. There's a cute tile imprint on his cheek."

"And you didn't think to call me when you got home at midnight?"

"I thought he was taking a middle-of-the-night trip to the toilet! I didn't know he was in there puking his brains out!" he shouts, grinning when a laugh sneaks through my pursed lips.

"So, you texted me to be on sick patrol?"

"Of course. He's *your* boyfriend, which means it's part of your job description. I got him into bed, but that's all he let me do. He kept demanding to see his Eddie or he would, and I quote, never drink another sip of water again and wither away like sand in the wind."

I wish I had put the mask on to hide my smile. The word boyfriend is so junior high, but has that stopped me from grinning every time it's said?

Nope.

"Plus, you're good with things like this. You know I can't handle vomit," Cade continues. "*At all.* When people around me puke, I puke!"

I fake a gag, and as always, Cade gags too.

Growing up with a dad on dialysis, vomiting was a regular occurrence in our household. Every other morning he would wake up sick, often after my mom had already gone to work. It was one of the times I felt closest to him.

"Does he have a fever?"

"No clue. When I tried to take his temperature, he almost bit my finger off."

Men turn into the biggest babies the moment they feel under the weather. It must be some universal guy thing.

Placing the mask in his hands, I roll my eyes. "You don't need a mask for food poisoning."

Cade ruffles my hair and heads in the opposite direction toward his room. "I know you'll take care of him, MalPal. Call me if you need me, but not if it's a vomit-related need."

I take a single steadying breath to collect myself as I push open Kenneth's bedroom door. Scattered empty bottles of water cover the floor, and a mild smell of sickness lingers in the air.

"Kenneth," I say, placing my hand on the unmoving lump on the bed.

He doesn't give any indication that he hears me, so I sit beside him and pull the blanket down. Freckled cheeks are red and splotchy, with beads of sweat gathered along his brow and upper lip. Affirming my suspicions of a fever, he's got on the thickest hoodie and sweatpants he could find to fight the chills. I mentally curse Cade for not calling me earlier.

"Baby, it's me. Can you open your eyes?"

This time a single eye pops open. His icy glare thaws instantly when he recognizes me. "Eddie?" he croaks, trying to sit up. He rubs his eyes before giving me the pleasure of showing me both beautiful emeralds. "You shouldn't be here. You're going to get sick—"

"It's just food poisoning, silly," I interrupt. "And even if it was contagious, I still wouldn't let you be sick all by yourself."

He takes me in slowly, my big T-shirt, big sweatpants, and big hair. Pushing his fingers into the fluff, a small smile appears. "Where does all this hair come from? It just keeps going and going and going and going and..."

After the eighth *going*, I slap my hand over his mouth. "You're delirious. I need to take your temperature."

"No thanks. I'm positive I don't have a fever." He tries to sit up again, and I place a hand on his chest to gently push him back into the mountain of pillows.

"Stay still. Do you remember the last time you threw up or ran to the toilet?"

"Like three hours ago? I slept on the bathroom floor for most of the night. Remind me to never eat food from a sketchy food truck aga—"

I sneak the thermometer between his lips before he can finish his sentence. Defiantly, he pushes his tongue against it, but I don't budge. Finally, he loosens his lips and lets it slide beneath his tongue.

After a moment, the thermometer beeps. "Like I thought, because I'm so smart." Kenneth rolls his eyes at my braggy tone. "You've got a fever, and those layers aren't helping. Would you mind taking them off for me?"

Even food poisoning can't keep Kenneth from being smug.

"I knew you couldn't wait to see me naked."

Without sitting up, thick fleece slips over his head with a quick *whoosh*, while I pull down his sweatpants. Silly taco briefs are tight on his strong and toned thighs.

While he complains about how cold he is and that the food truck behind the gas station, which would have been my first red flag, will never know peace again, I slip out of the room to grab an electrolyte drink from the fridge. When I return, he's sprawled on the bed like a starfish. I take the moment of calm to admire this sight. Even with his entire body damp and flushed, and his hair sticking up in all directions, Kenneth Gray is the most beautiful man I've ever seen.

As if he can feel my eyes, he looks up and grins at the drink in my hands.

Or at me.

Who knows, but the butterflies in my belly are kicking up a storm.

I am a sappy mess for this man, and there's nowhere I'd rather be.

After a bit of convincing, Kenneth agrees to a lukewarm shower. I offered to warm up some chicken noodle soup, but it's clear the word chicken will likely trigger his gag reflex for the foreseeable future.

I drop a slice of bread into the toaster, struggling to shove the knob down when Cade's arm reaches around me and expertly pushes it into place.

I grab a banana and point it between his eyes. "It's been three years. Get a new toaster. They're less than twenty bucks at any store."

Cade affectionately pats the hunk of junk. "No way! We've got history. Almost catching the dorm on fire. Falling out of Kent's truck on the highway. Annoying the hell out of you."

"That last one is your main reason for keeping it."

"You know it." He rests his chin on the top of my head. "How's he doing?"

"Good. I think we're out of the woods. After he showers, I'll see if he can hold down some food and water."

Cade looks down the hallway. "I've known Kenneth since before we could write our own names, and I have to say, he's never been like this. Not once."

"Sick?" I ask. "Sounds like you guys haven't hit all the friendship milestones. Are you sure you don't want to clean his vomit?"

"Tempting, but no. And I'm talking about the way he looks at you." Snatching the banana, he sets it aside and steals an almond from my plate. "We haven't gotten to talk just us in a while. How are you feeling about dating again?"

Cade may be Kenneth's best friend, but he's also mine. I know whatever I say today will never leave these walls.

I take a quick peek at the hallway and sigh. "Honestly, I was perfectly content never dating again, Cader Tot. Celibacy and singleness were going to follow me to the grave. To be honest, I'm the weirdest mix of entirely secure and freaking the hell out."

He chews on an almond before snapping his fingers. "I have an idea. Tell me the worst-case scenario when it comes to dating Kenneth?"

"No way, Cade," I groan. "I'm not doing this with you. I'd rather not think about it."

Any more than I already am.

"You already are. I know you, MalPal." He back pedals until he reaches the counter behind him. "What's the worst thing that big brain of yours is torturing you with?"

I avert my eyes. "The past—"

"Nuh-uh," Cade cuts me off, and I yelp when an almond hits my forehead. "Jordan is an asshole who didn't deserve you. Kenneth is not him, and he never will be."

"I know that," I swear. "Kenneth is perfect, Cade. I would never compare them."

"Good." He tosses an almond into the air and catches it in his mouth before continuing. "Then tell me your best-case scenario when it comes to dating him?"

I don't even have to think about it. "I want it all. The best-case scenario is getting to be with him. To be his."

My voice is so soft that I barely realize I said it out loud, but every part of Cade's smile tells me he heard it.

"And your worst-case scenario?"

I pause. Originally, my biggest fear was losing control of my heart, but that's not the case anymore.

"Not being fun enough for Kenneth. To me, he looks like freedom. I've never met someone so fun, Cade, and I'm not. It's nice when I'm with him though, because I feel like I can be. Then I wake up and remember that I'm scared, inflexible, and everything he isn't. What happens when he realizes that too?"

He looks over his shoulder toward the bathroom. "MalPal, that guy in there believes you're the best thing to ever happen to him. Kenneth wasn't going to be okay when the Brain Bowl ended. For him, graduation wasn't just the finish line for undergrad. It also meant losing you, which I was sure would shatter his heart."

I freeze. "Then why did he keep playing if he knew it would hurt him?"

"For you. Seeing you celebrate when you win. Watching you pout when you lose. To him, it was always worth it because he got to be around you. He got to have fun with you. Your worst-case scenario will never, ever happen."

My cheeks burn. "Are you lying to make me feel better?"

"I would never do that to you," Cade promises, wrapping his arms around me.

The bathroom door creaks open, and soft footsteps pad across the floor. Cade keeps me hidden by his massive body and looks over his shoulder to face his friend.

"You look good, Kent. Upright and not threatening my life."

I'm sure Kenneth gives him the finger because Cade takes one hand off my back to return the gesture.

A moment of silence passes before Cade speaks again. "All good. Just chatting about how I'm never throwing out the toaster."

Apparently pleased with that answer, Kenneth shuffles back down the hall. Cade drops his eyes back down to me.

"Feeling better?" he asks.

I don't know what it's like to have a sibling, but if I had to guess, it would feel a lot like my friendship with Cade. He uplifts me, brags about me, picks on me, pisses me off, and loves me hard. He's the brother I never had.

"Yeah, I am. I love you, Cader Tot."

He presses his lips to my forehead. "I love you. Now go take care of your boyfriend before he starts feeling left out."

When Cade leaves me, my heart clenches at the wasted time I lost keeping Kenneth at a distance. I wonder how different things would be if we started dating freshman year.

Would he have held me after I got a C on my first college exam because I studied the wrong material? Would he have stayed up late helping me prepare to ace everything else to get an A in the class? Would he have taken the day off to hold me on my dad's remembrance days? Would he have sat with me through endless endocrinologist appointments and meetings and held me while I navigated the new changes in my life?

I smile because he would have. I'm sure of it.

With his food in hand, I knock on his door and push it open. The sick smell is gone, a woodsy candle burning at his bedside. The muscles of his arm bulge as he lifts the trash bag, tying it in a knot before looking at me. I'm staring like a creep, but he's my boyfriend, so it's allowed.

"Do you ever worry this will stop someday?" he asks softly.

"What?" I slip off his extra-large slides and set the plate of toast and banana slices on the dresser.

"Us."

My eyes search for the thermometer, just in case his fever spiked in the shower. "Are you feeling okay? I should take your temperature again."

"No, that's not necessary. I feel good. Actually, I don't think I've ever felt this good. Food poisoning be damned." Kenneth sits down on the bed, letting out a gentle laugh. "To be honest, I'm not worried about us. The way that I feel about you, Ed, it consumes every second of my life. Wanting you. Needing you. Missing you constantly, even when you're in the same room. Craving the feeling of your hand in mine. The warmth of your fingers on my skin when you count the freckles on my shoulders. The way that kissing you makes time slow down. I want all the days with you, Eddie. Every single one."

I cross the room, and he pulls me in by my waist. "Good, because I want all of that too. We will never end, baby."

His lips quirk up. "That's a big promise there. You sure you're okay with that?"

I nod, pushing my fingers into his hair. "Absolutely. You are my copilot after all."

Kenneth's fingers dig into my skin as he sucks in a sharp breath. "Are you serious?"

"Deadly. Easiest decision I've ever made."

Taking my hand, he places a gentle kiss to each knuckle before holding them against his chest. I'm reminded of why I'm so into him when he ends the sweet moment by saying, "Shay's going to be so jealous. I can't wait to tell her she's been replaced. Dethroned. Banished."

I swat his chest. "You better not! She's your fellow Guardian of the Blood Sugar. Don't get on her bad side."

He kisses my cheek and moves to the dresser. Popping a piece of banana into his mouth he asks, "Will you lie with me?"

I quickly agree, crawling onto the clean, lavender-scented bedspread while he picks at the food.

Once he's eaten all he can, the mattress dips as he falls onto it, burying his face in my thighs. "First order of business as your copilot, we should discuss your sick day routine. I read that people living with diabetes can have personalized routines. Testing ketones and whatnot."

And just like that, it's official. Kenneth is my copilot, and I feel like the luckiest person alive.

By the time he drifts off, my legs are on fire. While he sleeps peacefully, I work to finish my last donation letter for Dr. Martin. I originally was worried working with him would take up too much time, but I have appreciated the distraction. I love asking rich people and companies for money that'll go to a good cause.

A phone buzzes beneath my leg. I reach for it, trying not to wake the sleeping beauty.

Lifting the phone to my face, I expect an endless amount of eggplant emoji texts from Shay, who probably assumes I ran out of the house this morning for some fun.

But the phone in my hand isn't mine. It's Kenneth's, and the message on the screen makes my stomach churn.

Dad

Getting your office set up for your summer internship. Looking good.

What the hell?

Chapter Thirty-Nine

Kenneth

"Mr. Gray should be out any moment now, Kenneth." My father's longtime secretary covers the microphone on her headset. "I let him know you're here."

I give the woman a polite smile. "Thanks, Mary."

Gray Construction is busy as usual. In the years since Dad took over, the small-town, family business shifted into one of luxury, only focusing on high-profit projects. Multi-million-dollar deals are his specialty.

I should be out celebrating with my classmates because we submitted our final projects along with our applications for the internship this morning. Finals are almost over, and the semester ends next week.

The application I handed over to Dr. Martin was a cumulation of everything I had. I spent years going against my dad to prove I didn't want to be like him, and for once, I don't care to prove anything to him. My grades speak for themselves, and my athletic career has been full of ups and downs, but this is my journey.

Winning this internship is something I want for myself. Even though there was a chance I wouldn't be able to see it all the way through, I needed to know my dreams weren't too far out of reach. That I could make it all the way to a Doctorate in Biostatistics, and straight to the

CDC. I'm not ready to let it go. Which means it's time to share my decision with my dad.

"Kenneth?"

My head lifts at the quiet voice. I stand, but don't approach the woman in front of me. "Hey, Mom."

"I'm meeting your father for lunch. I didn't know you were coming."

I shake my head. "I'm here to talk to Dad, but it shouldn't take long."

Crystal blue eyes pierce mine, and if I didn't know better, I'd say they were filled with worry. But I do know better. Ellen Gray hasn't worried about me in years. I don't expect her to do so now either.

"Kenneth!" The booming voice of my father rounds the corner, followed by his suited minions. "Come and say hello to the team."

After shaking everyone's hand, answering overly-personal questions, and being the center of attention for way too long, I look at Theo. "Can we talk in your office, Dad?"

"Sure!" He gives me a toothy grin. My mom steps forward to give him a quick kiss. "Let's make this quick. I've got a gorgeous lunch date."

My father's office is massive. His gorgeous oak desk gleams, covered with blueprints and paperwork that he keeps meticulously organized.

He ushers me into a chair and makes his way to the fridge. "Would you like a drink?"

"No thanks."

He grabs two water bottles and hands one to my mother before walking around to admire the photos of completed projects that cover every wall. "You'll be part of this soon, Kenneth. My children and I running the business together. You should see the blueprints I had Karla draw up for the office expansion. I'm going to put you right down the hall—"

"I'm not doing the summer internship, Dad."

The harsh click of his expensive shoes halts, seemingly frozen behind me. For a tense thirty seconds, the only sound in the room is the clock on the wall. I've managed to catch him off guard, which makes me raise my guard even higher. When blindsided, Theo Gray attacks, pulling all the stops to make sure he ends up on top.

"Excuse me? I'm not sure if I heard you correctly." If I turn around, I'm sure he will be mockingly cleaning his ears out. "Did you... Are you giving up on your family?"

"No. I'm betting on myself."

"Betting on yourself?" He barks out a laugh as if I've told him a joke. "What does that even mean?"

"That I'm going to risk it all for my dream, and my dream isn't to work at Gray Construction. I don't know if I'll get into a biostats PhD program, but I'll regret it if I don't try. Even if it means I have to lose some things."

"Some things? Boy, you're about to lose everything. All over some silly dream?"

"Yes," I say simply, deciding not to fight him on the word silly. It would be pointless.

After sitting in the financial aid office and speaking with an advisor about scholarships and grant opportunities, I devised a plan. My athletic scholarship will be increasing for senior year, which will help a little bit with the financial aspect, and I'll be working as a lifeguard this summer and tutoring during the school year. I'll do whatever to make it work.

The hairs on the back of my neck rise when I catch a whiff of my dad's Tom Ford cologne. He rounds the long desk and sinks into his leather chair, lips twisted in a menacing curl.

"This decision wouldn't have anything to do with Mallory, would it? I'd hate to think some girl is the reason you suddenly feel so passionate about going against your family. I never expected you to be so easily distracted. Pretty face or not, she's nothing more than that."

"Don't—"

He cuts me off. "A crush is all this is. Something you'll forget the moment you get your diploma and join us at Gray Construction. This, your family, will last forever. Mallory?" Her name rolls off his tongue like a curse word, and my stomach clenches. "She is fleeting."

"Keep her name out of your goddamn mouth," I hiss, slamming my fist against the desk. "This is *my* decision, so leave her out of it."

Mallory may have helped me get the courage to do this, but he has no right to have her name on his lips. I need to get out of here and get back to her, because tonight I'll tell her everything. My dad's plan. My uncertain future. The fact that I love her.

Holding his hands up, he leans back. "I feel like you've got a lot to say, so say it. Tell me how terrible I've been to you when I've given you everything. A roof over your head, which you decided to leave as a teen. A vehicle with no payments. Free rent for you and your friend in a house that's much too nice for two college kids. A check every month for whatever you need, not including tuition each semester for a degree that I didn't agree to. Hell, without me you'd be nothing, Kenneth. So please, go ahead and tell me how I'm the world's worst father."

I shake my head. It won't be that easy to pull me back in this time. "I'm not doing this with you, Dad. No more back and forth. I'm done."

"Done?" he asks, his cool demeanor shifting into boiling rage as he stands. "There's no being done when it comes to your family. The people who took care of you and still do to this day! All I asked was that you would prioritize your family and the plan I have spent years setting in motion, and you couldn't even do that right!"

"I never wanted any of this! Not once did you stop and ask me what I wanted."

"Because I shouldn't have to! I'm your father. I sacrificed—"

"No!" I cut him off. "You did those things for *you*. Not because you loved me. Not because I'm your child. Not because you wanted to be a good, caring, or supportive parent. But because one day, you wanted me to repay you by giving up my dreams to help you meet yours."

As if I'm nothing more than an annoying child, he waves me away. "Karla would do anything for me, but I didn't even have to ask Keaton."

"Well, I'm not Keaton."

He rolls his eyes. "That's obvious. Keaton listens."

Months ago, my biggest fear about going against my father was losing the people who raised me. Now I'm questioning if being my parents means anything at this point. The people who feel like home don't make me feel like this.

"You said I would lose my family if I turned you down, but I don't think you ever cared about losing *me*. All you cared about is losing a future partner and employee. Losing the perfect father title you've created by minimizing the passions of your children for your own benefit and coercing them into a life they never wanted."

He bares his teeth. "I didn't coerce Keaton and Karla. They made their decisions."

"Yet you thought you could force me into one."

He drops back into his seat with a huff. "You've never been one to make the right choice. You were always the most difficult child. I was only trying to help steer you in the right direction."

It almost sounds like he's being genuine, but I know him. All he's doing is trying to pull me back into his web of manipulation.

"My decision-making skills are great. In fact, this is one of the best decisions I've ever made."

While I'm often hasty, my actions have brought me nothing but fortune. Asking Cade if he wanted to come swim at the lake on our first day of kindergarten. Switching my major to biostatistics. Making Mallory mine.

That one is my favorite.

"We'll be moving to Lake Anita when the semester ends in a few weeks." I stand and head for the door. "Goodbye, Dad."

Each step feels like a breath of fresh air. I did it. I stood my ground and now I'm free. Right outside of this door is freedom. A new start. A life with Mallory doing exactly what I want.

With only a few steps separating me and the door, my father claps. The three pops make me freeze, even though I know I should run.

"I wouldn't be too sure about that, Kenneth," he says, voice dripping with malice. "Maybe you're not as smart as I thought. Your grandmother may own the lake, but do you think upkeep is free? Electricity? Who do you think pays those bills?" He smacks his teeth. "You're sadly mistaken if you think I'll allow you to stay somewhere I take care of."

My body whips around, and I almost trip over my own feet. "What?"

The sneer that takes over his face tells me I've fallen right into his trap. "I'm not sure why you sound so surprised. Lake Anita is part of the Gray family, right? And you're clearly abandoning it." He shrugs. "It wouldn't be hard to sell. Would definitely go for a pretty penny."

He wouldn't. That's Nan's home. *My* home. *His* childhood home.

A gasp from my mother reminds me she's been here the whole time. As much as I dislike my father, their relationship has always been strong. He may not love us, but he has always loved her.

Without a word, she grabs her purse and runs out of the office.

He gives me a conspiratorial shrug as he hooks his suit jacket over his shoulder to follow her. My body trembles with rage when he closes the distance between us.

"I need to check on your mother. She's always been a bit dramatic." His palm pats my cheek roughly. "Maybe you should take some time to think about your decision. I'm sure we'll talk again soon, son."

The door closes and he's gone, but I feel even more suffocated than I did before.

CHAPTER FORTY

"HOLY SHIT. I WAS right," Shay whispers. "Jo owes me ten bucks!"

For a second, I'm excited for her newfound wealth. Then she rams the shopping cart into my ankle, which effectively shatters my happiness.

"Ouch!" I scream, jumping out of the way. "Watch it!"

Shay waves apologetically at an older woman grabbing deli meat. "Stop yelling like a maniac in the middle of a grocery store, Mally. You're going to get us kicked out of here."

"You ran over me, but you're worried about me getting us kicked out?" I check my ankle for damage, happy to find nothing more than a scratch. "And why does Jo owe you money?"

Shay reaches up and pinches my cheeks. *Hard*. "You're literally glowing right now. Even under these gross fluorescent lights, you look like a million bucks. Meaning you either started using that highlighter I got you for your birthday or..." Her lips curve into a sly smirk. "You got laid."

My mouth gapes at the absurdity of her logic. Are those really my only two options? I mean sure, I look put together with my hair slicked back into a ponytail, violet pants, and skin that isn't revolting against me for once, but that's because I felt like dressing up.

"No and no! Neither of those! Can't I look good without it being related to a dick?"

I attempt to get around her small frame, but she pulls the basket around to block me against the cheese display. I must have forgotten my dear best friend is a defender, a center-back at that, so she's trained in the art of making big stops and tackling if necessary.

"Don't bullshit me! I know what someone who got boned looks like."

"Really?" I flick her between the eyes as hard as I can. "*Boned*? You've been spending too much time with Adri. She's rubbing off on you."

Shay shivers, rubbing her forehead. "Gross. Don't tell her I said that." She recovers from her moment of disgust and gives me a sharp look. "And don't think that's the end of our conversation. Did you have sex with Kenneth?"

"Oh my god, you're insufferable. Can we not do this in public?" I hiss, attempting to squeeze through a small crack. In an instant, she covers the spot before I can break out. "Don't you think I would have told you? Gave you a post-coitus bestie phone call while he was most likely still in bed with me? Hiding my sex escapades from you isn't part of our brand."

"Well yeah, but the tell-tale signs are all here!"

"What signs?" I look down at myself. Nothing about me physically has changed in the short time I've been dating Kenneth. Other than upgrading my underwear drawer with more lace options so I'm not caught in cartoon undies again.

But Shay can't see those.

She waves her arms. "Everything! I said his name earlier and you literally giggled. *Giggled*! You're buying his favorite snacks for when he comes over. You've got that twinkle in your eye that I've only ever seen when you're on the field, eating good food, or playing a game for the Brain Bowl."

I pat her head. "Sorry, babe. My celibacy streak hasn't been fully broken, and you already know about that. You'll be glad to know that I'm very happy though."

There's a moment of distracted silence as she gapes at me, so I slip out of the cage she created. She's frozen to her spot as I pick up a bag of cheese sticks and take over as the cart driver.

"What's next? We need noodles and ricotta for lasagna night, laundry detergent, a bottle of white wine, the good toilet paper, and—"

"Love," Shay says.

Ruffling her braids, I laugh. "Yes, Shay. I do love you. Very big, in fact, but I don't think we can purchase that here."

She shakes my hand off. "No... You."

"Come on. You've got to use your words. I what?"

"You are my best friend in the world, so how did I miss this? It's so obvious." Her eyes blow wide, darting around my face. "You love him."

I level her with a fierce gaze. "You have officially lost it. Help me finish shopping so we can go home."

"No, I'm serious. You're glowing. You're sleeping better. You're going out without having to be bribed. It's been *weeks* of this! You. Love. Kenneth."

I steer the cart toward the household products. "Okay, I'm putting this discussion on hold. You're acting worse than Adri did when she found out about you and Cade."

Shay clomps in her bright pink Crocs until she's in front of the basket, and I screech to a stop. "Answer this, Mal. Does he make you happy?"

I wince as a fellow shopper walks by, definitely judging us for having a full-blown conversation in the middle of the aisle. Even though I would scream about how happy Kenneth makes me from the rooftops, I'm sure nobody in this store would appreciate that.

"Yes, *Shaylene,*" I hiss. "I already said that."

"Does he make you feel safe? Valued? Cared for?"

"Very much so."

"Do you?" she asks.

I sigh. "Do I what?"

"Love him. Do you love him?"

"Shay."

"No." She holds the basket tight, stopping my attempt at a U-turn. "Do you love him?"

"We haven't been dating for long," I say, because it's the truth.

"It's been like three years since you met him. Do you love him?"

"It's not that simple, Shay."

"Bullshit. Do you love him?"

"Yes."

I cover my mouth, but my confession is already out. Shay jams her finger into my chest, and I'm saved when my phone starts ringing. The most annoying tone I could find three years ago is still set for Kenneth. Now it makes my stomach flip with pleasure instead of wanting to vacate all its contents.

"You didn't hear that," I say in what I hope is a threatening tone. It's hard to be serious and smile at the same time.

"Oh, I heard you. Maybe I should channel my inner Adri more often. She may be extra, but the girl knows how to get answers." Shay puckers her lips when she sees his name flashing across the screen. "And don't forget to tell him you *loveeeeee* him."

I hold a finger up to my lips, my middle finger, and click the green button. Those words will not be spoken over the phone for the first time.

"Hey. We're at the store and Shay is acting up—"

"Eddie," he whispers, and my whole body tenses. "I need you."

Three words was all it took to send me running. Out of the store. To the car. Up the driveway. Through Kenneth's front door. I feel along the wall until my finger finds a light switch, slamming my palm against it before racing down the hall.

When I make it to his bedroom, the moon illuminates his hunched shoulders, resting on the edge of the bed with his head in his hands. Everything feels dull, as if the usual energy of the room has been sucked out, replaced with what feels like dejection.

"Kenneth?" I whisper, struggling to catch my breath.

Bloodshot eyes meet mine. "Ed. Hi. Is Shay alright? I'm sorry—"

"There's nothing to apologize for."

I leave out the fact that my best friend was equally worried when I hung up and asked her to leave. In true Shay fashion, she was ready to go the moment I asked, abandoning our cart and running out of the store beside me.

Pushing the wheeled desk chair, I move to sit in front of him and let our knees touch. "What's going on?"

The deep exhale he lets out tells me all I need to know. This is the end of us.

It's ironic that only a few minutes ago I identified my feelings as love, and now I'm going to lose the person responsible for it on the very same day.

Since that text from his dad, Kenneth has been different. Not distant, but distracted. Constantly scrolling through websites on his phone. Scheduling meetings after class. Every time I questioned him, he'd kiss me and promise an explanation was coming soon. That there was something he needed to take care of first.

"Are you breaking up with me?"

"No!" He grabs my hands and holds them tight. "God, no, Eddie. Losing you is the last thing I want." His finger pauses its stroll across my wrist as he looks at me, a crease forming between his brows. "I never thought you and I would be here right now. Like this. I thought you were going to laugh in my face when I brought up the idea of being more than people who played the Brain Bowl, but it's evolved into so much more. If I had known, I would have told you immediately, I swear. I just wanted to make sure we were okay before everything changed."

My shoulders tense as I blurt, "Told me what? Why would things change between us?"

"It's... I don't know. I wanted to fix it all on my own. This semester was important for a lot of reasons, and telling you that the Brain Bowl could be ending early would've ruined things. I didn't want to upset you, and I didn't want you to know that I'm a coward who can't even stand up for myself."

I'm so confused that I lose my ability to form sentences. A coward?

"I'm sorry, Ed," he continues, and I hate the sound of guilt straining his voice. "There's an internship for Gray Construction this summer. I tried to find a way out of it, but my father isn't budging. This internship is only the beginning though. It'll change everything. My career plans. My goals."

There it is. An explanation for the text from his dad.

Summer internship.

What's worse is that for some unknown reason, he's more worried about disappointing me by having to end the Brain Bowl, rather than the reality that everything he's worked hard for is being ripped away.

Gut-wrenching fear transforms into something I can't accurately describe without wanting to scream at his father. It twists and churns nauseatingly until I finally have to break the silence and tell him the truth. Something I realized long ago, but haven't admitted out loud.

"I..." I swallow hard. "I don't care about the Brain Bowl."

His head pops up, saddened eyes full of worry. "What?"

I'm not surprised by his shock. We've spent years putting so much time and energy into this game. Fighting to win. Dreading the losses. Making it our sole mission to beat the other. And while competing with Kenneth is important to our history, what matters more than anything is our future.

"I don't care about the Brain Bowl," I repeat. "Even if it has to end earlier than planned, I'm okay with that. I care about *you*, Gray. Being with you. If the game went away right now, forever, I'd be perfectly content because I'm completely and whole-heartedly yours."

I take a seat on the bed, pressing our thighs together. His head falls heavily onto my shoulder, and a noticeable shift in the air is felt as he lets out a shaky exhale.

"I don't deserve you," he breathes.

I push my hand through his hair, calmed by the soft strands. "You're right. You deserve so much more. Now, tell me what's going on."

With a kiss to my shoulder, he explains. "If I pursue MS research, I'll essentially be cut off by my family, which means I'd have very little time for the game. I would have to work to make sure I can afford senior year, my PhD aspirations, and life on my own." Kenneth fiddles with a frayed string on my pants. "And if I go with my dad, I'll be back in Bryan almost every day preparing for my job as one of the suits for Gray Construction."

My mouth gapes. "So, it's your dream or your dad... That means—"

"It would all be over. Every thing I've worked so hard for."

There's no way he's serious. No parent should do this to their child. Kenneth has spent years working his ass off to be at the top of his class, setting his sights on working to change the lives of people like Nan. All Kenneth has ever wanted from his dad is love and support, and Theo continues to give him the complete opposite.

He clears his throat and continues. "It would be tough without them, but not impossible, and I had it all planned out. Financial aid, moving out of the house he pays for, getting two jobs. It was all going to work out."

"What changed?" I ask.

Kenneth's eyes land on the photo of Nan by his desk. "He told me that while Nan may own Lake Anita, he's the one that pays the bills. I didn't know that. I thought Nan... I don't know what I was thinking, but I didn't think he'd threaten to sell it." Anger radiates from him as he stands and starts to pace back and forth across the carpet. "It'll be gone, Eddie. All of it. The dock. The lake. The place where Nan taught me to swim. The place Cade and I grew up. Where it all started for us."

My hand flies to cover my mouth. Lake Anita is Kenneth's soft spot. It's the place he cares most about because it's part of him, and his father is threatening to take it all away.

"That's fucked," is all I can manage.

He gives me a weak laugh. "So fucked."

The curse word leaving his lips makes both of us laugh for real, breaking some of the tension in the room. Kenneth comes back toward me and kneels between my legs. Looking at him hurts every part of me. His eyes are so somber that I have to close mine to keep myself from crying for him.

"I hope you can forgive me for not telling you sooner. I'm sorry, Eddie. I'm so sorry."

I want to tell him that I don't feel upset or slighted. I'm sad. Sad for the loss that he will have to deal with no matter what decision he makes. His passions or the place he calls home. All semester he held onto the pressure of this ultimatum while acing his classes, being a star in the pool, and working hard for an internship he knew he might never get to complete.

"Apology accepted, but not needed." I guide him up and bring him onto the mattress with me, lying on my back with his head on my chest. "You've got to do what's best for you, Gray. Not your dad. Not me. Not anybody else. Because you're the one affected by this decision. Just remember that no matter what path you choose, I'll be right here by your side. I'm not going anywhere."

For the first time all night, his heartbeat slows, dulling to a soft thud against my hip. "You promise?" he asks.

I choose the three-word phrase I know is safe to say and hook our pinkies.

"The biggest promise."

Chapter Forty-One

Kenneth

My Google search on how to steal property and suing a parent for emotional damage came up short once again, so I'm back at square one.

My home or my dream.

I sink into Nan's leather chair and prop my feet onto the coffee table, which sends our partially-done puzzle to the ground. Nan enters her room with a wheeze, which would worry me if she hadn't just finished physical therapy. Copper hair is pulled into a ponytail at the top of her head like one of those adorable troll dolls, flopping as she shakes her head at me.

"Kenny Boy! I've been working on that for weeks!" She strides toward her mini fridge with ease, and I can't help but smile at the progress she's made since moving into Eberly Assisted Living.

I bend over to pick up the pieces of gorgeous bluebonnets and rolling green hills, placing them in the box. "It's less than five hundred pieces. You used to put these together in no time."

"Yeah, but that was back when I wasn't blind as a bat and my temper wasn't as short. Being old is really killing my vibe." She lets out a yelp as she stretches her back. "How's my girl doing?"

I smile for the first time all day, thinking of my beautiful girlfriend. "She's okay. Mostly oscillating between letting me come to terms with everything and threatening to go down to Bryan and talk to Theo herself. But with the gala tomorrow night, she has been busy with last-minute touches."

She grunts, falling into the seat beside me. "Wow, is it already that time? Your junior year really flew by. Have you gotten your internship letters?"

"Not yet. Dr. Martin said the committee needed extra time. We should get them tomorrow before the gala."

Regardless of the winner, we've already decided to go to the gala together, which, of course, doesn't feel like a punishment to either of us. I don't mind fetching Mallory those little quiches all night. As long as she's beside me, I'll be happy.

With one last smile, Nan asks the question I wanted to avoid. "What are you going to do, Fishie?"

I shrug, sinking deeper into the couch. "No clue."

"You only have a few days left. What's holding you back from making a decision?" she continues.

"So many things. Lake Anita is *our* home. If it's gone, what's left?"

Nan falls silent, seemingly mulling everything over. After a moment, she says, "The memories. That's what is left."

I scoff. "The memories? Nan, come on."

"You must've forgotten that I haven't been able to live at my home. It's been *years*, Kenny Boy. My bed. My kitchen. My garden. My lake. The place I love most is only three minutes down the road, but some days it feels like I'm thousands of miles away. I'm only able to go home on the lucky days when you take me, which I love, but it hurts every single time. Memories are all I have now." Nan gives me a disappointed head shake, and regret sits heavily on my chest as she shuffles away from me.

"I'm sorry. I shouldn't have said that," I say quickly. Fracturing my relationship with Nan is the last thing I need right now.

When I turn around, Nan is on the ground reaching for something under the bed. Without wincing, she stands and dusts whatever she found off. She still doesn't speak to me as she walks back to the couch and drops something heavy in my lap.

It's a photo album, worn from years of flipping through it at the dining table with Nan and Karla, stuffed with photos we took on disposable cameras. I smile at the first picture. It's so familiar. Red hair, a mess of freckles, and the dock that looks like it could collapse. Beneath the photo in Nan's messy handwriting reads "*Kenneth, 4.*"

"I know it sounds silly, but this is what I hold tight to. The moments I'll cherish long after Lake Anita no longer belongs to us."

She flips to a photo of Cade pushing Karla on the swing-set, moments before she accidentally kicked him in the stomach, and he tossed her into the lake. The next is of Nan, replanting tomatoes in her garden because I kept picking them before they were ripe. A rare photo of Keaton surrounded by Easter eggs makes me pause. He's seated on Nan's lap, smiling at whatever she whispered into his ear.

"It was impossible to capture every moment on camera, but I'm holding onto the ones in here and in my head for dear life." She rubs her finger over a photo of my mother and father, their smiles wide and arms wrapped around each other. "Your father had just proposed to Ellen. Right there on the dock at Lake Anita. I sat inside, patiently waiting so we could all celebrate. Theo was so happy that day."

"Wait. They got engaged at the lake?" I ask.

She nods. "Your dad loved Lake Anita. He still loves it, even though he may not act like it. That's why he pays for it and takes care of it." Flashes of nostalgia hit me as she flips through the pages. "Still, using it as a means to control you will never be okay."

After a few minutes, she closes the book and puts it aside. "I think you know what you want, but you're afraid to tell me, so I'll say it for you. Let Lake Anita go."

My eyes widen. "What?"

She leans up to pat my cheek and sighs. "Let it go and treasure the good things Lake Anita brought you. The shared experiences, meaningful conversations, and emotional connections with the people you love. Your future is the only thing that matters to me, Fishie. I'd give it all up for you."

Disappointing Nan is the last thing I want to do, and I believed that no matter what I chose, both options would do just that. But here she is, letting go of her home to free me of my father's games.

I stand and pull her up, resting my chin on the top of her head. "I love you, Nan."

"I love you more. Memories may fade, but your love for Lake Anita will never die."

There's one specific memory that I never want to lose. Mallory's first time at the lake plays clearly in my mind. There was so much uncertainty in her eyes as we stood on the dock hand in hand, but she allowed me to take the plunge with her. That day, she gave me a piece of her I never thought I'd have.

Her trust.

Three quick knocks pull us apart as the door slowly creaks open, and I return the confused look Nan gives me. She isn't expecting any visitors today. Auburn waves and the massive diamond ring tell me exactly who is walking into Nan's room, but I can't believe it.

"Mom?"

When she looks up, she doesn't seem surprised to see me. Actually, she looks relieved, shifting the large gift basket in her arms. "I was headed to Clear Lake to speak with you and saw your truck in the parking lot."

Ellen walks over to Nan and hands over the basket. It's similar to the ones Nan has been receiving once a month since moving into Eberly Assisted Living, filled with her favorite snacks and other goodies. "I wanted to deliver this in person today. I'm sorry for leaving them on your doorstep for so long, Sandy."

After pressing a quick kiss to Nan's cheek, she looks at me. "Can we talk, Kenneth?"

Nan stands before I can say no, heading for the door. "Thank you, Ellen. I always knew it was you leaving these for me. You've always indulged my love of sour candies. I'm going to see Titus, so I'll be back." She throws me a glare that says "*be nice*" and closes the door behind her.

I've never really understood my mother, and this moment compounds my confusion. The same woman who sits idly by and allows my father to run rampant in his children's lives also sends her mother-in-law monthly gifts?

We take a seat on the couch, keeping a respectable distance between us like she always has.

Always there, but never close.

"Your father—" she starts, and I hold my hand up. Every excuse she has made for him over the years started like this, and I'm over it.

"No. I'm not going to sit here while you continue to make excuses for him and tell me how I'm being a terrible son by wanting to get out."

"Kenneth—"

"No!" I shout, shocked by the anger that slips out. On the tip of my tongue are words I have never been able to say. Betrayal I haven't been able to express to either of my parents. "You've never been on my side. He's so worried about his image, and you've always been ready and willing to help him push that agenda, even if it means letting your kids suffer. Instead of helping, you were silent. And you've stayed silent for years. You saw everything and did nothing. How is that right, Mom?"

The spacious room feels cramped as my words fill the empty space. The fury I've been sitting on for years is finally out, and even though I want to see exactly how my words affect her, I turn away and focus on the show playing silently on the television. Along with the feeling of satisfaction, guilt weasels its way into my heart.

"I know," she finally croaks, her voice thick. The way my frustration cracks from the two words makes me pause, because that's not what I was expecting. "I know, Kenneth. I wish I could go back to fix things with you and Keaton. I regret not showing up for you both every single day."

I force myself to look at her. "Keaton? What are you talking about?"

For the first time, my composed mother looks distraught. "You don't know?"

She grabs the photo album from the coffee table and drags her finger along a photo of Keaton. "Your father was so excited about Keaton joining the family business. His oldest child. Theo had such high expectations for him. Then Keaton came to me right before his college graduation. He said there were things he wanted to experience and do on his own. Things that didn't include working for Gray Construction. All he wanted was a way out, and I did nothing to help him."

My brain struggles to process this new information. Keaton didn't want this life either? Why wouldn't he say anything to me about it? He was the first person I called when I changed my major. Not because we were close, but because I hoped he would understand my struggles with not wanting to join the family business. Wanting something more for myself.

He never even called me back.

"Is that why he's based out of state?" I ask.

She nods. "The least I could do was get him out of Bryan. I told your father it would be a good opportunity to expand the business. After that, Keaton stopped speaking to me."

My heart breaks for my brother. I bet he's a million times happier not having to be in town with our father, but he didn't truly escape. He may be hundreds of miles away, but he's still stuck under Theo Gray's thumb.

"Is that what you came here to tell me?" I ask.

"Yes and no." Pulling a piece of paper from her massive purse, she hands it over. "I can't watch another one of my children go through this, so I struck a deal. Your father either lets you go and continues to take care of the lake for you and Nan, or I leave and ruin the family image."

Disbelief slices through my chest as I open the letter, morphing into relief as I read the terms of their agreement. While there will be no contact, no financial help from my father for my education or career pursuits, and I'll be on my own, Lake Anita will be safe from his threats.

"Mom this is..." I choke out. "Why?"

"A mother is supposed to protect her children, and I didn't do that. I spent so much of your childhood silent because I believed that it would be easier that way for everyone. I see now that hiding away only caused more harm for you all. And I know I'm too late, years late, but I'll spend the rest of my life trying to make it up to you and Keaton. I don't deserve your forgiveness. I never will, but I truly am sorry." She reaches for my hand, and I let her take it. "I'm so proud of you, Kenneth. You'll forever be my bright boy, always fighting back. I'll be in your corner for anything you need moving forward."

A warmth spreads through me at her words. These are words I never thought I'd hear. Words that make me feel like there's a chance to still have a parent and chase my own dreams. Squeezing her hand, I feel like a kid again. But instead of staring up at my mother and trying to figure out whose team she is on, I'm sure that she's truly on mine.

"Won't that violate the agreement?" I ask. "Talking to me."

She points at a piece of text. "Nope. Ellen Gray, mother, may continue a relationship with her son, Kenneth Gray, as long as he is agreeable."

It feels foreign to laugh with my mom, but damn it feels good. After years of working in the legal department for Gray Construction, writing and reviewing contracts, she knew exactly how to make sure she was protected.

"Are you sure you want to do this, Mom?"

She stands. "I love your father, but I've spent too much time watching my family be ripped apart over unrealistic expectations and my inability to speak up. The only thing that matters to me is my children's happiness. You being happy is enough. Are you happy, Kenneth?"

I smile. "I really am."

Standing, I link our arms as we head to find Nan. I'll invite her to lunch at Sunshine Junction, and maybe Dr. Hope will let us take Nan too. I'm not ready for my afternoon with either of them to end, and I'm sure Nan and my mother have a lot to catch up on.

"Now tell me all about Mallory. I need to know about the beautiful woman who went off on your father. I like her already."

Chapter Forty-Two

Mallory

Today's the day.

The sheet of paper inside this envelope will tell me if all my hard work was enough.

If I was enough. Smart enough. Determined enough.

The click of my heels against the hard floor gains Winry's attention, watching me pace back and forth across my bedroom as I lift the envelope up to the light. I move to the window, but it's too cloudy to give me a hint at what's inside. Maybe I could steam it open and read the results. Kenneth would be none the wiser, and I would be able to go into the night knowing.

I shouldn't have agreed to wait for him.

Standing in front of the full-length mirror, I smooth out my dress for the gala. Before Mama left, she surprised me with a gown she deemed positively perfect for tonight. I had planned to wear a shade of green, but when she held up the satin, navy dress and emotion pooled in both of our eyes, I knew that dark blue would be my color for the evening. Slender straps crisscross around my neck, the asymmetrical hemline leaving one leg mostly bare and my back open and exposed.

There isn't much more time to stress out about the letter because Shay and I are supposed to be leaving for the gala in ten minutes.

Kenneth is my date, but there are a few things he wanted to get done before and promised to meet me there. I know he's still deciding what to do about the whole issue with his dad.

Coming to terms with the fact that the Brain Bowl could end early was easy. The information that lies inside this envelope is what's driving me crazy.

I'm not a risk taker. Never have been, but if I've learned anything about Kenneth's dilemma, it's that my dream is worth every risk. No matter what happens tonight, I'm proud of myself.

Win or lose, I will be okay.

Winry rubs her body against my leg, purring what I assume is approval of my appearance for the evening. Bending down, I scratch between her ears and press my lips to her head. I give my reflection one last look before poking my head into the hallway.

"Shay!"

There's no response. For someone who exclusively gets ready while blaring classical music, it's eerily quiet on her side of the house.

I heard her while I napped. The unmistakable sound of her rummaging through my closet and dressers, likely to borrow a pair of shoes or a shirt, woke me for a moment. But now that I think about it, I haven't heard her since I started getting ready. I assumed she was charging her social battery since we'll be out late with our friends and every CLU athlete, celebrating the end of another great year.

My heels click noisily as I storm down the hallway to her room, but the doorbell stops me from banging on her door. Winry sprints to the front door like a dog, scratching at the gap until I yank the door open.

"I'll get it, but hurry Shay! We're going to be la—"

My voice shuts off at the sight before me. Standing on the porch with a bouquet of flowers in hand is Kenneth. The combination of yellow, pink, and orange is gorgeous, but I'm in awe of the man standing in front of me.

Kenneth's eyes travel from the gold heels on my feet and up my legs, gliding across my body with adoration and desire. By the time his eyes meet mine, my heart is pounding so hard that I have to lean against the doorway to catch my breath.

"Don't be upset with Shay. I asked her to help me surprise you."

"You know how much I hate surprises," I laugh.

The May sun has nothing on the warmth of his touch as he swiftly pulls me against him, dragging his fingers up my spine before snaking his hand around the back of my neck. He's extra careful not to mess up the complex bun I spent an hour on.

"How can one person be so perfect? Brilliant. Gorgeous. Vibrant. Kind. You're everything."

His lips meet mine for just a moment, and he groans his displeasure when I cut our kiss short. I step back to get another good look at him. Red tufts curl slightly at the ends. Silver puzzle-shaped cufflinks add a pop of Kenneth's nerdy and adorable personality to the ensemble. The navy suit he's chosen for tonight looks like it was made for him, making his eyes pop like rare jewels.

Wait a minute.

"Hey!" I yell. "We agreed we weren't doing punishments since we're going to the gala together. Which means you're breaking the rules by matching with me."

He does that silly grin that makes my stomach flip before he closes the distance between us again. Snaking his arms around my waist, his lips ghost the shell of my ear. "Matching you isn't a punishment, Eddie.

Actually, it's an honor. I get to walk in with the most gorgeous woman in the room, and she's all mine? I call that a big win."

He has a point, so I just laugh and pull him inside by his tie. The door clicks shut, and it takes everything in me to not drag him to my bedroom and skip the gala. Instead, I jog to my bedroom to grab my letter.

"Let's open our envelopes before we leave!" I yell over my shoulder.

It seems heavier in my hand as I walk back into the kitchen where he waits, my finger already beneath the tab.

"Ready?" I ask.

"Nope." He plucks it from my fingers and holds it hostage in the air.

I jump up and try to snag it, but even in three-inch heels, it's impossible to grab. "Come on, Gray. I thought we were going to open them before the gala? If I don't get an answer soon, my head is going to explode!"

My feeble attempt to garner sympathy fails, but his eyes do soften. "All I want is one night with my perfect girlfriend and our friends. As much as I do care about what's in these envelopes," he leans down and presses a soft kiss to my forehead, "I also couldn't care less. Being with you is all I want tonight. It's our first gala together where we aren't trying to maul each other. It's a special night for us."

I roll my eyes. "That's stupid." *And incredibly sweet.*

"Maybe, but it doesn't change my decision. Let's open them tonight at Lake Anita. Where it all started."

My head falls back and I stare at the ceiling. Kenneth's sentimentality somehow turns this situation from annoying to romantic. He's really good at that, and I want nothing more than to kiss him until we need to leave.

"After karaoke?" I ask, desperate for a win.

He lets out a groan. "One song."

"Three," I counter.

"Two."

I smile, leaning up to press a kiss to his lips. "Deal."

Stuffing my envelope into my bag, I weave our fingers and let him lead me out of the house and down the driveway.

"By the way," I say. "What happened with your dad?"

Kenneth turns back and his joy makes my worry melt away. Not only does he look good, he looks free.

"Fuck my dad. Now come on, gorgeous. We've got a party to attend."

Chapter Forty-Three

Kenneth

I TAKE A DEEP breath, letting the smell of cedar wrap itself around every bundle of nerves and slow my racing heartbeat.

My finger lazily traces Mallory's shoulder with her head resting on my leg. Even in a fancy gown, she plopped onto the splintered dock without hesitation and beckoned me down to join her.

I would have been a fool to decline.

The second my feet hit the gravel road, I took a moment to appreciate the place I call home. Mallory being here with me makes it even more special because I am home with the woman I love.

God, I love her so much.

Deep blue, smooth as midnight, clings to her body like a second skin. My eyes trail up her legs, starting at pale blue toenails and then travel toward the cloud of curls she released from its bobby-pin jail halfway through "Raining Men" at karaoke. When I reach her face, honeyed eyes are already on me.

"You watching me?" we say at the same time.

"Jinx!" she screams, beating me by only half a second. "You owe me a hot chocolate!"

I hold my hands up in surrender. Little does she know, I plan on buying her one every day for the rest of my life.

Halfway through the gala's award ceremony, Mallory's impatience won out. Twisting her body away from me, she started to peel open her envelope, unaware of her name being called for the Women's Captain of the Year award. I handed her my envelope as a peace offering for taking hers, before walking to the stage to receive the Men's Captain of the Year award.

Tonight gave us both another point, making it 12-12. The tie breaker is in these envelopes.

"Ready to find out?" I ask.

"Honestly, no." Mallory sits up. "I'd rather hear about your decision."

I planned on telling her everything before the gala. Then she opened the door and the only thoughts I could articulate were how alluring and ethereal she is. And how lucky I am to be the man beside her all night.

Tonight was about us. Two student-athletes celebrating a phenomenal year. It was the first gala where we didn't spend the entire evening at each other's throats. Whispered adoration and soft touches replaced passive-aggressive comments and avoiding each other.

I didn't want to taint the evening talking about the man I'll never speak to again.

"I spoke to my mom," I finally admit.

"Really?" Mallory squeaks, placing a supportive hand on my knee. "Are you... Did it go well?"

I can't blame Mallory for her apprehension, but after my mother dropped by Nan's facility, we went to Sunshine Junction alone. Although everything wasn't fixed in those few hours, it felt like a good start.

"I have her to thank for why we're able to come here tonight. I'll still move out and work next year, but I'm free of my dad, and Lake Anita is safe. I thought about looking at some houses in Clear Lake, but Nan said if I didn't move here, she'd drag me here by my ears."

Mallory gives my knee a squeeze. "I think that's the best idea. I'm glad everything worked out for you."

At that, I have to look away. It's not that I regret my decision, but there is one thing I can't shake.

She places a hand on my cheek and guides my head into the crook of her neck. There's always a softness in the way she touches me, coaxing me into a calm state with her sweetness. "Where did you go, baby? What's on your mind?"

Keeping my face hidden, I press a kiss to her collarbone. "I talked to Keaton. He didn't seem upset, but he also didn't sound happy." I shrug. "I can never tell with him. But the guilt is eating me alive."

I didn't want him to find out I was no longer coming to Gray Construction from anyone else, so I called my older brother.

I got out, and I'm worried he never will.

"He'll come around," she promises, letting out a grunt as she stands. "Even if I have to fly out to wherever he lives and convince him to."

That pulls a real laugh out of me, and once I'm standing, I pull her against me. "I hear it's supposed to be a beautiful summer, and I'm looking for a lake buddy. Know anybody who would be interested?"

Her eyes glitter as she looks up at me. "I can't think of a better person to spend the summer with."

I want so badly to kiss her, but her smile tightens, and I'm sure the envelope poking out of my pocket jabbed her. A reminder of the next thing we need to talk about.

She pulls my letter from her bag, but when I reach for it, she holds it tight against her stomach.

"I was thinking we could open each other's."

"Any particular reason?" I ask.

"Emotional support, maybe? I don't know. I'm freaking out, and having you open mine might relieve a bit of the mess in my head."

I nod in agreement, sliding a shaky finger beneath the tab. This single piece of paper will not only declare a winner for junior year, but it will also be a defining moment for our futures.

Everyone in the Hilliard School of Public Health knows the insane rule for health administration and policy majors. It's the only degree plan that has a mandatory internship requirement before senior year. An internship is the only thing threatening Mallory's perfectly curated schedule.

It's scary and intimidating to think about how much might change after we open these, so I look to the person I know will stick around no matter what.

"Hey, Eddie," I say. When our eyes meet, my body relaxes. "No matter what's in here, I need you to know that I'm so proud of you. I couldn't have asked for a better partner. Project or life. Being by your side means more to me than whatever is in this envelope. There's nobody that I have more fun with."

"Screw you, Gray," she sniffs, attempting to hide the rush of emotion with her arm. "I hope you know that making me cry before receiving life-altering news is a breakup worthy offense." Then she drops her arm and smiles. "There's nobody I have more fun with either."

Just like her first trip to Lake Anita, we count to three.

"One..." I say.

"Two," we say together.

"Three."

Chapter Forty-Four

Kenneth Gray,

We are pleased to offer you the Internship Position with the Hilliard School of Public Health.

A sudden stinging behind my eyelids catches me off guard, the arrival of tears following. It's impossible to read the rest of the letter now, everything blurred by the rush of emotion that won't stop.

But these aren't tears of anger, disappointment, or even sadness.

Tears of bliss stream down my cheeks, each drop a testament of my overwhelming happiness for Kenneth. Against all odds, he did it. He's proven not only to his dad, but to everyone that he's on the right path. Now he has the much-deserved opportunity of a lifetime to work with a mentor that could launch his career. This is truly the cherry on top of his whirlwind semester.

"Congrats, Gray," I whisper. "You did it, baby. The internship, and you won junior year. 12-13."

"Ed..." Kenneth's voice cracks, holding my rejection letter in a vice. It's not pity he's looking at me with, which makes me love him even more. Every emotion I assumed I would feel is evident on his face: fear, sadness, shock, and hurt.

All for me.

Yet none of those are what I feel. They're all shoved aside as I look at him. Nothing but pride is felt as my fingers twitch impatiently, desperate to slip into his hair and hold him close while we celebrate his win.

As if snapping out of shock, Kenneth stumbles forward and throws his arms around me, effectively trapping my arms against my sides. I giggle, freeing my arms and snaking them around his neck.

"I hate this," he says, voice thick with emotion. "This doesn't feel good. It doesn't feel like a win."

"Don't say that," I beg. "We should be celebrating right now. Screaming from the mountain tops and swinging from the vines in the trees. Cedar trees don't have vines, but we can make do. You deserve to be happy."

"I am happy," he breathes, "but at the same time, I'm not."

"Talk to me," I urge him, sinking my hands into his hair. "Tell me what's going on in your head."

"Of course I'm thankful. I'd be selfish not to be, but I'm not okay with this decision. What about your dedication and hard work? Your application was perfect, and the judges are insane to have missed that!"

"But none of that means you deserve it any less. Do you know who else's application was perfect?" I kiss his nose. "Yours. Do you know who else works hard and is incredibly dedicated?" I kiss his lips. "You, Kenneth. I read your application. Hell, I recommended you for this internship because that's how much faith I have in you as a person. It's almost infuriating that on top of being brilliant, you have the kindest heart of anybody I know. You deserve this, baby."

Red tufts flop as he shakes my words away. "What about you? They're going to put you on probation and change your graduation date. You've got plans that will all be put on hold. Why are you so okay with this?"

I pause. Realization hits me that I *am* okay with this. I know I told myself that I'd be okay no matter what, but now that we're here, standing on the dock and discussing how my future is no longer going to plan, all I can do is smile at him.

"Don't get me wrong. I am sad, but I'm able to have all those emotions and still be ecstatic for you. I'm okay because I bet on me," I say simply, and my dad's words ring loudly in my head.

"Always bet on yourself, baby girl. There's nobody you should trust more than yourself."

"I've always been the person who takes care of everything and everyone, but I never trusted myself *with* myself. Doubting everything I did, said, ate, and drank, but that all changed this semester. I knew the risks from the beginning. Going up against you has never been easy, and I didn't expect it to be easy this time. Honestly, even if I knew this is how it would turn out, I still don't think I would change a thing. I prefer this over doubting myself ever again."

Kenneth tilts his head to the side, his lips lifting slightly at the corners for the first time since we opened the envelopes. "Who are you and what have you done with my Eddie?"

"I know. I've grown so much over the past few months," I chirp, wiping invisible dust off my shoulder.

Kenneth laughs, dragging his hands up my back and into my hair, massaging the thoughts swirling around in my head. They're heavy and conflicted. Happy and sad. Worried and calm. But when I open my eyes and see him, the heaviness vanishes. The only thing I feel is something I can't hold back anymore.

"I love you."

Kenneth freezes. "What did you say?"

I drag my finger over the freckles on his cheek that I would like to spend forever counting. "I used to hate when you called me Eddie, Ed, or Edwards, but now I don't care what nickname you choose, as long as you call me yours. And this probably seems like an ill-timed confession, but I don't care because it's the truth. I don't care if it's too soon or too sudden. I don't care about any of that. Because not only do I love you, I'm completely *in* love with you, Kenneth. Now please say something more than a question because I'm terrified that you don't feel the sa—"

He kisses me to shut me up. Or because he just couldn't wait anymore. Either way, I smile, because if I didn't know already, he says the words out loud for me to hear.

"I love you. From the moment I met you, I knew I was meant to love you, Mallory."

I roll my eyes, unable to stop the smile that takes over my face. "Don't exaggerate or I really won't believe you."

His chest rumbles against mine when he laughs. "I've never been more sure of anything in my life. You hadn't even said your name, and I knew you were going to change everything. To be honest, you scared me."

My smile falls, and my voice drops to a whisper. "Scared you? Why?"

He tilts my chin up, making me meet his eye. "It's terrifying to meet someone and know that you'll never be the same. I had no expectations when I came to CLU, and then I met you. After that day, I looked for you everywhere. Every party, study session, and athlete dinner. I gravitated toward certain places because I was sure you'd be there, even if we didn't cross paths. In that short moment on the stairs, I knew I'd be willing to let you break my heart if it meant getting a little bit of time to be yours."

On the stairs that day, I swore I'd never like this man, and now I'm in love with him. Our journeys were so different, yet here we are at the same destination.

This time when our lips meet, it feels like one story closes, while another is just beginning. His lips against mine elicit a burst of energy, the jolt fusing passion with a comforting promise that feels like the biggest one of all.

"You love me," I say when I pull back.

It's not a question. There's no doubt in my mind.

"I always have, Eddie. And I always will."

Chapter Forty-Five

Kenneth

Eventually Mallory and I made it into the house for the highly anticipated tour of the place I'll be living.

She glided around the living room, kitchen, and bedrooms, crooning over every baby picture, holiday card, school assignment, homemade knickknack, and elementary craft project she could find. The height markings on the kitchen door frame were her favorite part, tracing a finger over faded lines of permanent marker.

After heading back outside to grab the overnight bag Shay packed for Mallory, I lock the truck as we make our way back to the house, hand in hand. Spring has always been my favorite season. The smell of freshly cut grass and a chance of rain permanently in the air. I never cared much for winter, with its shorter days and loss of color.

But for the first time, I'm thankful for winter. This winter specifically. All because of what it brought me.

A swell of emotion wells up in my chest, in awe of the woman beside me. Bathed in the soft light of the moon, her delicate features are even softer and brighter.

We sat on the dock for hours. A moving truck was scheduled for next week. We checked our final grades that came out at midnight. Plans for the summer were discussed, traveling between Lake Anita and Clear Lake. Most importantly, every other sentence was those three words that have altered my brain chemistry.

Mallory Edwards loves *me*.

Standing on the front porch, I brush my hand over her cheek. All my life, love has been used as a bargaining chip. Something that was given or expressed only when I brought honor to the Gray image. I revel in the fact that Mallory's love is everything theirs wasn't.

Unconditional. Free. Safe.

"I love you," I say for the millionth time.

She pushes the door open, and I close it behind me. "I love you, but I'm a little worried you're going to wear yourself out saying it so much tonight. I'd rather you not run out of love for me anytime soon."

"I can promise you that won't ever happen."

"Good," she laughs. "Because I've been waiting to do this all night."

Our lips collide and her hands are on me. Pulling at my tie, I loosen it and toss it aside. She smiles mischievously as she unhooks the top button of my shirt. With every one that comes undone, her lips follow, leaving behind streaks of heat. She rubs her hands over my bare chest, peeling the shirt off until it's on the ground.

"Wait..." I say breathlessly, looking down at her hands on my belt. "Why am I the only one getting undressed?"

"Honestly? I wanted to see how far I could go before you noticed." With a clang of metal, my pants fall to the floor and she smirks. "I can't believe it took you this long to notice."

I was all too comfortable with letting her strip me naked in the living room. Mallory's victorious laugh follows us as I drag her down the hallway and into my childhood bedroom.

"How am I supposed to focus on anything when your lips are on me? Seems a bit unfair."

"Fine." Mallory turns around. "Would you like to make it fair?"

Peeling this dress off her body is exactly what I want to do. All I've wanted to do since I saw her in it hours ago. My hand drifts down her back, bare beneath my fingers. Even though the zipper calls my name, I stay a safe distance away from the tiny piece of metal. The last thing I want to do is push her into something because I'm ready.

"I don't want to push you—"

Mallory stops me by pressing a finger to my lips. "One of the things I love most about you is that you always put me first. My comfort. My safety. My happiness. It doesn't matter what you want, you're always thinking of me." Admiration fills her honeyed eyes. "So no, you're not pushing me. I'm sure this is what I want."

This kiss is different than the one in the living room. With her body against mine, everything feels right. There's no more Edwards, scared to ask for help, because she trusts me and knows I'll always be there. There's no more Gray, scared I'd never find a love that was unconditional or reciprocated, because I know she will love me the way I've always longed to be.

We love each other correctly.

I bend down and help her out of each golden heel. Unzipping the dress, I unwrap her body like the gift it is and let the dress fall to the ground. Hunger stirs as I straighten, taking in every inch of beautiful, smooth skin. But my eyes are on hers when I speak again.

"You are the most beautiful woman I've ever seen, Mallory. I can't believe I'm the man who gets to love you."

I sit on the comforter and pull her between my parted knees. My hands grip the back of her knees, roaming over the expanse of her legs, enjoying every inch of soft skin and toned muscles. A thin strap of emerald at her waist elicits a deep groan of approval from me.

"Truly perfect," I say, before using my mouth for something other than talking.

A whine leaves her lips as my teeth graze her nipple, sending Mallory grinding against my cock, hard and straining against my briefs. The contact is simultaneously too much and somehow not enough. I need more.

I need all of her.

As if reading my mind, Mallory's hand drifts down my stomach, stopping at the waistband. Her fingers move across the elastic in a teasing pattern.

"Scoot back," she commands.

I do as she says, backing up until my back hits the headboard. It's exhilarating to watch Mallory move across the bed, cheeks flushed and crawling toward me.

Her confidence seems to swell as she pulls off my briefs in one swift motion and wraps her hand around my cock. She bobs her hand up and down, and my head falls back against the headboard. Shit, I'm already so close to breaking, and this is only her hand. I've thought about this more than I'd like to admit. The real thing is so much better than anything my brain ever conjured up.

"*Fuck*, Eddie," I breathe, baring my teeth as she kisses the tip of my dick. She grins wickedly, licking me from base to tip. The comforter scrunches in my hands as her lips part, taking me all the way in. I move to tangle my fingers in her hair, letting her move as she pleases, but desperate to touch her in some way.

She's not timid, humming around me and sending every nerve into overdrive as she moves. Faster and faster until my hips buck at the overwhelming sensation, and I hit the back of her throat. God, it feels so good. The perfect mouth on the perfect woman.

My body tenses, and I pull at the coiled strands, only stopping when she whimpers.

"Shit. I'm sorry, honey," I say, wiping my thumb over her cheek. "Are you okay?"

Eyes dark as soot meet mine. With a single wink, she continues, sending me closer and closer to my release.

"Mallory... *Please,*" I beg, my voice unrecognizable and needy as I pull her off me. "I need you right now."

"Who's the impatient one now?" she teases, moving to straddle my waist.

"Me. Come here." I wrap my arms around her middle and pull her to me, pressing kisses across her chest, stomach, collarbones, and every inch I can reach.

The sound of a drawer opening pulls my eyes to my bedside. "Looking for something?"

"A condom." She ruffles through the drawer, but I'm positive there are none in my childhood bedside table. "Do you have one?"

I rub the back of my neck. "No. I didn't expect this to happen tonight. I'm sorry."

"Me either," she mutters, rolling off my lap. The headboard creaks and she leans against it.

"Do we need to stop?" I ask.

"I don't want to. I'm on birth control and, this should go without saying, I'm not sleeping with anyone else. It's been well over a year since my last time."

I clear my throat and look at my hands. "This is... This would be my first time," I admit, my voice quiet.

"Oh."

I expected that.

Then she takes me by surprise, straddling my hips again before she kisses the tip of my nose.

"I love you. Thank you for trusting me with that."

"I love you, and I don't want to stop either."

"Good," she whispers, threading her fingers in my hair. "Tell me what makes you feel good."

With her here in my arms, my answer is easy. "You make me feel good, Eddie. That's all I need."

Mallory kisses me one last time, long and soft. Her hands holds my face as she sits up and aligns herself with me. "Ready?"

I can't find my voice, so I nod through a shuddering breath. My fingers dig into her thighs as she lowers herself onto me, and I'm glad we're sitting because I'm sure my knees would have given out from the feeling of being inside her. The room is frozen for a moment, soft gasps leaving her pretty lips as she adjusts to the tight fit.

I lose my breath as I sink deeper and deeper into her perfect pussy, desperate to move, but also desperate to stay here for as long as she will let me. "Oh *fuck*, I'm not going to last long."

"Me either," she gasps. "It'll be perfect."

Placing her hands on my chest, we move together. Even now, she's not afraid to tell me exactly how she feels about me, whispering promises into the space around us. How much she loves me. How special I am to her. How much she trusts me.

It's in this moment that I know I'll never be the same.

Like that day on the stairs, I'm reminded that Mallory's the one who started it all. The want for a life more than just surviving. The need to love and be loved.

I'm entirely hers.

From below, I watch as she bounces, skin damp and glittering in the pale light. Coils fall over her eyes, sticking to her cheeks and neck.

"*Baby*," she cries with a stifled breath.

"I know, honey. Me too."

I pull her chest to mine. My name falls from her lips like a prayer, and the sound of skin against skin fills the room as our movements turn desperate. A sharp bite on my shoulder sends a shudder of pleasure down my cock, but I need her to come first. I thrust harder, following her pleas to not stop, and hitting the perfect spot over and over until she falls.

And I fall with her.

Our breathing is labored, damp foreheads pressed together as we catch our breath. Mallory's hair hangs around us, creating a shield between us and the outside world. It's just us in our own little bubble, and I want nothing more than to hide here for a little while longer.

Against my protests, Mallory unhooks herself from me with a quick kiss and slips on my dress shirt before leaving the room.

I'm not sure how long my eyes are closed, but when they reopen, Mallory is dressed in my—now her—hoodie, with her hair wrapped, resting on the edge of the bed. She watches me carefully, returning my wave with a cautious smile.

"I love you." I sit up and take her in. "How are you?"

"I love you, and I feel great. As tired as I am, I wouldn't be opposed to going again," Mallory says with a wink.

I hop off the bed and toss her over my shoulder, letting the sweet sound of her laughter wrap itself around my heart. She talks a big game, but her voice is thick with sleep, eyes already fluttering as I rub circles on her lower back. This is one of those memories I'll hold close. I'm going to sit here all night, wrapped up with the love of my life.

My Edwards.

My Ed.

My Eddie.

Chapter Forty-Six

Campus being empty feels weird.

I hook my tote over my shoulder, trudging down the sidewalk to the Hilliard School of Public Health building. It's been a week since we found out Kenneth won, and today is the day I discuss my new schedule and graduation date with my advisor. I can already hear Ms. Silva's smug laugh and the uncomfortable conversation that awaits me.

Right now, the only thing I care about is getting this meeting over with, crawling back into bed, and finishing off the pint of ice cream I started last night while hanging out with Shay and Kenneth. It feels as if everyone is walking on eggshells around me. Like they mutually agreed to not bring up the Brain Bowl or my loss, as if not talking about it will make it all go away.

I still talk about it though. Sometimes it's all I think about.

Mama says she's proud of me. Kenneth and my counselor Sharon haven't stopped saying it either. I'd feel like a coddled child if it wasn't for the fact that I am proud of myself too. Emotions are weird, because I am proud, frustrated, scared, sad, and worried all at the same time.

I just keep reminding myself to hold on tight to that sliver of pride.

Kenneth keeps saying that although everything looks bleak right now, he's sure something good is coming. Something that'll turn this all around. While my boyfriend is adorably optimistic, the realist in me is struggling to believe him.

A blast of air conditioning hits me as I step through the doors, a great relief from the humid hell outside. I swipe a bead of sweat from my brow as I walk toward the waiting area, ready to get this meeting over with.

"Mallory!"

My spirits lift at the familiar voice, turning to find my favorite professor jogging toward me. He's clearly in summer mode with his tourist outfit on, frayed denim shorts and a Hawaiian shirt. I wish I could take a picture for Kenneth. He would love this. "Hi, Dr. Martin!"

"I'm sorry about the internship," he says, stopping in front of me. "If it helps, you and Kenneth were truly neck and neck the entire time. Two of the brightest students that internship panel had ever seen. You also turned out to be a great pair, don't you think?"

My cheeks flush at the knowing tone of his voice. I'm sure he noticed the shift between Kenneth and me over the semester. Our hands clasped together under the table, bragging over quiz grades with a smile, secret laughs shared when Dr. Martin did something funny, and the kisses Kenneth pressed to my forehead as we walked into class. He never said anything, but I'm sure *"I told you so"* is on the tip of his tongue.

"We really did." I grin. "I'm proud of him."

"Me too." Dr. Martin looks around the empty office and checks his watch. "Who are you waiting to see?"

"Ms. Silva. We have a meeting in ten minutes."

"Perfect. I have a meeting at nine too. I wanted to thank you for the work you did with the donation letters. I wouldn't have been able to get Type All off the ground without your help this semester."

I bounce excitedly. "You got the funding for camp? That's amazing!"

Dr. Martin nods, distracted as he rummages through his bag.

During our first meeting, Dr. Martin asked me about life as a student-athlete living with diabetes. Something about the man had me pouring my soul out to him. Maybe it was the salt-and-pepper hair that reminded me of Mama, but Dr. Martin was suddenly privy to my doubts, the highs and lows when it came to my self-confidence with managing my diabetes, and the real fear that I felt like I was never doing anything right despite my constant efforts.

At our third meeting, he asked about my old job with the diabetes camp in my hometown. I explained my duties under my former boss, Saul: reaching out to donors, editing donation letters, processing applications, assisting with cooking classes, and becoming a counselor at sixteen. I connected him with Saul for the operational details, and it all paid off.

"It'll be a small group, but it's really happening, all thanks to you." Finally, Dr. Martin finds what he's looking for in his bag and hands me an envelope. "I've got to get going. If I'm late to one more meeting, the Dean might put me on probation."

"I bet your probation will be better than mine," I joke, stuffing the envelope into my backpack as he jogs away. He mentioned wanting to pay me for my help, so tonight I'll treat Kenneth to dinner on Dr. Martin's dime. It'll be my way of paying him back for letting me wallow in sadness for the past week.

When I turn around, the office door is wide open. Ms. Silva's eyes glisten like a predator stalking its prey. "Mallory, hello. I'd say what a surprise to see you, but it really isn't."

I roll my eyes and walk past her, keeping my curse words to myself like I promised Kenneth I'd do.

Kenneth's hands in my hair feel like heaven, massaging the headache away after that terrible, too-long meeting. With each knead of his fingers, he smooths out the bumps of shame Ms. Silva hammered into me this morning.

Irresponsible.

Overly hopeful.

Reckless.

"You're none of those things, Eddie," Kenneth promises, his voice soft. He's trying to keep it steady for me, but I know he's livid. "I don't care what that vile woman says."

The smell of cedar fills my nose, drifting in through the window that gives me a spectacular view of the lake. Kenneth and Cade moved to Lake Anita right after the semester ended, making their new home my little escape. Being here calms me as much as his words, but I'm still having a hard time believing them.

"What if she's right? I should've applied for every internship under the sun, but I was picky. Look how that turned out for me."

"We've been over this. You weren't picky. What you did was smart, because you, my intelligent, driven, and perfect girlfriend were made for so much more than what you were offered."

"Maybe. Part of me would rather be graduating on time," I huff, blowing a stray curl out of my eyes.

Kenneth sighs, and I assume he's giving up on me and my whiny attitude already. I would too if I were him. While I'm still incredibly proud of him, coming to terms with my new reality is tough.

Then he sweeps me into his arms and across his lap, his face incredibly serious. "Look at me, and tell me the truth. Would you really have been okay with accepting an internship that didn't push you or challenge you? Where you wouldn't learn or grow?"

My answer is quick. "No. I wouldn't have been okay."

"Exactly. Because the woman I know and love will always aim for the top of the mountain, never settling for anything less."

"I would have hated myself if I settled," I say, affirming everything he's been trying to drill into my head for the past week.

"I know, honey. You're not a settler. Just like you're not irresponsible, or overly hopeful, or reckless." He pokes my chest, right where my heart is. "You're Mallory Edwards. There's no amount of bad luck that can bring you down because every situation has the opportunity of turning itself around. What do we call that?"

I roll my eyes, unable to keep my lips from reacting to his silliness. I never should have taught him this saying. "Fortunate misfortune."

"Exactly," he says, and I mimic his goofy grin.

It's been hard to accept that betting on myself didn't pay off. I wanted that internship more than anything and wasn't going to let anything get in my way, but it didn't work out.

In the words of Mama, shit happens.

There are so many good things in my life. Here I am, snuggled up with the man I love, attending the school of my dreams, and working toward being the person my dad needed on his medical team. I'm more comfortable with my diabetes management, constantly working to accept the bad days as easily as the good days. I've got one more year of soccer with my favorite ladies, and I plan on making every second count.

With Cade out of town for the last week, Kenneth and I have had the place to ourselves. Our days are spent under the warm sun and our nights filled with stolen kisses and captivating touches. It feels oddly domestic,

Kenneth and I here at Lake Anita, doing everything and nothing together, but it feels right.

Things may not have worked out how I would've liked, but I'm thankful and grateful for the things I do have.

I kiss Kenneth slowly, reminding myself of these facts one more time before I stand and head into the kitchen to find the takeout menu. I've got pad Thai and spring rolls on the brain.

"Hey, can you open my backpack and take out the white envelope?"

He does as I ask, waving it in the air. "What is this?"

I pause outside the kitchen, wiggling my hips. "That's how we're paying for dinner. Courtesy of Dr. Martin for writing and reviewing those donation letters."

Kenneth does a goofy little dance that matches mine. We love free food. I would say it's a college-kid thing, but I think free food will make me happy no matter how old I am.

"Can I open it?" he asks.

"Sure!" I grab the menu from the drawer and scan it even though I already know what he wants, yellow curry with lamb. Pulling open my group message with the girls, I call out, "Also, Shay, Adri, and Jo are coming over to eat with us so—"

"Holy shit," Kenneth chokes out, cutting me off.

"Wow. Must be a lot," I laugh, dialing the number for Thai Garden to make our order. "How much money did he give me?"

One thing I don't like about the house at Lake Anita is that I can't see the living room from the kitchen, making it impossible to gauge Kenneth's reaction. The longer he stays silent, the more I worry. For ten seconds, the only response is the wind rattling the chimes on the porch.

I step away from the counter and head back to him. "You're scaring me. What is it?"

"It's..." He pauses. "Come here, Ed. It's not money. It's a letter."

Chapter Forty-Seven

Mallory Edwards,

Type All will be up and running this summer. Clear Lake will be a safe place for kids living with type 1 and type 2 diabetes. I aim to create a safe community for these kids, restore confidence in their abilities to care for themselves, and create a place people want to come back to summer after summer. That being said, I would like to extend an internship opportunity to you. Your life experience, tied with your passion for people, makes you special. I would love to have you on my team.

"What the..." I mumble, trailing off to reread from the beginning.

Kenneth waves a hand in front of my face, waking me from my trance. "What is it?"

I open my mouth to answer but nothing comes out, so I hand him the letter and start pacing. The worry lines in his forehead soften with every dart of his eyes. I'd bet anything Kenneth only reads until he sees the word *internship*, because at that moment his head shoots up, that pretty smile of his lighting his face.

In an instant, his hands grip the back of my knees and he lifts me up and starts spinning us in circles. I should stop him before we fall onto the coffee table and ruin the Lake Anita puzzle we've been working on for the last two days, but I don't because I'm too busy screaming to care about anything except what's on that paper.

I did it. I got an internship. Betting on myself paid off.

A flash of grief shoots through me. I wish my dad could see me right now. If he were here, he would find a way to turn this into a hilarious lesson about why I should have started listening to his advice years ago. He'd wrap me up in a big hug, letting his full-bodied laugh shake the room. He always said the wisdom of a father is the best kind, and I definitely believe he was right about that.

"Does this mean..." Kenneth trails off, looking up at me.

"I can graduate on time."

Every low I felt over the last week comes back with a vengeance in the form of wild giggles and pure excitement when Kenneth starts spinning us again. I'd bet the sound of our joy can be heard from the highway as we celebrate together.

"*We* won, Eddie," he says, hoisting me up higher.

My head is still spinning as I try to catch my breath, moving hair away from his eyes. "We won what?"

His body vibrates excitedly. "It's 13-13. You tied it. We're tied for junior year."

"No!" I scream, trying to wiggle out of his grasp. His hold on me tightens, but I keep fighting. "I see what you're doing, Kenneth, and no. Actually, hell no! You won fair and square. *You* got the internship that we agreed on. I'm not going to let you—"

"Let me," he cuts in. "Please. I may have gotten the one we agreed on, but you're being offered the perfect internship, and you didn't even have to apply for it! How can you not call that a win?"

He's not wrong, but still. "I can't—"

"But I can," he breathes, and the earnest tone of his voice makes me finally close my mouth and listen. "I used to think our game was the most important thing in the world. I lived for the thrill of competition and constantly working to outdo each other. Eddie, you will always be my favorite rival, but fighting to win will never be enough for me again. The chase and the rivalry kept this interesting, but I want so much more. To be your cheerleader and your biggest fan. Winning isn't everything anymore."

I'm glad I'm still in the air because there's no way my wobbly legs would keep me upright.

Winning isn't everything anymore.

I repeat the phrase a few times in my head. Not because I'm trying to convince myself of this fact. I've felt the same way for a while. The mind-aching need to beat Kenneth at our game weakened as the months went by, and I fell for him a little more every day.

"Does that mean we should end it?" I ask. "The Brain Bowl, I mean."

He shakes his head. "I've been thinking, I know next year will be different with me working every day, but I'm not ready to let it go."

Hope leaks into my words. "Really?"

"Yeah. I can't guarantee that we will be able to play twenty-plus games, but I want to finish college the way it started. With you, Ed. How does that sound?"

I grin. "I don't care if we only play three games the entire year. I just want to play with you."

"Good, but if we continue, it has to stay how it was this past semester. Mutual support and encouragement. We treated it like something fun, to be enjoyed, rather than an endless battle. This is the first time we worked together, celebrating each other's wins, and comforting each other after the losses. My main goal isn't to beat you anymore. Is yours?"

"No. I want to keep growing and be able to do it with you. What are we going to do after graduation though? The Brain Bowl will be over."

Kenneth chews on his bottom lip, pausing to think. "Next May, we get a fresh start, but I want to play and experience every thing with you for the rest of our lives. Finding new things to compete at. Weekly tennis matches, bowling, board games, seeing who can puzzle the fastest."

"That last one is definitely not fair," I breathe, resting my forehead against his. "For the rest of our lives, huh?"

"Is that too forward? Actually, I don't care. Me and you, Eddie."

"Forever sounds good to me, baby," I whisper. And it does. It's all I want.

But if we're going to continue the Brain Bowl, I need to know what this means for junior year. "So..." I say. "A tie?"

Kenneth nods. "I know the possibility of finishing the year in a tie used to feel like the end of the world, but right now, I can't imagine this year ending any other way. So, I'm calling junior year a tie, and I don't want to hear another word about it. It's 1-1-1, Eddie."

We both secured an internship that's somehow perfect for us. Kenneth with Dr. McGregor, where he will research MS, and me with Dr. Martin, building a safe place for kids living with type 1 and type 2 diabetes in the town I love. It may not have been the one I wanted originally, but it's exactly what I was looking for all this time.

Today, a tie doesn't feel like the worst thing in the world.

It feels like the start of something new with my best friend.

Epilogue

Kenneth

One Year Later

"Good afternoon, esteemed faculty, honored guests, proud family and friends, and most importantly, the graduates of Clear Lake University!"

Mallory's eyes roam the rows and rows of black graduation gowns and decorated caps before landing on me. Even with hundreds of people around, it feels like it's only us in the room.

"Breathe," I mouth. "I love you."

Mallory's shoulders drop slightly, lips parted to take a deep breath before diving in.

"Today we gather to celebrate a commencement. Many may call it an ending, but I believe it's a continuation. Your next chapter of life starts now, and as we step into this newfound time of life, I want to take a moment to explore a paradoxical theme that has resonated deeply with me over the last four years. One I'm sure we've all experienced in our lives and time here at CLU. Fortunate misfortune. To put it simply, fortunate misfortune is the idea that challenges, which originally may seem like inconveniences or hardships, can ultimately lead to positive outcomes. In the spirit of joy and festivities, I've chosen some lighthearted examples, but I don't want to take away from those who fought to make it here today. Your strength, grit, and perseverance deserve to be celebrated.

"During her freshman year, my dear friend Libby fell off her bike in the middle of campus. All of us can agree that nobody ever wanted to be that person. In that moment, Libby was badly bruised and embarrassed, but she was even more shocked when a kind soul rushed to her aid. They've been dating ever since."

Libby hoots from the audience.

"This source requested to stay anonymous. Every Hilliard Public Health student took Chemistry 101 with Dr. Mona, and we can all agree that it was a rough time. Sleep deprived and distraught that their medical school dreams seemed impossible, they stumbled out of the library and ran straight into someone they had never met before but had seen in class. Trauma bonded by Dr. Mona's pop-quizzes, they forged a forever friendship. Sorry, Doc. We love you."

Mallory's confidence soars as Dr. Mona struggles to contain her laughter.

"Life has a weird way of presenting challenges. At times, it feels like they're *too* daunting. Whether it's friendship problems, financial struggles, burnout, health issues, or academic setbacks. It's in those moments of adversity that you discover the strength not only to keep moving forward, but also to grow. Every time you overcome an obstacle, you acquire a new skill set to help you in every endeavor. Your time here at Clear Lake University has undoubtedly exposed you to many struggles, but that also came with new friends, experiences, personal growth, and chasing your passions and dreams."

The beautiful, emotional, and vulnerable woman I'm in love with pauses, wiping at her eyes. This speech means so much more to her than the people here truly know.

It's the story of her journey and us wrapped up in two words.

"May you carry a spirit of resilience into the world and far beyond campus. When faced with adversity, may you see not just misfortune, but the seeds of your future successes. Congratulations, and may the misfortunes of today be the stepping-stones to the triumphs of tomorrow!"

The applause is deafening, surprising Mallory with the reaction. It takes some time to reel the crowd back in before getting to the names, and before I know it, it's time to say goodbye to undergrad.

I toss my cap into the air, the sky black for a brief moment, signifying the first step into our new journeys.

"Kenneth Gray!"

There she is. Standing in front of me is the woman I still don't know how I convinced to be mine. My hands immediately pull her to me so I can sink my hands into her hair and kiss her.

Nan screams, "*Get a room!*" through her megaphone, and Mallory pulls back with a smile.

"Keep kissing me like that and Nan is going to get kicked out of here." Mallory drapes her arms around my waist, never taking her eyes off me. "How did I do? Did I look like I wanted to pass out? Because I swear, I was *this* close to fainting."

I press my lips to her forehead. "You did great, Ed. It was a beautiful speech. Don't you want to thank your ghost writer?"

"Nuh-uh. Editor," she corrects me with an eye roll.

"Same difference."

"Big difference. An editor is someone who—"

"Please don't Mal-splain something to me while I'm holding my summa cum laude diploma. I get it. You're the smart one in this relationship."

Mallory grins. "Me? Whatever, baby. In four years, you'll be Dr. Kenneth Gray."

Come August, I'll start my Doctorate in Biostatistics studying under my mentor, Dr. McGregor. A partnership bloomed after my summer internship, giving me an opportunity to continue research with one of the leading MS scientists.

"Even then," I say.

Type All had an outstanding turnout for their first summer. As expected, Mallory immediately became a co-director with Dr. Martin. Throughout the school year, she offered education and support to campers and their families virtually, and she begins her Dietetic Internship and Master's in Public Health in August.

Mallory's the hardest working, kindest, and most intentional person I know. It's why she demolished me senior year, taking the Brain Bowl with her, 1-2-1.

One win for me. Two wins for her. One tie for us.

"We've got a few minutes until we need to leave. Are you almost ready?" I call out, taking a seat on the couch.

Mallory steps into the living room and smooths out the emerald dress she let me pick for tonight. The satin material clings to every curve, accentuating the perfection of her fluid figure. I almost want to bail on our own graduation party because there's no way I'll make it through tonight without thinking about taking it off.

I grab her wrist as she walks by and pull her onto my lap. "You are so beautiful, Eddie. I don't want to go to the party. Let's just stay here tonight. What do you say?"

She smiles, allowing me to drag my finger up her inner thigh, toned and smooth legs parting slowly for me.

Then my perfect, incredibly punctual girlfriend checks her watch and sighs. "If we're even a minute late, my mom and Nan will never let us hear the end of it. Imagine how bad it would be if we didn't show up at all. Rain check?"

"Rain check, honey," I say. "So, do you want to open gifts now or later?

Mallory crawls off my lap and grins. "Who says I got you a gift?"

I lean over and pull out the box she tried to hide under the couch. While looking for a puzzle piece, I found it this morning. Like every gift she's given me over the past year, it's covered with gray wrapping paper. I run my finger along the smooth edge, admiring how far her wrapping skills have come. For the twins' birthday, she expertly wrapped all their gifts.

"Damn. I need to find better hiding spots. Go ahead and open it. I want you to have it for tonight."

Liquid sloshes around inside and a million options run through my head. I rip the paper and surprise fills me. It's definitely not what I assumed it would be. Heavy and cold in my hand is a glass bottle in the exact color of the dress the woman smiling at me is wearing. I trace the two words engraved on the glass.

"Lake Anita," I breathe.

Mallory takes the bottle and spritzes the cologne on my inner wrists. If I wasn't close to crying before, the familiar smell of cedar and citrus does the trick. "Now, no matter where you go, you'll always have a piece of home with you. Check out the surprise on the back."

I flip it over, overwhelmed with emotion at the drawing on the backside. Wonky cedar trees, a crooked dock, and violet water make the gift even more special because it's drawn by Jaxon and Julie.

"This is... How do you... You're too good at gifts, Eddie. Thank you."

"I'm so proud of everything you've accomplished so far." She presses a quick kiss to my lips. "Congrats, baby."

From my suit pocket, I pull out a maroon box and place it in her hands, suddenly feeling inadequate. Every gift from her feels like winning the lottery. All the joy and pleasure without the increased funds, but it's somehow even more exciting.

"You go through all of that work to make me a custom cologne, and I get you—"

"Holy shit," she gasps. The dainty, gold chain hangs from her fingers. A small pendant in the shape of a four-leaf clover shimmers in the sunlight. The moment I saw it, I knew it was perfect for her.

A good luck charm for my good luck charm.

I clasp the necklace around her neck, and smooth gold nestles beneath the hollow of her neck. It's gorgeous against the deep, velvety backdrop of her skin.

"It looks perfect on you, Eddie." My eyes lift from her throat to her face, before searching for the maroon box. I place it back in her hand. "There's a second gift in there for you."

Mallory's brows dip, as she pulls back the satin slip that separated the necklace from the final part of her gift. Then she gasps and shoots off the couch, pointing at me with the small gift clutched between her fingers.

"You want me to... Here? With you?"

"Yes," I chuckle. "I want to make Lake Anita *our* home."

She's no longer looking at me, wrapped up in the key. She rolls the metal between her fingers, memorizing every groove and curve. There aren't many things that can render Mallory speechless, but I see that asking her a big question is one of those things.

Noted.

"I don't need an answer right now, nor is there any pressure to say yes, Eddie. Because no matter where you live, I'm happy with you."

This catches her attention, finally bringing glassy eyes back to mine. I stand up and wrap my arms around her waist, my nerves melting away when she loops her arms around my neck and sniffles. Happiness blooms in every softened feature as she looks up at me.

"Yes. Absolutely yes," she whispers against my lips. "I'll talk to Shay."

"I can't wait to create a home with you."

"About time you get here!" Nan shrieks, even though we are ten minutes early.

"Yeah!" Jaxon yells, hopping off my mother's lap. "What took you so long?"

Mallory releases my hand and crouches down to wipe his ruddy cheeks that are streaked with dried tears. "We went home so I could give Kenneth that special gift you helped me with."

Home. Lake Anita is going to be *our* home soon.

Jaxon's stormy eyes shift to me, calming as he remembers the cologne bottle. "Did you like the picture me and Jules drew?

"Loved it. It's the best gift I've ever gotten. Thank you." I look around to find my other artist. "Where's Jules?"

"In the restroom with the girls," Jane says, appearing behind us. "She wanted to watch Adri fix her makeup. Shay and Adri convinced her and Jo to wear eye shadow too."

Mallory's mouth falls open. "Jo too? You're kidding."

Jaxon grips her cheeks, forcing her to look at him. "No more talking to them! Did you hear me screaming for you? I was super loud. I got a video! Come see!"

Mallory sighs. "Jeez, you're so impatient."

"I wonder where he gets that from," I tease.

She gives me a quick jab in the side before being whisked away. As much as Jaxon likes me, he isn't used to the fact the Mallory and I are dating. Jane says he's jealous about having to share his favorite girl. Julie on the other hand is already planning the wedding.

"Sorry," Jane says, patting my shoulder. "He's fussy today. Julie too. They equate graduation to leaving, and neither can fathom you two leaving Clear Lake, even though I've already made it clear you guys are staying. Now if you'll excuse me, both of my kids are occupied, and I need a drink. *Bad*. Pearl, wait!"

It's no surprise we're having our graduation party at Ida's Kitchen. After eating here with Riley and Mallory, it became a regular occurrence for the three of us. Riley flew in once a month to visit. All the people in our life love it as much as we do.

Heavy doors slam as two more guests step through them. Their matching purple outfits are a blur as they cross the room. One pair of arms hug my leg, with the other around my shoulders.

"Kenneth," Billie Owens beams. "I am so proud of you, son."

Cade's mother was the first woman to show me what a real mom looks like. Calling me son is natural because it's the way she's always treated me. When I left for college, she stepped in for me with Nan, stopping by throughout the week with treats and love. Even now that Nan's living with Titus and Cade is in California, Billie is still a constant presence in our lives.

"Thank you for being here, Billie." I ruffle Violet's pigtails. "Hi, Vi. You look very pretty. Are you excited to meet Julie and Jaxon today?"

Violet nods, grinning in that lopsided way that reminds me so much of her brother. The only person missing today. Cade's decision to enter the Major League Baseball draft after junior year wasn't a shock to anyone. What was shocking was how quickly everything changed after that.

Within a few weeks, he was under contract and on a plane to California for pre-season training, and he and Shay ended their arrangement.

My phone buzzes in my pocket, ESPN alerting me that his game will be starting soon.

I search for the remote to turn the game on, but my attention is frozen on the man standing at the front door. I blink once. Twice. Three times.

There's no way. I must be hallucinating.

"Keaton?" Nan asks from behind me, which proves that I am not seeing things.

Nan, Karla, and my mother rush across the room to him, immediately touching his hair, smoothing out his tie, and commenting on the bags beneath his eyes. Keaton's groans and grumbles, but I'm surprised that he doesn't push them away.

With Mallory's encouragement, I mustered the courage to invite him. I stopped believing he would come when he didn't respond to my original text or the two follow-ups.

"Can you guys give us a second?" I say, stepping behind the women.

From the back corner, I catch Mallory's eyes on me, even though she's mid-conversation with Riley and Jane. She gives me a thumbs up before looking away to give us a moment of privacy. The boost of support has an immediate calming effect as I face my older brother.

With a four-year age gap, we never seemed to be on the same page. Even as kids, Keaton was the peacekeeper, and I was the reason he could never have peace.

He breaks the long silence and holds out a card and large box. "Mom has been texting me updates on you and your plans. The box is for you, and the card is for Mallory. Congrats on graduating."

"Would you like to give it to her yourself? I can call her—"

"No!" He clears his throat and shakes his head. "I can't stay long. I just wanted to drop by."

Disappointment nips at me. He isn't here for me. "You're in town for a work thing."

"No," he corrects me, meeting my eye. "I came here for this, but I am meeting with Dad before my flight."

Reading Keaton is nearly impossible. His poker face is perfected after years of growing up with a father like ours. I can't tell if he's lying or telling the truth. Still, I'm thankful he's here.

"Well, thanks for coming. I know Mallory would love to meet you. Maybe another day? We could come visit you if that works. I know coming back here isn't ideal."

"I'd like that." His grim aura softens at my olive branch. Looking over my shoulder, the tiniest of smiles lifts his lips. "By the way, she's the perfect girl for you. On the bad days, I replay her putting Dad in his place on a loop. Mallory finally said what nobody else in that room had the courage to say. She's protecting you better than I ever could, and I'm sorry I never did. I should have done more for you."

My heart breaks. The most words my brother has said to me in years, and it's this.

I reach for his arm. "Keat—"

"I'll see you soon, Kenneth. I'll text you so we can schedule a trip. Congrats again. I'm really proud of you, little brother."

The door slams behind him before I can say another word.

Mallory steps beside me and laces our fingers. "Is everything okay?"

Instead of responding, I hug her. Keaton was right. Mallory protected me long before we became this.

I've always been safe with her.

Nan's eyes glitter with excitement as we walk toward the table, and I glare at her.

"Stop looking at me like that, Nan. I am not proposing." My eyes shift across the table. "And I'll have to ask Riley for her blessing first."

Riley winks at me. "That's my boy."

I clear my throat, pulling everyone's eyes to us at the end of the long table. "We want to thank all of you for coming out to celebrate with us today. In our four years at CLU, it wasn't always easy, but each one of you played a significant role in getting us here. To our families, thank you for encouraging us from afar and up close. To our friends, we'll never be able to thank you enough for laughing, studying, crying, and partying alongside us."

I drop my head to Mallory. Her eyes already glistening, and I haven't even started speaking to her.

"Eddie, you are the reason I'm here right now. You gave me the courage to bet on myself. You encourage me to fight for myself and the things that I want. Thank you for always pushing me to reach for the stars and being my constant. You're the best friend, partner, and rival I could've ever asked for. I can't wait to see all the good you will continue to do in the world."

I kiss her, not caring that we're in front of our family and friends. Mallory smiles against my lips as the adults shield their eyes, our friends holler, and the kids pretend to gag.

Right on cue, Pearl begins to drop off family-style platters. The delicious smell of all my favorite meals makes my stomach rumble with hunger, but I can't look away from the woman in my arms.

"I love you, Eddie."

"I love you." Mallory brings her fingers to her necklace, rubbing the smooth pendant. "Maybe I was never cursed after all."

Acknowledgements

It's equally terrifying and exciting to be writing an acknowledgements section in a book that I wrote. The book that reminded me that the greatest things in life aren't meant to be easy. The book that taught me to be patient and listen to myself. The book that showed me what a labor of love looks and feels like. Fortunate Misfortune is truly my pride and joy.

To my mom, thank you for always being my biggest fan. When I told you I wanted to write a book, you were immediately supportive in a way I'll never forget. For over a year, you've listened to every writing-related thought that crossed my mind. You are my best friend, Momma. I love you.

To my dad, thank you for showing me what it means to be hardworking and determined. Because of you, I know that I can do anything I put my mind to. My whole life, I've watched you fight for your dreams, which is why I can too. I'm forever your Sweet Pea. I love you, Daddy.

To Emma, I love you so much it's insane. You were the very first person I called when I realized I wanted to turn a half-built story into a full-fledged book. I had no experience, no plan, and was running completely on excitement, but you matched that energy. You encouraged me, pushed me, and fueled my fire, and for that, I am forever grateful. This book wouldn't be real without you.

To Megan, thank you for everything. When I think of friendship and found family, I think of you. I consider myself very fortunate to call you my best friend. There's a comfort in knowing that no matter where life takes us, we will always be us. I love you, Meg.

To Marianne, Elisabeth, and Clarissa, you three have been with me since day one, and you're stuck with me until the end of time. When I came up with the idea of the Clear Lake Quartet, I realized I have my very own quartet. From junior high/high school to now, we're four girls who have gone through every stage of life together. You are my soul sisters. You three are pieces of me, and I love you so much.

To Tyler and Cheyenne, thank you for being there for every step of this long process. From the first outline, to the sixth draft, to every second in between. Talking me through tough spots and hyping me up day in and day out. I love you both endlessly.

To Marja and Vai, you two have been my rocks in the indie author world. It's a very stressful and scary industry, but you two make it feel like home. Marja, it feels like it's been years since the day you sat on the phone with me, a total stranger, for an hour while I rambled. I love our long voice memos, the person you are, and how much we've grown together. Vai, you match me in all the best ways. Within an hour of talking, I knew we were in it for the long haul. I admire you and everything about you. Marja and Vai, *Fortunate Misfortune* wouldn't be where it is today without you and your encouragement. There are author-friends and friend-friends, and I'm thankful you two are both of those.

To my alpha and beta readers: Erica (book club bestie turned bestie bestie), D.J. (the person who told me exactly where I needed to dig deeper and push this story), Presley (my hype-gal from day one), Elaine (the sweetest human who helped in so many ways), K.C. (thanks TikTok for this friendship), Elisabeth (I would be lost without you), Marja (thank you for keeping me sane and reading twice), Vai (thank you for offering to read hours after we first started talking), Sarabeth (my sensitivity reader and a soon-to-be-dietitian), and Gina (my first friend in the world of indie publishing). Each one of you gave me such amazing feedback that helped turn *Fortunate Misfortune* into something so much more than I ever imagined. From your silly comments, to catching details I would've never spotted, to helping me improve. Thank you from the bottom of my heart.

To Tracy Pope, this book wouldn't be where it is without you. When I decided I wanted to write a book, finding an editor terrified me. Then I was lucky enough to have the opportunity to work with you. You talked me down after many anxious moments, hyped me up, and gave me helpful and necessary comments that helped me grow as an author. You made *Fortunate Misfortune* a real book, and I will never be able to thank you enough for that. Thank you, thank you, thank you.

And lastly to Boone. Writing *Fortunate Misfortune* took up time, space, and energy that neither of us expected, but you rolled with every punch. You smiled, supported, shared my work, and experienced every high and low right by my side. Thanks for listening to every nonsensical ramble that came out of my mouth, taking on extra duties at home so I could write, and being the best dog dad to our fur babies. You win the award for "Best Husband" in my book. I love you, honey. You are my very own good luck charm.

About the Author

Miah Onsha is a romance author and lover of books. She is dedicated to not only crafting stories of real love, but also to filling a gap she keenly felt in her own youth. Through her writing, she endeavors to provide the representation and affirmation that she yearned for as a young reader. As a registered dietitian with a passion for nutrition education, each story she writes holds a piece of that love through the eyes of real characters and real experiences. In each book, you will find healthy relationships, found family, and a whole lot of love.

Miah is based out of Texas and surrounded by her wonderful family, two perfect dogs, and the best friends a woman could ask for.

For inquiries, contact Miah Onsha at hello@authormiahonsha.com.

Made in the USA
Las Vegas, NV
05 August 2024